POWER OF THREE
THE NOVEL OF A WHALE, A WOMAN, AND AN ALIEN CHILD

BY CATHY PARKER

Second Printing 2019
Cover Design by Karli Foss
Edited by Nicole Matthews

This is a work of fiction. Names, characters, places, brands, media, and incidents are either the product of the author's imagination or are used fictitiously. Any resemblance to similarly named places or to persons living or deceased is unintentional.

PRINT ISBN 978-1-950282-90-6
EPUB ISBN 978-1-5137-0805-8
Library of Congress Control Number: 2015921051

ACKNOWLEDGMENTS

I am deeply grateful to my publisher for giving me the thumbs up, to my editor, Nicole Matthews for making this novel shine, and for the invaluable expertise of my teammates in toil, Olivia Howe, Karli Foss, and Karen Alcaide. This novel would never have existed at all without the superb guidance of Northwest Institute of Literary Arts faculty members Bruce Rogers, Kathleen Alcala, and Wayne Ude. Special thanks to the wonderful and insightful Vonda McIntyre. I am indebted to Dr. John F. Hurdle, M.D., Ph.D., and City of Roy Chief of Police Darwin Armitage for technical advice. And fond thanks to all my friends at the Northwest Institute of Literary Art for their wisdom, encouragement and understanding.

*for Kimmy, Catie, Madi, Austin and Justin, Steven
and of course for the beautiful beluga whale Mauyak*

*and In loving memory of Quiddity
large and slobbery mastiff extraordinaire*

PART ONE

LAVENDER LIGHTNING

CHAPTER ONE

SUNDAY

SHANNON KENDRICKS BURST THROUGH the SeaQuarium fish house door, whipped her unruly hair behind her shoulders, and spun around toward the towering figure following close behind.

"'No' means 'no.' We're quits. Leave it alone. Now go," she said, her voice firm, louder than she intended. She slammed the door in his face. Stood and scowled for a moment, poised for the mother of all pitched battles if the man dared open the door.

Do it. Double dare you.

All remained quiet. The hapless fellow stood outside, still and scowling, a distorted mirror image of herself. Then an angry fist knocked along the fish house wall, tracing the path of his footsteps back toward the Admin Building.

Shannon smacked the last of the fish buckets onto the counter and, with great splashy fanfare, filled the sink with hot steaming water to grind through scrubbing of the last of the day's feeding containers. She spared a moment to catch her hair in a loose ponytail.

On her path back to the fish house from the last otter feeding, she'd been waylaid by her would-be suitor. Nice guy, good looking, bright, one of the marine biologists over at the Aquarium. But in recent weeks he had started asking for "emotional closeness," as he put it. Where did they hide all those guys who wanted nothing to do with emotional closeness? She wanted one of those. But she always ended up with the softies most women would kill for. *There's irony for you.*

Emotional closeness? Shannon refused to go there. Ever. And this fellow didn't want to hear the message. Steam arose from the hot water in the sink. She plunged her hands in. Well. Now he understood.

But she hadn't handled it well. She sighed.

"You always want to let them down gently. You're too nice about it," her supervisor and best friend Becky Anderson said from her stool without looking up from her logbooks, always knowing her friend's unspoken train of thought much too well, to Shannon's ongoing discomfort. "Cold. That's the way to clear them off. Act as cold as a frozen mackerel."

Not just cold; keep clear of relationships altogether; that's the ticket.

The grit of her encounter still scraped on her mood and, she suspected, her voice. *Poor guy, not his fault she preferred going it alone.* Tears clouded her vision. She didn't to turn around when she spoke.

"Otters looked good," she said, in a raspy effort at normal. "Nome chittered up a storm, took everything I offered, but didn't eat much. Katmai ate enough for both of them. Shuyak waited her turn like a good girl. The usual."

Shannon could feel Becky's gaze on her back at the sink.

"Okay," Becky said.

Neither spoke for a moment.

A volunteer breezed in, grabbed his backpack, and as he took off out the door, hollered behind him, "Walruses all present and accounted for. Cleanest underwater windows this side of the Windex Company. Been fantastic as usual, ladies. See you Monday after classes, Becky. Next weekend, Shannon. Ciao."

Even Shannon had to laugh to herself. *Oh, for the untroubled energy and irreverence of the very young.*

Silence resettled on the fish house, broken by the periodic scratchings of Becky filling out the daily paperwork and Shannon scrubbing buckets.

"You want to talk about it?" Becky asked at last.

"No." The angry edge to Shannon's abrupt answer surprised even her. Becky raised her hands as if to deflect her words.

"Okay. Don't bite my head off."

"I'll deal with it," Shannon said.

Becky nodded at her and kept right on nodding. "When're you gonna get it through that brilliant yet thick head of yours that (a) some things come along that one person just can't deal with alone, (b) even if people *could* do some things for themselves, others would love to share the load and thus make the load lighter, and (c) even if people could do some things for themselves, if they try, they make a piss-poor job of it? Not to mention any names, Shannon."

Shannon muttered to herself. She wasn't *some people*. She'd deal with it. She always did.

"If you say so," Becky said, and returned to her paperwork.

The minutes stretched on without the usual banter between the two friends at the end of Shannon's weekend volunteer duty. Was it Shannon's imagination or had the second hand on the wall clock started ticking like Big Ben? She listened, poised for each next click, as if hoping that something, anything, would disrupt the rhythm of the clock's beat.

Tick. Tick. Tick.

Tick.

Odin's eye, as her Norse grandmother would say, and as Shannon always said in loving memory of the kind, patient old woman. *Enough.*

"What's called for here," Shannon said, "is some non-toxic glue to keep these scales *on* the fish." She glanced over. Did Becky take the bait?

Her friend didn't look up from her paperwork. "Mmm hmm," she said.

Shannon made a face at Becky and returned her attention to her fingertips. She needed just one fingernail long and stiff enough to pry that last stubborn fish scale off her stainless steel bucket. A difficult task for a woman whose fingernails sported the tensile strength of wet tissue. Those damn scales stuck like a bad reputation on a fun-loving girl.

"Ah ha," she said, spying an eighth-inch of nail, little finger, left hand. She applied it to the sticky translucent oval. "Victory is mine." She dried the bucket and added it to the stacks on the rear shelves of the fish house.

"I will wash absolutely, positively, and unconditionally no more buckets today," she said, trying one more time get a rise out of Beck, who looked up from her log sheet and said, "Okay, *Ms.* Kendricks, what if I absolutely, positively, and unconditionally will no longer permit volunteers to fraternize with any creature in the Ocean City

SeaQuarium Marine Mammal Center unless said volunteers wash as many buckets as I say? That ban would include the sea otters, the seals, the sea lions, the orcas, and yes, my dear, the beluga whales."

Shannon ran her fingers through her long dark ponytail, as if pausing to ponder Becky's words. "Then *I* would say—hand me another bucket."

"Thought so. Lucky for you everything's clean. Go away."

"I still need to wash this counter...." Shannon said without enthusiasm. She'd worked her patooti off today. She slumped against the counter searching for one last tiny spark of energy. No luck.

She sighed. And yet, even a hard day at the SeaQuarium rated higher than the one facing her tomorrow. Back to her "real" job. She must finish a difficult legal brief on one of her cases, conduct a deposition, attend a staff meeting with her petulant, petty, pasty-faced boss, who was, unfortunately, the head of the County Legal Department, and work her way through a mountain of legal paper sitting on her desk. She once loved days like that. Where had the joy gone?

Ah well. Who needed joy? People admired her, respected her. Some of the jokers she faced in court even feared her. Satisfaction enough.

Becky bent over her logs, her feet curled over the bars between stool legs, her head nodding to music she alone could hear. After a moment, she put down her paperwork and looked at her friend. "You sound tired. Why don't you skip Juneau tonight and get on home to your big-eyed kitty and giant dog—what kind of dog is Indy again? Elephant dog?"

"Elephant dog? *Elephant* dog?" Shannon crumpled a wet paper towel sitting on the counter and aimed at Becky's head. "Sofa-sized, max."

Becky watched the wad fly off to her left. "You are one lousy shot, lady. That the best you've got?"

"I missed on purpose. Lucky thing I know you love my babies as much as I do, or—right between the eyes, kiddo," Shannon said.

"You dream. So go home and feed your sofa."

As Shannon opened her mouth to protest, Becky lifted her hands in defense. "Don't say it. What was I thinking, suggesting you go home without your dose of SeaQuarium's most stubborn, most intelligent, chubby white whale? You're addicted, sweetheart, might as well face it. Go see the spithead."

Addicted. True.

No need to ask twice. "All righty then," Shannon said. "And thanks." She picked up her backpack and headed for the door. As she left, she turned and caught a glimpse of Becky burying her face back in her paperwork, one hand waving in Shannon's general direction, a leg jiggling to that unheard beat.

Shannon called a farewell, pushed the fish house door closed and made her way down the behind-the-scenes pathway.

Eager to see Juneau, the infamous spitting beluga, she struggled to pick up her pace.

Wouldn't happen. She'd run out of pizazz. A squashed-flat penny on a train track. She surrendered to her exhaustion, and ambled past the equipment lining her route, taking comfort from its familiarity.

The whales' enrichment toys—hoops as blue as the deepest ice, slick and squeaky balls, hose sections, buoys.

The stretcher designed for the belugas, with soft padded holes for short beluga fins, hanging on the generator room wall. For emergencies. Never needed during the ten years Shannon had volunteered. With any luck, it never would.

Heading downhill, she could see Juneau floating alone in the middle of the back whale pool, the rounded top of her head, her blow hole, her wide, white back, bobbing above the water. The other four belugas lingered out front in the big public pool; Juneau chose to remain in the private pool. A loner, Juneau, just like Shannon.

"Becky called you a spithead," she said as she approached the rim of the aqua-colored tank. "Feel free to give her a whacking big spit bath next time she comes down. But you won't spit at me, right, my bright yet moody friend? I'm your favorite volunteer, right? And you're, no question, my favorite whale. Pals don't spit at pals, right?"

Right. Odds, maybe 50/50.

And the worst part—the staff biologists had started it all by design, when they encouraged the belugas' natural ability to press ice-cold mouthfuls of water through their lips in forceful streams, creating lovely upward spraying fountains. The belugas performed the behavior on cue, a good husbandry measure and crowd pleaser. However, Juneau would often spit without warning to send messages like "take a hike." Shannon's kind of girl. Except when the whale lobbed a torrent of salty water right at *her* face.

Shannon reached the rim of the tank, three feet high on her side, and twenty feet down on the whales' side. Juneau swam to greet her, the whale's snow-white, plump body gliding through the water. The beluga raised her head, with the broad, unmarked forehead, ebony button eyes set well back on each side, short soft curving nostrum, and the mouth that reached so far around each side she always appeared to smile. Beautiful as ever. Shannon grinned at the sight—she couldn't help herself.

Shannon studied her for a moment. No sign of her pebble today. Shannon had no idea where the whale hid it. For safety reasons, the staff removed rocks of any size from the pool area whenever they spotted one, yet they'd never found this little round pebble the size of a pea that Juneau loved to bring to Shannon. Clever girl. Shannon should've taken it from her, but she couldn't bring herself to do it. Often she would take the little stone off Juneau's tongue and drop it for Juneau to dive and find. Perhaps she found the pebble hunt more of a challenge, preferring to search for this tiny dull-colored object rather than for those big bright rings and buoys the trainers sent her to retrieve. In any case, Juneau had elected not to play today. Today she wanted rubs along her back and fluke, and scratches under her small pectoral fins. She did love her back rubs.

Shannon reached out to give Juneau's smooth white head a gentle stroke.

The whale floated closer to the pool's edge.

Fingers met forehead.

At that instant, a bolt of lavender lightning flashed over the pool and surrounded them. A jolting pain, like the electric shock of grabbing a live wire rippled through Shannon. The crackle of a hundred firecrackers erupted. A strong scent, spicy and exotic, filled her nose. The taste of salt water bit her tongue. Her ears rang as if the lightning had touched off sirens.

What the—? Can't move, can't breathe.

A second piercing shock ripped through her, shaking her like hands on a jackhammer. She jerked as shimmering, lavender energy captured her and Juneau in a tight net. Flashes of lavender branded miniature strands of light on the inside of her eyelids and scalded her eyes. The pool began to slide up.

Correction.

The pool remained stable; *Shannon* began a rapid collapse. *No!* She gripped the rough, rounded pool rim until she couldn't feel her fingers. She fought the dizziness.

No good. Blackness circled inward from the edges of her vision, stealing the view of a hazy twilight sky. Her legs buckled.

Shit. She *never* fainted.

She dropped to the concrete like an anchor in shallow water.

* * *

Shannon fought her way from a thick black void toward light. Her head hurt. Thor had taken his hammer to her skull and continued to pound. She raised a shaky hand to explore her scalp. Her fingers found a hard lump the size of a dinner roll. She must have cracked her head when she fell. An exotic aroma floated on her skin, mingling with the familiar bleach-washed smell of the pool deck.

What had happened? Why was she sitting on her keister next to the back beluga pool with a knot on her head and her mind imitating twirling helicopter blades? So confused…she was missing something important…oh no, Juneau! What had happened to the beluga when the lightning hit her? Shannon grabbed the pool rim with aching fingers and pulled herself to her feet.

So weak.

Panic bubbled toward the surface. She clung to the rim of the pool. *Steady.*

Steady.

She squinted down into the well-lit tank.

The water. Dive into the water. Safe. Cold water. Go. Now.

No! That made no sense. She stiffened her arms and pushed hard against the rim. She took a deep breath, then forced out the air and tried to push her head fuzzies out with it.

She surveyed the results. Urge to swim gone. Good. Head fuzzies just where she'd left them. Crap.

Forget that, focus on Juneau. She peered down again. One of Juneau's listless eyes stared at her. The beluga's body floated on its side, sinking, the blow hole inches from the water. Water in Juneau's blow hole meant water in her lungs. And that meant death.

"Juneau," Shannon said, her voice a whisper. She listened. The whale exhaled a weak breath. *Still alive.* She pulled the whale's head toward her. Juneau's tail fluke sank another few inches. No good. Shannon spun and stumbled toward the fish house, screaming for Becky and the SeaQuarium vet Andy Fernandez.

The wind had picked up. It pressed her back, like an ocean wave. She leaned into it, but too far—she fell forward, flat on her forearms, skinning them on the rough cement.

Tired. Dizzy. Hurting. Hungry.

Wait. Hungry? At a time like this? Forget hungry.

She rested her head on the pavement for a moment.

Her mind swirled and jumped, as if a greyhound ran around a race track inconveniently located in her mind. As if something inside her fought to escape.

Her head would explode. No joke. She would shatter.

Afraid, so afraid…water, get in the water….

Then, out of nowhere, a humming rose in her whirling mind, slow, calm, like a rich, musical blanket to warm her shivering spirit. Shannon's wild thoughts quieted. She experienced the strangest sensation, as if some small…something had brushed across her mind with a velvet glove.

The chaotic internal bouncing and battering departed. Not so much died down as *went away,* deep into her mind somewhere.

The humming hadn't dissipated the confusion, dizziness, nausea, and headache, though, so she continued to rest her head on the walkway. The cool concrete soothed the side of her face. She'd just lie here until she stopped hurting and her head stepped off the merry-go-round. *So tired.* She closed her eyes. Lavender lightning flashed through her vision. Her eyes flew open.

Right. Juneau needed help. *Get up and move. To the fish house. Go.*

Shannon pushed herself to her hands and knees. *Shaky.* She scooted over to the generator room and pushed with her hands and legs until she could lean against it and stand. Still woozy, but she could walk. Her ponytail whipped in the wind. She kept one hand on the uneven unshimmery gray wall as she took one halting step at a time.

Unshimmery?

She wove back and forth and faltered, her steps unsteady, as she advanced toward the fish house. "Becky," she shouted, her voice straining, "Juneau's in trouble." Her words blew back in her face, thrown by the wind as if by a petulant child.

Just as she reached the fish house, Becky opened the door. "Get Andy, it's Juneau," Shannon said, exhausted, leaning on the nearest counter. Without a moment's hesitation, Becky whipped out her radio and called the vet.

"Come down to the pool and tell me what happened," Becky said as she raced by Shannon.

Becky would handle it. Shannon relaxed. What little energy she'd mustered seeped out the soles of her boots.

Can't rest. Get back down there and help. Well. Maybe she would grab an energy bar from Becky's stash. She pushed off the counter with a groan, stumbled to the cabinet where Becky kept her snacks, unpeeled the energy bar, and began the slow, unsteady journey back to Juneau.

Andy rushed her way from the walrus pools. He charged past as the hare would pass the turtle, but she kept moving, wobbling, the wind swirling around her. At last she reached the pool. Becky barked into the radio she held in one hand, and into the cell phone she held in the other.

She didn't shimmer either. This troubled Shannon. *But why?*

Shannon found herself looking at Becky's legs. Andy's too. Two legs. Her eyes wandered to her own legs. *Yes, two.*

She blinked. *So strange, these thoughts.*

Becky stepped in front of her, grabbing her under both arms and easing her to the ground. "You sit, girlfriend. Our friendly neighborhood paramedics are on the way."

Then Becky turned back to Juneau. More staff arrived, other people Shannon didn't recognize.

Shannon chewed on her energy bar and tried to focus on bits of conversation over the next few minutes, voices raised above the noise of the wind, but she couldn't concentrate for more than a second or two.

"…some kind of biochemical leak?"

"…getting hazmat down here right now."

"Juneau can't breathe on her own. We haven't got the equipment to deal with it…."

"The research center has agreed take the whale; they've got their water tank truck coming."

"Where's the woman who saw it happen?" an unidentified voice asked. Becky pointed at Shannon and took a step over to her. "Are you feeling better? Can you tell us what's wrong with her?"

Shannon mumbled, but didn't know if anyone understood her, didn't even know what she'd said.

Someone, maybe Andy, said, "…don't see anything obvious, but *something* happened here."

*   *   *

Dizzy, her thinking jumbled, her head still throbbing from the fall she'd taken after the lightning strike, Shannon huddled cross-legged on the concrete and watched as rescuers swarmed around Juneau. From long habit, she flipped her ponytail over her shoulder from her back, and ran her fingers through her dark, fine hair. Harsh lights circled the pool, rigged by the SeaQuarium maintenance crew to counter the growing darkness. The SeaQuarium had never outfitted this behind-the-scenes pool area with lampposts. The belugas could rest in silent, dark quiet here.

But not tonight. Now her eyes ached from the bright glare.

Unable to rouse the whale, they'd made arrangements to transport her to the Dickson Marine Mammal Research Center. A specially-equipped truck with a large built-in tank sped toward the SeaQuarium. As soon as an SQ electrician had assured Becky and Andy that no electric current remained in the pool, they'd donned wetsuits and adjusted Juneau to the stretcher designed for belugas. They prepared a hoist to lift the stretcher into the truck tank.

Juneau remained motionless.

Their words sifted through Shannon's consciousness but she couldn't quite catch the meaning.

Why couldn't she understand?

"Let me say, I mean stay and help, Beck. I'm fine." Not a lie. Not entirely. Well, essentially a lie. "Want me to do some jacking jumps, I mean jumping jacks to prove it?"

Becky nodded and smiled—and said, "No way, kiddo. Be a good girl and stay put until the ambulance comes for you."

Shannon exhaled a small cry of frustration. Becky, her best friend, would welcome her help—if Shannon *could* help in any way. She couldn't.

But she'd go to hades before she'd go to the hospital.

She hesitated, confused. *Why not?* Any sensible person would go. *Couldn't remember. But she must run. She longed for the sea.*

As soon as Becky turned away, Shannon stumbled to the back gate, let herself out with her key, and wobbled downhill on the steep wooded park path. At the bottom, she crossed Boardwalk Avenue to the wide sidewalk next to the ocean, then disappeared beyond the glare of the street lights.

She clambered down the huge, slippery boulders below the boardwalk into the shadows and sank, shivering, her arms clasped around her knees.

Come on, brain, wake up.

No good. The lightning had fried the gray matter, crossed the wires, turned out the lights. Left her tired, so weak, she might never move again. She should've grabbed a few extra energy bars when she had the chance.

At least she could find solace in the quiet here.

And then her solitude dissolved.

* * *

Like a rogue wave, the urge to jump in the water and swim far, far north startled her calm. Before she realized it, she'd scrambled to her feet and moved down the rocks toward the inky water.

Wait! Jumping in the water solved nothing. What on earth planted that idea in her mind? She couldn't jump into the water; in her condition she'd drown before she could swim twenty feet.

And yet the urge pushed her, pushed hard. An image flashed in her mind: Juneau, her beloved beluga. Not at SQ in a coma, struggling to survive, but here, arcing into the sea and swimming, the glorious sense of water flowing along her body, bending her powerful fluke to propel her, adjusting her pectoral fins to steady herself as she raced free. *Free*.

Shannon's legs, like jelly fish tentacles, ceased to support her weight. She sank hard onto a boulder a foot from the water.

Sweat dripped into her eyes; she wiped her arm against her forehead.

The image of Juneau at sea had flashed in *her* thoughts. But she hadn't generated it; the image had a foreign feel to it, as if someone had described it to her.

How could that be?

Had she developed some psychic link to the beluga because of the lightning? No. She'd sensed nothing from Juneau as she sat helpless on the concrete watching her friends' frantic work.

Remembering the scene, Shannon's stomach pinched.

Before she could puzzle out these strange thoughts, she noticed a ribbon of silvery lavender floating on the water. The wisp rose into the air and formed a mist. A child, a little girl, five or six years old, emerged from the mist and floated forward to stand on the sandy beach staring with huge, round eyes at Shannon, as the incoming tide brushed the child's bare feet. She wore no clothes.

Shannon blinked. The child must have swum along the shore and waded in from deeper water.

A beautiful but strange child. Her skin glistened silvery lavender even in the faint glow from the street lights up on the boardwalk. Her hair, the palest blond, the tint of the early evening moon, floated around her face, Albert Einstein style. Her lips quivered below her tiny nose, between her tiny ears. And those eyes. Those huge, anime-like, silvery-green eyes, deep as forest moss, eyes brimming with tears about to flood her cheeks. Her child-plump little hands rubbed her eyes and wiped her face, as if the mist has dampened it. Her mouth crumpled, and she cried. Poor thing. Shannon fumbled her way to her feet and took a step, her hands reaching for the girl.

"Who—"

Sirens wailed. Dozens of them. The sound converged on SQ; then the shrill, rhythmic howls spread over the entire area. Loud. Insistent. The racket assaulted Shannon's ears, increasing tenfold the already pounding pain.

She crouched, pressed her her hands to her ears. Even so, she couldn't miss a blasting siren above her on Boardwalk Avenue.

The sound stopped.

Uh oh. She craned to look up the rocky slope. Dark silhouettes appeared against the street bleached yellow by lamp lights. Quiet voices competed with the soft lapping of the incoming tide and the receding sirens. A bright flashlight explored the boulders near Shannon in a systematic pattern. Inevitably, the light paused on her huddled form.

As her Norwegian grandmother would say, *By Odin's eye.* Couldn't they just leave her be? Her grandmother. Shannon hadn't thought about her in a long while. A tall, proud woman, tanned by long hours of following the reindeer herds she loved so much—a true scientist, a skilled photographer, a gentle and laughing babysitter for Shannon, whose mother had always found so many reasons to go away. Perhaps the old woman had believed in the Norse gods. The child Shannon believed. She swore oaths by them, cursed through them, sought comfort from them still. Of course she no longer believed they'd answer her. Now she called out Odin, Thor, Loki, and the others to honor the rough hand that had caressed her face and wiped away her tears, the fierce blue eyes that had captured the sky in their depths. Odin's eye, her grandmother had told her, saw everything in Asgard and on Earth. Well. *What do you think of lavender lightning, Odin?*

Shannon glanced back at the child. She stood unmoving, eyes fixed on Shannon. The dark shape of a man silhouetted against the streetlights picked his way down the rocks.

"Don't worry. I'm a police officer," a deep, quiet voice said. "I'm looking for someone who may be hurt. Can you tell me your name?"

So much for solitude. Shannon didn't much care. Too exhausted.

But some part of her rebelled.

That wild urge to plunge into the sea returned.

Not again. *Why? Why would she dive into the water?* She fought down the urge. Not a problem—she could summon no energy to jump into the ocean anyway.

Shannon listened to the officer's scrambled approach down the slippery rocks and watched the child at the water's edge. The little silvery-lavender girl showed no outward reaction to the officer, as if no one mattered but Shannon.

Afraid. The child's panicky fear coursed through Shannon.

Wait. She could feel the child's fear? *How?* The little girl stood as still as a clam. As if she'd gone into shock. But Shannon felt her fear all the same. She rocked back from her crouch and thumped her backside onto the beach.

The police officer arrived.

"I'm the one you're kooling, I mean, looking for," she said. "Shannon Kendricks." She made no move to stand. Her hand reached for her pony tail, the loose ends now tangled in the humid ocean air.

The officer eased down beside her. "My name is Lucas Quintana," he said. His voice, low and calm, conveyed an unspoken message: *nothing urgent, let's sit and gather our thoughts;* a conversation as clear as if he'd spoken aloud. A half-crazed runaway hiding in the shadows, and this officer remained unhurried. A rare quality in a police officer. Rare in anyone.

"There's a lady up at the SQ frantic with worry," he said.

"My bend—best friend Becky. She's the supervisor at the SQ Marine Mam, Mammal Center. I'm her volunteer." *Great. Now she'd taken up babbling.* She never babbled.

"Pretty good friend. She jumped on her cell and fought her way up the chain of command until she reached the Chief. I have it on good authority that she told him how many ways she could make him hurt if he didn't send a search party out. Claimed she knows the Mayor *and* the Governor."

Shannon managed a small smile. "She's the best."

They sat in companionable silence for a moment.

Shannon, uneasy, hadn't taken her eyes off the child.

"You should take that little girl over there up to the Boardwalk too. Locate her mother." Shannon said, pointing.

"What child would that be?"

"Right down there in the water." Shannon pointed.

"Can't see anyone."

"You're sure?"

"Quite."

Hallucination?

"She doesn't need any help then."

"Unlikely."

More sweat broke out on Shannon's forehead. *Something very wrong had happened here. If she could think straight, she could work this out.*

In time, Officer Quintana came around to the point. "How're you doing? Ms. Anderson said you ran away when they tried to send you to the hospital."

"Yes I...." Her voice trailed away. "I'm not sure why I ran. Well, I don't like hospitals much. Bad memories." Yet instead of her bad memories, images of a whale desperate to return to the sea and of a frightened little silvery-lavender child flashed in her mind.

In his gentle voice, Quintana said, "You need to go get checked out, though. Lightning can cause serious damage. Should I call for a stretcher to carry you up to the road?"

"No, I can walk."

But she couldn't.

Not until Quintana lifted one of her arms over his shoulder and held it with one large hand while he gripped her around the waist with the other and picked his way up the rocks. Shannon's feet didn't touch the ground.

Back on the boardwalk, his partner, a short, round woman, quick to laugh and quick to sympathy, radioed for an ambulance. Then she offered her hand.

"Officer Taney."

"I'll stop by the hospital later, if you like," Quintana said as she sat in the back seat of the police car, her feet hanging out, elbows on her knees. "Give you a lift home when they release you." The words sounded casual. Yet Shannon detected an undertone, a hopefulness. She turned to study him, to *see* him for the first time. Unruly black hair and neat bushy mustache, deep dark eyes, thick long eyelashes. Strong face. Confident.

"Thanks. But that's above and beyond."

Quintana broke out a broad grin and whispered, so that Officer Taney couldn't hear, "It's the perfume, Ms. Kendricks. Hard to resist."

Perfume? She didn't wear perfume.

* * *

Shannon arrived at St. James Hospital, verified that yes, she was Shannon Kendricks, one of the county's deputy attorneys. She correctly identified the day of the week and the sitting president.

The doctors tested her, poked her, and x-rayed her. Made her recount the lightning story again. And again. Tucked her in a bed and, at last, left her alone. All the while, her head spun and her confusion refused to vanish, while she proclaimed over and over that she felt quite good enough to go home.

Once they'd closed the door on her room, she relaxed. At first she rested and waited. They'd let her go home soon. She hoped. But she waited some more. Time passed at the pace of a baby snail with a sore foot.

She asked for something to eat. The nurses promised they would arrange something soon. Nothing materialized. *Liars.*

* * *

Not her favorite place, St. James. Her six-year-old best friend had died here. Her ex, Scott Cross, had ended their relationship here too, moments after her emergency appendectomy. The tears she'd cried within its bleak yellow walls. And now this nightmare visit.

Her mind couldn't settle, sticky, like cotton candy swizzling onto a paper cone. She craved a nice cod dinner.

Cod? Where had that come from? She didn't much care for fish.

The one good thing about the hospital tonight? The smell. Like a delicate perfume. Quite wonderful. She'd smelled it before. *Where?* She couldn't quite remember….

She closed her eyes.

Long ribbony wisps of iridescent colors in a river of light flowed across her mind and threw off silver glints as if mirroring a bright sun. Ribbony wisps just like the one that she'd seen before the little girl waded ashore.

The translucent wisps glimmered in every shade and tint she'd ever seen, and some she *hadn't*. Wisps entwined in a psychedelic river. A wonderful scent arose from the river—the same one she could smell in the hospital room.

The sight mesmerized Shannon, lifted her spirits, as she hummed along with the river's own music.

selador came the whisper.

And there, standing by the river, stood a child. Shannon's eyes flew open. The same little silvery-lavender girl who'd appeared by the ocean. An exotic aroma arose from the water, the perfect blend of thousands of spices.

Again, the soft whisper.

esssii.

Essi?

Goosebumps skittered into platoons across Shannon's skin. *What in Odin's name?* A beautiful hallucination or two, okay. She'd bonked her head when she passed out at Juneau's pool, so she could accept a little mind warp, but whispering in her head? She shuddered.

Shannon fastened her gaze on a crack in the ceiling, determined to ignore all whispers. A moment later, out of the corner of her eye, she glimpsed a mist forming at the door of her room. A lavender haze.

What now?

A doctor whisked in through the haze.

"Shannon Kendricks?" she asked, looking at a clipboard. "I'm Dr. Bennett. All your tests have come back normal except one. I would've expected quite different results with a lightning strike. Are you sure that's what happened?"

"Quite sure. Um. Did you see that smoky haze over by the door? An electric outage somewhere?" She pointed, but the haze had disappeared.

Dr. Bennett glanced that direction. "No. Nothing." She pursed her lips. "I'd better have a look at your eyes." She pulled a light from a chain around her neck, where other instruments dangled, and peered into each eye. "Hmm. Looks fine. Do you see this haze now?"

"No, it's gone. Forget it. But hey, it's great news that the tests came out okay. I'm much better now. Good enough to go home. Right now."

Okay, the full Pinocchio, that last bit. But she wanted out.

"I said all but *one* came back normal." Dr. Bennett pulled up a chair beside the bed and sat down. "Your temperature has remained quite high since you arrived, and I wanted to know why, so I had some additional work done. Some unknown agent is causing your metabolism to accelerate at a phenomenal clip. Your body is burning your energy stores faster than you can replenish them. We've asked a number of specialists to study what we're seeing. We want you on a glucose drip under observation until we discover what's going on and can reverse this process. Any questions?"

Shannon gripped the loose end of her ponytail and stared at Dr. Bennett in numb silence. "Do you mean," Shannon said, "that if you can't stop the calorie burn, I'll waste away? I'll die?"

*   *   *

Dr. Bennett looked Shannon in the eyes. Her gaze didn't waver.

"That's right. You *would* die. But," she said, rising, and patting Shannon's arm, "It won't come to that. We'll sort this out. I'll check on you later. Nice perfume, by the way. Never smelled anything like it." With that Dr. Bennett sailed out the door.

This perfume business bewildered her. Shannon wore no perfume. She never had. Perfumes gave her headaches. Yet Officer Quintana had smelled it too.

Still, Shannon found Dr. Bennett's other comments much more pressing.

Dying? How could she wrap her mind around that? She stared at the crack in the ceiling. *Do not fall to pieces.*

Again she caught a glimpse of lavender haze at the door. A nurse bustled in to take her vitals.

"Nice perfume," she said. "Bet that stuff brings in the guys like wasps to a picnic." The woman scribbled on a chart. "Need anything?"

"Yes, I need to go home," Shannon said, and meant it.

The nurse smiled, shook her head, and left.

Minutes later, the lavender haze materialized once more. *Wait for it; someone will come.* Just as she expected, a young volunteer from the SQ appeared with the backpack she'd left at the Fish House. The kid didn't mention the perfume but he leaned in and inhaled.

Fifteen years your senior, child, back off.

When he departed, Shannon picked over what had happened—puzzling over the strange happenings on this most improbable night beat worrying about dying. So. This weird lavender haze predicted arrivals. People around her smelled perfume where none should exist, the same scent given off by a multi-colored river in her imagination. A silvery-lavender child haunted her mind. She heard unexplained whispers. *What had happened to her?*

Odin knows, as her Nordic grandmother would say.

She tried to focus. Couldn't. She drifted off to sleep…

*   *   *

…rising, as if to the surface of a lake, her awareness thick and spinning. Her eyes opened.

No silver shimmer…Afraid…Where is this place? Trapped.

She screamed.

A nurse hurried in. "What happened?"

Oh. The hospital. No silver shimmer here, never had been.

en selador, the voice whispered.

And sell a door. Uh huh. Sure.

"Sorry, nothing. Bad dream."

The nurse fussed around Shannon's bed, adjusting the covers, straightening the drip line, checking the needle taped to Shannon's wrist.

Shannon eyed the glucose drip. Where had that thing come from? They must have hooked her up while she slept.

The nurse blurted out her next words, looking embarrassed but determined to speak. "If I could ask, why did you hide down on the sea shore when you ran away?"

Shannon frowned at her. A bit nosey.

As if Shannon had voiced her resentment aloud, the nurse, fiddling with the edge of Shannon's bedcover, said, "I just wondered. I go down there sometimes and wish I could swim away and never come back."

Uh oh. Too much information. Yet…that exact thought had flashed through Shannon's mind. A light bulb blinked on. Correction: Shannon hadn't imagined *herself* swimming into the sunset; *Shannon* didn't long to swim away. She'd imagined *Juneau* swimming off to deep water; the *whale* longed to escape to the sea.

True, she supposed; but why would some imagined longing of Juneau's overwhelm Shannon? *Not a clue.*

In the meantime, this young nurse had shared her own pain. Shannon couldn't ignore the woman's hurt.

"I hear you," Shannon said to the nurse, placing her free hand on top of the nurse's. "Sometimes life is just too much, right?" *Like right now.*

"Yes," the nurse said, straightening up, relief on her face. "Love the perfume, by the way," she said as she left.

The perfume. Of course she loves the perfume. But what *perfume?* She sniffed her wrist. Then her arm. She lifted her sheets, pulled up her knee, bent forward, and inhaled. Yes, the scent she'd attributed to the hospital's efforts to hide the real hospital smells *did* emanate from her instead, and from everywhere on her.

The lightning must have brought it.

Sure. Blame it all on the lightning—the appearance of the child, channeling Juneau's longing for freedom, and the unidentified metabolic agent that now killed her calorie by calorie. Lightning always did that to people. *Sure.*

Wait a second, though. She'd meant the lightning blame game as a little joke. But now that she'd brought it up, of course she should attribute these odd occurrences to the lightning. Fried brain led to hallucinations and…who knows why the lightning had caused her to emit a pleasant scent. Better than burnt toast, anyway.

Shannon's groggy mind drifted. She wanted to sleep, just for a minute…. Her eyes closed. Her worries softened and melted away. A dream filtered into her mind.

* * *

…Shannon's favorite living room reading chair, big and pillowy, enfolds her like a giant doughboy hand. She sleeps. Good lord, her mouth looks ridiculous gaping open, like a big raspberry doughnut.

Her soft white blanket covers her lap. The little girl, with her pale hair and silvery lavender skin, snuggles in Shannon's lap and smiles at Shannon's snoozing face with its doughnut-O mouth.

esssii.

The child cuddles a small stuffed animal in her lap. A round white beluga whale. A toy Juneau.

zhoo.

The head of the stuffed animal rotates, and its little black eyes, alive, stare straight at Shannon. The whale's forehead moves. A sonar sound reaches her mind, a long desperate cry. The child watches her too. *Watches.*

*   *   *

Shannon bolted upright in her hospital bed, clarity arriving as if hand-delivered in the dream.

So—lavender lightning. Then a lavender *child.*

o, esssii, the inner voice whispered.

And Shannon touched Juneau just as the lightning struck and then *Shannon* longed to return to the sea, as Juneau would, while at the same time Juneau sank into a coma…

zhoo.

…Juneau in a coma, her conscious mind hidden. Everyone assumed her conscious mind had buried itself deep within her own brain. But what if…if Juneau's conscious mind was hiding *in Shannon's mind* instead?

Well, too crazy to contemplate.

Right, too crazy.

She eased her head back onto her pillow.

On the other hand, though, she was carrying an unidentified metabolic agent, as Dr. Bennett had called it. *Something* was gobbling up all Shannon's energy.

She bolted upright again.

Juneau? Her Juneau?

Her whisperer seemed to think so: *o, zhoo.*

No way. How would the whale's consciousness have moved over to her?

The lightning? Possible. Shannon snorted to herself. As possible as anything else on this bizarre night.

But where did the child come in? The lavender haze? In her dream, the child had cuddled with Shannon and Juneau.

Oh no, no, no. *Her too? In Shannon's mind too?*

The whispered voice said, *o esssii.*

Essi? The child is Essi? Impossible. Totally and completely impossible.

Well.

The presence of the whale and the child in Shannon's mind did explain a lot of things. And what did she know about lavender lightning anyway? It could happen. *Holy Odin.*

No, no, no. Just listen to her. *Crazy. Impossible, right?*

*   *   *

Run. And this time, the urge *did* originate with her, not Juneau, not the child.

As if she could outrun her thoughts, outrun Juneau and the child. As if she could be alone again. And not dying. Of course she couldn't.

Still. Although she could control little this night, she could control whether she remained in the hospital, and now she wanted nothing more than to leave. Now.

She pulled out her glucose drip, threw on her clothes, peeked through her hospital room door. No sign of Dr. Bennett. She limped to the elevators, stumbling like a drunk as she fled to the main floor.

Shannon made for the front entrance, but caught the smell of cafeteria food drifting over the hallway. Her stomach grumbled like a bear waking from hibernation, rousing a ravenous appetite in Shannon, unlike anything she'd known. She wanted food. She *needed* food.

All right. She'd stop, but just long enough to grab a bite. And then she'd return to her quick escape.

An hour later, Shannon shuffled along, still dizzy and clumsy, but undiscovered, out of the hospital. Perhaps no one had thought she'd escape to the cafeteria. *Hah.*

Shannon caught the bus in front of the hospital and returned to the SQ to retrieve her VW bug from the parking lot. She drove her unsteady way toward home...

* * *

...and in the next instant she found herself in her kitchen staring at her amber-tiled floor with the glittery copper grout. She loved that grout. She...

Wait. Focus. Grocery bags lined her counters. She peeped into one. Fish and pastries and who knew what. How did they get there?

How did *she*?

She remembered nothing. Grocery store, unloading the car, nothing. *Eye of Odin. Not good.*

As Shannon stood straining her memory, holding a box of chocolate cream doughnuts in her hand, her mastiff, Independence—her big, slobbery, lovable Indy—stalked into the kitchen, head lowered. The dog bristled and growled, a deep rumble.

Run. Shannon backed toward the garage door, her eye on the dog. Images flashed. Juneau swimming away in the sea, far away from this unknown creature. A silvery lavender child cowering against a wall.

No. She *wouldn't* run. Not from her Indy. Juneau and, and what's her name, Essi—is that her name?—notwithstanding.

Juneau and Essi notwithstanding. *How bizarre to even think that.*

Shannon crouched and, in her softest, calmest voice, said, "It's mommy, sweetheart. Do I smell funny? Not surprising. Come here. It's me."

Indy's whip-like tail wagged in a slow, tentative pendulum that quickened as the dog sniffed Shannon's hand. Then Indy's tail wriggled her whole giant rear and she greeted Shannon in her usual leaning, licking, delirious way.

Indy settled onto the floor by her food bowl just as Shannon's cat Narcissus slipped through the cat door, paused with a black paw in the air and stared at Shannon with her big blue eyes, ready to bolt. Narci too? Shannon popped open a can of cat food, and called her over. Narci hesitated a second, then pattered in. A slave to the food dish, that one.

Shannon should talk. She had a feeling food would become her own lord and master in the hours and days to come.

As Shannon dished out the cat food, she sniffed the can. It smelled quite alluring. A strong suggestion of fish with a hint of corn-starch and wheat gluten. She might give it a little taste. She dabbed a finger in it, which emerged with a brown wet lump. Reminded her of a chopped, broiled slug.

Of course she would *not* taste it.

Well. Perhaps a tiny lick.

She licked. She rolled the flavor around. Tender savory shreds. Nice sauce. Not so bad.

Odin's eye. She'd just eaten something that smelled like fish guts. She stumbled to the sink, spit, grabbed a water glass, squished water around and spit again.

What was the matter with her?

Forget the cat food—she craved a human meal. True, she'd eaten a large meal at the hospital, more than she'd intended, but her body cried out for food again. She settled for a tableful of left-overs from last-night's dinner, and ate until her plate glistened. She wanted more. She pulled down a box of graham crackers and polished it off. The whole box.

Dr. Bennett had said she couldn't shovel food in as fast as she burned it. So, the more she ate, the longer the dying process would take. She hoped.

The dying process. Her shaking fingers found her ponytail. She pulled it over her shoulder and ran her fingers through it again and again.

Narci had jumped into her lap. The cat sniffed Shannon's hands, nose pressed to Shannon's skin. Yes, her new scent of rich, blended aromas, unfamiliar and exotic. *That* she could learn to live with.

If she lived.

Juneau's rubbery skin brushed her mind. *Her mind. What was she saying?* Shannon wanted someone to talk some sense into her.

She grabbed her phone and tried Becky's cell phone. No answer. Home phone. Nothing.

When the message beeper sounded, Shannon said, "Beck. Something terrible happened to me and Juneau when the lightning struck. Well, you know something terrible pan, I mean happened to Juneau, of course, but what I'm trying to say is, and I know this sounds crazy, so don't hang up and no, I'm not jerking your chain, but I think the oterapive—operative—word being *think*—that Juneau's mind or her consciousness or her spirit or whatever you want to call it, left her body and came over here into my mind with me. I know how that sounds, but call me. And let me know how Juneau's doing. Love you."

Even before she disconnected she regretted every word. It sounded ludicrous. Becky would call the men in white coats. In fact, Shannon should call them herself.

As she sat frowning at the phone, the door bell rang. She rose and, using the wall for support, made her way through the front hall. The door, with a large glass arch in the upper half, afforded a view of Officer Quintana. A pleasant view. Shannon looked beyond him to the lit porch. No Officer Taney as far as she could see. She let him in.

* * *

"Hey," Quintana said. "Your place is on my way home from work, so I thought I'd check in, see how you're doing."

"Thanks. Come on in. I was just getting ready for bed. Oh. I didn't mean come in *because* I was just...I meant come in *until* I...I won't go to bed now of course until later..."

Burbling like a pan of water about to boil. *How infuriating.*

Officer Quintana smiled. "I understand."

Indy trotted up and sniffed Quintana's belt buckle.

"Hey, buddy. You're quite the big boy. You taking good care of your mommy here?" He rubbed the dog under her ears. Indy's tail wagged in quick time.

"No stereotyping, now," Shannon said. "Indy's a girl. A big girl, but a girl."

"Oops, mea culpa. Sorry, girl. Indy's an interesting name. She reminds you of one of the cars in the Indianapolis 500?" Quintana asked.

Shannon pretended to take the question as a serious one. "She's the right size but not fast enough." She shook her head. "Short for Independence. We're loners, Narci, Indy, and me. Well, except for each other," Shannon said. "The name proclaims our nature."

"And Narci is—?"

"She's my cat. My little Narci tends more to the extreme end of independence. More like, 'I am the center of the universe. Bend to my will.' So I call her Narcissus."

Why would she tell him that? She didn't tell people that. She played with the loose ends of her hair as they talked, braiding and unbraiding it in a loose weave.

"I stopped by the hospital to see you and ran into a doctor, Julia Bennett. On a rampage. Reminded me of your friend Ms. Anderson. She said she ordered you to stay put and then you left. I told her I'd give you her message, which is, 'You march your stubborn ass right back down here, young lady.'" He paused. "I'm paraphrasing."

Shannon laughed. "Message received. I'm not going back though."

"Why not? The doc thinks the lightning may have caused some damage."

"Oh, she's right." Shannon gestured to the couch and Quintana sank into the cushions. "You need coffee or anything? A piece of cake? I might eat a piece."

"No-ho. Not for me. Not this time of night. Wouldn't sleep."

"Ok, well, give me a send, that is, a second then."

Shannon returned with a quarter section of a three-layer chocolate cake. Quintana watched her dig in. He made no comment.

For one crazy minute, the impulse to confide in this tall, self-assured police officer the whole story overwhelmed her. But no, Shannon never confided in anyone.

"You remember that child you didn't see on the beach?" Shannon asked, poking a drop of icing back into her mouth.

Don't talk about that.

"Yes, the child I didn't see."

Tell him nothing.

"The silvery-lavender child, yes. Well, um, as best I can tell, she came in with the lightning that struck at the SQ pool and she landed in my mind. I can't quite wrap my head around it."

Did she just say that to a stranger?

Quintana's face remained placid. "I can't quite wrap my head around it either. So, the child I didn't see, the lavender child, arrived on a bolt of lightning and landed in your mind?"

"'In.' In the lightning."

"'In,' sorry." Silence. "She still there?"

"Yes and I'm pretty sure she's the reason my metabolism's out of whack."

"Is that what has the doc worried? Your metabolism?"

"Right. I can't shovel food in as fast as she burns it."

Quintana looked at the diminishing quarter cake on Shannon's plate. "I see."

Did Shannon detect a slight patronizing note in his voice? *That burned.* She shook the loose braid in her hair back out and let the pony tail swing loose down her back.

Silence followed. Quintana stood. "Well, I'd better head on home. If it's okay with you, I'll radio in that I've located you. Again. And that you're all right for tonight. Dispatch will get the message to Dr. Bennett. Maybe you'll check in with her tomorrow."

Shannon stood too, and limped toward the door. "Doubtful. Look, I realize I sound a bit weird here. I'm trying to figure out this bizarre night, that's all."

"Sure."

Sure? What did he mean? Sure, she struck him as a bit off? Sure, he found her loonier than a bird on Walden's Pond? Or sure, the night had indeed turned bizarre.

None of those answers offered anything promising. She didn't ask him to elaborate.

And *why had she blurted out any of this, anyway?* She *never* confided in anyone. Except Becky. And never about something like this.

"So. A lavender child. Not from around here, then." Quintana said after a pause.

Good point. Where *did* the little girl come from? Another planet. Had to be.

There. She'd said it.

Simple.

Shannon shared her head with an alien.

*   *   *

An alien. The full impact of those words penetrated the confusion and pain Shannon had suffered all night. She gripped the edge of the hallway table. The sound of static blitzed her mind, buzzed in her ears and grew louder and louder.

"Shannon, what is it? You're as pale as a snowflake."

His voice came from a long way off.

Something alien and alive inside her.

Don't panic.

So scared.

Hold on.

"Hey, you need to sit down, come back into the living room."

"Don't touch me," Shannon said, throwing up her hands to warn him away. "Just don't."

Disintegrating.

No, damn it. Hold on to something solid.

She struggled down the hall into the kitchen with Quintana at her heels. Indy had returned to her spot next to the screen door to catch the cool evening breeze. Shannon reached the mastiff in five unsteady steps, fell on her knees, and hugged her sweet dog in a tight grip. Indy's big head lifted and her great floppy muzzle brushed the arm wrapped around her neck. The dog's long wide tongue licked Shannon's face, knotted her bangs into a ball of slobber. Indy leaned in close, her eyes patient, as Shannon wrapped her arms around the dog's neck and held tight. Shannon inhaled the familiar musky scent of Indy's skin. Her Indy. The mastiff's great muscled shoulders and the heaviness of her bones grounded Shannon. Solid Indy.

I'll can always count on you, my baby, no matter what.

Quintana stood motionless in the kitchen door, at a complete loss. Shannon forgot his presence.

She became aware of vibrations in her head, pulsing low and steady. Calming. The child.

At least she had a kinder, gentler alien on board.

A child.

Yes, Shannon could tolerate a child alien without going insane. Maybe. Well no. But as body snatchers went, Essi could've been worse.

She remained nestled over Indy, her arms stretched around the dog's shoulders. After a moment, she sat back and made room for Indy's big head in her lap.

"I'm okay. It's fine if you go now," she said, trying for calm confidence.

"You sure?"

"I'm sure." He didn't press her on where the child had come from. *Good man.*

Quintana looked dubious, but dipped his chin in farewell and said, "I'll check in later to see how you're doing."

Shannon remained on the floor with her dog. She would owe Quintana an explanation. When she recovered. If ever she did.

An alien.

All at once, Shannon's sense of her place in the scheme of existence shifted. She imagined herself, as if from far away, and growing smaller, a tiny figure huddled in her kitchen, in her house, in her world, in a strange and limitless universe.

Shannon remained still and quiet in that limitless universe for a long time before her awareness returned to her kitchen floor, to herself. She stood and returned to sit at the kitchen table. Narci jumped to her lap. She said to the little girl in her mind, "Well, sweetheart, since you brought Juneau in, you will now take Juneau back to her body and then you will go home. I'm too young to die."

No response from the child. *Why not?*

Shannon mulled over her conversations with the little girl to date. *Ah.* The child so far had communicated only in images and sounds. Shannon formed an image of a little Juneau shape and a little child shape inside Shannon's head. Then she pictured the child floating from Shannon over to Juneau's body and floating with Juneau back into Juneau's body.

The vibration tightened in Shannon's head, excited. The child understood! The little girl took up the image-making.

Shannon's hand touches Juneau, just like tonight at the whale pool, and the child, with Juneau in tow, flows down through her hand and into Juneau's body.

So that's how the little one would make it happen. Shannon must touch the whale. Outstanding. Now for part two.

Shannon formed the image of the child floating out of her head and away into the air. The girl erased the image. Nothing replaced it.

Shannon frowned and rubbed her forehead hard.

The alien child didn't know how to get home?

CHAPTER TWO

MONDAY

A NEW FEAR struck at Shannon. If the lightning strike had carried an alien to Shannon, had the lightning carried an alien to Juneau too?

Shannon formed pictures in her mind for the little girl. She used a wisp, like the ones in the psychedelic river, since she had no idea how the child's fellow creatures looked.

The little girl erased Shannon's concocted wisp and replaced it with another image. Juneau's head and Shannon's head. Shannon's head showed the little girl inside. But nothing showed in Juneau's head.

Well done, little one.

No alien. *Thank Odin.* Shannon's energy ebbed away. Her eyes drooped. Her muscles ached.

Her eyes wandered to the kitchen table. A cookie package lay next to a grocery bag she'd unpacked. Handy. She finished off the box.

Shannon yawned and checked her cell phone. 2 a.m. She slipped her hands under the purring Narci in her lap, stood, and eased the cat onto the seat recently warmed by Shannon's posterior. The cat settled while Shannon wove her way through clean-up, always with one hand on a counter for balance, restoring her kitchen to reasonable order, biting off big sections of a chocolate almond candy bar as she tidied.

Upstairs in her bedroom, Shannon pulled on her old oversized night shirt, SAVE THE DOLPHINS emblazoned on the front, and slipped under sheets as cool and smooth as, as—

selador.

Sell a door? Her groggy mind rebelled. No, that's not right, that's the lavender child talking…

…as smooth as her ex's fingers running along her back. Scott. Once upon a time.

Narci jumped on the bed to curl into Shannon's side. Indy climbed aboard to claim her half of the king size bed, her butt nestled against Shannon's leg. As Shannon drifted toward sleep, she checked fo—

esssii.

—for her little silvery lavender child. Oh. Essi? She called herself Essi.

Shannon slipped down into a deeper sleep.

…Cold black waters surge around her; her strong body flexes and ripples. *So good here.* Her arms move in short arcs. She tastes the water; *the others have fled,* moving away from land. Whistles and clicks echo through the water and she understands. *Trouble comes. Follow.* The sweetness of swimming free, racing, turning, diving in vast waters tingles along her spine. Her muscles stretch, strong, rhythmic. *So good.*

Pain! She bumps against webbing, hard, ropey. Like strings of intertwined kelp.

Fear courses through her. *Away, get away.*

The net surrounds her. Panic whirls like hurricane winds.

She struggles. Struggles.

Can't break through. She redoubles her efforts.

She flees downward, then up, then back, faster and faster, desperate to find a way out.

She twists, bucks, dives, but the webbing tightens.

The kelp becomes bars.

A tight little box encloses her. A coffin. *She can't move, can't swim.* It is as if she is dead.

Then the water becomes mud and the mud dries.

Can't breathe…

Shannon bolted out of bed, thrust out her hands, pushed hard. *Dig through the dirt. Escape the coffin. Can't breathe.* Her lungs expanded in a desperate attempt to fill with air. Her throat burned from ragged breathing…but wait.

Wait.

Her hands met no resistance. She stopped clawing the air. Her skin dripped with sweat. Cool fresh night air blew in a window.

Oh. Her own bedroom, her own bed.

She'd been holding her breath. She gasped it out and drew another in with a greedy gulp. Such wild fear, such a frantic effort to escape. She had *lived* that entanglement, a memory, not a dream.

She reached for the bedside lamp and clicked it on. The soft warm cone of light shining on her rumpled bed covers comforted her. As did the sight of one giant buff-colored mastiff, now stretched across two-thirds of the bed. Indy, long, wide tongue hanging from her panting mouth, lifted her huge head to study Shannon. A goopy string of drool dangled off her chin. Shannon relaxed at the sight of her sweet two-hundred-pound puppy.

Narci, who had tumbled to the floor when Shannon leapt off the bed, now perched on Shannon's dresser. The sleek, black cat licked a paw, flicked her tail, and pelted Shannon with withering looks.

"Sorry, kitten." Shannon slipped over to her and stroked her chin until the cat purred.

Still trembling, Shannon combed her fingers from her scalp through the long strands of her soft, fine hair, then wobbled to the bathroom, one hand skimming along the wall to steady herself. She leaned forward to check her face in the mirror. The lightning had not been kind. Pale, gaunt face. Eyes, with bags. Shannon of the Undead.

Wait a tick. Her eyes. She squinted. The night light on the wall provided dim interruption to the darkness. Funny. Her ho hum-colored eyes cast off a weird dark green glint in this light. She'd never noticed that before. Her irises never hinted of green in regular light.

And hey, in the semi-dark, her dark hair, which she had always refused to color any shade of blonde, shone like a stream of pale moonshine. Why had she never noticed these weird effects in the bathroom's half-light before? She studied the look for a moment, then gave her head a dismissive shake. Blonde, even this lovely shade with silvery highlights—not her style.

The lavender child—what had she called herself? Essi—whispered:

leemira.

Leemeera? Means what? The wheels in her mind had grounded to a halt.

"Nope, don't understand, Essi. And too tired to try."

Her empty stomach gurgled. Again. Shannon sighed and dragged herself downstairs to the kitchen.

* * *

The radio news erupted from her alarm clock at 7 a.m. Monday morning. Shannon responded with a long, low wail. Some jerk inside her skull slammed hockey pucks against her forehead—a leftover, no doubt, from the knock to the head she'd received when she passed out at the pool; moving her ribcage enough to breathe demanded effort; cogent thought lay in tatters. She checked her mind for the little silvery lavender child. Please no lavender child, please…*Hell*.

"I take it you're still there too then, Juneau?"

The feel of a long sleek form brushed against her mind. Beluga chittering sounded in her ear. Shannon smiled.

After she fed Indy, Narci, and herself, she sat at the kitchen table and mulled over her nightmare. She shuddered at the memory. Now that her brain was awake, she could see that *Juneau* had dreamed last night, a horrible dream, and Shannon had experienced the full terror of it. But why had Juneau shared her bad dream with Shannon? She stirred cream into her coffee as she wondered how Juneau had managed to get entangled. A fishing net? She must've been a baby, a few years old, since she'd come to the SeaQuarium at the tender age of four—

All at once the answer jumped like a racing dolphin into her mind: Juneau had dreamed about the day the SQ had captured her in frigid Canadian waters. A terrifying capture. Juneau had never forgotten. Nor would Shannon. Not after the nightmare.

She shivered, snatched up her cell phone, now clear about what she needed to do, and called the SQ Fish House. Becky wouldn't have arrived yet, but Shannon didn't have the guts to talk to her in person anyway. She took the coward's way.

"Becky? It's Shannon. I haven't had, I mean heard back from you since I called yesterday, so I don't know what you're even thinking right now, but there's something important I need to tell you. And don't go ballistic."

Shannon swallowed. "Juneau, who's in my head, as I mentioned last night, dreamed about her capture and so I dreamed it too. A nightmare, a terrible nightmare. And, and until this moment, I'd never *known*, never understood deep in my gut, the cruelty of Juneau's capture." Tears ran down her cheeks. "Now I do. And it changes everything. I'm resigning from my volunteer work at the SQ, even though I'll miss the marine mammals so much." Her heart pulled at her chest. "So much. Tons. I'm going to work to free Juneau. And after her, all the others." She hesitated. "Don't flip out, Beck. Please. I love you. Bye."

Shannon clicked off, put her hands over her face and cried a bucket of tears.

After a time, she grabbed a wad of tissues, wiped her face, and blew her nose. She plucked a yellow banana covered with a multitude of brownish spots from the fruit bowl. She sniffed. No good. Too soft and pungent.

But the only edible thing left within easy reach. She hesitated a split second, then gulped it down in five big bites. She looked at the left-over banana peel. *Why not?* Down it went, unwashed and....

And she'd just consumed a bad-tasting banana and its peeling.

Unacceptable, for Odinssake. Soon she'd have to check herself into an institution for the gastronomically insane.

Her feet unsteady, she clutched the stair railing with both hands and hauled herself in slow motion toward the upstairs shower. A strong and strange impulse led her to bypass the usual news channel on the radio that kept her company as she prepared for work, and flick through her CDs for humpback whale songs instead.

Hot steamy showers, the hotter, the better, the ultimate luxury. Shannon never dipped a toe in water less than 70 degrees. But today a sudden hankering for a chilly salvo of water seized her.

"You again, right, Juneau?"

With grave misgivings, she turned the water faucet to full cold.

Wow. The wet polar splash tingled her skin, jump-started her blood flow, and jazzed her spirits.

As the cold shower water ran down her back, she sang with the humpback CD. She couldn't mimic their squeaks, low moans, and haunting calls, but she fashioned the whale sounds she could, closed her eyes, and imagined herself in the dark waters, moving smoothly, gracefully, joyfully with the long-finned giants. Essi added a quiet hum, keeping time with Shannon. While Shannon scrubbed, another set of whale calls arose in her head, beluga sounds, creating a stereo effect with the humpback tape. Her heart quivered. She'd never conjured any music so forlorn yet exquisite before. Well. *She* hadn't conjured that beautiful music. *Juneau* had.

As Shannon listened, shivers iced through her body. She stepped out of the shower and grabbed her towel.

The whale song persisted, echoed louder; her shivers grew more violent, until her arms twitched and jerked. She wrapped her giant white bath sheet around her and pulled it tight. Though plush and soft next to her skin, it failed to warm her. Essi hummed low.

So. Juneau's way of sending another message. She wanted her own kind, and not in a tiny pool where her fellow captives grew anxious, depressed or mean-spirited, but out on the open sea.

Still wrapped tight, she sank onto her bed, pulled up the cheerful blue and yellow-flowered quilt her grandmother had crafted for her and waited for the shaking to stop. And waited. The whale sounds, and the shivering, died away.

Shannon pulled on black wool slacks. *Wow.* Even after everything she'd crammed into her mouth, not only did the zipper close, but she could slip her finger between her skin and the waistband. Impressive. Yet not good. Well, she'd just have to eat more.

She buttoned her white silk shirt, lurched to the bathroom, and grabbed her brush—then paused, brush in mid-air. She leaned over, drawing her face close to the mirror, and peered at her eyes. Shadows under them, yes, but what an excellent color of green. A strange, unfamiliar vivid dark green.

How?

Uneasy, she resumed brushing her hair, halted again and grabbed a handful of her long locks. Her mop had grown thicker, its dark luster replaced by a pale blond. And it shimmered.

Eyes, hair, transformed. Not the trick reflection of a half-lit room at night, but real.

No freaking way.

Shannon stared at the pale blond strands.

leemira.

"You did this, Essi? Well, undo it." Shannon set up an image for the child, replacing the new Shannon colors with the old ones.

Nothing.

leemira.

"Means nothing to me, little girl, and I'm too tired to figure it out. Just fix it, will you?"

Nothing. Shannon sighed and exited the bathroom. Time to get dressed for work.

As Shannon slipped on her comfortable black work pumps and headed downstairs, she listed the people she must call.

She dialed Becky first as she plunked down at the kitchen table.

"Hey. How're you?"

"Ugh," Becky said.

Shannon grinned. "I hear you. Did you listen to my messages? I don't suppose there's any change in Juneau?"

"Yes, I listened to your messages, and dismissed them as the ravings of a lightning-struck lunatic. We'll talk more later. I've been glued to the Dickson pool for most of the night. It doesn't look good, girlfriend." Becky said, her voice flat and hoarse. "So, you might want to prepare yourself, in case—" She paused. "—you know."

Shannon's guts roiled. "I can save her," she answered. "I'm sir, I mean sure of it. She's here with me."

"First, you will not go to work today, right? You can't even talk."

Not go to work? Of course she would go to work. She always went to work. She touched her silk blouse.

"Uh. Yes, the nightning, lightning, scrambled my speech center a bit. But otherwise I'm fine." Well. Not fine. More like holding her own. More like hanging by a thread.

Becky went on. "Uh huh, I noticed. Anyway, the Dickson experts have researched lightning victims. They've contacted other marine mammal centers. Tried everything. Total failure."

"Yes, but they don't know anything about *this* lightning. Here's the thing: this lightning didn't travel *through* me, it travelled *into* me, and *brought Juneau with it.* I just need to get over to the Dickson and send her mind back to her."

Shannon pictured her mind clear of Juneau's nightmares, of the lavender child. Her appetite back to normal. No confused vocabulary. No dizziness, no gibberish. Hooray.

No scent, no dark green eyes. *Oh.* Foo.

The whisper floated across her mind again:

en esssii?

Shannon's heart twinged, but she tried to ignore the child. However, the waif didn't ignore her. Lavender lightning flashed inside Shannon's eyelids. Flashed and pulsed. Her alien child's vibration stepped up the tempo. Splendid. Her little guest, pitching a fit. Shannon rubbed her temple and waited. After a moment, the vibration settled back to a low grumbly hum.

Becky said, "No offense, but if you still had a lightning bolt rattling around in your bod, it would've fried your brain. I can picture it; your eyes glowing yellow, your body jerking like a marionette, and your brain a briquette after a pig roast."

"Nice talk. But..." Shannon closed her mouth. Only someone who'd experienced this phenomenon would believe her.

Maybe no one ever had.

Never mind. If Shannon couldn't persuade Becky with words, she'd go down to the Dickson and prove it.

"Listen, Shannon. Kidding aside, I wanted to prepare you for...probabilities."

Shannon's gut twisted as if the cleaning lady was squeezing them like rags.

"What proba, probabilities?" she asked, her voice vibrating with the first note of panic.

"Very low chance of survival. They're telling us she's fading. They won't keep her going much longer. They'll take her off the respirator soon."

Shannon tried to stand, tipped sideways in her kitchen chair, and grasped the table edge at the last minute. Even after she regained her balance, her white-knuckled hand continued to grip the table edge.

She imagined the whale's bright eyes; her fingers caressed her palm as she relived her being-to-being connection with the beluga whenever she touched Juneau's rubbery skin. But now, she saw Juneau, lifeless, the breathing apparatus disconnected. It hadn't occurred to Shannon that Juneau's body might die before she could return the whale's mind!

zhoo.

The whisper echoed her pain. Shannon answered without thinking. "Yes. Juneau." She laid her face on the table, one ear down, holding the phone on top of the other ear. Juneau couldn't die. *Couldn't.* Shannon would reach her first, send her mind back.

Or was it already too late?

Becky and Shannon remained silent for a moment. A desolate whale call reverberated in Shannon's head.

"How long?" Shannon asked after a time.

"If there's no change by Friday morning, they're pulling the plug."

Friday? Four days. Not enough time. Shannon lifted her head and banged it once on the table. The child's hum slowed into a low mournful throb. The sorrowful whale call echoed again, deep in Shannon's mind.

At the other end of the line, Becky took a shaky breath.

Oh man. Shannon hadn't given much thought to her friend since last night. Not kind.

"You okay?" Shannon asked.

"You'll hurt more than anyone when…. Juneau connected with you," Becky said.

"Connected," as in past tense? Shannon's head lifted from the table. Becky had already given up?

Shannon straightened her back. *By Odin's eye,* Shannon wouldn't write Juneau off just yet. And she'd see that Becky and the Dickson didn't either.

"Listen, I have a big favor to ask. I need to see her. Please. Just a few minutes. Can you get me into the Dickson today?"

Becky remained silent for a moment.

Say yes. Say yes.

"With Juneau…failing now, I don't see why not," Becky said. "She's fragile, so some jerk in SQ Admin might get his panties in a knot but screw 'em. I'll call the Dickson and give the research team a heads-up. When do you want to go?"

Shannon reviewed her schedule for the day. A deposition she couldn't miss. Everything else she could rearrange.

"Right after lunch? And thanks. You're the best."

"You bet I am and don't you forget it. Hey, I forgot to ask you— why aren't you in the hospital?—Oh wait, sorry, Andy's here. Weighing walruses today. Gotta go. We'll stay in touch, sister." Becky's phone clicked off.

Shannon sat staring at a piece of paper in her hand, seeing instead Juneau's round white head, laughing black eyes, and deceptive smile.

She blinked. *Earth to Shannon.* Focus.

Oh, right. Her list of calls.

Next: Dr. Bennett. Voice mail picked up and Shannon detailed her tale of woes. "I need some help to sable, I mean stabilize soon, Dr. Bennett. I can't afford to function at anything less than a hundred percent right now. Thanks."

A hundred percent? Hah. She'd settle for half that.

She glanced at her watch. A window of time remained before she must arrive at work. If she hurried, she could flip some pancakes, and throw together a bacon and avocado omelet. Biscuits. Coffee cake. A second breakfast.

Wait. She rechecked the time. She'd last eaten just an hour ago. *And already famished?* Loki be damned. Hah. No, she couldn't blame her new hyper-metabolism on Loki, the dark Norse god of mischief. Then Odin and Thor could take care of him for Shannon. But Loki wasn't the culprit here. Odin and Thor could do nothing for Shannon.... Loki? Odin? She snorted. *For heaven's sakes, focus, Shannon, focus.*

After she'd filled her stomach again, she packed some casual clothes for this afternoon's visit to Juneau, along with a snack bag, gathered her keys and briefcase, and kissed her babies good-bye.

"Your favorite dog-walker will come at ten, Indy. Be good."

And now to work. She never missed work. It should go fine, right? Sure, she'd become a little addled and carried a wild whale spirit and an alien child around with her, but what could go wrong? As long as she just acted normal and didn't open her mouth often, she might get by. She wrapped her hair into a tight french twist.

When she reached the Mannheim Building, which housed all the county offices including the Legal Department, she walked with slow, deliberate steps to the elevator, keeping her balance with fair success. Well, with some success. Okay, she wobbled like a top just about to stop spinning.

She scanned the crowded elevator space for colleagues who might have watched her trip her way across the smooth marble floor. The fates were kind. None of the faces around her belonged to coworkers. She did recognize her paralegal's husband, a Bluto-looking fellow in alligator-hide cowboy boots, but today she bypassed the opportunity to shout a friendly hello.

The elevator contained the usual 9 a.m. crush. The walls crammed the nine occupants together. They could count each other's facial pores. Without warning, icy claws of claustrophobia clamped her skull and torso. Too much like the nightmare coffin. She fought the impulse to scream.

Concentrate. Breathe. Focus. She looked straight down and, right next to her own pumps, she could see the bony ankles and red high heels of a skinny woman in an orange-and-yellow plaid suit. The crowd had pressed the woman close to Shannon.

Hold on. No screaming. Focus. Bony ankles. Red shoes. Hold on.

A moment of welcome distraction came when the Bluto look-alike stepped on the foot of the man behind him, who groaned as if a steel girder had fallen on his toes. Heads turned. Murmured apologies followed.

Bony ankles. Red shoes.

At last the elevator reached her floor.

Shannon worked her way to the door of the Legal Department and reached for the handle, then halted. She had no desire whatsoever for her boss, Matt Portman, to spot her. How to avoid him? Shannon performed her job well, extremely well. The attorneys of Ocean City held her in high regard as an intelligent, well-prepared, fair-minded counselor. But she'd had a few run-ins with her boss. She did not suffer fools lightly, and in many ways, Matt's personality and his lack of intellect made her suffer. Not lightly.

Nor did she want to lay eyes on Scott Cross. The sight of his soft, pale blue eyes still transformed her into a witless pudding. And yet when she and Scott had been together, she'd shut him out. She wanted him and she didn't. *Idiot.* Why was it that she could freeze an opposing male attorney into a hapless popsicle, but personal relationships? She brought no power to that game.

She looked at the Legal Department door. Come on. She could do this. *Go in, act casual. Remain cool.* Don't dally. She straightened her spine.

The elevator chimed behind her and disgorged a batch of chatting attorneys and staff. Without thinking, she turned to the sound. As if conjured by her thoughts, Matt Portman led the pack, and right behind him, Scott Cross.

* * *

Portman. Big-shot County Prosecutor with designs on the mayor's office. What a bumbling, interfering, buck-toothed donkey. Well. Not buck-toothed. At least not in the literal sense. But he did want to butt in on her current big case, the Paradigm litigation. Portman knew she'd crafted her case into a winner, and of course he lusted after the coming victory to prime his political ambitions. Shannon didn't mind if he took the credit. Just as long as he kept his plump, oily fingers off her actual work. She did not want to give the man even a tiny opening to wreak havoc on her crucial Paradigm legal brief. If he suspected that a Hereford with mad cow disease could outperform her today, he'd grab her brief and make off with it so fast Shannon would still be saying "no way—" to the empty air.

And Scott. Looking like a million dollars. Well, a thousand maybe.

She couldn't move. Her stomach dropped to the first floor; her forehead broke out in a sweat. Sweet mother of Thor. She'd left her heart stuck in the past where it didn't belong. She'd pushed him away; he had moved on. Now she should do the same. Because—she blinked as she began to see it—because she didn't really yearn to have Scott back. No, she yearned for something else. Something to heal a great wound she refused to admit even existed. Scott had been a bandage and without the bandage, she couldn't ignore the open hole it hid, deep with bittersweet emptiness and stone heavy silence. She–

Then—an adrenaline rush. Fight or flight.

A roaring whirlwind, a hurricane, awakened her mind. Out of the roar flew a wildness without words but Shannon understood: *enemy - protect - fight.*

Uh oh. Juneau, picking up on Shannon's emotions, had kicked into gear.

A strong urge flashed through Shannon to grab Portman's fat jowls and then swing her leg up and kick him. The whirlwind roared. She shook in its grip like a teacup in an earthquake, and it frightened her.

A faint, soothing whisper, *en, en* arose in the midst of the roar,.

Essi. Trying to calm the whale.

Portman spotted her and hurried his step, lifting a finger to catch her eye. The unobservant idiot-not-savant desired a word. Disaster loomed. In a millisecond Shannon would lower her head and charge right into his quivering double chin. He approached. The will to defend, every wild, irrational drop of it, poured through her shaking hands and trembling body.

She fought for control.

Portman came nearer and nearer, unaware, grinning like a body-wrinkled bulldog. When he drew near enough to take a good look at her trembling anger-filled face, he dropped his finger. His grin faded. He stopped, causing a bevy of office workers behind him to stumble into him and each other. An uncertain, even fearful look crept into his eyes. He tried to step backward, but the elevator crowd behind him pushed him forward.

Do not kick him between the legs. Do not kick him —

Shannon looked at Scott Cross's tall form just beyond Portman's shoulder, his eyes trained on her, his look one of puzzled curiosity. She spun, grabbed the door handle, pulled it back just far enough to escape to the other side, and slammed it in Portman's pompous, pear-shaped face. She jerked toward her office.

That feral rage. Way over the top. Her face still blazed, her heart pumped a mile a minute. She leaned against the wall.

Juneau, calm down. Shannon struggled with the whale's wild instincts. She imagined rubbing the whale's gum, her tongue. Juneau loved that.

Soon Shannon's firm grip on Juneau's emotions and her images, aided by the child's humming, slow and gentle, settled the whirlwind, lowered Shannon's heart-beat, soothed her racing thoughts. She slowed her pace, drained and dizzy, aware again of her growing fatigue.

Shannon bumped toward her paralegal's cubicle and Jane glanced up. Jane's bottle-red, curled bangs marched in stiff formation across her forehead, the teased mound of hair, sprayed to ensure it would hold against an F-5 tornado. Loose long locks fell from the wind-proof mound to midway down her back. She wore a Western checkered shirt with a bolo tie, an oval of turquoise in the knot. Jane and her husband Picker—Shannon had never dared ask how he got that name—ran with the rodeo crowd.

Cowgirl ensemble aside, Jane had developed into the best paralegal in the county, bar none. Maybe the best on the West Coast. Shannon cherished her.

"Hi ya, darlin'. How're you this fine morning?" Jane said.

Shannon fiddled with the name plate attached to her paralegal's cubicle wall, the words "Jane Strand" printed in neat gold letters. "I spotted Picker on the elevator," Shannon said. "He, um, pest, I mean, stepped on some little dude in the back."

"Oh my lord, did they have to scrape the poor fella off the floor with a putty knife?"

Shannon grinned. "I couldn't bear to watch," she said.

Jane laughed, then sobered and said, "The Boss called in from home about forty minutes ago. Regarding your brief." Since Jane's cubicle wall extended a foot and a half above her desktop, she peeked over it, and asked, "I watched you coming down the hall. What's wrong with your feet?" As she waited for an answer, she returned to her typing,

"Nothing. I'm fine."

"Your voice sounds as thick as Momma May's molasses, you're moving like a marionette on a bad day, and you claim you're fine. Whatever you say." Jane looked at Shannon and her eyebrows lifted. "Bless my stars, you've bleached your hair. It looks bee-oot-ee-ful. Something else's different, too. I can't quite put my finger on it." She frowned, eyeing Shannon up and down, her fingers curled beneath her chin while her index finger tapped her lips.

Problem. Everyone would assume she'd *bleached* her hair. Not the professional image Shannon had always projected. Well, what else *could* people assume? That the hair fairy had visited in the night?

"Thanks for the compliment. I think. So when Portman clal, I mean called, what did he say?"

"Said that he wants your brief on his desk today so he can shape it up and make revisions before we file on Friday. He'll sign it. A direct order," Jane said. She waved at the document clipped next to her computer. "I've finished this set of revisions. I want to check a few things and it'll come back atcha later this morning."

"Damn. He told me Fur, Friday that he's decided to take lead on my case. *Now,* when I've done all the hard work." She slapped Jane's cubicle wall. "And we know what happens when he takes the reins."

Jane puffed her cheeks and made a pffft sound with her tongue. "Cow patty," she said.

"Exactly. Listen, I don't want him messing with my brief. If he comes around asking for a copy, say you can't assess, access it because I have it up on my computer. He wouldn't understand it if he read it, but that wouldn't stop him from changing something critical."

She might not understand the brief so well herself if she read it this morning. "He never makes revisions on my work. Why now?"

Jane looked around to check for eavesdroppers and said, "He knows you have Paradigm Industries right where you want them, a firm grip on los cojones. He wants his actual imprint, not just his signature, on the brief so he can take the credit and nobody can call him on it. He's picked up the rumors, same as the rest of us. On the street they know he's botched about everything he touches. Could mean his job. He needs the Paradigm win to save his hairy you-know-what."

The paralegal leaned back and examined her fingernails. "But I never said that. What I said was 'Why does he want to revise it? Why, as he is the County Attorney, all work leaving this office must meet his rigorous standards.'" Jane snorted. "Like he could analyze his way through my four-year-old's *Baby Boo Counts to Ten.*"

Shannon grinned despite her fatigue and frustration. "Indeed, Baby Boo might overwhelm him at seven silly seals slurping sardines."

Jane's mischievous eyes sobered. "You know I can't keep him off your back for long, though," Jane said. "He may be a tiny flea on a horse's ass, but he *is* the boss flea."

"Understood." Shannon turned to leave and then, curious, she said, "You notice anything about my eyes?"

"That's it! Shoot, I should've caught that. Green contact lenses. I've never seen them in that color. They'll get you a man, just you wait and see. Done mourning Scott Cross, are we?" Jane winked. "High time."

Shannon winced.

Jane continued, "Now run along and let me finish this draft." Shannon had started toward her office when Jane added, "Oh, and Paradigm's attorneys are already in the conference room prepping their witness." Shannon could feel Jane's eyes on her back as the paralegal added, "And something is too wrong with your walk. And your tongue."

"No there is not," Shannon said as she slammed her office door and leaned against it.

The dep. Due to start in fifteen minutes. She'd never get through it.

*   *   *

She bumped her head back on the door three times. Dyed hair. Colored contacts. Tangled tongue. Paradigm's pricey hired guns would quake in their collective boots when she stumbled in. Not.

Her eyes settled on her desk. Five untidy stacks of papers cluttered the surface screaming for attention. The sight depressed her. She continued past the desk to her west-facing windows, which she kept ajar a couple inches at night. Contrary to office policy, which stated that all staff must close and latch windows when leaving for the day. But then, Shannon had never been one to sweat over office policy.

The air soothed her skin. She watched kids play at the little park across the boulevard. The ocean beyond the park spread along the beach, like a deep blue coverlet; she loved how some days the waters turned deep sea green; other days, dark gray.

She sighed. Time to give her deposition materials a hasty review.

Yet she lingered at the window. The children in the park, all so colorless, pitiful that...*wait. What?* Oh, another intrusion from her guests.

"Correction, Essi, not silver lavender like you, but here colorless is normal."

...the sea, so inviting...she should go for a swim...

"No way, Juneau."

Shannon massaged her forehead. Managing these two would challenge even the Dali Lama.

The dep. Focus.

Shannon settled on the window seat. Just for a minute. She closed her eyes....

"You all right? Did you hear me?"

Shannon jerked, squeaked, and teetered on the edge of the window seat before steadying herself. She looked up. She was swimming, far out in the ocean. Jane stood on a sandy beach in the distance.

Wrong.

Shannon squeezed her eyes tight, gave her head two tight, quick shakes, and peered again.

Jane stood by Shannon's desk, paperwork in her hands. *Better.*

"I forgot to mention the Leeberg Agreed Order. You need to sign it."

Right. "Sorry, I didn't hear you come in."

"I noticed," Jane said.

Watchful of that first step, Shannon pushed off from the window seat, picked her wobbly way to her desk, dropped her briefcase, plunked down in her padded chair, and signed the order.

"Anything new going on in the office?" Shannon said, as if desiring a bit of idle gossip.

If a butterfly fluttered its wings anywhere in the department, Jane would know the color, pattern, size, sex, location, and flight plan of the subject butterfly within the hour. Had word spread of her bizarre behavior at the office door?

"Not a whisper. Since the Boss tubed our last big case, the place has stayed as quiet as a mouse at a wildcat convention. No one wants him to even notice they exist. If anything comes up, I'll let you know." Jane winked, and checked the paperwork in case Shannon had missed anything—which she had. The paralegal whisked another page in front of Shannon's face and she penned her name on the overlooked signature line.

"So," Jane continued, "What's responsible for your current state of dilapidation? A big date last night? About time." Jane said as she headed out without waiting for a reply.

Dilapidated. Fair description. Falling asleep minutes before an important deposition!

She liked to go over her materials one last time right before a dep, but she'd already pored over the file for days and her question list and exhibits lay stacked in a neat pile. No time today. She packed her triplicate copies of documents for the witness, thick case binders, note pads, pens, sticky notes, cell phone, and lucky brass whale tale into her briefcase to lug over to the conference room.

*   *   *

Shannon tottered into the small conference room near her office, taking little steps with barely-raised feet, touching the wall for support, but no more than three or four times. *Good.* Now just that little bit of open ground to the conference table. Push off from the wall. A few steps. And…grab the chair back. *Not too bad.*

Had anyone noticed her unsteady entrance? She looked at the four people seated at the table. Everyone had busied themselves with the tasks of setting up, except the Paradigm exec there for his deposition. He gaped at her with a look of alarm. Shannon stared him down without a word until he lowered his eyes to his hands, which he'd folded on the table. She noticed his nostrils flaring.

Ah. She'd forgotten the scent.

"Counselors," she said to the two gentlemen flanking her deponent. She offered her hand, and one of the two half rose and gave it a quick hard crunch. Shannon had expected the macho hand squeeze and returned it with equal gripping gusto. The attorney winced, just enough for Shannon to catch sight of it. She allowed herself a tiny smile. But it cost her. Her hand had gone numb.

"Beguiling perfume. But at a deposition?" he said and clucked his tongue.

A feeble counterattack. *Jerk.*

The other attorney feigned extreme interest in a document on the table in front of him and never looked up, as if she didn't rate his time and attention. So typical of him. She could hear him sniffing, though. He'd picked up the scent as well. And if they found the scent distracting, all the better.

Bad Shannon.

Their client gave her a nervous nod, unsure which of his two watchdogs to emulate.

The court reporter sat behind his machine ready to start. Shannon slid her business card to him.

"Good to see you," she said.

He returned her smile and gave her a small salute.

"Shall we begin?"

Before she could go on the record to establish the proceedings and participants, that now-familiar longing pulled at her like an outgoing tide.

The yearning slipped in and out of her consciousness like an eel. *She could survive this if she could return to the sea.* Her chest jerked with pain. The ache flowed out of the pain like blood, deep, urgent. *Trapped.*

The image formed in her mind once again, the white beluga swimming just under the surface of the water, her powerful tale fluke flexing up and down, propelling her away. Nearby, a little silvery lavender wisp, Essi's river form, flowed along, keeping up with Juneau.

sela esssii o zhoo.

Shannon drifted…

* * *

"—I said, are you ready Ms. Kendricks?" Lead counsel's booming voice cut into Shannon's haze. "My client and I can't twiddle our thumbs here all day while you stare at your notes."

How long had she sat there like a blond rock? She glanced at her watch. Ten minutes. *Odin help her.* Shannon's hands shook. A cool sheen of sweat broke out on her forehead. Her stomach lurched, about to heave.

"If you will exclu," said as she cleared her throat, "I mean, excuse me for just a moment." She didn't—couldn't—wait for a response. Stumbling against the table, Shannon made her way out of the conference room and down the hall to the ladies' lounge, walking as fast as she could, pushed through the door. And lost her breakfast. Given how much she'd eaten, she had little to heave. Essi and Juneau had converted it and used it in record time.

She applied cold water in large quantities to her face, slapped her cheeks hard three times and waited until the trembling stopped.

Day dreaming right in the middle of her dep? Not Shannon, never Shannon.

Every time she breathed in, she shuddered. *No good.* Propping her hands on the edge of sink, her arms straight, she leaned her head down for a minute and tried to regain her clarity and her calm.

She fought Juneau's wild desperation.

She couldn't finish the deposition.

Of course she could finish. Keep on breathing, slow in, slow out.

After a while, she popped a handful of sugar cubes from her bag into her mouth.

All right. She—the longing for the sea hit her again, so hard she curled over her gut, her stomach cramped.

No, she couldn't finish the dep.

* * *

Fifteen minutes later, she mustered enough control to return to the conference room.

"My sorry, I'm, my apologies, everyone," Shannon said. "I think I must have picked up a touch of the flu. I'm afraid we'll have to cancel."

"It's your money," the second attorney said, looking up from his paperwork with an ugly smile. Shannon kept her face neutral and sagged into her chair. *Jerk.*

The attorneys hustled their client away. The court reporter packed up his gear. Shannon sat.

"It's your money," the Paradigm attorney had said. All bluff. Paradigm had been running up the legal fees, sure, but the court wouldn't require Shannon to pay them if she won. And she *would* win if she could keep Portman away from her brief.

Even so, Paradigm's lead counsel, one of Portman's golf buddies, would call and give her boss grief for Shannon wasting his precious time. He might even say she'd acted drunk. Not a bad guess, now that she thought of it.

Portman would become irate. To say the least.

Trying to rise, dizziness overtook Shannon again. Her head pounded like Godzilla on Tokyo. More leftovers from her concussion. Or her hunger. Or her rapid energy loss. She dragged herself back to Jane's cubicle, collapsed on a short file cabinet and lamented the aborted deposition.

"You need to get on home now," Jane said. "Fix yourself some green tea with chamomile and honey, and tuck up in your quilts. Read a nice romance novel. I've got Heather Anderson's latest right here. It'll make your toes curl. You want it?"

"No thanks, I'm good for books, but I might take a break and get out of here for a while. I'll come back this afternoon."

Jane pursed her lips but said no more.

Shannon slipped into her office. Her desk phone message button blinked, an ominous portent: Portman. *Uh oh.* Shannon hit "play" and Portman's voice sizzled down the line.

*   *   *

"Portman here. You closed the door in my goddamn face this morning and I want to know why. In my office this afternoon at…just a minute, let me check my schedule…" The phone clanked onto his desk. His muffled voice floated through the line as he yelled out the door to his admin assistant Cynthia. He didn't know how to use the hold button—that figured. A muffled voice answered— Cynthia's—then Portman again. Shannon chewed her fingernails for something to do until he picked up and continued his message. "It, uh, I can't see you today, but tomorrow at 11 a.m. sharp. Or, Paradigm case or not, I will send you out the door for insubordination." The call ended with a crack as his phone slammed down.

She erased the message and put her face in her hands. Oh man. Nothing Shannon could say to Portman about the door incident would make the slightest sense. Or appease his sense of pride. He'd bluffed about sending her out the door. He wouldn't fire her before Paradigm wrapped up—he couldn't afford to—but after the win? Plausible. Even more plausible if Paradigm's attorney called and described the dep. And if anything else happened, she was cooked. She'd have to tread lightly.

In the meantime, Shannon must eat. What a surprise. Time to get out of the office and out of Portman's sight.

*   *   *

Shannon wanted a restaurant where she wouldn't run into her colleagues. Her favorite Thai hole-in-the-wall, The Thai Game, fit the bill. She hopped a bus headed for the International District.

As she helped herself to curried vegetables, pad thai, rice, and pot stickers, she relived the horrors of her run-in with Portman and Scott, and her catastrophic deposition. Her body hurt all over, as if she lay at the bottom of a rugby scrum.

Forget work. Let it go. Get down to the Dickson, return Juneau and Essi to the whale's body. Juneau revives. Simple.

Very good. Thinking like the old can-do Shannon. Now some progress—

—Essi's hum, urgent, insistent, rose in Shannon's mind. The child formed an image in Shannon's mind. Essi and Juneau's spirits flow back to Juneau's body, but Juneau loses her ample beluga fat, thinning down and down. The whale looks like a long white eel and sinks lifeless to the pool floor.

Oh. Of course. If Essi stayed in Juneau's body, Juneau couldn't eat enough to survive, same as Shannon.

By Thor's thunder. Not an option.

Juneau took over the image. Shannon watched as Juneau revives and is hoisted above her SQ pool. Juneau bucks, her powerful fluke flings her out of the hoist. Slamming onto the concrete. One final act of defiance, of escape from captivity.

A jolt of revulsion shocked Shannon. *Holy Odin.* Message received: Juneau would rather die than go back to her little pool.

She stirred her rice around her plate, frowning, lethargic and unable to shake the shock. *Juneau would rather die.* Then the now-familiar pull to lift her eyes drew her focus from the table. Lavender haze floated beside her chair: in the next few minutes, someone would pay her a visit.

But no one knew where she'd gone. No one bothered her here.

Shannon had seated herself with her back to the door. She laid her fork down and waited. A moment later, Scott Cross appeared from behind her chair. Scott Cross, former lover. Scott Cross, whose face still sent her into nervous spasms as if she were a thirteen-year-old in puppy love, even after three years apart. And the stupid part was that Scott wasn't right for her; he never had been. But for a long time, he'd stayed around without asking for the commitment thing. She'd grown at ease with him. Like a comfy old couch. Then he'd up and taken the couch away. Only then did she want it—or rather him—back. Yep. Stupid.

So. Not him, not now. Anybody but him.

"Hi. Mind if I sit down?"

Go away.

"Sure. I mean no, I don't mind. How'd you know I'd come here?"

He lowered himself into the seat. "Jane said you'd gone to lunch. I checked the cafe in our building. I didn't see you and remembered that we used to come here when we were in law school. You always liked their pad thai. And voila."

Shannon studied the man she'd once loved. He looked better than ever, the bastard. Pale blue eyes bright and clear. A glowing tan. He looked content. She'd like to wipe that happy look right off his face.

Now Shannon. Stay cool, attractive, professional. She flashed a big smile. She lounged back in her chair. *Casual, now.*

Scott perched on the edge of the chair opposite her and said, "You look terrible."

Shannon's smile faded. *So much for cool, attractive and professional.* She pulled the comb from her french braid and shook loose her long curls. Let it tangle, then, free.

"Look, I just have a minute; I'm on my way to court," he said, as he twiddled Shannon's thin white straw wrapper into a small ball. "I just wanted to check that you're okay. Have you seen a doctor?"

Feeling wonderful. Tell him that. *Never better. Better and better ever since he'd left.*

"Yeah, something's messed up my health, for sure," Shannon said. "I'm taking a few days off. My doctor's working on the fix."

Now go away.

"Thanks for asking, though."

"Well, the flashy hair and green contacts. I know you're trying to hide the problem. But you still look pretty bad. So." Scott's words faded out. He turned the paper ball in his fingers over and over.

Could she sink through the floor now? Could she run screaming into the street? Could she smack him across his placid-looking kisser?

She said, "Well I expect I've picked up the flu. Great to see you. "

Now disappear.

"Yeah, well, I've got a motion on the calendar this afternoon." Scott checked his watch, said his good-byes and rushed off.

By all the gods of heaven, earth and sea.

Shannon sat there, surrounded by the emptiness Scott had left in his wake. Her concentration had followed him out the door.

"You look terrible," he'd said. Time to face the facts. The lightning had blasted her out of her normal life. No use pretending she could carry on as if nothing had happened.

A great weariness settled in, as if she'd just finished swimming the English Channel. A warmth brushed her mind and wrapped her thoughts. Essi thrummed low. For now, she could do no more than sip her green tea and gaze out the window at the colorful foot traffic on Honshu Street.

*   *   *

After a time, she phoned Becky, who turned on the phone's camera image of herself so she could talk as she filled food buckets from the thawed herring in the sink at the SQ. Shannon clicked on her phone camera as well.

"Yo. How you feeling?" Becky said.

"Not so good. Disastrous morning at work. I'm going to see Juneau now, then home. How about you?"

"You went to work? Fool. Did I not tell you? As for me, I'm surviving. I've mastered the sleep-working technique."

"How's—" Shannon stopped herself before she could say, "How's the body?" "How's Juneau?"

A grim look passed like a shadow across Becky's face. Shannon's heart sank.

"Getting worse."

"Dickson's staff should…should *do* something," said Shannon.

"They're doing their best, kiddo, believe me." Becky squinted into the phone display. "What's that on top of your face? Looks like that blond wig you bought when we went underground to research prostitutes in college."

"It doesn't look that bad, does it?"

"I'm teasing. It looks good. Just surprised you'd go blond."

"No, I—it's comli, complicated." Someone in the background called Becky's name.

"Listen, I can't talk now," Becky said. "Ron told me I could leave early if I finished all the feeding. So generous. Remind me I need to resign when this is all over, would you?"

Shannon nodded. Her friend threatened her boss, Ron Forrester, with her resignation once or twice a week. "A woman with a mind like a seal strap, shit, steel trap like yours won't need a reminder. You'll get out of there soon. Today, I hope?"

"I should escape in less than an hour. Then it's lights out for me before I go out to see Juneau. Go home and rest."

Becky's face disappeared.

Shannon dialed Dr. Bennett's private office number. Still no answer. She punched the phone's off button, voiced a few choice curses, grabbed her purse, and took off to see Juneau.

She stopped at her office just long enough to pluck the flash drive off her computer, avoiding Portman by taking the long way around the square hallway to her office so as not to pass his door.

Jane called out as Shannon brushed by. "Do you have the brief for the Boss Man?"

"Not ready yet. I'll fish in it, crap, finish it at home. Portman wants to see me tomorrow. I won't make it. Tell him it's because I'm sick, will you?" Shannon called back to her, brandishing the flash drive.

"Yes I will, and good for you. You should've never come in today. You look like you ran with the bulls in Pamplona and stopped to tie your shoelaces."

Jane too. Fine.

Next Shannon stopped at home, downed a couple of sandwiches and packed her biggest picnic cooler to the brim before she left for the Dickson.

"The dog walker will come back for your afternoon walk in less than an hour, big girl," she said to Indy. "Come on, Essi and Juneau, we've got places to go, whales to see."

But what would she do when she arrived? Send Juneau's mind back in the hope of saving her body? Even if that meant the Dickson would send Juneau back to the SQ, where the whale would rather die than go?

*   *   *

"Let there be a parking spot near the Dickson's front entrance. Parking spot. Parking...."

No such luck. As part of the Dickson's partnership with the University, it had located its main facility on the campus along with the U's 32,000 students. And their cars. She'd have to drag her tired ass seven or eight blocks to reach the Research Center. Good thing she'd brought provisions.

Popping a toffee bar into her mouth and hefting the strap of her snack bag over her shoulder, she scanned the horizon and aimed for the Dickson's tall blue-peaked roof towering above the campus.

The late afternoon sun warmed her skin; the slight wind smelled of ocean-salt. If the lightning strike hadn't left her mind and body in shambles, if it hadn't dropped an alien-child with the appetite of the Roman Army on her and if it hadn't left her beloved whale comatose, she could've enjoyed playing hooky on this mild, breezy day.

If.

Shannon arrived at the front steps of the Dickson and hesitated. Juneau, nearing death, would look terrible, emaciated, limp, those lively eyes gone dim.

Well, she would deal with it. She passed through the revolving entryway doors into the building's soaring three-story glass atrium.

The moment she stepped inside, fear poured over her like an arctic waterfall. She froze, as if an invisible hand on her chest had stopped her dead in her tracks.

So afraid. A forlorn call echoed on her mind.

Juneau's fear playing out in Shannon's mind. Well, who *would* want to see her own dying body?

Understood, Juneau.

If Juneau could comprehend how serious the situation had grown, though, perhaps Shannon could persuade the beluga to return to her body and trust Shannon to somehow come up with a way to win her freedom.

Shannon fought back Juneau's urges and ordered her legs to move. She headed down the main hall muttering curses. At the end of the hall she found a small sign beside a set of stairs leading to the next level down and labeled "Auxiliary Pool."

As she started down the steps, shivers again shook her, like another watery avalanche of ice. Nausea punched her belly. Hells bells. She couldn't risk barfing her breakfast; it would take the entire Dickson staff to clean it up.

Essi, can you help Juneau? Shannon imaged the child, her arms around the beluga's neck, humming.

Essi's beautiful music filled Shannon's mind.

Shannon lowered herself to sit on the step, clutched the railing, and leaned her cheek against the cool iron support post to wait out Juneau's panic. The thought of going farther made Juneau want to run; her fear fought Shannon like a marlin on a tight line.

Shannon struggled to wrestle Juneau's wild instinct to flee, then slapped the cool iron railing; she *must* go; she *would* go. Once she focused all her willpower on moving forward, Juneau's icy panic subsided. She rose, gripped the iron banister with white-knuckled fingers and descended to the basement.

On her left she spotted a set of metal doors big enough to roll a whale through. She couldn't see much through its window, crisscrossed with tiny wire mesh. Shannon pushed. It didn't budge. She scanned the area. A button set in the wall on her right looked promising. She pressed it. A hollow voice floated out of a six-inch brass square:

"Yes?"

"Shannon Kendricks. Becky Anderson arranged for me to send, I mean spend a few minutes with Juneau?"

A rustling of paper. Checking the guest list.

"Right. Come on in." A buzzer, a click, and Shannon pushed the door open. She paused for a second to gather her composure.

*   *   *

The auxiliary pool room smelled of damp walls and chlorine—someone must have recently been cleaning the concrete decks. The humidity in the air increased to an uncomfortable level. A researcher in a white coat stepped away from a table that held a computer, a printer, and a binder thick with notations. He moved toward the pool and beckoned her to follow. The chlorine and the dampness ramped up their assault. She pinched the bridge of her nose as another headache formed.

At the edge of the pool perched a black six-foot-high machine. The respirator. A black plastic wall had been rigged between the respirator and the pool to protect the equipment. Not that Juneau could spit or splash now.

The whale floated just behind the protective wall; Shannon could glimpse the tip of Juneau's inert white fluke on the surface of the water, but no more.

zhoo.

Yes, Essi, that's Juneau.

Nausea rocked Shannon.

A soft black belt encircled her tail. The belt looped through a ring attached to a cable hanging from the rafters. Something similar, no doubt, supported her torso and head, so she floated with her back just above the surface of the water. Belugas floated due to their body design, so they must use the belts to steady her blow hole and keep it above the waterline.

Okay, move on, take all the time Juneau needs to come to grips with this. Her flat extra-grip Nikes slipped along the smooth cement floor without a hitch.

The working side of the artificial breathing apparatus rounded into view. She could hear the ghastly manufactured breaths that kept Juneau alive, like Darth Vader inhaling, exhaling, forced in, forced out. *So vital. So artificial.*

As she moved from behind the respirator, Shannon gagged at the sight of the tubes attached to Juneau, and again at the sight of Juneau herself, yellowish, her layer of blubber already thinning, her eyes filmy and neither quite open nor quite closed.

Shannon's knees wobbled, her face grew hot, beads of sweat seeped from her forehead. First ice cold, now tropic hot. Her hand groped for the smooth protective wall, Juneau and Essi echoed Shannon's revulsion at seeing the helpless whale at the mercy of machines. Shannon gagged again.

Shannon stood waiting for equilibrium. Essi rallied and pulsed her calm hum. Shannon's stomach settled, the heat in her face cooled. She could think of nothing but stopping the whale's death spiral. Every other consideration would have to wait.

Take her home Essi and then come back to me. She's too weak to support you.

Shannon crouched down. Her hand reached out to touch Juneau's forehead.

She stretched. Closer now, an inch or two more—

—Ten strong firm fingers gripped her upper arms and jerked her back to her feet.

"Sorry. Protocol. No tactile contact. Coma cause disputed. Unknown effect on her, on you."

Shannon turned on the researcher who'd just delivered this abbreviated speech. His hazel eyes, magnified by the think lenses of his glasses, blinked back at her from a round, red-bearded face. The outside edges of his bushy brows bent down, in perfect unison with his unsmiling lips. His hands had flown off her arms the moment he succeeded in pulling her away from Juneau. He focused at a point over her shoulder and fidgeted.

"Nice perfume." He took a step back. "I'm married." His face turned the color of his beard.

A surprised laugh burst from Shannon. "That's good to know." Then she moved in close to him. "Look, the cause of the coma isn't in dispute, as you said. I know what claused, that is, what caused her coma. Lightning caused it. And did you say no contact? She *needs* contact. She's so sensitive to touch. Maybe rubbing her would bring her around. Please, just let me try. I—"

The researcher's head swung back and forth like a clock pendulum the entire time Shannon talked. He interrupted when Shannon ignored his negative response and said, "Doesn't respond. Electronic sensors, small shocks. Feels nothing. Could hurt you both."

Shannon's eyes squinted, dark with anger. "I don't care what might happen to me. Give me a lerease, um, release, I'll sign it. And you gave her shocks? What are you talking about, shocks? A shock got her into this mess, for Odinssake."

"Stop," Todd said, no irritation in his voice; just the facts, ma'am. "We're going in circles. *Our* equipment, *SQ's* whale. We say, SQ says, no touching. For her sake."

Back off. Don't upset the guy. Shannon took a step back. "Yes, I see, you're being cautious for her sake. But, you're planning to pull her off life sport, support in a few days. What harm can *I* do that's worse than that?" Hysteria crept into her voice. So unlike her, but if the situation called for hysteria, she could do hysteria. "Please, uh—" Shannon read the tag hanging from a chain on the researcher's neck. "Todd. Are you going to let this whale die if you could do one more thing to try to save her? The lightning struck me at the same time as Juneau. Let me try to get through to her. Please."

Todd shot her a curious, interested look for the first time. "You the one? Touching at the time? Just a minute." He hurried back to his desk, flicked some pages of the notebook until he found the one he wanted. He read through it for several minutes.

Why wait for him? The temptation to touch Juneau while Todd stood too far away to stop her squeezed Shannon's chest like a giant's fist.

No, she should wait for permission. Maybe she *would* hurt Juneau without meaning to. She didn't even know for certain, after all, that Essi could ferry Juneau back to her body.

Juneau remained quiet, as if, now that she'd seen her deteriorating body, she couldn't decide whether to go back or hold out for freedom.

Hell. Touch her or not?

Shannon would make try for it; the Dickson might never give her another opportunity. Shannon drifted toward the pool as if wandering. She watched Todd, mental fingers crossed.

Todd's head snapped up.

Run. She took three fast—okay, slow—steps toward the pool. In five quick, long strides, Todd stepped to her side. No time to bend low enough to reach Juneau. *Damn.*

Todd eyed her, but said nothing about her movements. "Yes. Shannon Kendricks. Didn't connect the name. Makes no difference."

Makes no difference? Shannon prepared to punch Todd right in his scientific hairy face. She squared up and curled her fist. She'd learned to jab a punching bag for exercise and stress relief over at Jimmy Luck's boxing center. *See if* this *makes no difference—*

Shannon paused. On the other hand, the Dickson *had* kept Juneau alive. She wouldn't have made it if they'd left her at the SQ. This guy had helped that effort. *Oh, all right.* Shannon relaxed her fist.

Todd, unaware of the narrowly-averted blow, continued. "Will talk to Dr. Moon. He's exhausted every measure trying to save her. Soft spot for whales. Time in the field. Humpbacks. May let you. If no, you can say good bye. Fair?"

"Who's Dr. Moon?"

"Who's...." Todd stood openmouthed, looking startled by the enormity of her ignorance. After a beat, Todd found his tongue. "Dr. Moon is *the* Director of the Dickson. Makes the final decision on everything. Personally working with this project."

Oh.

A lot of words for old Todd.

Did she dare wait? Or should she perform a running cannonball into the pool right now? *No.* What if she didn't have enough time to send Juneau back? Todd would haul her out of the pool and this time he wouldn't apologize, and this Dr. Moon would never permit her within a mile of this place again.

"How long do you think it might take to get his permission?" she asked.

"Today. Tomorrow latest."

She'd risk it. If this Dr. Moon said no, she'd march in here tomorrow and dive in.

Juneau? Shannon imaged walking away today, coming back tomorrow. Juneau responded with gentle shove against her, *away* from the pool.

"Then yes, thanks, great, please talk to him."

She would force herself to wait. Force herself to leave Juneau's poor dying body. Concentrating on the exit doors, she slid one slow step after another away from the pool.

"Wait. Phone number. I'll call," Todd said to her departing back.

Shannon stopped long enough to holler her number, then fled.

Once she had broken free of that terrible room, she and Juneau both calmed, and she fled the Dickson in short order.

Outside, she stopped at the large fountain in the square to quell the shaking that assaulted her as she left.

She'd made the right choice. Right?

The whale brushed against her mind in a slow gentle pass, Juneau answering "yes."

*   *   *

Up the block from the Dickson, Shannon found a little Russian cafe and ordered a plate of steaming pirozhkies to eat while she mulled over the day.

A couple of teenage boys burst into the cafe, a jumble of arms and legs, laughing and jostling each other. The woman at the cash register barked at them in Russian, and shooed them into the back with a fond pat. The owner's kids.

A sigh escaped Shannon. Not her sigh, but Essi's. The little girl sounded forlorn. Juneau's precarious state had affected her too.

tosss.

Toss? Toss what? Toss it where?

Essi imaged Shannon taking one of the child's hands, and a young teen boy taking the other.

tosss.

Poor thing. She missed the comfort of somebody. Her brother, maybe. The kids in the cafe reminded her of the boy. Toss? Was that his name? Shannon imaged a big hug for Essi. After a few minutes, the intensity of Essi's vibrations loosened. As Essi calmed, her vibrations worked their magic on Shannon as well. By the time she finished eating, her certainty that she'd taken the right course had solidified.

Her phone rang. She picked up. Becky's picture flashed in the view screen.

"Something's happened to Andy. We went down to take care of Wally, and Andy fell into a—" Becky waved her hands, searching for a word to describe it. "—a trance. Like you, last night. Get over here now. The fish house. Hurry."

The dial tone sounded in Shannon's ear. *What on earth?* Why would Becky call her and not 9-1-1?

Shannon replayed the conversation in her mind. Becky's every word had shaken as if she tried to talk while jack hammering. Becky hadn't sounded that terrified since the time in college when the coke dealer caught them trying to tape transactions. Andy's condition had terrified her. As Shannon gathered her belongings, Becky's words rang in her ears: *like last night.*

Shannon had told Becky that she believed Juneau had come into her mind. Maybe now her friend wondered if Shannon could've been right. Maybe now it had happened to Andy. That would explain why Becky had called her instead of 9-1-1.

Andy in a trance. The laid-back SQ vet approached life as if he aimed to be the best human being, the best vet, the best lover, and the best friend in the world. Everybody loved him. Becky more than anyone. Shannon wouldn't let him, or Becky, down.

And, of course, Becky would rip Shannon's heart out if she let anything happen to her main squeeze.

Shannon ran to the car, inhaled a lovely whiff of cinnamon from the dessert in her hand, popped the last sticky sweet bite of apple dumpling into her mouth, and unlocked the door.

"I'm counting on you two for help, whatever's going on, and—" Shannon stopped, as an elderly woman walked past on the sidewalk next to the car, a young child holding her skirt. They shot Shannon a look halfway between confusion and alarm. "Oh, sorry, not you two, I was talking to…some other two…so, so enjoy your walk." Shannon ducked into the car and made her escape.

*　　*　　*

Fifteen minutes later, Shannon rushed, out of breath, still plaiting her loose braid so that no stray ends distracted her, into the familiar chlorine-and-herring-smelling SQ fish house and absorbed the scene at a glance. Becky and Andy alone in the room. Becky hovered near Andy, her arms folded across her teal SQ tee shirt, the fingers of each hand gouged into the skin of the other arm. Andy, in his matching tee, perched on the edge of a tall stool near one of the stainless steel counters. He grasped the rim of the counter in a death grip.

Shannon ran to them and folded Becky's hands, stiff and cold as ice, into her own.

"By the curse of the Ice Giants, woman, you need some warm coffee in you. Now." A pot of Becky's French vanilla brew sat on the counter, and Shannon pushed Becky toward it.

Then she turned to Andy, leaned close, and peered into his face. The smell of sweat dampened the air, along with a terrible putrid odor. Tears ran down his cheeks, so many tears that large wet spots soaked the front of his shirt. He stared into the distance, but his eyes registered nothing in the outside world; he focused inward, deep into places Shannon and Becky would never see.

Normally.

"Andy?" Shannon watched his face. No sign of recognition. No response. *Like last night,* Becky had said, but Andy's difficulties were playing out in a different way than Shannon's; she'd blacked out and come back dizzy but normal. Well, not normal. But not struggling like Andy. Not in the grip of some internal horror.

"Why didn't you take him to the hospital? What if Andy's suffering a seizure?"

"He said to call you. When this first happened, he said, 'Don't touch me. Don't let anyone.'" Becky's face had paled to the color of a kestrel's egg against her black curls and dark brown eyes.

Panic stirred in Shannon, but Shannon didn't own this panic. Nor Juneau—Shannon could recognize Juneau's wild emotional ride now and this wasn't it. This fear radiated from Essi.

Calm down, Essi. Andy can't hurt you.

Or could he? What did Shannon know about anything anymore? What if Andy's situation did mirror Shannon's? That would mean he had an alien on board. And not, it would seem, a sweet little lavender girl. Shannon had better go slow until she learned more.

Out loud Shannon said, "Why would he want *me* here?"

Before Becky could answer, Shannon's breaths shortened and shook. Essi again.

"Essi," Shannon said.

"What?" Becky asked.

"Uh, Share. Explain what happened."

In her mind, Shannon slapped some pictures together: Shannon takes the little girl's small soft hand; Andy reaches out for help; Shannon and Essi turn toward Andy, everybody calm.

But Essi erased those pictures and began sketching some of her own—

"Andy walked down to the walrus dry deck with David and me." Becky paced along the fish refrigerator wall, hands in a strangle hold on her coffee cup. "Andy called Wally out of the water so he could treat a gash. I chatted with Andy, sassing him like I do, and rubbing Wally under his flipper to keep him quiet. Noise crackled like firecrackers going off and the air smelled like fish rot."

Sounded like the crackling when the lightning hit Shannon. Except the tropical spice perfume she'd smelled beat out fish rot by miles.

"Did Wally collapse like Juneau? Who's out at the pen with him?" Bile rose in Shannon's throat at the notion that the smart old walrus might have fallen into a coma, destined for the Darth Vader machine at the Research Center.

"No, Wally's fine—that's the crazy thing. David stayed with him. David will call us right away if anything happens."

"That's David Fielding, right?"

"Right."

"What's he doing down here? I thought he volunteered up at the Brackish Water Center." David Fielding had volunteered around SQ for several years and he'd worked several times with Shannon at the Marine Mammal Center as a substitute. She trusted the affable young volunteer. He would take care of Wally.

As she talked to Becky, Shannon monitored Andy with a steady gaze. The tears still dripped, his counter-gripping knuckles still stood out, misshapen white knobs, and his eyes still stared hard, registered nothing.

"Oh, David transferred down just a few days ago. So, when I smelled that stuff on Andy, I looked over at Andy to say something about it, like make a joke. But he looked scared to death. That shut my smart mouth. I've never seen a person that scared. Ever."

Becky looked plenty scared herself, her eyes twice their normal size, double wrinkle lines across her forehead.

Meanwhile, Essi had finished putting together her images and Shannon took a quick look: the ribbon river of color flows in the foreground. And an alien Halloween monster stands beside the river. None of Essi's lovely silver shimmer. No sweet little girl with huge green eyes. A tall gaunt figure. A woman? A thick black substance like tar floats around her. The woman's skin looks flat and unhealthy gray, flecked with the color of watery rust. Thin, lusterless, ash-colored hair, with a few strands of bad-butter pale yellow-orange woven into it, sticks out from her scalp, dotted with bald patches. Her eyes glimmer coal black with a patchwork of bleary red lines around the iris. Deep furrows etch her face, a face that glares out at Essi's world, as if nothing in it could please her.

Despite her corroded condition, she radiates menace—the scowl, hardened jaw, puffed swagger, furtive jerks of the hands. She turns her head from side to side, never still, as if always on the lookout for danger.

A scent like swamp, like Shannon's decaying compost pile, assails her nose.

thsssarm.

Tharm. Just looking at the creature terrified Shannon. No wonder Essi had given Shannon the shakes.

Essi's image changed.

The alien woman Tharm arrives in a mist and floats over a pool where Andy stands. She sinks into Andy's head.

Andy would not survive that thing.

"Bloody hell in a hand basket," Shannon said.

*   *   *

"What?" Becky asked again.

"Did you see any lightning when this happened?"

"No, but I wasn't looking up. I'd just seen another little cut on Wally's rump and I kneeled to get a closer look. The sky darkened for second, Andy gurgled out a choking sound, and asked for you, talking so fast it was hard to understand him. Then he charged up here like a crazy man lit on fire. By the time I caught up to him, he'd made it to that stool and glommed onto the counter, just like you see him now. He's stayed like that ever since."

Speak calmly.

"Look, as I mentioned, something, oh, uh,…unusual happened to me after the lightning on Sunday. I think something similar has happened to Andy, so just let me try to get through to him for a minute, okay? You'll need to stay back."

The outside tips of Becky's eyebrows sank, the inside tips rose. She winced, as if Shannon had pinched her. Her friend took a step back toward the fish freezer and leaned against it.

Essi built another image. Now the alien kid showed a large image of Andy's head with small images of Andy and Tharm inside it—okay, Andy's mind, his spirit, his consciousness—along with this Tharm woman. The alien pushes Andy backward, keeps pushing, harder. Andy pushes back.

Essi, are they locked in this struggle now?

ysssss.

That explained Andy's beads of sweat, the grim concentration.

In the image, Andy loses ground inch by inch, and Tharm flings Andy out of his own head and he disappears into thin air.

Could Essi mean that the alien woman intended to push Andy's consciousness out of his head? Kill him? Could she *do* that?

ysssss.

In an instant, Shannon formed this image: a tiny Shannon figure—*her* consciousness—Essi and Juneau float down Shannon's hand, over to Andy's hand and up to his mind. She imagined all of them pushing the alien woman, pushing *her* out into thin air and *her* disappearing.

Shannon waited.

Essi didn't take away the image.

Okay. They would try it.

"I, um, I may go into a trance here too for a minute, to connect with Andy, so prop me up if I fall, but don't pull me away from Andy's hand, no matter what, okay?" Shannon said.

"What's going on? I don't—"

"He's in big trouble. Just let me help him or we're going to lose him." *Sorry, Beck. No time to explain.*

Shannon picked up the sound of quiet crying in Essi's pulsing thrum. And deep, primal fear.

Tharm scared the living daylights out of the child. No kidding. Should Shannon even ask Essi to do this? Shannon couldn't think. No time. She formed the image of the little girl holding the back of Shannon's shirt, staying behind Shannon, Shannon's arm out to keep her behind, with Juneau behind the child. They'd protect her.

Essi flashed a picture. In it, the little Tharm figure throws Essi, Andy, Juneau, and the child out of Andy's head and they *all* disappear.

A reminder. This creature would try to kill Shannon and her visitors. *Kill them.* As in forever. As in murder. *Odin's eye.*

She tried to grasp the death that might take her if she pitted herself against Tharm. She couldn't. Death by alien? In Shannon's ordinary work-centric life?

But she did grasp that Andy couldn't hold out much longer. He would die unless she helped him. *So get on with it.* Shannon smoothed her loose braid, settled herself on a stool and slouched over the counter so as not to fall, then placed one hand on Andy's tense, knotted shoulder. She moved her free hand to grab Andy's.

* * *

As soon as Shannon touched Andy, a new vibration flowed through her arm and entered her head, smooth, soothing, like Essi's hum, but in a low register. Tharm's vibration.

Wait a damn second. Did Tharm just invade Shannon's mind? Panic rose like a thousand frightened swallows. *Essi?*

Essi imaged a quick "no."

Shannon zipped down a long hill to stillness from her adrenaline high.

A new image formed—and not created by her, *or Essi or Juneau.* The swamp bitch could form images in Shannon's mind? *Holy—*

—Essi imaged: Tharm's pictures form in *Andy's* head and travel through Shannon's hand to her mind.

Okay, good. No Tharm images unless Shannon touched Andy.

Let go, then.

No. She'd hold onto Andy's hand. As long as this harpy engaged Shannon, Andy had a fighting chance.

Tharm images: Essi moves from Shannon's head through her hand to Andy's head, Tharm hugs Essi, and the two float off into the distance, leaving Andy safe and alone.

Shannon's eyes narrowed. *A trade?* Essi for Andy?

By the gods, no.

Just by looking at the alien, smelling her, Shannon could tell she couldn't trust Tharm farther than an inchworm's stretch. If that far. She'd think of another way to rescue Andy.

As Shannon thought, by long habit images formed. Images Tharm picked up.

The witch's hum sank lower, grew angrier.

Tharm spoke.

In English.

"Give me the child," she said, hissing like a snake.

Tharm spoke English? Shannon imaged to Essi. Puzzled, the child relayed no answer.

Tharm read Shannon's question and shrugged. "One as old as I translates languages, sounds, without effort. Give her to me."

"No," Shannon said.

Tharm's voice grew low and malicious. "I gather her. Now."

"No."

Tharm laughed, a low cackling grunt. "*You* will stop me? A puny worm?" A new note had entered Tharm's voice. The sound of cruelty. As if the alien wore viciousness like a comfortable old sweater. "We crush worlds. Suck them dry. And *you* will stop me?" She paused. The cruel undertone hung upon her words again. "In fact, our thanks for the opportunity to devour this world go to the girl."

Shannon's heart and stomach sank as one.

"Essi?"

The woman gave her head an impatient shake. "Her name signifies nothing. She signifies nothing. She is no more than a mote of dust."

"How can you—"

Tharm's voice thundered. "Do not question me." Tharm's grayish lips curved outward, the upper lip raised on one side in a venomous smirk. "How deliciously unfortunate for you that, of all the worlds in the universe, the fleeing girl you now shelter drew our attention to yours." Tharm sent images to accompany her words, ensuring that Essi would see her part in bringing the odious creature to Earth. Her laugh sounded more like high keening. "All her fault."

A stream of anguish, not her own, doused Shannon. Essi understood, all right. The witch had broken the child's vulnerable heart.

Shannon flashed to Essi: Shannon holds the child in a fierce hug and shakes her head no. No; Shannon didn't blame Essi. Tharm and her kind owned whatever happened to Earth.

Tharm observed Shannon's images. Her head jerked, her eyes glowing under lowered eyebrows, impatient with Shannon, as a child might lose patience with a baby. "Give her. I wish to feast." Again the cruel curve of dark gray lips. "We require a great deal of energy to stay alive. More and more fuel as the eons pass."

They require more and more energy to stay alive. Shannon could relate.

Did Tharm say "eons"? *Holy oldies.*

"Every morsel counts," Tharm said.

Essi shrieked in panic, a sound that resounded through the corridors of Shannon's mind. Shannon recoiled from Tharm's words. "You would…would, uh, make a morsel of one of your own people?"

Taken by surprise, Tharm said, "Oh no, Grodar no. We are *not* Seladoran, not of the Riverworld people. We stole bodies from among Seladora's inhabitants to move among them and defeat them unawares. But Grodar's mercy, we don't *belong* to such a simple race." Her voice dripped with disdain. "Why, the people of Seladora died within a century—even—" Her eyes turned to slits. "Even back when they lived to a ripe old age. *We* have lived longer than some worlds."

What did she mean, *back when* Seladorans lived to a ripe old age?

"Not Seladoran, no." Tharm jerked her head, as if to shoo away the thought. "We invaded Seladora. But we've consumed most of the Riverworld's life forms now. And so we will feed on this world." Tharm imaged herself leaning toward Shannon, her mouth twisted. "Until not a living thing survives." The alien relaxed. "We will *look* Earthan, but we will not *be* Earthan. Grodar forbid."

Shannon lifted her fingers from Andy and shuddered, Tharm's words burning like lava. After a second, she grabbed Andy's hand again.

Tharm's voice boomed. "Give me the child."

Tharm renewed her deep, invasive humming. Shannon's mind slowed, her thoughts thickened. The low vibration hypnotized, enticed, compelled....

...But didn't convince. Essi's frantic vibration interrupted Shannon's fuzzy mind, like a blaring all-hands-desert-ship alarm. Juneau flashed along the edges of Shannon's mind in a frenzy. Their fear quivered down Shannon's spine.

Shannon's fingers lifted yet again. Her thoughts flew to her friends. She couldn't bear to see them hurt. Andy, mute and still, fighting the battle of his life; Becky, smelling of French vanilla coffee and fish bucket mackerel, with her wide, tear-filled eyes and fear-tight face. Grief would destroy Becky if anything happened to Andy. And Essi, the little girl with silvery lavender skin and huge green eyes, helpless against this wretched demon. Juneau, who could never win her freedom in the world Tharm had planned for them.

Shannon would fight for them. She would fight this disgusting creature who had conquered universes. With her last breath, she'd fight.

Oh, that sounded good. Shannon gave her head a long, slow shake. *Had she just vowed to fight a powerful alien with her last breath?* Who in the real world said that? She could not, *would not* accept that Tharm existed. The stuff of science fiction horror, of the most terrible nightmares. But in this world? Tharm couldn't happen.

And yet there Tharm stood, occupying Andy's head and here Shannon stood, and she must force the alien out. Even if she couldn't believe it existed.

Right. Good luck with that.

Still, Shannon turned her mind to Juneau and flashed her resolve to fight. *Would the whale help?*

A wild call blasted back at her. Shannon could sense Juneau's fierce whirlwind gathering.

Okay then.

"Why're you just standing there? Do something," Becky said, breathing hard, her hands shaking, breaking into Shannon's deep concentration.

Shannon's determination swelled, her fingers dropped into place. She focused on Tharm's voice. She shook her head side to side in a smooth slow motion. "No, you may not take Essi."

The alien, furious now, crackled with energy. Her hum's vibration increased, the smell of decay intensified.

The vet's voice trembled forth from his parched lips. "Shannon? This thing *will* kill me."

At the sound of Andy's voice, Becky reached toward him. Shannon raised one hand toward Becky's chest to block her way.

"Shannon, what—" Becky said.

Oh, right. Becky had heard none of this exchange with the oily creature.

"I need room. Go over there by the freezer. And stay there," Shannon ordered, and pointed with enough grim authority to propel Becky back.

We'll give you Andy because we need to go away and figure this mess out, Shannon said to Tharm with her thoughts, but didn't speak aloud—or Shannon wouldn't have needed to wait for aliens to wring her neck. Becky would oblige.

She dropped Andy's hand, and counted to ten.

"Shannon?" Andy's voice shook with terror and betrayal.

Hold on, Andy, just hold on.

Then she grabbed Andy's hand again and, in a soft firm voice, she said, "Now!"

She imaged herself, Juneau and Essi streaking across to Andy. Essi blazed through Shannon's fingers, her thrum as shrill as a scream. Juneau's wild spirit followed with a high cry, as forceful and fearful as a tsunami. Shannon gritted her teeth, pulled along on Essi's thrum. Like light and energy, her spirit raced toward Andy's mind.

In that split second of surprise, they slid by Tharm and deep into Andy's mind.

But the monster turned on them.

Essi's thrum amplified. Louder and louder it grew, the tempo carried a steadiness and courage that stirred Shannon's heart.

The child heartened Andy as well: as Essi, Juneau, and Shannon rushed onboard, Andy redoubled, tripled his effort, his will power roared like the ocean on a stormy night.

"Andy? Where's Tharm?" Shannon spun around in a circle. No one stood there.

Well. Not literally. She couldn't *see*, but her own mind interpreted her surroundings *as if* she were using her senses: she stood in a vast, dark cavern. Empty. Andy's unused brain space. She couldn't see him, but she sensed him. His spirit smelled like her father's mellow old pipe tobacco, the musky masculinity of a man, lake edges, cut grass. His desperation dominated his mind, along with his deep, cold abhorrence of this creature.

Juneau floated beside Shannon as if this black space held an ocean instead of a cavern. Shannon reached out and stroked her side.

Essi stood as still as a beautiful Greek statue a few paces away, her arms pulled tight against her chest. Shannon swept the little girl in close behind her. Juneau maneuvered close to Essi, too.

"Andy, can you see us?" Shannon said, her voice directed into the dark.

"Yes." Andy ran toward them and grasped Shannon in a fierce hug. "Thank God you've come." His head, the one in his mind, the one Shannon saw, jerked as he said, his voice rising in near-hysteria, "She's coming."

Tharm rushed across the empty space like blinding light, a hurricane wind. Everything Shannon needed to know about Tharm thundered in her vibrations and that godawful smell: rage, power, corruption, dark hungers, swamp thoughts, madness. Shannon choked.

Something more: Tharm's vibrations hid a curious quiver, so faint that Shannon strained to catch it. Desperation in Tharm's pulsing drum beat.

Surprise washed over Shannon. Just as Tharm had captured Andy, some…thing…had captured Tharm, Shannon could feel it. A thing darker, more powerful than Tharm. A thing that forced to the surface Tharm's most primitive urgings. Blood lust. Despite Shannon's disgust, a thorn of pity stung her.

As if Tharm caught Shannon's sympathy, the alien halted. Shannon's compassion had, in turn, taken that foul creature by surprise. But Tharm hesitated only a beat, then charged Shannon and her allies. They squared up against the gaunt, gray-black figure and her large swampy spirit, so close to them that her reeking breath stirred their hair.

And they faltered.

The false body-image of Tharm's monstrous spirit rammed against them and pushed, pushed with unrelenting force, a huge shield held before her that spanned them all. She shoved the little group back. Back toward the edge of Andy's mind, the edge of existence.

The swamp that defined Tharm thickened around them. Shannon's strength ebbed, her will shriveled, her passion paled.

She could never defeat a being as powerful as Tharm. So foolish to think she might.

Juneau emitted a shrill cry. The call to battle buoyed Shannon up, out of Tharm's swamp, like a beluga mother pushing a newborn to the ocean's surface. Shannon inhaled fresh air, air pulled from the memory of night visits to Juneau's poolside. So fresh, so vital.

"Shannon," Andy said, adding to Shannon's growing understanding, "don't listen. It feeds you false images, it drains your emotions, it tries to replace them. Fight it. *Fight it.*" Andy, exhausted, pulled out, his hands slumping to his knees to prop himself up. Tharm had fought him to his limit.

That witch had tried to brainwash her? That did it. Shannon wouldn't give up. By all the heroes of Valhalla, she would fight this monstrosity.

Juneau's feral cry rocked the dark space. Her wild strength pulled Shannon and Essi forward with power and drive neither Shannon nor Essi possessed alone. Juneau, born wild and still wild, would fight to the death.

Tharm staggered, driven back by the beluga's savage intensity. An ocean spirit so exotic, so unlike Tharm's own that Juneau bewildered the alien.

Andy rejoined them. They rammed against the alien with every ounce of will they could muster.

Shannon, Andy, Juneau, and Essi inched Tharm toward oblivion, but the repugnant alien rallied. Tharm screamed in rage as they resisted her newest attack. She battled back. The little group pressed forward with every scrap of will remaining. For a moment, neither side could move the other.

So much power. Soon Shannon's troops would collapse. Shannon sensed them weakening. *She must end it.*

Shannon sensed Becky edging closer.

By Odin. Becky would *not* get sucked into this mess.

"Back off," Shannon barked, out of Andy's mouth with Andy's voice, a harsh, hostile warning. Becky jumped back. Astonishment, confusion, and hurt flashed across her face. Shannon couldn't let Becky's feelings matter. As long as she stayed safe.

In the short time Becky had distracted Shannon, Tharm regained the advantage and inched them toward the outskirts of Andy's mind, inched them toward nothingness.

An ember caught fire in Tharm's slimy thoughts, a victory fire—the swamp alien smelled their deaths.

No! Shannon would *not* let Juneau die here. Or let Tharm steal the child. Or would she venture back to the fish house without Andy.

She bellowed, loud and long, a terrible, bitter, furious sound.

Shannon summoned all the rage she'd buried. The rage of causing her childhood friend's death. Of losing Scott Cross because she'd shut him out. Of failing to walk away from work she'd come to resent. She'd held the rage in for so long. Now she poured it all out. Directed it at Tharm.

"You," she said in her loudest courtroom boom, "You slimy, stinking swamp snake. Get out."

Shannon boiled forward.

Juneau pressed forward with the fierce, beautiful savagery of an untamed creature.

Essi's dimmed thrum rebounded like a shrill whistle echoing through a narrow tunnel.

Andy's desire to live spurred him to dig deep.

Tharm stumbled back and back to the edge of Andy's mind and body. And farther. And then—

—a faint stirring, as gentle as the bending wing of a butterfly. A sigh. A sound from Tharm, as if, at last, she welcomed her release from whatever had shackled her.

Tharm vanished.

Shannon, Juneau, Andy, and Essi stood alone in the black cavern. Stunned by the silence, the emptiness. Shannon, exhausted, ran her fingers along her braid, surprised that it retained its tight weave during the battle.

For long moments no one stirred.

Andy looked like he'd been tumble-washed and hung out to dry. *Let's leave him be,* Shannon imaged.

Essi led Shannon and Juneau in a slow and gentle sweep from Andy's mind. Shannon relaxed into the flow, surrounded by Essi's silver-lavender shimmer.

Back in her own mind, Shannon's eyes opened and she dropped Andy's hand. She found herself wedged against the counter next to Andy's stool. Becky hovered next to her with saucer sized eyes.

Shannon stirred. An inch. Mount Rushmore could outrace her at this moment. *So tired.*

Essi and Juneau floated in her mind. No brush against her mind. No clicks or whistles. No whisper. A thrum so faint Shannon strained to catch it.

Andy looked terrible. No wonder. He'd struggled alone against Tharm for so long. When he lifted his head, aware of his surroundings, his eyes searched first for Becky.

"Honey?" Becky said.

The vet nodded his head one small fraction up and down and said in a soft monotone, "Yeah, I'll survive. I think."

Becky flew to him, threw her arms around his neck, and buried her face in his shoulder. "What happened?"

Andy mumbled over Becky's dark curls. Didn't make much sense to Shannon, but she nodded. She'd been there.

Shannon stood, swayed, and heaved onto the stool next to him. "Becky, do you have anything in here we could eat?"

"Are you kidding me? You're hungry at a time like this?" Becky said.

"You are, right?" Shannon asked Andy.

"I am," Andy said. "Baby, can you bring my leftovers from the refrigerator? And will you see what else you can dig up in my back pack? I don't care if it's moldy and black. I want it."

Becky brought over Andy's lunch leavings, along with her own colorful and nutritious stash from the cupboard. Shannon ate everything Andy didn't

"Okay, so, you two can just cease stuffing your faces. What happened?" Becky said.

"If I tell you, you won't believe it," Andy said. He turned to Shannon. "That thing. What was it?"

"What are you talking about?" Becky asked him. But he'd packed food in his mouth as soon as he'd voiced his question. She looked to Shannon.

So much to explain. Shannon spread a pack of butter on a cracker to give herself time to think. How to put this? Shannon puckered her lips. "Well, in a nutshell, Tharm, an alien, invaded Andy, and together we, that is Andy, Juneau, my alien Essi and me, ah, ended her invasion."

"Tharm, *an alien?*" Becky's voice rose an octave. "Essi, *your alien?* Juneau? For christ's sake, *Juneau?*"

"Yes, I already told you that part," Shannon said. "Essi I, um, forgot to mention. And I just learned about Tharm. Or that's as close as I can come to pronouncing it. She turned out nasty and vicious. Essi, my alien, is just a sweet kid. And brave," she added, imaging for Essi.

"Oh come on. That's bullshit." Becky said.

"No," Andy said as he munched, "This shitty alien creature Tharm *did* invade my mind and *did* try to kill me. And then Shannon somehow rode to the rescue by coming *into* my head, I mean really came *in there*."

"Don't try that bull hickey on me. You two playing an April's fool joke here? Not April and not funny. And what do you mean, when you say Juneau came with you?"

"No joke. I told you last night, remember?" Shannon said again. "Juneau's spirit or consciousness or whatever came to me during that lightning strike. So when I went to help Andy, she came with me. Huge help, by the way." Shannon imaged for Juneau's benefit. "And so she's *not* in the body down there at the Dickson, which explains why she can't respond. And won't until I can get her consciousness back to her."

"You're talking straight-jacket crazy," said Becky. She paused, thinking. "And how could you get your consciousness from your head to Andy's?"

Shannon began her answer when she noticed a smell like rotting fish. She took a deep, discreet sniff. *Uh oh.* Andy. While exotic perfume wafted from Shannon, Andy reeked of sewer. Poor guy. How long would that stink last? She imaged Essi.

Essi imaged nothing back. She had no clue.

Shannon turned her attention back to Becky, whose expression conveyed no sign that she believed a word Shannon or Andy had said. "Essi took us. We…we *flowed.* I don't know a better way to say it. And…." Her voice petered out as she watched Becky's face grow more and more skeptical.

"Look at me, Becky. Look at these fetching black rings under my eyes. Look at my hair and the color of my eyes. Look at my boney wrists. What I just told you is the reason for all this."

Becky glared at Shannon for several long moments. "True." she said, "You do look like a zombie with a hangover."

"Hey." Shannon swatted at her. "Unkind."

Leaning in, Becky plucked a couple hairs from Shannon's scalp.

"Ow. What, you need a lock of my hair to make a voodoo doll?"

"No, I want a look at the roots. Although the doll is not a bad idea."

Becky took the hairs over to her science desk and picked up her magnifying glass for a closer look. "They aren't bleached. Although that's impossible, since I know you're brunette."

Shannon flinched as Becky returned, wary of another yank on her hair, but instead her friend tipped Shannon's face toward the ceiling lights.

"No contact lenses, but, yes, strange, dark green eyes you never had before. Also not possible."

Becky cleared her throat. "Okay, preliminary scientific data supports you." She hesitated. "Although how can I believe either one of you? It's preposterous. And speaking of Juneau as part of this rescue operation," Becky said, "Why didn't you tell us right away that she'd allegedly slipped into your head?"

Shannon finished the crackers and licked the salt off her fingers. "I didn't know Juneau had come onboard at first. I—"

"—Wait, wait, wait. We digress," Andy said. Noting that Becky frowned, he added, "We can come back to that. But first, I need to know more about that thing we pushed out of my mind. Where is it now? How do I make sure it never comes back? I feel dirty from it. How in God's name do I scrub it off?"

Shannon formed an image: Tharm flies out of Andy's head, disappears, reforms as a black-orange cloud and floats around the fish house with them now. Essi reset the image: Tharm flies out of Andy's head, and breaks into a thousand little drops. The drops drift farther and farther away from each other until they all disappear. End of story.

"Dead," Shannon said, her voice flat. "Not a problem."

She put down the apple she'd just bitten into.

Dead. Shannon had been responsible for someone's death before. Her childhood friend. She'd never wanted to go there again. Shannon looked down at her long legs, feet tucked under the high bar stool at the counter. They looked the same as always, but she would've sworn she'd shrunk. Her mood sank.

This death occurred under different circumstances than Georgey's, of course. She'd never intended to hurt her childhood friend. This time she'd killed an alien who was trying to murder Andy. But a killing, even justified, would never sit well with Shannon.

Becky grabbed her car keys. "Come on, Andy, we'll stop and give David instructions for the rest of his shift and then you will tell me everything—e-ver-y-thing—on the way to the doctor. And *then*, boyo, you will go home and take a shower. You smell like the dump." She propelled Andy out of his seat. He grabbed a couple cracker packages that Shannon hadn't spotted, and gave her a wave.

"Okay, but we're stopping at Dairy Queen."

Shannon watched the door close. A shower wouldn't remove that smell. Any more than her morning shower had washed away her new perfume. Her eyes teared up. How would he live with that?

Shannon rubbed her arms. Cold in this damn fish house.

Picking up her bag, she followed the other two. She could just make out Andy's words as he and Becky walked down to the walrus pool.

"...okay, but we don't tell David what happened. I don't want anybody to know about the alien in my mind. Ever. Promise?"

Shannon had parked her VW behind the Marine Mammal Center. Before climbing in, Shannon paused with her hand on the open door to take a deep breath of air. A hint of dampness always permeated the SQ, with its pools and the nearby ocean. Sometimes Shannon found the dampness stifling. Today, after the swampish Tharm, she relished the relative freshness. A soft sea breeze blew in from the west, cool and gentle. She closed her eyes and the sun warmed her. *So good to still live.*

The sun-filled moment vanished as her weary bones folded onto the seat. She caught her image in the rearview mirror. Ew. She not only *felt* like an armored truck had run her down, she *looked* it. Maybe a whole convoy.

"Food time again, my friends. And while I'm eating, Essi, I want to know about this 'we' Tharm talked about. Will someone else show up here?" Shannon waited. Essi, though just a little kid, must know who had terrorized her world. *Poor baby.*

Essi's image formed: another alien comes into focus, bigger than Tharm, more ferocious. Gray skin shows a touch of dull burgundy. Black-gray tar clings to him. Bald, his black eyes streaked in red, hunched, fingers twitching. Male. Menacing, nasty, just like the last one.

The child whispered, *drrrmm.*

Drum was his name? No that didn't sound quite right. Drom. The best Shannon's thick human tongue could manage.

In the image, Drom turns to mist and reforms at the SQ.

Uh oh.

"Has Drom invaded a body too, then?" Shannon asked Essi. "Who?"

Essi imaged Drom sinking into a featureless head.

Great. The child had no inkling.

Shannon sagged, as if struck by a blow to the shoulder. This Drom inhabited somebody's brain, might have sent somebody's spirit to die. Maybe it had attacked one of her friends. Thrown her away.

Essi's hum tightened, shrill and anguished.

"It's all right. We'll figure it out. For the moment, I know a place that serves the best steak and lobster in town and that sounds like just the ticket for all of us."

* * *

When Shannon arrived home, she fed the babies, walked Indy, and bee-lined for bed.

"Don't look at me like that, dog," Shannon said when Indy eyed her as they climbed onto the mattress. "You've taken longer walks, yes. You'll take longer walks again. But mommy's sick."

"And no bad dreams tonight, okay Juneau?"

The longest Monday of Shannon's life faded into slumber.

CHAPTER THREE

TUESDAY

SHANNON OPENED HER EYES on Tuesday morning just as the sun began to lighten the sky through her skylight, her mind all fuzzy, in that smoky charcoal, not-quite-awake, hit-by-lightning way.

She needed food. *Dammit.* Of course she did.

Eating, eating, eating all the time had been a kick for about a minute and a half; not any more. Her jaw hurt. Her stomach lurched along, always tender and queasy. She pictured hours and hours of her future devoted to buying, cooking, eating food that would disappear as fast as a guppy at a shark party.

If she *had* a future. Sweat dripped off her face. Her hands shook. She must eat. She pushed up onto her elbows but flopped back down, her mind swirling as if she were circling the drain.

Too dizzy to stand. *She should call someone.* Scratch that. Any friend would do the right thing and send her to the hospital. And thus do the wrong thing.

Do it anyway.

No. If she landed in the hospital again, she might not make it to the Dickson in time to bring Juneau out of her coma.

Shannon crawled to the staircase. Indy lumbered off the bed and padded beside her, snuffling her face.

"I'm good, sweet girl." *Shameful lie.*

A whale called, weak and distant. Essi's hum had slowed to a near stop. And Shannon's own body had started shutting down. *Hurry.*

She put her butt on the top stair and bumped her way down, then flipped back to her hands and knees. Into the kitchen. Blackness rimmed her eyesight.

Don't pass out.

If she fainted, she wouldn't come back.

Keep going, just keep going.

From her knees, she opened the freezer door of her side-by-side refrigerator. *Grab something quick. There*! Her fingertips stretched for a quart of ice cream on the second shelf…a little more…she grabbed it. She scooted to the silverware drawer and nabbed a spoon. Sinking to the floor, she polished off the entire ice cream carton, too weak and famished to register the flavor. She crawled back for another carton—chocolate with cherry bits and almonds. Oh yeah. She emptied it.

And waited, her head back against the cupboard, her eyes closed.

Better.

Indy's strong shoulders and the cupboard drawer handles supported her as she struggled to her feet.

Leaning against the counter top, Shannon considered this latest crisis. Awake, she could eat all the time. She'd better make sure she kept the chow coming at night too. From now on, she'd carry cookies, candy bars, a sack of chips, a bowl of tuna salad, whatever she could, wherever she might find herself. And at night? She'd pack a cooler and keep it by her bed.

After a large satisfying bowl of mashed potatoes and a cheesecake, Shannon's mind had cleared enough for her to take her bearings. She could hear the tick of her black cat clock above the oven. The time registered 8:15 on its grinning whiskered face. That late? No wonder she'd awakened so ill. She'd gone hours without food.

She checked her phone for messages. No word yet from Moon. But what if he agreed to let Shannon attempt to revive Juneau? Should Shannon send the beluga to her body to save her if that meant the SQ would haul her back to a living death at the SQ? Juneau yearned for the sea, craved it. So she'd hijacked Shannon's dreams to force her to understand.

But how could Shannon make Juneau's freedom happen? Impossible.

No, nothing was impossible. Just look at what had happened to her. So think. *Think….* As Shannon leaned over her kitchen table, a plan formed. A long shot. A plan that involved taking a big risk with Juneau's life.

Shannon created a series of images for Juneau, setting out her scheme. She played and replayed its elements, struggling to help the wild creature, with a mind so different from hers, understand.

"So, what do you think, Juneau? Do we risk it? Risk you?"

Juneau formed an image. The whale plunges far below the surface of the ocean, turns, whips her powerful fluke, her body undulating. She rushes toward the light and breaks the water's surface, every inch of her body free and joyful above the waves.

Shannon took that as "go for it."

Shannon jumped into a quick, cool shower. As she dried off, she chanced a glance in the mirror. Hair still blond, paler perhaps, with a hint of silver. Eyes still green, bigger maybe. Skin pale, circles under her eyes black. Even her formerly round cheeks now showed the contour of bone. *Wait*—she had cheek bones?

Back at the table for a second breakfast, she spotted the lavender haze over her cell phone, giving her plenty of time to swallow her cereal and clear her throat before the first ring.

"Shannon? Dr. Bennett here. I've listened to your voice mail messages. I'm concerned. I want you back at the hospital for a battery of tests and observation. You will stay for a few days, so bring a small bag with your toiletries, but no valuables. Today."

"Oh. This week won't work." Shannon frowned out her kitchen window at the deep woods behind her house.

"You need to make this week work. I want you in here at 10 a.m."

"Can we put it off a few days? I have an important meeting coming up."

"What meeting?"

"To…well, it's about a whale who's—"

"Not good enough. The symptoms you've experienced may indicate a critical condition. The whale can wait."

zhoo. The sound, a whisper of urgency.

A whale call, mournful.

"I hear you," Shannon said.

"What?" Dr. Bennett asked.

"Oh, sorry, I didn't mean you, I was, the…someone…."

Dr. Bennett didn't comment. "Today at 10. Saint James." The phone went dead.

The incoming call ringer jingled before Shannon could lay the phone down.

"Hello?"

"Shannon Kendricks? Todd Zimmerman, the Dickson?"

"Right. Todd." The red-haired researcher she'd contemplated clocking.

"Good news. Dr. Moon's office 10 a.m. Don't be late."

Shannon pumped her fist in the air and mouthed a silent "yes!" Good old Todd. "That's so great. 10 a.m. sharp, I promise."

She clicked off, but clued again by the lavender haze, waited for the third call to come in.

Grand central switch board here.

"Shannon, it's Jane. The Bossman's called a meeting for 10 a.m. sharp. Another lecture about how many paper clips we're using. Yippee kiyay. We'll love it, like the clown at the end of the horse parade loves his shovel."

"Again? Didn't we just sit through this lecture last week?"

"Oh no, honey, *that* lecture concerned rubber bands and sticky notes. Weren't you paying attention?"

"I can't make 10. Or the one at 11 that I'm supposed to have with him in his office. I have a…well, a doctor's appointment."

"Better postpone. Portman's memo said attend or else. Cynthia said Portman told her to tell me to tell you to show up whether you're sick or not." Jane paused. "So you'll come, right? You don't want to get on his bad side. Not that he has a good one."

"Hey, the law says sick people don't have to come to work."

"Sweetheart, the law says no speeding. You wanna know how fast Picker drove his truck through downtown Ocean City this morning? I'll tell you how fast. As fast as a quarter horse that just stepped in a wasp nest."

Jane's husband Jim, but known to one and all as Picker, hailed from New York City. Shannon had never seen the giant man in anything but cowboy hat and western shirt. She imagined him speeding through town in his beat-up Ford, followed by a trail of dust. Well, not dust. Exhaust.

Jane and Jim. Made for each other.

When Shannon clicked off, she powered down the cell and slid it back into her pocket. No more calls.

Her black cat clock reported 9 a.m.: time to go—somewhere. She ran her fingers over the smooth cobalt and copper surface of her kitchen table, opened a can of peaches, and plucked one out. Then another.

Three urgent places to be, one time slot.

If she failed to appear at the Office, Portman would chalk up yet another black mark against her. Portman's tally contained quite a few black marks already. She couldn't afford to lose her job. She'd never be able to pay the grocery bills, for one thing.

If she failed to appear at the hospital, she'd lose another chance to stabilize her dropping weight, or cure the dizziness and the rest of it. She feared she could count on the fingers of one hand the days remaining before Essi and Juneau consumed too much of her.

And if she failed to appear at the Dickson, she might miss her chance to return Juneau's consciousness to her frail body and bring her out of her coma.

Right.

The Dickson at 10.

Time to dress for success. She pulled her hair into a tight French twist, and donned her best navy suit.

*   *   *

Shannon pulled into the Dickson's gated parking lot and gave her name to the guard, who checked her off his list. Mid-morning, smack dab in the middle of the university campus, and half this private lot remained empty. A vast improvement over parking out in the hinterlands.

Since she'd arrived a few minutes early, she seized the moment to deal with her *other* ten o'clock appointments.

Doctor Bennett. This time she prayed for the message machine. Dr. B. Such a bulldozer.

Voice mail. *Yes!*

"Hi Dr. Bennett. It's Shannon Kendricks. My boss just called. I must attend an important meeting this morning. Most important.

The boss ordered me personally to attend, don't want to get fired, of course, so I'll get over to the hospital as soon as I can. Bye."

She'd sped through the message and hit the "end" button in a hurry, in case Dr. Bennett sat listening in silence and had reached for the phone to countermand Shannon's plan.

A finger of guilt poked at Shannon's conscience. Well, technically she'd told the truth. Portman *had* ordered her in. Although she'd omitted the tiny fact that she'd decided not to go. She shook it off. She lived in difficult times. Different rules applied.

Next call, Portman.

She couldn't stomach dealing with him yet. She called his Administrative Assistant.

"Cynthia Weaver, Assistant to the County Attorney. How may I help you?"

"Hey, Cyn. This is Shannon. I just discovered from Jane that I should come into the office for a ten o'clock meeting. My doctor told me I may have a serious medical problem." True. "And I've been experiencing strange symptoms." Hah! Nothing more true. "I'm getting pretty sick and she wants me to check into the hospital." All true. Except for the tiny omission—oh forget it.

"Poor baby. You just get well. Don't come dragging yourself in here. Can we help?" Cynthia asked.

"Thanks so much, you're so nice to offer. For now, I can handle this end, but Matt needs to know I can't come in today." Or rather, she *wouldn't* come in.

"And tell him this medical thing might be long term." That one better *not* be true, but the longer she could keep Portman at bay, the quicker she could solve her…situation.

She ended the call and stepped out of the car. The cell rang. She checked the caller: Portman. *Don't answer.* Let him leave a message.

Remember the black marks.

She answered.

"Matt here. What's this about long term medical issues? Long enough to interfere with our big case?"

Our big case? Pathetic.

"No, the Paradigm case is in good shape. I'm walking into the hospital as we speak," she said, as she walked into the Dickson. *Bad,*

bad Shannon. "My doctor hasn't identified what's wrong with me. It could be serious." *True.* "Do you want me to sign a medical release so she can talk to you?" Shannon waited. Portman remained silent. The sound of him chewing his pen crackled down the line.

"Leave it for now. I know you wouldn't dare lie to me," Portman said.

Don't lose control. Don't call him the back end of a camel. Don't do it.

"And my—our—brief is just ready for the finishing touches," she said after a moment of struggle.

"I don't know about that," Portman said. "I got a call from Jack Davis yesterday afternoon. He burned my ear for half an hour about the mess you made of his deposition."

She recognized her location and turned for the elevator bank.

Matt continued. "So you hear this and believe it: I'll make it clear to one and all who blew the case, if it blows. And *that person* will find herself on the street with her reputation hanging down around her ankles."

Shannon looked at the receiver, wishing that Portman's arrogant face might materialize where she could smack his fat, smarmy lips. Her temper flared.

"Remember the Americans with Disabilities Act, Matt? You might want to go study it. Soon. Keep this up and I'll ask my attorney to talk to your attorney."

"Now don't be like that. We'll work something out. Just do not blow this case"

"Thank you, Matt," she said.

He slammed his phone down.

More black marks, but Shannon didn't much care.

*   *   *

Shannon arrived at a door marked "Administration Office" and asked for Dr. Moon. A student in jeans and a University tee shirt pointed across the room. The gold lettering on the door proclaimed, "Dr. Moon, Director of the Dickson Marine Mammal Research Center." At two minutes to 10, Shannon slipped onto a straight-backed chair next to the door and clutched her purse in her lap. She'd attended the University. The familiar collegial atmosphere fit her like her favorite well-worn cardigan and eased the knots in her tense shoulders. All that private money to throw around, and Moon had settled in a modest, casual college office. Way to go, Moon.

She reviewed her main talking points. Her arguments sounded strong.

The risk, though. To Juneau.

Juneau's image, head raised above the ocean waves, with her wide unknowable smile, dominated Shannon's mind. A series of clicks and calls echoed in her mind.

Shannon set her mouth in a straight, hard line. She would pull this off. For Juneau.

Voices drifted from Moon's office. Shannon detected Todd's voice, a certain positive and persuasive lift in his clipped tone. A stand-up guy. She would've regretted clocking him.

Precisely at 10, the door opened and Moon appeared. He stepped out and offered her a welcoming hand. "Ms. Kendricks? Please come in."

* * *

Shannon and Becky had attended several of Moon's marine mammal lectures. He struck Shannon as brilliant and ambitious. She counted on both. She took a deep breath. Show time.

Shannon clenched her purse in one hand. She wiped her free palm on the side of her skirt as she stood, and offered Moon a firm, dry hand shake.

As she preceded the scientist into his office, an invisible force propelled her forward and she stumbled.

Juneau! Settle. She imaged the whale floating in a pool in Shannon's mind, calm, lazy. The rush from Juneau's high emotions subsided.

Shannon's gaze scanned the furnishings. The familiar ambiance of the spare and functional university office ended at Moon's door. Plush burgundy carpet covered the wide expanse from wall to wall. Antique furniture, authentic Tudor to Shannon's eye, filled the generous space: Moon's huge desk at one end, a large round meeting table and chairs in the middle, and a cozy conversational grouping at the other end. Early Dutch Masters and Impressionists dotted the walls. A few originals, perhaps. A pungent scent hung in the air, overpowering Shannon's own new perfume.

This office reeked of money.

Moon steered her toward the three inviting navy armchairs and a pillowed couch nestled around a low table, where four well-dressed people sat staring at her with expectant faces. Not a problem. Shannon faced intent, even hostile, faces all the time.

Shannon considered the four as she approached. Todd sprawled in one chair in his white lab coat, beaming at Shannon. He winked, one big red bush of an eyebrow dipping in sync. A woman relaxed in another chair, dressed in an elegant, vivid red sari, and welcomed Shannon with an open, smiling face and a nod.

Two men in navy tailored suits lounged in the deep cushions of the couch. One detached and cold. One politely interested.

"Please be seated."

Shannon perched on the remaining armchair, her back stiff.

Sit back, for Odinssake. Ease up.

"Coffee or tea?" Moon asked. As he spoke, he wheeled his desk chair to the group.

"Do you have water?" Shannon said, her lips already as dry as her throat.

Moon lifted a crystal pitcher, filled a tall, elegant glass with iced water, and introduced the others. Then he sat back, his tea cup in hand, studying Shannon's face. "I didn't know that you had fallen ill. Todd should have informed me." He turned a reproachful eye on the researcher. Todd squirmed and looked at her, then back at Moon.

"She looked a little tired yesterday, but not as bad as this." When he swung his gaze back to Shannon, he mirrored Moon's disapproving glare, and stole Moon's line. "You should've told me."

She pictured herself as the others would see her. Black half moons underscoring her eyes. The weight she'd lost revealed in the looseness of her suit. If these people perceived her as frail, they'd also see her as weak.

That wouldn't do.

She rode to Todd's rescue. "I didn't mention my…my condition to Todd. Sorry, Todd, I didn't realize it would come up," Shannon said with the slightest hint of reproach, aimed at Moon for mentioning her health. "My doctor assures me I'm not infectious. It's nothing." She waved a hand through the air, as if her health didn't concern her at all. *Lie.*

Moon emitted a little bark of a laugh. "I would not say your condition is 'nothing.' Perhaps you need a new doctor."

Shannon threw him a broad smile. "I appreciate your concern. You're very kind. But I feel quite well." *Huge whopper.*

Moon pursed his lips.

"Now," he continued, "the whale. The Dickson Board consists of twelve members, but these three, with me, form the Whale Research Subcommittee. The bulk of our discussion today involved Juneau, of course. Since you suggested you can revive her, I invited the Subcommittee to stay for our discussion." Moon's expression settled into a mask. "Juneau is a costly asset. We don't want to lose her."

Shannon's concentration broke when Moon referred to Juneau as "an important asset." *Asset?* She opened her mouth to protest, but he continued.

"You must understand that I see her as beautiful and fascinating—" The smile returned and disappeared. "—if moody—whale."

Shannon awarded grudging points to Moon; he had Juneau's personality pegged.

Moon continued. "I have visited the SQ belugas on many occasions. Juneau piqued my interest most of all. I hope you understand why Todd could not allow you to interfere with her care. We want to help her, but I will not allow her to die even minutes prematurely because a woman unknown to me desires to say her last good-byes." His mouth set into a grim line. "Although her death looks inevitable at this point."

Shannon's hand jerked at the word "death." The glass in her hand slopped water onto her suit. She ignored it.

Moon leaned forward and handed her a linen napkin. "The specter of her imminent death is why we," he said, nodding toward the others, "agreed to listen to you. Tell us, why would your efforts result in any better outcome than ours?"

Shannon paused long enough to draw the attention of them all before she said, "The difference is this: I can reach her mind; reactivate it, you might say."

"I understand from Ms. Anderson that you formed a close bond with Juneau, closer than anyone else, even the SQ staff."

"Yes. And we *still* have a close bond. Extremely close." *Oh yes. Two peas in a pod.*

Shannon's strong affection for the whale radiated in her thoughts and Juneau responded with a long high call.

"So you can arouse her from her coma by mere physical contact?"

One of the navy suits snorted. Shannon's head swung around to the couch, but both men wore calm, interested expressions now. Shannon returned her attention to Moon.

"Yes. When I touch her, she'll respond."

Shannon paused again and cleared her throat. She calmed her nerves. She willed the tenseness in her shoulders and mind to drift outward and away. She focused. *Shannon, all rock, no sand.*

She edged forward and stared at each of them.

"However, I want to make a broader proposal."

Moon and the others stirred, their faces flat with surprise.

Shannon suppressed a smile. It always gave her such a rush to flip over an unexpected card.

The Director looked at her with intelligent curiosity. "Please continue."

"I'll try to keep it short. When I bring Juneau out of her coma, she'll go back to the SQ. However, I know — and I'd like to emphasize the words '*I know*,' because I don't mean 'I suspect' — I *know* that Juneau despises the whale pool. For a decade it's crushed her will to live. I don't want her to go back there."

"Well," said Thomas Tremaine, navy suit number one, his voice as chilly as a November New Jersey beach, "I afraid what you 'want' carries no weight here."

"Or perhaps it does," Shannon said, scowling at Tremaine. "As I shall discuss."

"How would you know Juneau 'despises' the beluga pool, as you put it? Such a declaration sounds rather anthropomorphic." Tremaine shot back.

"Not at all," Shannon said. "I'm not imagining how a human in her position would feel; I have observed her anxiety, the extent of her desperation to go back to the sea."

"But what other choice than captivity exists, if we assume she revives?" asked the woman, Ambika Chidambaram. "She cannot survive in the wild, and no facility in the world cares for the whales better than our SeaQuarium."

Good for Chidambaram. No personal attack and no interest in Shannon's wishes. She focused on Juneau. Shannon liked the woman already.

"You're correct, the SQ has built a world-class cetacean center. If we must house a whale in captivity, I'd pick the SQ hands down, Ms. Chidam, Chidambaram" Shannon said, smiling at the small, dignified woman.

"Call me Ambika, please, no one uses my unpronounceable last name," Chidambaram said.

"Ambika, my apologies, and thank you. As to your first point, I, too, once thought that Juneau could never survive in the wild, but I thought wrong." Shannon paused to assess her audience. Tremaine looked at his watch and used his suit cuff to polish its face. The rest paid close attention.

"We assumed that Juneau must either remain captive at the SQ or disappear, unequipped, into the wild to die. One or the other. Black or white. But what about black *and* white? What if we could set Juneau free *and* give her husbandry care?"

Ambika cocked her head toward Shannon. "You mean set her free in a sea pen?"

"At first. Then, in stages, set her free without limitation. But she'd reappear on a regular schedule, where we can examine her, conduct tests, treat her for illness or wounds, feed if she hasn't caught fish—" Shannon imagined Juneau at large in the ocean, then swimming in to eat extra fish, "cared for her *and* where the public can see her." A gentle bump slapped her head—Juneau, confident in her fish-catching abilities.

"I know this concept," said Kip Saunders, navy suit number two. "Animal activists once touted it as the zoo of the future. Uninhibited marine mammals wander in of their own volition to interact with humans as they choose. The idea's rather gone out of fashion; exorbitant cost, I should imagine. And well-founded fears of our whale and dolphin friends pulling disappearing acts."

"But we must at least attempt it, for the sake of the species. And Juneau's the perfect candidate," Shannon said. "Like Keiko—you know, Free Willy. He provides a strong case study."

"Not a good one, I'm afraid," said Saunders. "He died, you know."

"He died of pneumonia, which might've been treated. And Keiko's health always suffered from all the time he spent alone in a tiny pool in warm water in Mexico."

Ambika, head still cocked, asked, "But what makes you think Juneau would indeed return to us from the wild once we freed her?"

"The same way I know I can bring her out of the coma. We're that close." *Oh yeah, that close.* "We'll prove it to you together." *She hoped.*

"Keiko did travel a thousand miles from Iceland to Norway on his own. He socialized with wild orcas. At the time, I thought these achievements impossible," said Moon. The fingers of his free hand tapped his tea saucer one at a time in quick succession, as if different unspoken thoughts pulsed down each digit. "We would not, of course, send Juneau to sea until she regained her heath. If she ever does."

"Yes, that goes without saying. And I know of another interesting comparison," Shannon said. "Dr. Birute Galdikas's work with orangutans at Camp Leakey in Tanjung Puting National Forest."

"Where in God's name is that?" asked Tremaine.

"Borneo. Southern Borneo. Part of Indonesia."

"Borneo?" Tremaine said with a laugh, looking at Moon as if to say, *Get rid of her, Moon, she's a cracked egg.*

"I don't know of—what was her name again?" Saunders asked.

Shannon shifted into lecturing mode. "You're familiar with Jane Goodall who researches chimps and Diana Fosse who researched mountain gorillas until her death, right? Well, Professor Louis Leakey sponsored their work, and also sponsored Dr. Galdikas's work with the orangutans. She started in 1971 and she's still there, rehabilitating orphans and injured orangutans to the wild."

"I have some vague recollection that she's controversial," Saunders said. He tapped his knuckled on his thigh as he tried to recall.

Shannon nodded. "Yes, so I understand." Shannon looked at the floor. "The same people unhappy with Dr. Galdikas would not approve of us for caging the belugas at the SQ."

"I shall have to read about these orangutans," said Chidambaram. "Borneo—a hot and humid jungle. And Dr. Galdikas still lives there after all these decades! She must love these creatures very much."

"Just as we love the belugas," Shannon said, seizing the opening. "Anyway, even after the orangs go out on their own, the option exists for them to come to a number of feeding stations. Dr. Galdikas can study them while they're at the platforms and—" Shannon raised her voice just a touch and paused, "—that's when tourists in limited numbers pay for the chance to go look at them. People don't catch glimpses of them in the wild, with the forest so dense. Just as they don't catch sight of belugas when they're out in the open sea."

"Perhaps she's set up such a unique operation no one can replicate it," said Tremaine.

"Oh no, the Malaysian government has set up rehabilitation centers in northern Borneo as well, in Sarawat. Like Bako National Park. We could create something like that."

Chidambaram said, "Well, if people will trudge out into the steamy jungles of Borneo to see orangutans, I believe they will come to the northwest coast to see belugas."

The muscles in Shannon's neck relaxed. The tide had turned; Shannon had dragged them inch by inch toward her side, and she'd won Chidambaram and Saunders. As the two directors continued to think out loud, Shannon turned her attention to Moon, who'd remained silent.

Shannon struggled to follow his thoughts. She centered all her powers of observation and concentration, watching for any slight sign that might reveal her strongest arguments, her most potent silences, her next move.

A lavender haze formed around Moon. *What? Why now?*

All at once she could experience, *sense,* Moon's emotions, just as she sensed Essi's and Juneau's, and she could view images from his mind, just as Essi and Juneau showed her theirs.

No way.

Shannon blinked. Her water glass slipped from her hand, fell to floor, and took a soft bounce in the deep carpet pile.

Shannon gaped as Moon's excitement and his intellectual enthusiasm buzzed in her mind. She caught other snatches of emotion: kindness, eagerness to help Juneau. Greed, maybe. She watched an image that Moon had painted for himself of Juneau, swimming strong and free. An image of Moon, standing on a podium in front of a vast audience, nodding to thunderous applause. Glimpsed an image of a Tudor hutch that would fit quite well along a bare wall to Shannon's left.

Stop. This display, stolen from Moon's mind, smacked of spying, of voyeurism.

She forced her eyes—and her lavender haze—from Moon and gazed down. *Oh.* Her water had spread in a wide circle on the carpet.

"I'm so sorry—" Shannon said.

"No need to worry. No harm done." Moon stepped to a credenza, and pulled more napkins from a drawer. While Moon sponged up water and rescued his crystal, Shannon fought to recover from the shock: *had she just peeked into Moon's mind? How the hades could* that *happen?*

Other people's images and emotions. By Odin, the next best thing to mind reading.

She took a deep breath. However astonishing the discovery of this new mind-reading ability, she couldn't afford to let it distract her. She must focus. For Juneau.

Tremaine, with a perpetual pout on his face, spoke again. "SQ would never go for it. The whale means money to them."

"Keiko won over the people of Iceland and Norway as well as everyone who visited him in Oregon. You could design the program to maximize a wonderful—and *paid*—viewing experience, in partnership with the SeaQuarium," Shannon said. "And the more whales in the project, the more lucrative the viewing experience would become."

"Do you not see?" Ambika asked the others. "If this plan is designed with scrupulous care, it will bring publicity and more funding. It will also be the correct thing to do." Shannon didn't need a lavender haze to read Ambika. The woman from India had grasped at once that they could win Juneau's liberation if the movers and shakers perceived it in terms of profits. And Ambika burned to see Juneau free. An excellent ally.

Saunders said, "There's grant money in this, I can smell it. Donations from all over the country. All over the world. All the better if we can procure seed money to provide the momentum."

"Yes, we will be needing a fund-raising structure," Ambika said.

"We'd have to build the facility further north. The water's too warm here," Tremaine said, determined to take the pessimist's role.

"The Dickson owns land in Alaska that would suffice." Moon looked at Shannon, his hands now clasped in front of him, his elbows resting on the armrests of his chair. "We must deal with the SQ, of course," he murmured.

Yes!

"But," he continued.

Shannon grasped the arms of her chair. *But what?*

"But I agree with Mr. Saunders that I must uncover seed money in an attention-attracting way to move this project off the ground."

"I can offer—" Ambika began, but Moon raised his hand to stop her.

"Thank you. I will greatly appreciate anything you offer—in due time."

"We know our previous donor contacts," Saunders said. "Ask your secretary to print the list. We can divide the names and put the pressure on."

"Again, in due time. But for the initial donation, I believe our full Board and our partners must see support from beyond the usual suspects." He smiled at his little joke.

"What about *her*?" Tremaine stuck his chin toward Shannon. "Just how committed to this project are *you*?"

Uh oh. The rat had teeth and meant to bite.

"I say if she wants Juneau free as much as she claims, she should put up or shut up. She's an attorney. Let her put her assets where her mouth is."

Odin's eye. Shannon hadn't seen that one coming.

"Ms. Kendricks practices government law, I believe," Saunders said in mild rebuke of Tremaine. "With not quite the resources of your friends in private practice."

Grateful, Shannon slipped him a weak smile.

"Then let her raise it," Tremaine said. "A million dollars seed money."

Shannon hoped for a word from Moon telling Tremaine to stuff it, but Moon wore a mask that revealed nothing. He waited for her answer.

Sweat broke out on her forehead, on the palms of her hands. Trickled down her shirt under her arms.

Although she yearned to know Moon's thoughts, she didn't dare focus too intently on him. She didn't understand her newly-discovered emotion-and-image-reading talent well enough. What if he could sense her spying? No surer way to sink the project. She frowned at Tremaine, hoping she conveyed icicles.

No! Smile and decline. Laugh it off. You haven't got a million bucks, can't raise a million bucks. End of story.

"I'll bring it to you by Friday," she said.

Say what?

Moon allowed himself a slight smile.

"I don't believe her," Tremaine said.

If looks could kill, Tremaine would have melted into a tiny puddle of goo on the floor.

"Write the check," he said, goading her. "I won't cash it until five o'clock on Friday. On my honor." His hand raised in the boy scout pledge.

Like the boy scouts would ever accept him.

Without batting an eye, Shannon pulled out her checkbook and wrote a check with nine zeros. *Nine. Odin help her.*

"I'll tell the bank I'm willing to take as much as they can get from your account. Even if it isn't a million. But *if* it isn't, you don't get it back and you're out of luck here."

Why? Why would he do that? Abandoning her caution, Shannon focused on him, probed for his emotions and images. Tremaine harbored a great deal of anger, jealousy…an image of a woman appeared in Shannon's thoughts, a strong, confident woman, dressed in a British barrister's wig and robe. She held the hand of a little boy who looked like a ten-year-old Tremaine, his mother, Shannon guessed. An attorney like Shannon. Something complex going on there, and Shannon didn't want to know the details, but it appeared she was going to pay for choosing the same career as his mum.

Anything else? She probed again. Distrust—strong, pure and straightforward, it radiated from him like a furnace blast. Conviction to the point of absolute belief that she meant to cheat the Dickson in some way. Determination to trip her up. He meant every word he'd said. He'd ruin her because he *knew, to a certainty,* she planned a con. *Wow.*

Shannon sat in stunned silence as the group continued to discuss the matter. She took six sugar packets out of her bag and dropped them in the new glass of water Todd had brought her. Dr. Moon observed her with a puzzled look but handed her a spoon. She stirred, sipped, and listened to the sentiment flow first in favor of the venture and then against it. Back and forth. Momentum gathered.

But she must raise the seed money. What had she been thinking? No way could she come up with so much money in so short a time. Sure, her friends loved her and the whale, but they didn't have that kind of money either. She could remortgage the house, but it wouldn't bring in half enough. Even an online fundraiser would fail, since she couldn't reveal to the world that to revive the whale, she'd need only return Juneau's mind. Which she safeguarded. In her mind. That kind of talk would get Shannon a ticket straight to the padded cell.

Well, she'd get the money. Somehow, some way, she'd come up with it.

She snapped back to the discussion as Moon turned to her and spoke. "You understand that we will need confirmation of the willingness of the whale to return to station?"

"Yes. Of course." *Hell, she'd climbed so far out on a limb, she might as well venture the rest of the way onto the tiniest twigs.*

"What if you don't restore her to consciousness?" Tremaine asked in a thin, over-confident voice. He reminded Shannon of Portman.

Shannon's face didn't change. She must convey utter confidence. "Irrelevant question. I can and will do it." *With any luck.*

"We keep your million dollars either way, or however much of it we receive," Tremaine said. "Agreed?"

Never.

She gulped. "Agreed."

"And if we decline to pursue this proposed project, Ms. Kendricks?" Moon watched her with unblinking eyes.

The moment had arrived. She'd prepared herself. The success of her proposal depended on her next words. If they suspected Shannon would help Juneau regain consciousness whether or not they agreed to free the whale, they'd wait for Shannon to revive Juneau, then turn the whale over to SQ. After that, maybe they would broker a deal, maybe they wouldn't. But in the meantime, Juneau would rot in her little whale pool.

Pull it together. Concentrate. Her heart beat faster; she clasped her hands to hide a slight quiver. She breathed in the calming incense that permeated the room. Then she gathered herself like an ace pitcher about to throw the game-ending strike.

Are you with me, Juneau?

Energy burst upward through her chest with a rush of passion, real and fresh, and her spirits lifted, as if she'd broken free of her chair and burst into the air.

Shannon's face showed none of her elation. It tightened into stiff, grim determination. She looked first at Moon and then at each of the others in turn. "If you won't free Juneau, gentlemen, and madam, then she will die here. I place her life on your consciences. I will not bring her out of the coma so that you can send her to SQ where she suffers. Suffers," she added in a louder voice for emphasis. "Think about my proposal and discuss it with all necessary parties, but remember this: Juneau goes free or goes nowhere. In addition, before I leave today, I'll need your word that you'll keep Juneau on the breathing apparatus until you reach a final decision."

She rose. Her calm exterior would shatter like the surface of a pond in a hail storm if she loosened her grip on her emotions even a fraction. She stifled her trembling as she took a shaky breath. The others sat immobile, pinned to their chairs by her ultimatum. Then Ambika stood in one graceful motion, gave Shannon a small smile, a slight nod, and held out her hand. Shannon shook it. Moon also rose. He shook her hand and escorted her to the door.

"You are an interesting woman. It has been a pleasure, I assure you. You bring us a fascinating proposal and the possibility of an unexpected and generous donation—if, as you say, we can get the necessary paperwork together. Our subcommittee and the full Board will discuss it with the thoroughness it deserves. You have my word that the whale will continue on life support until this matter is settled."

"Thank you." Shannon squeezed the words out of her constricted throat.

"You understand that the key to this project is that once she revives, Juneau must return to home station. At this time, we have only your word for this. We will require you to demonstrate the truth of it soon."

"Right." Shannon had dug herself in deep here. Miles deep.

"It is my opinion that I can push through the most important decision, whether to even set the project in motion, by Friday at the latest. It is always better to work against a deadline in negotiations, isnt' it?" Moon asked, as a half smile reached his lips.

"Right," Shannon said. Her knees wobbled and her neck blazed. Assuming a casual pose, she propped her arm against a work counter to keep herself upright.

Moon's smile faded. "In this case, however, the deadline is not artificial. Juneau's internal systems have not adjusted well to the apparatus. We must revive her by Friday, I believe, or we will lose her."

Shannon processed the words as if she were underwater.

Lose her. Friday.

Friday would come too soon. *Too soon.*

Moon couldn't pull the project together in four days, could he? And she couldn't scrounge up a million bucks. Not in four days. Not in four years.

Moon continued. "I will make her precarious condition known, and your ultimatum. These facts, will, I feel certain, contribute to a speedy and positive outcome. The Board, you understand, may resent your—" Moon hesitated, then said, "—blackmail, if you will."

Oh, like Shannon didn't resent Tremaine's blackmail.

"For Juneau's sake," Shannon said, "resentment means little to me."

Moon hesitated. "I hope your words do not come back to haunt you." She brushed the thought away; right now Juneau's life mattered more than the anger of a few of Ocean City's wealthiest and most powerful.

"Todd will contact you when all relevant parties have come to a decision."

* * *

Shannon shambled out of the Dickson, sweating and exhausted. She pulled off her suit jacket, and wiped her face and neck with it. Where could she cool off? *There*, the plaza fountain. She eased onto the pool ledge, dipped her jacket in the water, and wiped her face again. Better.

"Did I do the right thing, Juneau?" she said, her words a quiet murmur. Her hand dangled in the pool, sliding back and forth. She watched the sun's reflection ripple in the waves she'd set in motion, like wide, flat lightning expanding across the sky. Students sat along the pool rim, or propped their backs against it to bask in the late morning heat.

Sure, Shannon loved the game of bluff, but with Juneau's life as the bargaining chip? The hairs on the back of her neck prickled.

The whale, calm and steady, rubbed along her mind.

Yes. She'd made the right move, despite the risk. She'd thrown the plan into gear. Now she'd give the wheels time to turn. *No panic.* Keep the goal in sight. Freedom for Juneau.

Odin's eye, how she hated having to depend on others. She slapped her thighs and stood. Well, she couldn't accomplish Moon's part. She must trust him to win over the SQ and the Dickson. She'd force herself to wait and watch. No matter how crazy it drove her. Her hand flew to her french twist. Removing several long pins, she shook her hair, pulled it over her shoulder, and braided it in a loose weave.

The task of scaring up a million dollars would keep her plenty occupied. *Was she crazy?* She could kick herself. How could she have written a check with nine zeros, *nine zeros*?

Never mind. Damage done.

Now, where around here could a woman win a fortune in a mere day or two?

She snapped her fingers. Tremaine had been so convinced she meant to pull off a con. Well, maybe she would. *At the casino. The White Wolf Casino.*

*   *   *

The fountains in front of the White Wolf Casino outside town on the Native American reservation featured fifteen-foot twin waterfalls.

Shannon had always loved them. Their tumbling currents reflected colored lights in the pools below. She drove between the two cascades, lifted her foot off the gas pedal, glided between the water walls, and eased off the gas to prolong the ride. Mist drifted onto her windshield. The muffled plink of the tumbling water floated through her car like a work of magic.

selador.

Essi, attracted to the colors in the water, crowded up to Shannon's eyes—blurring Shannon's vision. Of course: the fountains reminded Essi of all those wisps flowing together in the child's shimmering chromatic river.

A wash of emotion ran through Shannon—Essi's emotion—a feeling of *home,* reminding Shannon she must send the child home, somehow, some way.

But first, Juneau. And for Juneau, first, the casino.

Shannon parked, stepped from the car, and straightened her evening gown.

Could she feel any more uncomfortable?

In her work, Shannon dressed for business, or for power, or for the trust of the jury. At the SQ, she dressed for dirty, smelly chores. Waterproof and washable overalls and chlorine-stained sweatshirt all the way. But *this?* Seductive vamp? Not her style. So *very* not her style.

And yet here she sat, embarrassed and uncertain, her pale blond hair fell in soft curls down her back, flowed across her shoulders, and rested on her chest. This resting place, not coincidentally, emphasized the bosom Shannon preferred to keep tucked beneath sensible blouses buttoned well above her cleavage.

She looked down. *No, no, no—too much of her damn self on view.* Maybe if she—but when she tugged the bodice upward, none of her chest disappeared. Okay, what if she arranged a big curl of hair down the front? She tried it. The locks fell back to their natural resting place as soon as she lifted her hand. *Bloody hell.*

What in the world had tempted her to gussy up in this unlikely attire? Her mouth wrinkled in a wry smile. Not hard to explain. This afternoon, she'd hit all the best formal wear shops in town, unimpressed, until she came upon this form-fitting, shimmery, deep emerald gown in a tiny, high rent district boutique. The price tag, ten times more than any garment she'd ever owned, should've stopped her cold. But the clerk had seduced her with murmured admiration. The stunning gown fit her so well. Complimented her eyes in such enchanting fashion. Would take men's breath away.

"Like a runway model," the clerk had said. "And with that perfume you're wearing, they'll never know what hit them."

And Shannon, so desperate to win big money for the sake of Juneau and her bank account, had swallowed the hook, like a salmon on herring bait.

For the first time, she occupied the skin of society's vision of a beautiful woman, and here at the casino to flaunt it, Shannon weighed her emotions. On the one hand, measuring up to the Gold Standard of Beauty for once in her life bestowed upon her a new brand of feminine power, confidence, and nerve. On the other hand, she didn't want this brand. She couldn't wait to return to her jeans and tee. She'd spent her life becoming a woman who earned her power and confidence. No, she's shed this garb at the earliest opportunity.

Shannon shook her head as she remembered her afternoon expedition. After the dress, the clerk sold her the four-inch spike heels.

"With your long legs and this slit along the side of your dress, you really *must* have them. Like the girl on the vodka commercial."

Uh, who?

Her torturous emerald footwear. *Yeah, vodka might help.* She'd worn them for one crummy hour now, and they already squeezed her toes when she tottered forward, and they demanded such anti-wobbling machinations that her knees screamed at her to kick the nasty things off.

She'd gone to Becky for the finishing touches. She'd recounted Tremaine's challenge and Moon's unsettling silence when she'd looked to him to put the bastard in his place.

Becky and Andy still insisted that Juneau couldn't survive in the wild. But Shannon's friend agreed to help her with her hair and make up for the sake of her bank account.

"You know I've got your back, girl. You're in good hands."

The coup de grace came in the form of a sparkling jeweled necklace. A for-real, huge emerald pendant, encircled by shimmering diamonds.

"It's beautiful. I can't borrow that," Shannon had said, pushing the necklace away in protest.

"That belonged to my mother, girl. It's treasure to me. You lose it, you scratch it, you breathe on it wrong and you die," Becky had said as she placed the necklace around Shannon's neck. "My god, you never told me you had cleavage, honey child, even though you look too skinny today. Are you losing weight?"

"Sure I am. I expect we all are, with Juneau hurt and the scare with Andy. Plus that lightning strike knocked me for an extra loop."

Becky frowned. "I can see that. You should go home and jump in bed, but if you insist on going, you need a longer chain so the jewel rests right there." Becky poked at a point just north of Shannon's newly-uncovered décolletage. Becky sifted through her jewelry box until she emerged with a silver chain of the perfect length, fastened it behind Shannon's neck and stood back to admire her handiwork. "You want to distract the other card players, my curvaceous friend? This should do the trick."

Shannon hated it. Well, not the necklace. It sparkled. It lent her eyes a rich viridescent depth. But drawing attention to her body? Yeah, she hated that. Real talent involved winning with one's wits.

However, not tonight. Tonight she would cheat, if that what it took.

Cheat, and not only with her feminine wiles, but with a bit of image-spying and emotion-reading. Desperation had driven her to it.

Guilt riddled her conscience. Shannon, the straight arrow, stooping to distraction and mind-reading. Gah.

Yes, she planned to pick out the players who could afford to lose. Yes, She believed her cause, Juneau's cause, worthy. Still, she'd washed her hands three times before she left the house, and yearned to wash them again. Now.

She sighed, and pushed her memories of how she'd come to this sorry pass away.

Well, she'd come to the casino. *No sense standing here.* Moving toward the casino entrance, she picked up the hem of her dress and clutched her silver purse. It contained every penny from her savings account, withdrawn from the bank this afternoon, plus a sizable loan from her 401k plan. It even carried a fiver from Becky, although that didn't count, because Shannon had promised to pay her friend any winnings it earned.

She peered around the parking lot. Now, where was her escort?

*   *   *

As Becky had applied Shannon's silvery eye shadow earlier in the evening, she'd convinced Shannon an escort *must* attend her.

"Why?" Shannon had asked. "I swear I'll turn into a radish if anyone I know even *sees* me in this get up, let alone watches me slink around batting my eyes at the high stakes poker players."

"Don't argue with me. I know these things. You go alone, and it shouts 'cheap pick up,'" Becky had said.

"Yeah? And how is it that you know these things?"

"Never you mind, girl. Now close your eyes so I can blend the shadow."

Since she allegedly must have an escort, Shannon had tried to convince Andy to do the honors as he sat at the kitchen table watching Becky work.

"Don't think so," Becky had said, eyeing Shannon's cleavage again.

"Not interested, Shannon," Andy had said. "Don't feel up to it."

Shannon frowned. Andy hadn't acted or sounded—or smelled—right since Tharm's invasion. Either angry, fearful, bitter, or lethargic—like now. She resolved to cook up a way to help him if she survived this night.

There. She spotted her escort. Not bad. The tuxedo looked splendid on his tall, lean frame. Nice shoulders.

All her misgivings returned.

How crazy was she to go into a casino intending to cheat the table blind on the arm of a police officer?

To talk him into this little adventure, first she'd apologized for her bizarre behavior when it had dawned on her that an alien had invaded her mind. Which hadn't gone swimmingly. No surprise there. She explained that the revelation had stunned her, overwhelmed her.

Quintana had said, "I see."

Which left her where? What did he see? A deranged woman? A ruined shell of a human infested with oddities? He didn't say. She didn't ask.

Instead, she'd proceeded to throw out four or so shameful whoppers. She said she couldn't send the alien home until she found a secret portal that Essi believed existed somewhere inside the casino. Said that since Shannon didn't know its location, she'd need to arrive prepared for even the inner sanctums of the gaming house, where they required formal wear. And where she couldn't bear to go alone, fearing the kind of men who might frequent such places. Said please, please, would he rent a tux and help her? Like a maiden in distress, batting her eyelashes and wringing her hands.

Disgusting.

Shannon could take care of herself. She always had.

Quintana made his way to the entrance where she waited. At first, his eyes passed over the bejeweled woman in green. Then he froze mid-step and blinked. His eyes returned to her, moving first to her face, then along her svelte dress to her bosom.

Shannon's face face flamed like blistering sunburn.

Thor's hammer. If Quintana's gaze could turn her as red as a scarlet letter, how could she tolerate the looks of strangers with greasy hair and yellow teeth?

"You look good," he said. "Really good. But I didn't think you were…the type."

The type what? The type to look really classy? The type to look like a dressed-up slut? No answer could be good. She didn't ask.

"Thanks. You too." There. Let him think he wasn't the type either. Whatever type they were talking about.

When she passed through the casino doors, the vast gaming rooms smothered her like a polluted cloud. She'd forgotten the noise, hundreds of machines chiming in discordant rhythm. The smoke, gamblers puffing endless cigarettes to take the edge off their losses. The worst thing about this tribal casino—it didn't adhere to the state's ban on indoor smoking. And the crowd, hundreds of people playing the machines or roulette or craps or cards.

The urge to turn and run amplified in her head like a loudspeaker with the volume rising. The urge, though wordless, screamed, *Get out. GET OUT.*

Juneau in a wild panic.

Shannon spun and bolted for the door, but just as she reached it, she pulled herself to a stop. Sure, Juneau had experienced nothing like this in the wild or at the SQ, but who was in charge here, anyway? She closed her eyes, and imaged to Juneau, surrounded the whale with gentleness. *We need this, my friend. Without it, I'll never win your freedom.* Shannon filled her mind with confidence, assurance. Essi hummed. The whale stilled.

Quintana, caught by surprise at Shannon's reverse run to the door, had taken several seconds to catch up with her. "You okay? Second thoughts about trying to locate this portal? We could go to my place instead. I have some etchings I could show you." He raised his eyebrows three times and flicked an imaginary cigar.

Shannon smiled at him. "Not at all. I…I thought I'd forgotten my lipstick, but I found it in my purse." She rubbed her lip with her tongue. Might as well practice.

He stood close to her shoulder, his eyes intense. "I really didn't think you were the type," he said again, mumbling, as if to himself. As if saddened.

But he rallied. "You're wearing my favorite perfume. I hope you wore it for me." He offered his arm. "Shall we? Where do you want to start?"

Shannon hated this. More and more every minute. *Get it over with.*

"Let's go straight into the high stakes game room. I have a feeling that I'll come up with what I'm looking for there." She hesitated. "No, wait a sec. Why don't we hit the buffet first?"

After an hour among the meats, casseroles, and breads of the Fine Dining Buffet, Shannon dabbed at her lips a cloth napkin and stared down at the empty plates from her latest trip to the pastry bar. Quintana watched her without comment. They'd said little as Shannon ate. And ate. Quintana helped himself to salad, roast beef and mashed potatoes, and called it good. He then found himself with nothing to do but watch Shannon pile it in.

Shannon blushed under his stare, put her fork down, and swallowed a large mouthful. "I know," Shannon said, unable to look into his solemn eyes, "You're wondering if I'll still fit into this dress when I stand up."

"You told me already. The child alien is taking out more than you can put in. I'm beginning to believe it. That or you're suffering from a serious metabolic disorder. Either way, you should leave. Your make up, although beautiful, doesn't quite hide those dark shadows under your eyes, or the paleness of your skin. Portal or no portal, we'd better go."

Yes, she should *leave, but she had no choice.*

"I'm all right," she said, waving his concern away with a flick of her wrist. "But thanks." She tossed a rueful look around. She wished she could remain parked here at the buffet all night. "We might come back before we leave. I want to try that ice cream parlor." She stood, laid her napkin on her chair, and took a breath. "Let's get started."

A gentleman at the door to a room called The Inner Sanctum gave them the once over, liked what he saw, and let them pass. Several conversations stopped as the usual Ocean City elite gamblers craned their necks to see who'd entered.

To Shannon's chagrin, many a game player gaped at her with the appreciative glances she dreaded. *Might as well play it all the way.* One hand came to her chest to touch her emerald. She moved several more steps into the room, swaying her hips, a coy smile on her glossy lips.

Out of the corner of her eye, she caught Quintana frown. His protective hand touched her back. If the stakes weren't so high, she'd quit the charade in a split second right now, rather than lose the respect of this Ocean City Police Officer, Lucas Quintana.

Don't believe in this fake Shannon, Quintana. Please.

"Quintana, I want you to know I—"

"Don't I know you?" asked a tall, pole-thin man who'd stepped in front of them. He stared at Shannon's chest for a moment, then at her face. "If I don't, I can't imagine how I've lived without you all this time." He extended his hand. "Tom," he said. "Tom Willingham. Aussie. Jetted up this week from Sydney to see my auntie." He winked.

Shannon, a professional hand shaker, reached for his offered palm. He snatched her fingers and kissed them.

Oh for Odinssake.

As if he'd just noticed him, Aussie Tom looked over at Quintana, his square, tan face feigning surprise. "Oh, and you are...?"

Quintana offered his hand. "Luke Quintana," he said. The two men froze in a long, tight hand shake. Neither appeared to want to let go.

"Yes, well," Shannon said, "We've never met. Nice to meet you, Tom. Perhaps we'll see you again sometime." She put her hand on Quintana's arm, gave his sleeve a firm yank, and guided him away.

Neither of them spoke.

Quintana also garnered his fair share of admiring looks from the female population in the room. Shannon's teasing smile faltered, but she plastered it back on.

The couple drifted about for a few minutes, watching the tables. While she concentrated in mock earnestness in the search for the portal that didn't exist here, Shannon focused on players, house dealers and croupiers, other observers. She studied the games, concentrating hard. Some of the games involved too much risk. Five card draw might work.

"You know," she said to Quintana, "Since we're here, I think I'll play a few poker hands. You want to watch?"

"Hoo. I don't think you want to try that here," he said. "You can't even get a chair at the tables without a stake of thousands of dollars. These people play in a different league than us normal folk." He returned his hand to the small of her back.

"Oh, I brought plenty, see?" Shannon said, opening her purse to give Quintana a glimpse of its contents.

Quintana's eyes narrowed. "You came here to gamble with that kind of money? So you fed me all that nonsense about aliens and portals so I could be your ticket in here? Well, you're in. Good luck."

Quintana's hand dropped from her back. He turned and disappeared from the room before Shannon could squeak out an answer.

Go after him.

No, she couldn't. She needed money. Badly. She'd already written the check. Unless Moon intervened, Tremaine would bankrupt her. She steadied herself, her hand on the back of a chair.

"Oh dear, my escort has vanished," she said with a tiny pout. "Might I sit here and play a few hands while I wait for him to cool off and come back?" A seductive smile spread across her face. "Which he will," she said.

A young man stood and said, "Take my place, before I lose my last dollar."

The dealer said, "Sure, if you have the $20,000 to buy in."

Shannon's blood rushed to her stomach. Shock. *Twenty thousand to buy in?*

"Of course," she said, opening her purse. "Gentlemen, let's play."

* * *

Three hours later, Shannon had gained ground. Her winnings tipped $600,000. *Good, but not good enough.* At this rate, she wouldn't reach a million until dawn she'd never last that long.

Shannon hadn't played poker before, and her emotion-and-image reading skills took her only so far, even though she read each player's hand right along with him the moment he set eyes on his cards. She made errors. And poor cards happened, of course. Too many. She couldn't win with a measly nine high, for Loki's sake.

She needed time to learn the players' reactions, emotions and facades: the flatline bluff; the black fugue that preceded folding; the ill-conceived rush of bravado that led players to raise the stakes when they shouldn't.

And it took time to tease out their strategies. Like that bird-like guy in the paisley vest and black jeans next to her, who drew little attention to himself and placed small bets, even when he held winners. And that bear of a man in the cheap beige suit across the table, with his hair parted in the middle, combed down like a 1930's gangster, who never revealed his hand if he folded and even folded on smaller pots that should've been his. He kept his cards tilted, top toward him, preventing onlookers from peeking into his hand.

At first, she'd been so busy watching everyone else that she'd mismanaged her own hands. After a time she tried out several of the tricks she learned from eavesdropping and her strategies improved.

People had learned about her, too. A house detective appeared behind her to watch for signs of cheating. Shannon clutched her cards with white fingers. Okay, she *had* cheated. All night. The detective *should* accuse her, *should* arrest her. *Should* make her give back every penny. But he couldn't catch her. Couldn't prove a thing. Still, he unnerved her, until at last he moved along.

"I see your $10,000 and raise you $50,000," Shannon said. Her hand showed a full house, aces over tens. After a long dry spell, Shannon held winners at last. She wanted to reach her million on this pot. Two players had already folded.

Paisley Vest also held a full house, kings over sixes. A surge of adrenaline hit his veins as soon as he picked up the final king. His thrill rolled through Shannon like a thunder clap. His face, his posture revealed nothing, but his excitement told her he'd abandon his usual careful play on this, the biggest pot of the night.

"See you," he said, "and raise you another $50,000." *Gotcha.* Shannon made a show of frowning.

Once word spread about the size of the pot, a crowd gathered, whispering among themselves. At Paisley Vest's bet, someone behind her inhaled sharply, audibly.

The bet moved to Cheap Beige Suit, the last player remaining. Cheap Suit's emotions flat-lined; Shannon read nothing. She cocked her head. *Not one image, flat line emotions.* He'd gathered himself for some move, a move so difficult he dared not even think about it for fear of betraying himself. Shannon panicked. She couldn't read him!

Calm down. He held a poor hand: the king, queen, and ten of hearts, seven of spades, two of diamonds. Shannon squinted at him. He meant to bluff her into folding. That had to be it.

"See your $10,000," he nodded at Shannon and tossed the money in with a flourish, "your $50,000," he nodded at Paisley Vest, and raise you $200,000."

Now a man in the crowd said, astonished, "no way." The murmurs turned to raised voices. Shannon couldn't think.

She read nothing from Cheap Suit. *Nothing.* He was damn good. And yet he didn't hold winners. It made no sense.

"I will see you and raise you another $100,000," she said.

Paisley Vest's elation vanished. He slapped his cards on the table. "I'm out. You two have at it."

She allowed her lip to quiver. She took a sip of water and licked the last drop off with her tongue. Her free hand played about the emerald on her chest.

Nothing. She couldn't distract him. He focused on his hand, never looked up.

"Here's your $100,000 and $100,000 more."

The room erupted. Other casinos in more affluent locales might see this action all the time, but not in modest Ocean City.

He can't win. Shannon didn't get it.

"I call. Show us your hand," Shannon said. As she placed her hands over her chips to move them to the center of the table, a large, square hand covered her own slim fingers. She knew that hand; Quintana had worked his way through the crowd behind her. She had no idea how long he'd been standing there.

"Don't, Shannon. You can take money home tonight, a sizable chunk. Don't throw it away."

She lifted his hand with a soft squeeze and moved the chips.

Cheap Suit, who'd held this hand below table level, now lifted the cards and spread them on the table.

"Ace, king, queen, jack and ten of hearts. Royal flush." He pushed back in his chair and grinned. "Never thought that'd happen to me in this life time."

A few in the crowd cheered and slapped him on the back. Many more patted Shannon's back with sympathy.

Shannon froze, rigid, stunned. *He couldn't win.* She'd seen his hand. No ace, no jack. Then the truth sank in.

He'd cheated, pulled the cards in from some hidden pocket.

She stood and turned to Quintana. "He cheated," she said, her voice rising and cracking. "He didn't have a royal flush."

Quintana looked at her as he might look at a limping puppy. "How would *you* know? Why do you think he bet up the pot? He suckered you. He had a rich dumb blond in his sights and he took you to the cleaners."

"No, I *know* he didn't have the cards, I...I..." Should she tell Quintana she'd looked at Cheap Suit's cards through his mind? If he didn't believe her, he'd write her off as a fruitcake. If he did believe her, he'd brand her a cheater. Neither option appealed.

Beaten by an even bigger cheater than herself. *How droll.* She'd lost so much. "I'm not a dumb blond, and I'm sure not rich," she said, looking down at her chips; not even enough to replenish her 401K. Her knees gave out; she collapsed back into her chair.

"You're blond, but you're not dumb, I give you that," Quintana said. "Look. I know some people. I can get you support for the addiction. Let me help you."

In a dazed and absent voice, Shannon answered, "I'm not addicted. I've never gambled before and I sure as hades will never gamble again."

As Shannon stood to leave, the lavender haze appeared over the roulette table.

jjjo, Essi whispered. *jjjo.*

Go? Now? Why now?

nnnowwwaaa, Essi answered.

Shannon slid her night's take into her purse and bee-lined for the roulette table, Essi's anxious hum in her ear.

Shannon jerked to a halt, just as the croupier grasped the wheel.

One last time with the girly-girl thing. She plunked down her chips. "Please. I just have the strongest feeling. Please let me play." She blinked at the man in the house vest with her big forest green eyes under long lashes, a little moue on her lips, her fingers twirling her hair right above the emerald."

He winked at her. "If the lady has a feeling, we'd better let her play. How much and where?"

"I want all of it on—" She read the number under the lavender haze. "Black sixteen."

Quintana touched her hand. "Are you crazy? Take your winnings and go home," Quintana said. "Don't do this. You don't need to do this."

The croupier raised his eyebrows. "Yes or no?"

Shannon took a big breath, held it, and said, "Yes. Black sixteen." Sweat ran down her back, dripped from her chin into her cleavage. Everything rode on one spin of the wheel. Everything.

Time slowed. The wheel spun. The ball bounced. It landed.

Black sixteen.

Onlookers, some of whom had followed her over from the poker table, screamed.

The croupier signaled a runner. "Odds are 35 to 1. You're a rich woman."

As if answering a bell, two large men in red blazers swooped in and swooped her out. They would take care of her, they said, just come with them. You, they said to Quintana, wait in the lobby.

"Why can't he come with me? We're together," Shannon said.

"He didn't play, he didn't win. You did. He tried to stop you, in fact. We're not sure you're on the up and up just yet. You want your money, you'll come now," one of the men said.

"Wait," Quintana said, pulling out his wallet and showing the men his police credentials. "We're all on the same side. I'll just sit in the back and mind my own business. What do you say?"

"Your credentials don't mean squat here," said the same man. "And we may or may not be on the same page. Nothing's going to happen to her, unless she's running a scam."

"I'm not," Shannon said, indignant. Well, okay, what she'd done might qualify as a scam. All right, it *was* a scam.

"Just meet her in front," the man said.

Quintana began to protest further but Shannon interrupted. "It's okay, Luke. I can handle this. You don't need to come."

Don't ask for trouble, Luke. Not on Shannon's account. Better that he stay away from her problems.

He threw up his hands. "Right, then," he said, and turned his back on all three of them.

*   *   *

They rushed her into a plush white office and settled her in a black leather chair, her purse on her knees. The men in red departed.

The silence in the office after the circus outside eased the tension in her shoulders. A long quiet sigh escaped her. Then her big win and what it meant sank in at last. She cried. She cried as if her world had collapsed. Until she shook with the sobs. Until she sagged from her seat onto the floor. *Juneau, we won it. We won your money.*

Two more men in red arrived, looked surprised to catch her on the white carpet crying, but said nothing and helped her back into her chair. They demanded she empty her pockets and her purse, scanned her body with a metal detector, took her driver's license, left.

Shannon envisioned a glum guy in a white shirt, his sleeves rolled up to the elbows sitting in a dark room nearby reviewing the video recording of her movements. Uneasy guilt stole over her, even though she hadn't committed any crime. No law against following a lavender haze around.

Essi, you're a miracle worker.

Visitors. Phone calls. Roulette wheels. What else could Essi predict?

No images formed in her mind. Essi wouldn't say.

The minutes ticked on.

She couldn't believe it. Juneau just might—*just might*—return to the sea. Shannon shivered, her teeth chattering, until a man swished in, startling her; a different one this time, in a costly, rose-colored, silk suit fashioned for the young and hip.

The man, whose tag read "Casino Manager," and whose name Shannon never caught, grasped her hand in both of his, gave it a squeeze, then gave her papers to sign; she signed them; he sped through some words of congratulations and handed her a check; a photographer took a picture of the man shaking her hand; and then the manager whisked her to a back entrance. Before she could utter more than a thank you, she found herself alone in the parking lot staring down at a check for three and a half million dollars. *Odin be damned!*

The unmarked private door from which they'd booted her didn't open from the outside; she couldn't re-enter. The casino wished her gone.

Uh no. Not happening. *The ice cream parlor awaited.*

She folded the check, put it in her purse and circled around to the front to search for Quintana.

Quintana had disappeared. She'd last glimpsed him when she looked over her shoulder at his retreating figure as the two men led her away. And what a glimpse. He turned back, as if he felt her gaze. His face stormed, his eyebrows and mustache down and dark, his eyes flashing. He had reached into his pocket, maybe for his car keys, as the manager's door closed on Shannon's view.

Shannon wandered out to the parking lot to search for his car.

Gone.

As she turned back toward the ice cream parlor, her adrenaline high crashed, and extraordinary exhaustion welled up. Dizziness overwhelmed her. She leaned against the nearest car, a sleek, metallic black Jaguar, and closed her eyes. She'd never make it to the casino.

PART TWO

MISFORTUNE ENCOUNTERED

CHAPTER FOUR

WEDNESDAY

SHANNON SWAM IN DARK WATER, ink, a universe of dead stars.

A smooth, rubbery form with a slightly rising ridge swam beneath her and lifted her with slow, careful undulations.

A low, musical hum filled the water, vibrated in soothing pulses, surrounded her. *Safe,* it whispered to her, *safe.*

Shannon knew this place, although she couldn't quite name it. Not just yet. If she could awaken enough….

She watched the blackness above her. After a few moments she detected a lightening; the black softening, yellowing. A surface. Somewhere up above the early morning had dawned.

Closer, brighter.

And then she awoke, lying on cold asphalt. Juneau and Essi had brought her out of a deep faint. Still exhausted, and now weak from hunger, she turned over and tried to sit up. Too weak. She lifted her head and scanned the casino parking lot. The black Jaguar had gone. She reached for her necklace and the comfort it would give her, her connection with her friend Becky.

Gone.

No, no, please Odin, not Becky's heirloom.

Panic mounting, she turned her attention to the pavement. The necklace chain must have broken. Her purse, her check—rather Juneau's precious check. *Not stolen, please Odin, not stolen.*

Nothing. Except broken glass all around her. Someone had broken a bottle out here and she'd fallen right into in. She looked at her hands. Blood. She'd cut herself. Not important. The necklace and the check. Where *were* they?

She searched hard, every inch of the lot she could distinguish from squinting eyes and her low vantage point.

Nothing.

Turning halfway on her side, she checked the ground that her body and gown had protected from view.

Nothing.

Shannon, who never cried, wailed, a long, loud, desolate cry.

An elderly couple appeared out of nowhere and loomed over her. Mid seventies, perhaps, wrinkled faces that spoke of hard times. Dressed in plaid shorts and bright orange tee shirts, they looked as if they'd just abandoned a brutal all-night session of gambling and it hadn't gone well. The man knelt beside Shannon and took her soft hand in his calloused one. He wore a Proud Veteran pin on his shirt emblazoned with the American flag. She wore a cut out of fuzzy kittens.

"What's wrong, miss? Are you hurt?"

Shannon gathered her thoughts; then the words rushed out. "Yes, please, I need help; I fainted last night and just came to; I've been robbed. Can you call the police? And I need food; I have a disorder; I need to eat every hour. And then I have to tell the casino to stop payment on a check."

Without a word, the woman opened her huge denim-washed blue purse, its rhinestones sparkling in the early morning light, handed her cell phone to her husband and fished further until two king-sized chocolate bars with almonds surfaced in her hand.

"Here. We was saving these for this afternoon when we go back, but you need 'em worse'n us. Just going out to the car to let the dogs stretch their legs. Tea cup poodles we have. Lucky we cut through this space. I'm Dorothy. He's Jack."

"Thank you so much, Dorothy," Shannon said, tearing the wrappers off. "You're so kind. Do you see my purse anywhere? Matches my dress? Sparkly, like your bag." Chocolate smeared her upper lip and chin as she pushed the first bites in—but she didn't care, except that she would remember to lick every last smidgeon off her face.

Dorothy gazed around. Her features remained placid, but Shannon caught a sudden glint in her eyes. Without a word, she picked her away around Shannon and her husband, and disappeared behind a red convertible dented as if an orchestra of drummers had borrowed it for timpani.

"—yes, at the White Wolf south parking lot, 'bout halfway from the street to the building. Can't miss us. A pretty girl in a fancy green dress and a couple old geezers. Bums next to her." The man kneeling beside her listened for a few ticks. He noticed Shannon staring at him and winked. "Okay. We'll stay put."

He clicked off and said, "Police're on the way, and paramedics. When—"

Dorothy returned, Shannon's purse in hand, battered like a paper cup on the highway.

"Think somebody ran over it," Dorothy said. "There's a few things inside." She poked through the contents. "No check from the casino like you mentioned. Comb, hanky, five dollar bill, so they didn't take everything," she said in a bright voice. Trying to perk Shannon up.

Not working.

The quickly-consumed candy bars set off a tiny spark of energy, and Shannon struggled to a sitting position, Jack easing one hand to her back to assist. She wiped the chocolate off her face with a finger and then licked the finger clean.

"That's about it," Dorothy said, handing the purse down to Shannon at last. "I'll go on back into the casino and get someone out here about that check." And off she sped, with a slight limp in her gait.

Shannon removed each item in her purse and placed it on the asphalt. The check *must* be there. When she'd finished, she surveyed her work. Dorothy had missed one measly dollar bill that had been crumpled into her hanky. *No check. No necklace. Odin's eye.*

Six dollars to her name.

"Look," she said, "You take this six dollars for the candy bars. If you go back in again this afternoon, you'll need nourishment." She held out the bills.

Jack smiled, wagged his head back and forth and said, "People don't help people for mon—"

Shannon interrupted. "Do not argue with me. I am a woman in a fragile emotional state. You must humor me." To her dismay, she *did* sound fragile.

The old man pushed out one huff of soft laughter and took the money. "So long as we're all clear we didn't stop in the hopes of picking up a reward."

"Not much of a reward," Shannon said, glum, her shoulders falling.

The sound of sirens drew their attention to a police car pulling in the lot, and on its heels, a Medic One unit.

A tall, skinny officer with a brush of acne scarring his cheeks approached them, his partner remaining behind to have a word with the disembarking paramedics.

He pointed to Jack. "You the one who called it in?" As Jack's head bobbed in the affirmative, he continued, "Let's get your statement first while the medics have a look at Miss...?" He made it a question.

"Kendricks. Shannon Kendricks. Please, we need to get word out at pawn shops and jewelry stores right a—"

"One thing at a time, Ms. Kendriss." He turned his attention back to Jack, who stood and stepped away with the officer.

Oh, one of *those. May Odin's thunder bolt strike him—no wait.* No bolts of lightning. Forget it.

The paramedics treated the cuts and bruises Shannon had accumulated on her fall, including a tender scrape and cut on her cheek, which stung and throbbed and burned, all at the same time.

She must look a treat. So much for Shannon the sexy vamp.

"May need a stitch or two. Better take you into the emergency room."

"No thanks. Give me the refusal form. My own doctor can deal with it."

Lie.

Another patrol car screeched into the lot, curving a tight circle toward the group huddled around Shannon. *Good grief.* Looked more like a response to a mass murder than one lone chick robbed in a casino parking lot.

The car jerked to a halt. Quintana jumped out the driver's side door. Officer Taney pulled out of the passenger seat in a more orderly fashion.

Quintana strode over, his long legs moving fast. "You. I knew it was you the minute they mentioned the pretty girl in a fancy green dress. I shouldn't have—what the hell happened?"

The skinny officer left Jack—and Dorothy, who'd just returned with a man from the casino.

"You need something, Quintana? This is my call."

Yep, one of *those.*

"She's a personal friend, Mike. Just need a minute." Quintana's eyes never left Shannon.

The paramedic returned with a refusal form, as his teammate finished bandaging another cut on her leg, which Shannon hadn't even noticed. Now that he'd brought it to her attention, it throbbed.

"Quintana, I'm sorry about last night," Shannon said, her voice cracking. "I'll explain later. But right now, we have to get word out that someone stole a for-real emerald and diamond necklace. They'll try to dump it in a hurry. It belongs to Becky." Shannon's eyes welled up and this time the distress was genuine. "Can you help me? *He—*" She glared at Skinny Mike. "—isn't in any hurry."

"But you're okay? No one—"

Shannon flapped her hands. "I'm fine. Well, I'm okay. No one hurt me. I fainted last night. Just woke up and found everything gone."

He knit his dark, unruly brows and hesitated, as if he'd rather stay, but said, "I'm on it. Give me Becky's number in case she can give me any more info about the stone." He stood, spoke a word or two to Officer Taney and they left.

Shannon gazed around, the victim unattended by anyone, as Officer Skinny Mike spent quite some time with Dorothy and Jack. His companion, a red-headed woman who looked about twelve, took notes from the casino rep.

"Hey, I don't want to interrupt or anything," Shannon said in a weak and unimpressive voice, "but I have an eating disorder. I need food and I need it now, or somebody's going to get their socks sued off." Shannon didn't pull the litigation card often. Today, her mood had sunk so low, she might even mean it.

Becky's necklace. Odin's eye, how can I tell her?

Dorothy said, "Oh I'm sorry, bless your heart, I forgot with all this drilling going on over here. They think we're suspects. Can you believe that? We sat in that place all night," she said, pointing to the casino. "We got drinks, we talked to other gamblers. We had something to eat in that snack bar. And they think we're suspects. Anywhose, I brought you these." She wrestled the contents of her rhinestone bag again and this time pulled out a sandwich, a wrapped salad, and a huge piece of lemon cake.

"Bless *you*," Shannon replied, taking the food from Dorothy and digging in.

Skinny Mike suspected Dorothy and Jack of the theft. A shiver of doubt wriggled through Shannon. *Dorothy and Jack—the thieves?* Shannon hadn't even considered the possibility, even though she knew from experience that bad people could mimic good behavior when it served their purposes.

Essi built her an image, her hum impatient, startling Shannon. Juneau and Essi had stayed so quiet, she'd forgotten them for a moment. The image showed Shannon throwing her purple haze at Dorothy and Jack, reading their emotions, watching their mind images.

Essi hummed and imaged the lavender haze.

Oh. Of course.

She concentrated on each of them in turn, her fists balled, her back straight. She found that she could eat and throw lavender haze at the same time. So she did. After some minutes, she relaxed. No, these two simple people suffered from a wheelbarrow full worries, about money, work, relationships, even their fashion wear, but, judging from their mind images and emotions, they hadn't robbed Shannon.

The casino rep broke away from the red-headed officer and stood over Shannon. She craned her neck, looking up at him, shadowing her eyes from the rising sun with her hand extended, shading her eyes.

Jerk. She didn't say that out loud, although she wanted to, but rather asked him to place a stop order on the check they'd given her, and do it right away, then issue her a new one.

Of course, he replied, but they must assess fees. Cancellation fee, reissue fee, handling fee. If the check had been cashed, complications….

Blah, blah blah. Shannon, out of long habit, had tucked her credit card away for emergencies in a private place on her person that the thief had missed. He'd have had to undress her to chance upon it.

That, thank Odin, he hadn't done *that*. She could at least pay the fees.

She prayed to all the gods of earth, sea and sky, that the thieves had not deposited her check.

She rose to her feet with the help of Officer Red Hair and Casino Man and told them both that she was going to the buffet to fill out forms and give her statement. They insisted on helping her limp to the dining room and steadying her while she dished up.

A cop and a casino guy watching her every move from seven inches away. A ripped and soiled evening gown at seven a.m. Scrapes, bruises and bandages. Even more embarrassing than her entrance last night.

Her humiliation, however, had no effect on her appetite. Shannon ate, filled out forms, gave a long, tedious statement to Skinny Mike, answering often irrelevant questions, ate. The casino manager informed her that it appeared the first check had not yet been deposited.

Thanks be to Odin and also whomever.

However, when the casino manager arrived, a different one now on shift than Rosy Suit guy, he explained that the casino would not issue the new check until all doubt dissolved as to whether anyone had or would deposit the old check.

How long would *that* take, Shannon asked. She needed that money by Friday afternoon or, she said, lives could be lost and litigation could ensue.

The casino manager, without batting an eye, told her he would do his best to speed the process along.

* * *

Shannon exited the casino in a low mood. She'd managed to lose three and a half million dollars plus cash and she might not get it back in time.

And she'd lost Becky's beloved emerald. She retrieved her car and headed straight for Becky's house. Shannon hoped that Becky had gone to the SQ, which would delay Shannon's ordeal, but no such luck. A quick cell call from the curb confirmed Becky hadn't left the house yet because of late hours with Juneau.

This would go badly. Very very badly. By Thor's hammer, Shannon would rather walk across the country to Hoboken right now in her four-inch spiked heels than face Becky.

* * *

"Oh my God, Shannon. You look like New Orleans after Hurricane Katrina. What happened? We've been so worried," Becky said when she opened the front door to Shannon.

"When I came out of the casino, I fainted and some jerk robbed me. Took my check for my winnings, took my cash, and—" Shannon hesitated. "Can we sit down? I'm still a bit shaky."

"Sure, baby, come on in the kitchen and I'll get you some coffee. Did you see a doctor? You need aspirin or anything? That must've been horrible."

Shannon couldn't tell her. She had to tell her. But how could she tell her?

She joined Andy at the dining table and smiled a wan hello. He nodded back. He wore an old torn sweatshirt, a pair of shorts and flip flops. He hadn't shaved this morning. He didn't smile. The odor of the swamp still floated about him like a fog.

Damn Tharm. Damn her damn eyeballs.

Becky poured Shannon a cup of coffee, placed a cinnamon roll in front her and sat down.

"What can the casino do about the check? They can fix it, right?" Becky asked. "How much did you win?"

"They can fix it, but it'll take time. Time Juneau doesn't have. I'm sick about the whole thing." Shannon sipped her coffee.

Tell her.

"I won a lot of money. Even for you, from the fiver you gave me. Much more than Tremaine even demanded. And also…." Shannon couldn't breathe. Couldn't speak. Moved her lips like a gold fish.

"Also I lost your necklace. The thief stole it."

"You *what?*" Becky asked. "He what?"

"I'm sorry, Becky. I know how much it meant to you. But Quintana, that police officer I told you about? He's looking for it right now."

"Shannon, it was my mother's. My mother's," Becky said, her face blotchy with rising sorrow. "I need you to give it back to me, Shan. Please. I…And now I'd like you to go." Becky rose, trembling.

"Beck," Andy said quietly.

"Andy can drive you if you don't feel up to driving yourself," Becky said, never taking her eyes off Shannon.

"I'll bring it back, I promise. Just let me stay and talk to you."

"Shannon," Becky said, the words held a warning; Becky's mother had died when she was a teenager. She'd never moved past that missing part of her heart. *Odin knew*, Shannon could understand that.

"But—"

"Better go," said Andy.

Shannon stood, circled around Becky and fled the house.

On her way home, Shannon stopped at the fast food place on Commercial Way and ordered four sacks of grease and fat. Hamburgers and fries.

"You're sure hungry tonight," the kid with thin hair and acne at the drive through window said, joking, as he handed out the food and took her money.

"Yeah," Shannon said, her mind elsewhere. "Yeah. I am hungry. I have a cheesecake at home to go with these, though, and there's just me, so this will do."

The kid's grin faded. He looked at Shannon's skinny arm. "There's treatment for booloomia, ah, beleemia, oh, you know, that disease where you stick your finger down your throat? You should see a doctor."

"Yes, right, thanks, I'll get that looked at. And it's bulimia." Shannon drove on, unperturbed, and a curious exhaustion-fed airiness filled her head. A good kid. He cared.

Not bulimia, but she damn well better make some progress with her health soon or her poor dying Juneau might outlive her.

*   *   *

"You're fired," said Portman.

"I'm what? What did you say?" Shannon asked. She couldn't have heard right. Portman couldn't mean that.

She'd just come in her door from Becky's house when her cell phone rang. She pushed straight on into the kitchen, her giant wriggling mastiff at her heels, and sank into a chair at the table. Narci jumped up on the table and purred into her face.

"You slammed the door in my face when I came in on Monday. You made a mockery out of a key deposition. You disobeyed a direct order to attend my meeting. You lied about your whereabouts—I just checked with the secretary at the office of your doctor what's-her-name and you never showed up at the hospital on Tuesday. In fact, the doctor thought you'd come here instead. And you failed to produce your brief for my inspection and input. I've had it. You're done."

Busted. Doctor Bennett's office shouldn't have given out that information but a lot of good that did Shannon now.

Portman radiated hostility. Sure, she'd wounded his oversized ego, but she'd counted on his famed false veneer of civility to keep him in check. Well, it seemed ego had trumped civility in her case, and she'd better mend her fences, fast.

"I'm sorry. I have been sick; Dr. Bennett's office must've confirmed that, and I've had a lot on my plate, with the summary judgment coming up and—"

"All my attorneys have a lot on their plates. They don't take it out on me. They don't lie. They don't play hooky. They don't disobey me."

"Yes, I wasn't thinking straight and I'm sorry Matt. I've been under a lot of strain."

"The brief. Is it ready for me to revise?"

Stall. He can't fire you until the brief's done. No one else knows the issues.

"Um, no," *Think of some excuse to keep the brief, any excuse.* "I, I haven't yet put together a good argument for one of the issues. I'll have to wrestle that puppy right down to the wire."

"Just send it to me. I'm sure I can deal with it."

Portman starting from scratch on a complex issue? In his dreams.

"Would love to talk longer," he said after a pause, "but I too have a lot on my plate. Just get down here, pack your things, send me the brief and get out."

Shannon racked her brain for something to say, to change his mind. "Please. Let me get well. It may take a couple weeks, but once I'm back, you'll see my old self."

"That's what I'm afraid of. Don't think I don't know what you say behind my back, what you think of me, Miss Way More Intelligent Than Everyone Else in the World. Well, if you're so smart, how come you're the employee being fired and I'm the boss firing you?"

Busted again. He was acting like an adolescent, but once again Portman's hostility shook her. He'd known? That made her feel like a middle school bully picking on the nerd.

"I tell you what, and believe me, this is the best you're going to get. Have a letter of resignation signed and on my desk tomorrow morning along with the brief and I won't fire you." He slammed his phone down.

Shannon remained frozen and still her chair for a moment. Juneau flipped her fluke in long powerful jerks and passed back and forth in Shannon's mind.

"Calm down, Juneau, sweetheart. Anger won't help us here. We just continue on: eat, sleep, plan, fix things. Recover Becky's emerald; explain everything to Quintana; wring a check out of the White Wolf; free you; send Essi home; get well. No problem." Shannon stared unblinking at the kitchen tile for several moments, as the phone buzzed its disconnection in her ear.

She called Jane.

"Where've you been?" Jane said. "Gracious, I thought you'd died and gone to heaven. Or somewhere. I've been calling for an hour."

"Sorry, I turned off my phone last night."

"So you could sleep, poor lamb. That's okay."

Shannon didn't tell her that sleep had been low priority since Sunday night. No need to muddy the waters. Shannon winced. Scratch that.

"Important items first. A cute feller asked about you. Officer Quintana, I think? Nice looking, eyelashes to kill for. One of those guys who gets midnight shadow three hours after he shaves?"

If Shannon had been there, Jane would've been winking and nudging her in the ribs.

"Did Quintana say anything about an emerald necklace?" Maybe he'd already recovered it.

"No. He just asked about you." A wink and a nudge. "Oh, while I'm talking to you, I need to tell you I'm taking a four-day weekend starting tomorrow so Picker and me can attend sheep shearing classes."

"Wait. You don't own any sheep."

"Well, that's why we go, silly," Jane said. "We can't practice otherwise."

Vintage Jane. Shannon lifted her eyes to stare at the line between ceiling and wall for a long moment.

She should tell her paralegal Portman had fired her. She couldn't. Not yet. Why ruin Jane's four-day sheep-shearing extravaganza? Shannon would leave a message on their home phone so no one would blind-sided Jane Monday morning.

Coward.

Shannon let Jane talk for a while. Her friend, as usual, peppered the conversation with loads of office gossip, but the people Jane mentioned now felt like distant acquaintances. Even strangers. They didn't interest her much.

So strange—two days ago she'd sat in the conference room to depose Paradigm's pudding of a client, as if the case mattered more than anything in the world. She'd gnashed her teeth over Portman's ineptitude. Scott had sent her into paroxysms of embarrassment. Now, the Paradigm case, Portman, Scott—all the things that had engulfed her every waking thought just last week—existed in the vague far-away, like ghost ships in the fog, like desert mirages. A year could have passed since the last time she'd laid eyes on the office, judging by the dim spark of interest she could muster now.

Interrupting after ten minutes or so, when Jane paused to take a breath, Shannon said, "Listen, Jane, I'm still not well. I need a couple days before I can come in." True, but talk about a lie of omission.

"Wow. You must be on death's bed. The Shannon I know would crawl in here on hands and knees before admitting to illness."

Shannon sat with her head in her arms on the table, the phone propped up next to her ear, dejected, exhausted.

On death's bed. May be.

*   *   *

Shannon fed the cat and dog an early dinner and emptied her fast food sacks in record time. Swirling a last piece of pretzel bun around her plate, soaking up catsup from her curly fries, she gazed from her kitchen table out at her back yard. The kitchen smelled of burger grease with a slight tang of key lime from the cheesecake.

It would turn dark soon.

Behind her tree line and beyond a copse of eucalyptus trees stood Eisner City Park, a big 800-acre wood with miles of trails and forest, brush and ball fields. The city closed the park at dusk; no light filtered from there.

A sudden thought chilled her: anybody could hide there. Drom, anybody.

She rose to lock the house up tight, her great mastiff by her side. Then she curled up on the couch with a book, *The Host*, by Stephanie Meyer. The book resonated with Shannon—aliens invading human minds, taking over the world? Of course it resonated. However, the day's events had turned her power of concentration into a bag of confetti. Her foot tapped as she tried to read. The couch fabric scratched her back. The light from the standing lamp hurt her eyes.

Forget it.

Throwing her book on the end table, she revisited the window and door locks again and refilled her cooler with her night time snacks. Her weariness set about its slow work of dissolving her limbs and leaving her a helpless puddle on the floor.

Shannon picked at the emotional scab where her feelings about the death of Tharm festered. Death by her hand. How different did that make her from any murderer?

Holy Odin. Where had that idea come from? Was she kidding? Way off base.

Ok. Self defense. Not at all the same. But that didn't mean she'd made peace with it.

She slept as soon as her head hit the pillow. As her consciousness drifted into dream, Essi projected images to her: Essi and Tharm and the beautiful river Selador....

Essi, shimmery, silvery, lavender, stands in the tunnel of a dark cave outside a door-like opening that glows and flickers with light from the room beyond. The little girl stands off to one side and peeks in. Holes—windows? portals?—dot the walls, filled with bright white flame, flashing with white lightning. Essi's young friend Toss stands before a portal studying something on a glowing rectangle floating in the air in front of him. Essi ducks back to avoid being seen. As she leans even further forward to see more of the room, one of her hands gripping the edge of the entryway skids across the stone and slips through a beam of light that stretches from one side of the entrance to the other.

The instant her hand crosses the beam, Essi flies into the room, her arms and legs flailing, as if hurricane winds hurtled her through the room, pulled by the portals themselves. Essi grips the edge of a portal that threatens to swallow her, her eyes wide, her mouth open in a scream Shannon can't hear. Invisible force tears the child's hands loose. The instant Essi enters the portal, her form turns into the familiar misty wisp; the lightning turns lavender, and Essi disappears.

The image of Shannon stands by the edge of the whale pool. Juneau rises to greet her. The lavender lightning flashes and branches out; a terrified Essi shoots *through* the lightning bolt from a portal that opens above the pool, into Juneau, and then the child and the thrashing, bucking Juneau flow with the lightning through Shannon's hand to her mind.

Emotions flooded Shannon, overwhelmed her even while she slept. Not *her* emotions; the shock, fear, loneliness, and utter desolation that spilled from Juneau and the child as they relived that moment.

So that's how Essi arrived. No wonder Shannon had wandered around dazed and confused during those first hours.

Mother of Loki. A colossal accident. An accident that might lead to the destruction of the world.

Shannon stirred. Essi dreamed on. The scent of the Selador River, the scent of all Selador's people within it, blended into a glorious unity. The hum of the Seladorans rises above the river and together the vibrations turn into sweet ethereal music, intertwined in a harmony that would wring tears from stone gods.

Shannon's cheeks grew moist. Teardrops ran down the sides of her face, onto her pillow. Still asleep, she blew her nose on her sheet.

The Riverworld's music rinsed Shannon's mind clean.

Yes, Essi. A wonderful world.

But then Essi's thrum turned to a low slow beat, which quickened and grew intense; the child's anguish vibrated in her humming, as if Essi couldn't contain her grief and it burst, pulsing, from her.

Essi's next set of images explained why she grieved.

The Seladoran slope behind the river morphs into a set of wide walnut-brown steps, two hundred, perhaps more, that flow and curve around the hill to either side, stretching until they disappear in both directions.

Below and some distance off, where the ribbon river should be, a few inches of muddy, mucky, green-brown water extends along the river bank. Swamp.

Great Tree of the Universe. What in hades had happened to the Selador River?

Gone. A pang of sorrow shot from Shannon, as if someone had reached in and torn the Selador from her own chest. A small cry burst from her, like a frightened chickadee from a hedgerow. Such a loss. She couldn't bear it. She wanted to throw herself to the floor and wail.

No, she wouldn't mistake Essi's feelings—or Juneau's—for her own. She could lose herself, become more Essi and Juneau than Shannon. She shivered at the thought. Essi grieved and Shannon suffered as if the grief were her own. That was all. And yet Shannon's instincts disagreed with her: the grief over Selador belonged to *her.* To both of them.

Poor Essi. All this time she'd been showing Shannon the great river as it *used* to look, not as it looked after Tharm and her partner had finished with it.

Drowsy but awake now, Shannon imaged herself drawing the child close and holding her once more.

But Essi hadn't finished.

Once again the little alien built an image of Selador as it used to be. The child stands by the water, then pivots to look up a long slope of gentle, rolling meadow of grass and wildflowers, unfamiliar shapes, blossoming in unnamed colors, echoing the hues of the Selador. Above the slope rises a towering cliff face, glinting gold under twin red-colored suns.

Even as Shannon took in the bluff's glittering and impressive height, the cliff-top changes into a massive man-made structure. Gigantic. The front side facing Shannon stretches ten city blocks at least. It reaches several hundred feet high into a rose-white sky, like a New York skyscraper.

Within stone walls, Shannon could make out movement.
Something in the stone *flows*. Mud-brown. A flowing mud building.
A huge misshapen dome forms the top of the structure.
Great arches, perhaps fifty feet high, circle the base—
rrisssa
—arches circle the Rissa, all the way around the cliff top and disappear out of sight. One of these arches towers to twice the height of the others. The alien that Essi showed her earlier, Drom, passes under this dominating arch and into the darkness beyond. The arches, too, flow within their beams, like sludge in transparent pipes.

How had Tharm and Drom built that monster?

Essi showed her.

The planet's two suns beat down, intensely red. The Selador pulses in rhythm with the suns' pulses.

The river is made of Essi's people; they draw their energy from the suns through the river.

Drom and the lately-departed Tharm build a dam and divert more and more wisp water, with its sun-energy, through a tunnel under the cliff. The river shrinks and muddies. Its scent turns swampy. As the two invaders divert more and more of the river under the cliff, the building rises up.

Essi imaged the river flowing into a huge circular pool in a cavern carved out of the mountain's rock. Drom and Tharm float in the river, and inch by inch the river level shrinks. They absorb the river's energy through their skin. Almost nothing of the river remains. When they rise, the black tar on their skin has been replaced by their original vivid colors. But now the pool has emptied and the black tar begins to build on them again.

By the hammer of Thor. The ribbon river, the Selador, had consisted of Essi's *people*. Tharm and Dorm had consumed *her people*, just as Tharm had said. *But to see it*. Terrible.

The contents of Shannon's stomach lurched into her throat, burning it. She fought it down.

With the river depleted, Essi shows Drom and Tharm travel to the portal room. They startle as the little spy-girl-gone-wrong flies by them without warning and disappears through a portal. They wait. She doesn't return. First Tharm, and later Drom follow her.

Shannon bolted upright in bed. Indy lifted a sleepy eyebrow at her and Narci, displaced from Shannon's side, adjusted her curled shape just enough to fall back to sleep.

"Essi, did the two aliens kill everyone but you?"

The child imaged a group of people outside the—what had Essi called that big building—the Rissa? They move down to what is left of the Selador River to watch and mourn as its beautiful colors sicken to muddy brown. No wisp mists rise from the shrinking brown. Some choose to mist into wisps and return to die with their friends and families. Some choose to leave the River before the aliens consume every drop of its life.

Rows of small, dreary huts patched together from brown clay, not much more than lean-to's, huddle by the swamp, roofs thatched with dried, green-brown reeds. The new homes of the few remaining Seladorans. The sadness of it, the wretchedness, seeped into Shannon like toxic gas.

Unable to sleep, and despite the dead weight of her legs, the sluggishness in her mind, Shannon scooted her feet over the edge of her mattress to the floor.

So. The alien killers, Tharm, then Drom, had landed on Earth, and, with the Riverworld depleted, had begun their quest for world domination. World domination. Who used "world domination" in a sentence about their biggest worry of the day?

Tharm had perhaps deceived her when she referred to Essi as "a morsel." They wanted Essi out of the picture to prevent her from warning the people of Earth. *Too late for that.* But Drom didn't know Shannon had learned all about it, and his ignorance yielded a slight advantage to Shannon. She'd do her damnedest to keep that knowledge from him.

Another ugly thought—if Drom located Essi with Shannon, he might decide to commandeer *Shannon's* body, just as Tharm had hoped to pilot Andy's. He might push Shannon's spirit out into the ether, or, scarier yet, keep her in Shannon's body with him.

She ground her teeth in frustration. Before one single flash of lavender lightning, Shannon had lived a regular life, spending her time clashing swords with nothing more menacing than Ocean City attorneys. Her main preoccupations consisted of living under the thumb of her boss and dieting in repeated failed efforts to thin down to model standards.

But after the flash, the benevolent invaders of her mind, Essi and Juneau, had arrived, killing her minute by painful minute. No dieting worries now. And not-so-benevolent invaders, Tharm and Drom, had arrived to destroy the entire world of living things. If someone had told her all this a week ago, she'd have asked them what brand they smoked because it was wicked strong stuff.

She looked at her companions, Narci and Indy, darkening lumps in the evening light. Good thing Shannon had those two. She might melt like butter on a hotcake if this Drom caught her alone, but by the gods, if he hurt a hair on Indy's or Narci's head, she'd beat him to death with her bony fists. She'd never let anyone push Juneau into the ether either; nor, she might as well admit, would she ever let the alien hurt a soft, curly hair on Essi's head. She'd die first.

And maybe she would. Die. How surreal to stare into the face of her own death mask.

Shannon, still sitting up in bed, let herself slump back onto her pillow in the dimming light of her room.

Essi formed another image. Distracting Shannon again? Or lost in her own dream of home?

Essi holds the hand of a shimmering silver-turquoise boy. It's the teenager Essi showed Shannon before. Toss.

Yes, the child yearned for her friend.

tosss.

"Is he your brother?" Shannon re-imaged the child's own picture of Toss and Essi until she'd reduced them to babies. She constructed a little house and family. *Wait.* Essi's people lived in the Selador, thousands of wisps in a ribbon river. As Shannon hesitated, Essi erased the house and replaced it with a silvery purple woman who transforms into her wisp-shape and sinks into the Selador. A tiny strip of the wavy wisp breaks away, several shades lighter. Lavender. Wow. Essi's birth. *Easy peasy child birth.* The silvery purple wisp lifts from the river, turns back into a woman holding the baby Essi. Sweet. The silvery purple woman is her mother.

leemira

Her mother. Pale blond hair. Huge green eyes. Essi looked a lot like her.

Matter of fact, Shannon looked a lot like Essi's mother, with her new green eyes and pale hair. *Funny—*

—Wait. Shannon the leemeera?

Shannon the *mother?*

Holy Odin. Essi had set about remodeling Shannon into the child's mother? *Not good, not good, not good.* Shannon squinted in the dimness to check her hands. Nope, not purple like the leemeera's. At least not yet.

It made sense, in a way. Think of the fear and pain that had overwhelmed the child when Selador went to ruin and then, on top of that, when she'd plummeted by accident to a new strange, bewildering planet and life in Shannon's head. No wonder she'd set about re-creating her mother to care for her here until she could go home to the real thing.

Shannon's mind drifted. Now, what had she asked Essi about? Oh, right, Toss.

Shannon imaged Essi's mother turning into a wisp in the river and splitting off a little silver *turquoise* wisp who arises and turns into Toss. Yes or no? Essi erased that one even before Shannon could apply the finishing touches. Not siblings, then.

In Essi's next image, she crouches in the brown mud, crying, plunging her fingers into the muck. In the swamp water, several beautiful wisps have ceased to shimmer or flow, bubbling in their last efforts to turn to mist and escape the smothering swamp. But they're trapped, unable to lift, their energy stolen. Essi's mother, who has faded to a dull, plum-blue wisp, lies at the little girl's feet like a crumpled ribbon. The color fades, fades, and disappears, leaving a brown muddy twist of decaying matter.

Oh my Odin. Drom and Tharm had killed Essi's mother. Oh my god. No wonder Essi'd been looking for comfort. For a surrogate. Essi couldn't go home to her leemeera.

Shannon imaged: Essi cuddles in Shannon's lap, the child's head snuggles against Shannon's chest. Shannon can smell Essi's warm, spicy-scented skin. Shannon strokes Essi's hair, and runs her fingers down Essi's velvet-soft face as if her fingers are light, soft paint brushes. Essi's long thick silver-lavender eyelashes flutter and close.

But Essi wrestled the image from Shannon.

The child's eyes fly back open. Essi's leemeera, her mother lies dying in the river. The child thrums, at a pitch inconsolable and sad.

Shannon caught a faint hint of the musical tones of the leemeera's vibration, the hidden words within the hum that Shannon could never quite understand.

In the image, Essi cries and trembles, grief-stricken. She sobs on and on. A hand appears on Essi's shoulder. Toss hums to her, places gentle hands on her shoulders, turns her from the river and guides her up the hill to a hovel so small only Essi can fit into it. Toss kneels and smoothes out the reeds inside and the child goes in and curls up in a sobbing, heaving ball. Toss sits before the opening and hums.

A friend then. Good man, Toss. Another orphan, maybe. Juneau inserted herself into Essi's image—she could do that too?—

Juneau rubs along the child.

The whale had been a mother herself in her small set of pools at the SQ and had lost her newborn. Her own grief must've compelled compassion for the grieving child.

Essi hugs the whale. Her sobs quiet.

Those two could understand the loss of the mother-child bond in a way Shannon never could. The temperature in the dim room dropped and the darkness echoed with emptiness.

Shannon tried to sleep, tried to forget her calamitous world.

She vowed to send Essi home to her friend Toss no matter what. She imaged Essi inside Shannon's head down at the SQ, looking around. She pictured Essi showing her the portal, then Shannon lifting Essi close enough so that the child could float through.

Essi erased the picture and didn't rebuild. Either she didn't know the location of the portal or she didn't know how to get through it. Maybe they'd have to locate Drom and choke the answer out of *him*.

Anyway, what would happen to Essi even if Shannon found a way to send her back to Selador? Would Drom go back to destroy her as he finished off Toss and the others on Selador? That Shannon would not permit.

For Essi, for the Earth, it all boiled down to the same thing: Before Shannon could send Juneau and Essi home, Drom must be stopped.

*   *   *

Shannon had almost dozed off when a new worry intruded: her friend Andy. Neither Shannon nor Essi had weathered the alien invasion well. What kind of shape had Tharm left *Andy* in? She glanced at her night stand clock. 8:30. Her friends would still be awake.

She picked up her cell phone and dialed.

Andy said hello before his phone had even rung.

He knew the phone would ring. Uh oh.

"Hi, Andy. Hey. Fast pick up."

"Shannon. Hello. I was coming down the hall, so I just picked up on my way by. What do you want?" Andy's voice sounded hollow and harsh, like an angry wind bouncing along a cavern wall.

From the sound of it, Andy's recovery hadn't proceeded too well, either. *Not good.* Shannon looked at the bedcovers without seeing them.

"How do you feel?" she asked.

"How do I feel? Pretty much like I'll never feel right again. Thanks to you."

Back off, friend. She hadn't caused Tharm's attack.

Her elbows jabbed into her thighs. She opened her mouth to tell Andy what he could do with his resentment. "Andy—"

Essi pulsed, a quiet, sleepy thrum. Calmed Shannon down.

Shannon loosened her grip on the phone. She understood, of course she did. She'd experienced the sewer thing named Tharm. Andy would need time to recover, plenty of it. She could roll with his mood.

Deep breath.

"I'm so sorry this happened. You'll forget Tharm. It'll just take some time. I know you will."

"No, I don't think I'll ever scrub the oily, swampy feel of her out of my mind. That thing dripped with…well, stupid as it sounds, with corruption. Like the bottom of the otter pool, fish-rot bad. Like flesh-eating bacteria bad. Pit bull on your throat. Piranhas in your pool. Do I need to go on?"

endi, Essi whispered, pity stroking her whisper.

Poor Andy indeed, Essi.

Out loud Shannon said, "No, I'm clear on the concept. Hey, if you need help to, you know, cope, I can give you the name of an exceptional therapist."

"I'm not crazy. I don't need a shrink."

Ouch. It seemed Andy hadn't bought into the whole get-in-touch-with-your-feelings movement. Shannon hesitated a tick. "What did Tharm want from you, anyway? Did she want you to take her around the area so she could look for Essi or other people to take over? Like that?"

"What does *your* alien want?" Andy said, snapping back.

"Essi's nothing like Tharm. She just wants to go back to where her friends live, that's all."

"Yeah? Have you looked in a mirror? You look like death on a stick. It wants to eat you alive. Your alien's co-opted you and you don't even know it."

Fair assumption. But wrong. "No she hasn't," Shannon said in an even voice. "She needs my energy to stay alive, yes, and to keep Juneau alive, don't forget Juneau. Essi's just a kid. She's also the reason we could get to you and push Tharm out."

"It wanted me dead, the real me, even though the body would've stumbled on. And that's scary as hell."

"What went down when it first happened? Tell me every detail."

"After it took me over, down at the whale pool—I've ordered the pool cordoned off until this invasion stops, just so you know—I could see this black cloud behind my eyes, and I could feel it look around, check me out, study my body, read my feelings, I could *feel* it. By the time it finished, I'd already yelled at Becky to call you. I ran. I wanted to escape, like that made any sense."

Now that Andy had started, the words tumbled out.

"Then it—it talked to me. It wanted my body, but not *me*—it thought of me as a nuisance. It regretted for one nanosecond that it would have to snuff me out, like you might regret for one instant that you had to swat a fly on your kitchen counter, but you'd swat it anyway? As in, I'm the fly, and the alien's the fly swatter."

"Have you talked to Becky about this? Let her help you."

Andy ignored Shannon's interruption and went on, as if he'd never left the fish house, caught in his worst nightmare. "It rummaged around in my mind and played with my memories. That thrumming it made sounded like laughter, like it was mocking all the memories that made me feel bad or ashamed, dragged it all out and laughed about it."

Jesus. Poor Andy. For sure, Shannon had drawn the kinder, gentler alien.

"By the time it turned on me to…to kill me, I'd made it to the fish house. Nowhere else to go. I just grabbed the edge of the medicine counter and held on for dear life. I fought it with everything I had, every bit of will power. But I got tired, so damn, dead tired." Andy's words slowed to a stop.

"You beat her, though. You matched her. Screw her, you beat her."

Andy didn't respond. "I never felt so alone, like the last living being in the solar system except for *it*. Then you came with Juneau and the other alien, and I was never so glad to see anybody or anything, any damn thing." Andy's tone softened as he recalled how Shannon's threesome had charged into the fray. His words slowed, his anger spent. For now. "I'd forgotten that. Sorry I came on so strong. You saved my sorry behind. I won't forget again."

"Don't spend a second worrying about it. You'll recover. You will. It's just a matter of time." Maybe.

"Did you get into my thoughts like *it* did?" Andy asked. "Look at everything I don't want people to look at?"

Hells bells, Andy. Living with the knowledge that someone had intruded into his most secret thoughts. Ugly.

"No," Shannon said. "My word of honor on Juneau's round belly. Tharm kept me way too busy to peek at your thoughts even once." Shannon tried a small joke. "Too bad, really. Could've blackmailed you into letting me do some training with Wally."

Andy laughed, a small, tired, worn-out sound. "Good enough." Andy said something in a muffled voice. Then he said into the receiver, "Becky wants to talk to you."

"Shannon." Becky sounded surprised to find the phone in her hand. "I was just standing here thinking about grabbing the phone out of Andy's hand so *I* could talk for a while, and all of a sudden

Andy shoved the phone into my hand. You're psychic, boy," Becky said to Andy.

Uh oh. That sounded familiar too.

Andy had picked up Becky's image of herself grabbing the phone. Bad news: he'd performed the trick even after Tharm had disappeared. How disorienting would *that* be, with no friendly alien on board to help him figure it out?

Wait a second. Did that mean Shannon's lavender haze that could predict events about to occur would hang around after Essi left? She imaged, then Essi nodded.

Good or bad? Shannon couldn't say.

Before Shannon could dwell on that, Becky's voice dropped; her hand cupped the phone and muffled the sound as she continued, "Don't think for a minute that I've forgotten my necklace. But I want to talk to you about Andy. He's gone to the kitchen. I listened to the story he told you. My god. He hasn't uttered word one about it 'til now. I'm scared for him. You know what else? He can't get rid of that swamp smell. It's driving him crazy."

"Hang on a second," Shannon said. She imaged Tharm disappearing out of Andy's head, then Shannon, Andy and Essi looking hard to see if anything of Tharm had been left behind. They see nothing. Then she imaged Andy happy, smiling, in all ways fine. *He'll recover, right, Essi?*

Essi displayed black and orange powder on the black cavern floor of Andy's mind. In her image, Andy doesn't smile.

What is that stuff, Essi?

The child imaged that dark hour when Tharm had occupied Andy's head and Shannon and her team had fought to throw her out. As Tharm moves about his mind, the black and orange powder shakes off her and remains behind. In Essi's image, the powder glows with its own life.

Ugh and ew. That swamp witch had left some of her essence behind? The notion stunned Shannon. She imaged Andy sweeping out the powder, sending the particles away. Essi returned the powder, alive and glowing, to Andy. That little bit of living Tharm would always torment her friend. Repulsive, primal, stinky Tharm. Shannon didn't move, shocked.

"Shannon? You there?" Becky asked.

"Oh, sorry, I'm sitting here feeling bad about what Andy's going through. I don't blame you for being scared. Andy's shaken up. Who wouldn't be? Tharm's sure to give him nightmares for a while. But he should turn back into our same old intelligent, competent, efficient, easy-go-lucky joker dude, don't you think?" *Lie, lie, lie.* But she couldn't bear to dump the entire extent of the catastrophe on Beck all at once.

Tears blurred Shannon's vision. She blinked over and over. Andy would never ever again be the intelligent, competent, efficient, easy-go-lucky joker dude Becky loved.

Shannon choked off the tears, cleared her throat and said, "Take care of him."

"I will. How about you? You doing okay?"

"Fair to middling." *Lie.*

"Well, you take care of yourself, too. And you *will* bring back my goddamn necklace."

"I will. I promise." Shannon clicked off.

She sat on her bed and stared at nothing.

Did Andy possess all of Shannon's new skills then? She constructed the image, Shannon and Andy, side by side, see haze, people arriving; see haze, phone ringing. See the pictures in other people's minds.

Essi altered the image.

Shannon looks at someone far away, a tiny dot, and sees the figure's tiny images. Andy, on the other hand, sees images only from the mind of someone touching him. Shannon waits for long minutes from her first view of lavender haze to a person entering the area. Andy sees just a few sparse wisps of black haze the second before a person shows up.

Oh. The little bit of Tharm that remained made Andy's new skills weak. Maybe they wouldn't freak him out.

No they'd freak him out.

And the smell?

Essi shook her head.

Shannon's temper flashed. *Andy didn't deserve this.*

Essi imaged Andy's black cavern again. Essi, Juneau and Shannon stand there, then leave. Tiny scatterings of white, cobalt blue, and lavender living powder remain behind.

Shannon understood—Juneau's and Essi's living powder dotted the floor. The cobalt blue powder—Shannon's? Essi nodded yes.

Well even those little particles would help him, right?

Essi affirmed, but since they hadn't stayed as long as Tharm, they'd dropped a tiny amount compared to Tharm.

Shannon whistled a long, bleak note of frustration. Becky and Andy deserved to know what they faced. She tried out the conversation in her mind. "Hey Beck, here's a funny thing; you'll sure have a hard time keeping secrets from Andy now! And get used to the stink. And put him on aggression meds."

No, Shannon couldn't face telling them about Andy's new talents and problems yet. Although she'd have to spill the beans sometime, Loki's luck. Bad, bad, bad luck.

Another possible piece of Loki's luck struck Shannon like a falling piano. In less than a heartbeat, Shannon imaged her own head with Tharm powder. *Please say Tharm never made it into Shannon's head, Essi.* Please please, say no powder came back into Shannon's head when her group returned from Andy.

Essi erased all evidence of Tharm from Shannon's head.

There is mercy among the gods.

Shannon laid her head back down on her pillow and cried. From relief, from grief, from fatigue that clung to her day and night. Her shoulders heaved. Great sobs escaped her. Her eyes grew puffy and red, her sinuses swelled, packing her head with pain.

Could this day get any worse?

Essi could hear and feel Shannon's grief, which would do the child no good, but Shannon couldn't stop herself. Shannon's spirits sank lower than ever before in her life.

Indy picked herself up, moved over and laid down, positioning her big head on Shannon's feet. The mastiff's warmth seeped into her cold and shaking body. Narci's front legs stretched across one of Shannon's arms, and cupped Shannon's hand in her paws. Juneau brushed along Shannon's mind, but this time, the slight rubbery pressure didn't pass by and vanish; Juneau stayed, her touch tight and firm against Shannon's spirit. The child pulsed a gentle, quiet hum, and built this image: Shannon's head is the big one this time, and within it, the black cavern of her unused brain—

Bummer; she'd hoped *her* empty cavern would be smaller, what with all the activity she envisioned taking up space in her hard-working brain, but her empty space echoed, huge and dark.

—Shannon's little self stands with Essi, and Juneau floats with them. Then Essi and Juneau turn to clouds and float away. There on the floor lie huge mounds of living powder, a lovely blend of Juneau's white and Essi's shimmery silver lavender. Piles of the stuff.

She understood. The longer another spirit stayed, the more powder remained with the host. When Essi and Juneau managed to get home, Shannon would keep something of them. Something living. Less than their physical beings, yet more, much more than memories.

At this moment, nothing could have comforted Shannon more. Her sobs slowed, then faded.

She closed her eyes and shifted her pillow; tried sleeping on her right side, then her left. Maybe she needed food. She fished a snack out of her cooler, ate, and ate some more. Tried to sleep again. No good. Sleep refused to come but Shannon needed to rest.

She stood and headed for the bathroom. A growing headache pounded harder with every step, like dozens of pellets from a bee-bee gun bouncing back and forth off the walls of her head; signaling her body's accelerating deterioration. The pain made her woozy. She turned and sat on the edge of her bed so she could raid the cooler again, then waited for the infusion of calories to quell the headache. This time the food had no effect. She was losing ground fast. This called for stronger measures. She headed back to the bathroom. There she hesitated, her hand suspended at the medicine cabinet door. No choice. She reached for her pain killers.

Looking at her ravaged face in the mirror, Shannon brushed out her hair and plaited it in a loose braid. The braid fell over her shoulder and down her chest to her waist. Longer by at least five inches than just a few days ago.

She climbed into bed, her troops in their appointed places, and soon sank into a deep sleep, submerged by fatigue and medication. She dreamed the day from her past that years of discipline had taught her not to dream....

* * *

…Shannon sits at a child's table, long and low, in a large, loud school cafeteria with gray linoleum floors speckled in white, and bright posters on the wall. On the posters, red, yellow and blue cartoon dinosaurs pose, brushing their teeth, washing their hands, picking up clothes off their bedroom floors. A low-hanging, creamed-corn odor presses down on the lunch room. Shannon's grade school cafeteria.

The dinosaurs turn to stare at Shannon with sharp-toothed grins, to laugh, to point with short arms and claw-fingers. They know what happens next.

The cafeteria hums with laughter and the high voices of children, some eating, others rushing their empty trays to the wash-up conveyor and running outside to play. All at once, all activity stops. Every child turns and stares at Shannon. They, too, know the story. The children move, crowd close to her, dozens of them, all around her lunch table, so close she can smell spaghetti spilled on shirt fronts, strawberry shortcake on out-blown breath. No one speaks. Their faces lose all expression but their eyes become large, like the eyes of lemurs, marbles glued to puppet faces.

Her elementary school best friend Georgey sits next to Shannon. He pays no attention to the moving dinosaurs, the hovering children. He chatters away, as always. His carrot red hair sticks out every which way. On his freckly face plays a big smile. Shannon can't hear his words. Then he too stops. He holds out his hand, palm up. His eyes sag at the edges, his mouth droops. He knows what Shannon will put there. So does Shannon.

She doesn't want to. She tries to stop her hand when it moves from her lunch box. But she can't. A cookie, a snickerdoodle, swollen to the size of a pizza, turns shiny black, with a foot-long peanut in the center. She watches, a frozen statue, as Georgey takes the cookie. *No, no, don't take it,* she screams, but no sound issues from her lips. Her eyes move to his face. Tears everywhere, as if someone has splashed a bucket of water over his head. So many tears. Tears the size of soft balls.

He takes the cookie. Its blackness glistens as it spreads to his fingers, down his hand, down his arm. His face turns to black glass. The glass shatters into a thousand tiny pieces, and the pieces tinkle to the table with the sound of a breeze-blown crystal wind chime. Shannon grabs at the pieces. She scrabbles to put them back together; her fingers reach here, then there, then here again to match up the pieces. A bottle of glue appears on the table. She snatches it, spreads the white, sticky liquid over the black, crisp jumble, tries to stick them together, to bring Georgey back. The black chunks turn ice cold in her hand. They won't stick.

They won't stick.

One of the poster dinosaurs, a Tyrannosaurus Rex, jumps onto Shannon's table. It leans its huge head into her face and roars thunder at her.

Shannon doesn't look at the dinosaur; all her concentration focuses on those black shards. She must glue the pieces together. She works faster and faster, tries harder and harder. She must finish before the principal comes and takes her away. She looks up at the clock. The numbers begin to grow larger and larger, until the clock crashes to the floor.

Georgey's parents appear, and sweep the black shiny pieces of glass into a black box with a black whisk broom. Her own parents appear, as always, dressed in black. No one will touch her. No one ever does.

But now another child comes into the cafeteria, a little blond girl, with silvery lavender skin, as never before. And Indy. Indy comes with Essi. The children fall silent and part to let them through. One look from Indy and the children step back. Essi takes the black bag from Georgey's parents and empties the contents onto the table. The black shards move and pull themselves together and become Georgey. He smiles at Shannon and hugs her. Then Essi throws her little arms around Shannon and hugs her tight too. Georgey coughs, and a tiny single quarter of a single peanut pops from his mouth onto the table.

Essi and Georgey point. The peanut has caused her friend Georgey to die. A peanut that never should've been in her cookie.

Something deep, something that had been left to gnaw at Shannon long ago by careless adults shifted inside Shannon. A peaceful quiet in a small room far inside her head settled like a down quilt over a cold weeping form, warmed her, and dried her tears.

* * *

Shannon's sleep turned dreamless. But not for long.

Shannon is taking Essi home…She wanders the concrete walkways of the SQ looking for the portal…here somewhere…She searches along a path she's never seen before…The sun creates dazzling light all around her, as if she's immersed in a field of lightning. She can't see…Her eyes squint…There! Up ahead centered on the sidewalk is a door, pure black against the blinding light…Essi is no longer in her head, but on the sidewalk, trying to hurry, her hand tugging Shannon along…Shannon tries to shake her hand free, but Essi won't let go…Essi is pulling Shannon through the door…*leemira,* the child says, *Mommy.* No, this is all wrong…Shannon must not go through that door…Essi is frowning now…Shannon looks at her hand; ropes bind her wrist to Essi's…They approach the door….

Shannon bolted upright from her pillow, her breathing rapid.

"Essi, Essi," she whispered, accompanied by images. "You know I can't survive on your world. And you can't stay here, because neither of us would survive."

Shannon would've sworn she picked out sobbing deep in Essi's vibrating tones. She sighed and imaged herself wrapping her arms around the heart-broken girl, rocking her, murmuring to her.

"Remember," she imaged, "Toss misses you."

The sorrow of her little alien's hum softened. Yes, Essi would enjoy seeing her friend again.

Shannon slipped into sleep once more.

Then the dinosaur roared again.

Shannon groaned, even in her sleep. Not again.

The cafeteria lights went out. She couldn't see…*wait,* not the cafeteria, not a dinosaur…her room, Indy…barking, growling. Shannon couldn't open her eyes…couldn't think…the pain killer…Indy, not on the bed, where? There, by the window, the ridge of fur on her back standing straight. Indy howled like a Hound of Baskerville.

Shannon jolted upright, grabbed a packet of sugar cubes and threw a handful into her mouth as she stood and wobbled to the window. She blinked the sleep out of her eyes, opened her curtains a crack, and peered out toward the woods behind her house.

Even as Shannon stood there crunching sugar, Essi's dream hug came back.

"I owe you so much, Essi. I needed you. I needed someone, anyone, to hug me back then." Tears welled up. She wiped them with the back of her hand and gave her head a violent shake. No time to babble on now. *Wake up.*

She squinted, her face close to the window glass and stroked the mastiff to calm them both. As always, Indy grew quiet under Shannon's touch. Shannon yawned. Mind still foggy. If only she hadn't taken the pain killers.

She slapped her cheeks and wobbled back to her cooler, moved the crushed ice around, and popped open a chilled choco-latte. She'd stockpiled these caffeinated drinks for her morning wake-up call, but screw that; she needed one. Right now. Maybe two or three. She grabbed two more and returned to the window.

A hundred feet of thick and scratchy scrub brush stood between her back fence and the nearest trail of Eisner Park. She'd never caught anyone fighting through the bushes and onto her property from Eisner, but a determined killer with a big knife could make it.

On each side of her yard, a six foot fence ran to the back and across, then from the back all the way to the street sidewalk and then across the front. A retractable gate across the driveway. A locked pedestrian gate. *Secure.*

Indy continued to growl low in her throat. Shannon couldn't see anything. *Yes. There*—a shadow, a smidgen darker than the moonlit night, moved along the trees at the far back of her yard. Triple shitsky.

Focus on the shadow. She cast the lavender. Could she catch images and emotions that far away?

Yes she could. The intruder stared at the back of Shannon's house, skipping from window to window, the back door, the side yards.

Searching for the best way in.

And then a picture of Shannon formed in the invader's mind, which in turn gave rise to a swell of the invader's emotions. Shannon covered her mouth with her hand. Sweet mother of Loki. Such rage. Such a strange foreign mind. She'd never imagined anyone or anything could hate her that much.

drrrmm. en en en. Terror warped the child's whisper. The vibration connected to the alien words rang out so loud and tense it mauled Shannon's eardrums.

Could the intruder read her images too? No time to consult Essi. She backed away from the window. Focused on words.

Think in words. Do not allow pictures.

She checked behind her; she hadn't left any lights on in the hall. Good. No silhouette to alert the intruder to her whereabouts.

Shannon's eyes stayed glued to the inky outer edges of her yard. She didn't dare blink; her breathing slowed; she remained as still as the old oak dresser on her left.

The shadow she'd pegged as Drom—or rather some poor soul with Drom aboard—crouched as motionless as she did.

Her eyes burned now, but at length her night vision refocused the dark shadow. Yes, he squatted on his heels against a pine tree, right about dead center along her back fence. His body looked loose, relaxed, as if he had all the time in the world.

The wind had returned, much stronger than before. Leaves flew into the beam of her porch light, as well as loose bits of paper, cigarette butts, a child's heart-shaped barrette.

Essi's hum picked up her pace, vibrating in tighter and shriller notes, aiming for shriek level.

Hell. Why did she crouch there like a store window mannequin?

"Screw this. Let's get out of here. Come on, Indy."

She chugged down the last of the chocolattes and groped for her clothes in the dark. Yes!—still strewn on the chair where she'd thrown them in her hurting-head desperation to collapse into bed. She crept out the bedroom door and raced with silent steps to the spare bedroom where she kept Narci's travel kennel. Back to her room for the cat and the cooler. Down to the kitchen. She'd closed the kitchen curtains before she went to bed, but a telltale white beam would slip out over the curtain rod into the back yard if she turned on the light. She opened one of the side-by-side refrigerator doors and left it that way. The open refrigerator door kept most of the interior light from the window, but Shannon could see well enough to gather more food for herself and the animals. She opened a can of tuna, plucked out enough to lure Narci into the kennel and stuffed the rest in her own mouth. Coke. Dog leash. Brief case. Purse. What else? Think think think. Shannon grabbed a large carving knife and two steak knives from her silverware drawer. And a couple shish kabob skewers.

No gun in the house. She'd never learned to use one.

Once the utility room door closed behind her, Shannon turned on the garage light and hustled Indy into the back seat of the car. She heaved Narci's kennel down on the passenger seat. "Sorry kitten." Then she dashed around to the driver's side.

How to get out of here before Drom came around to the front? When she started the garage door opener, he'd hear her and charge before she could get away.

Oh. She smacked the side of her head with impatience; the stupid pain killers had made her so thick-witted. She jumped out of the car, flicked the garage light out and felt her way along the shelves stacked against the wall to the garage door. The chord that disengaged the garage door from the automatic opener dangled overhead. She pulled it, then bent to grab the handles on the garage door. She raised it with as little sound and as much speed as she dared. Any second now Drom might appear. Shannon's hands shook. When the door reached a height the car could clear, Shannon peered out.

Nothing moved. Crickets chirped and a dog barked far down the street. The air, crisp and clean, smoothed itself against her skin. She took another deep breath, and dragged down the driveway to open the gate, her kabob skewer clutched in her fist. She released the power lock and slid the gate over.

Shannon hustled, okay toddled, back to the car. Faster. Move faster. Her adrenaline rush had already spiked and plunged again, her new-normal exhaustion returning. Her limbs grew leaden, as if she'd landed in one of those dreams where she ran in slow motion.

Still no sign of the intruder. She reached the car, checked the back seat to make sure he hadn't climbed in, but that wouldn't happen, because Indy stood guard there. Shannon took a quick look at Indy; nothing alien-like lurked in the dog's eyes. She relaxed. No alien could look at Shannon with Indy's goofy, slobbery grin. Shannon jumped in, pushed the power locks, started the engine and backed out of the garage.

Just as they cleared the garage door, a figure ran full tilt around the side of the house and slammed into the passenger side of the car. Shannon screamed.

CHAPTER FIVE

THURSDAY

INDY LUNGED AT THE CAR WINDOW, snapping and snarling. The dog wanted nothing more than to break through the window and rip the intruder to pieces.

"Don't do it, baby. He's lethal."

Shannon pushed the gas pedal hard and shot in reverse down the driveway. The wind whistled around the car as if trying to break in.

The alien jumped to his feet, then charged after her.

Drom carried a long thin sword in his hand. He leaned low as he ran, the sword pointed straight at her head.

What the hell? He couldn't poke through the car's window with a sword. She assumed.

He jabbed at her right front tire. Ah.

No way. Shannon slammed the accelerator, juicing up her reverse speed, and turned to focus out the rear window. Once she'd backed into the street, she threw the car into drive and jerked forward.

Drom still ran at her. She aimed her car straight toward him. Her tires bounced over the curb onto the grass and hit him. He slammed off the hood, flew into the air, landed on the sidewalk in a heap, and lay motionless. Good. She hoped he'd broken both legs and his back. And his neck.

But no, as Shannon turned the steering wheel to drive off the grass, he lurched to his feet and ran into Mr. and Mrs. Ryan's yard next door. An unfamiliar dark sedan parked in their driveway. Drom's. She straightened the wheel and shot down the sidewalk until she could swerve back onto the street, where she gunned the engine and took off at full speed.

No other cars moving. Shannon blew a long breath from pursed lips. *Safe for a second.*

But Drom would catch her in minutes. And now he'd be one angry alien. She needed help.

And she'd forgotten to call 9-1-1. Everybody knows to do that. Little kids know that. She fumbled in her jeans pocket where she hoped she'd stashed the cell phone. Her frantic fingers slid over the denim; please still be in her pocket, please, please. *There.* Her hand landed on the phone's smooth, cool surface. She pulled it into her lap, dialed 9-1-1, and flew on down the road. With one-armed turns, she took a right or left every few blocks to throw Drom off her tracks.

The emergency dispatcher came on the line. "9-1-1. Please give me your name and the nature of your call."

"Help me. I'm driving toward downtown from the North End. Somebody tried to break into my house and he's armed. He's after me. This guy's a killer. Please, hurry."

"What is your location, ma'am?" the dispatcher asked.

"I don't know. I'm changing streets to keep away from him." Shannon peered up at the street sign as she made another right. "Okay, I just pulled onto Market Street from Spring. But I can't stay on it. He might see me." Shannon cried out the words in tight little bursts.

"Stay on Market, ma'am. A squad car is en route and will intercept you in approximately five minutes. I repeat, stay on Market so the officers can contact you. Do you understand?"

Shannon understood. But did she dare stick to one street? Maybe. She'd stick unless Drom showed up in her rear view mirror.

"Stay on the phone with me, ma'am. Are you with me?"

"I'm here."

"All right. What's your name and where did the break-in occur?"

"Shannon Kendricks. My address, uh, my address…oh right. Eleven-seventy-seven East Orchard."

"Can you give me a description of the attacker?"

She'd caught sight of him as he ricocheted off the car but she'd been frantic to shift into gear and get the hell out.

"Ma'am?"

"I'm not a ma'am," Shannon said, snapping the words out. What a stupid thing to say. *Calm down.* Calm down. She breathed in and exhaled. "Sorry. It was a man, white, don't know how tall. Average build. He had a ski mask on, so I couldn't see his hair or his face. Black clothes. Black shoes. Ordinary sneakers. Long sleeved shirt." She paused and tried to picture him. He'd smashed himself right against her window, for Odinssake. She couldn't conjure up anything more. "That's all I've got."

Tires screeched. She looked up. Off to her right, as she passed through the Oak Street intersection, Drom's dark sedan, two blocks over, fishtailed as it made a sudden turn toward her.

"Oh my god, he's found me. He's coming." Shannon turned on the phone's speaker function and threw the phone on the seat beside her. "I just passed Oak. I need the police."

"Try to remain calm, Ms. Kendricks," the dispatcher said.

"Remain calm? Are you kidding me?"

Okay, bring it down a notch.

"All right, I'm calm. Calmer. Not calm, but listen, I'm going to try to hide the car from this guy and then go back down Market the way I just came, toward Spring. Got that?" She could hear police sirens now. If she could just keep him away from her for a few minutes more.

Up ahead, she spotted a white RV parked in a driveway. The van would block the view of her car as the alien rounded the corner. She jerked right and pulled in next to the van, banging her bumper on the concrete as she left the road, and banging her head on the ceiling as she bounced onto the driveway. She turned off her lights.

Before she could draw her next breath, Drom's car screeched again as it turned left and raced down Market in the direction she'd been heading. She moved the shift stick to reverse. Wait for it, let him get down the road a ways, wait…wait….

When she could bear to wait no longer, she slammed on the gas, banged her car bumper on the curb again as she left the driveway, braked hard, threw the VW into gear, hit the gas and yanked the steering wheel around. The back end of the car fishtailed. Narci's kennel slid across the front seat and smacked the window. Indy thudded off the back seat in the same direction. "Sorry babies."

The car swerved, straightened, and Shannon floored it. The sound of sirens pierced the air. Close now. And she could hear two, maybe more, police cars hone in from somewhere up around Ocotillo Street. She flew toward that sound like a moth to flashing lights.

Venturing a glance in her rear view mirror, she watched as the dark sedan u-turned. It closed the gap between them.

"He's going to catch me," Shannon said, yelling at the cell phone.

"Stay calm, ma'am. A squad car should arrive any minute."

If Drom got his hands on her, he'd rush into her head, push her out, take her identity. The police would be none the wiser.

What if Indy attacked as Drom tried to reach Shannon? He would take Indy and then what would she do? Run from the car screaming for the police to shoot her Indy?

"Not in a million years," Shannon said, bent over the steering wheel, and pushed the car as fast as it would go. At last a police car careened around the corner just ahead of her, speeding toward her, blue and red lights flashing. Too close! Groggy from the pain killers she'd taken and slow as molasses ever since the lightning strike, Shannon lifted her foot and slammed it on the brake pedal, but she hadn't reacted fast enough. Her car fishtailed right into the patrol car, which had skidded to a stop.

Her head banged hard against the side window as her air bag deployed. Ow. Those things hurt. She sat unmoving for a moment then called out to the dog, who'd been loose in the back seat. Indy had crashed hard into the seat back first and then against the window, landing half on the seat, half on the car floor. But now the dog scrambled back up and stuck her head between the front seats. Tough dog. But Shannon would need to get her to the vet right away. She eyed the crushed front bumper and mangled side door. Not in this car, she wouldn't.

Shannon's head hurt worse than ever from all the battering it had taken. She touched the lump where head had met window.The bump had taken the shape of a baseball already and her finger came away sticky. Blood.

The squad car that sat next to hers, and the two vehicles in the middle of the road, Shannon's crosswise, would barricade the sedan's passage.

Shannon tried her door. No way it would open. Ever. She half climbed, half fell over the center console, grabbed one of her knives, and stumbled out the passenger side into the wind, which caught at her clothes, whipping them like sports flags. She locked Indy and Narci inside the car to keep them away from Drom, and watched the sedan coming right at them.

Officers had jumped out of the squad car she'd hit and took shooting stances over the hood, facing the oncoming sedan. Shannon hid the knife behind her back and staggered toward the police car. One of the officers, a big broad guy with a gut that sagged over his belt, shouted to her, "Get back in your car and lock the doors. Now."

Nuh uh. Drom could break a windshield, touch Shannon once—that's all he needed. Shannon would stick right behind the guys with the guns. If Drom came anywhere near her, they'd shoot him before he could get his hands on her. Shannon crouched down a few feet behind the officers.

A thought ripped through her like a second lightning strike.

Wait, now. Complications. She'd missed something big when she called the police. Now the ramifications hit her like a ton of tortellini.

She should have figured this out before. Damn pain killers. Damn lightning. If the police caught the man harboring Drom, they'd cuff him. Touch him. Drom would invade one of them. The police officer's spirit would vanish and no one would stop Drom if he, in his police officer body, then waltzed right over and destroyed Shannon's spirit.

By the moon and the sun, she wouldn't let Drom kill any of these officers if she could help it. She'd never recover if an innocent person died because she'd panicked.

Oh yeah, she'd proven a big help so far: she'd just drawn a dozen officers right to him.

A second crown vic pulled up. Two female officers joined the others.

A trailing police car closed the distance behind Drom's sedan. The cops' black and white touched the sedan's moving back bumper. As the alien approached the police barricade, he jerked his car to the right and into the yard of a small rambler. He flung open the driver's side door and raced toward the darkness at the back of the house.

How do you feel now, you scum? The cat became the mouse.

The trailing squad car overshot the spot where the sedan had turned, and braked to a halt. The officers scrambled out onto the street and shouted at the fleeing figure to stop. He didn't. They took off after him, shouting as they ran.

Drom disappeared around the back of the house and an officer raced down the walkway, using the cover of the house for protection; he stopped, his weapon raised, and peered around the corner, then charged into the back yard. The other officer pounded on the front door to rouse the residents and get them out.

More police cars arrived. Shannon watched as two more officers took off in pursuit of her pursuer. Others jumped back in their cars to patrol around the block. More fanned out on foot. Another uniform stood about ten feet from Shannon, intent on barking into the radio in his hand.

Shannon's shoulders sagged. The sirens, the shouts, the traffic noise, all faded. Her thoughts had room for nothing but the monstrous pain in her head. No wonder—banging it from every side these last few days. She stopped watching as curious onlookers approached and were herded away by officers. Her heart, which had been beating like a hummingbird's a moment ago, slowed and quieted until she couldn't tell for sure if it still beat. She looked down and noticed that in her haste to run, she'd left the house without her shoes. She lifted the sole of her left foot. A small sharp rock had lodged deep in her flesh, and blood dripped onto the pavement. She couldn't feel it. *Shock.* She limped to the nearest squad car and leaned against it.

None of the police had a clue that the "ordinary" guy they hunted carried an alien onboard who could kill with a touch. They wouldn't believe Shannon if she told them. Her head drooped. She didn't need any alien-infested innocents on her conscience. With the greatest reluctance, she crossed her fingers and hoped the police would shoot and kill her would-be murderer from a long way off, and if not that, she'd have to hope he escaped the police perimeter. She'd have to deal with him herself. Somehow.

Just now, though, Shannon planned to stay right here. Drom might try to circle around and come at her from behind, try to grab her before the officers could stop him. She wiped her sweating hands on her tee shirt and gripped her butcher knife with the sharp side out, but well hidden from the near-by officers.

Near Shannon, someone called for more back-up. Hey. Shannon knew that voice. Quintana. She looked around to see if he stood close enough to spot Drom if the alien came anywhere near her. There. He turned, identified her shivering form, and told her to get in his police vehicle and stay there.

Shannon hesitated. His voice had sounded cool, impersonal.

Before Shannon could say a word, he moved off down the street, running in a half-crouch, angling in along the lawns, trying to cut the alien off if he'd gone that direction.

More sirens bleated now; police units rushed from three directions. Shannon shook, more from shock than the night air. So she climbed into his police car. But not because Quintana ordered her to. Hah.

She tucked herself into the back, her feet up on the seat, her knees under her chin. Her back rigid, her knife clutched in her hand, her eyes darted everywhere. Her would-be killer could run at her any time, in one desperate attempt to take over her body.

On the other hand, if Drom escaped, she'd have to go after him, and she and Juneau and Essi would have to destroy him alone, just as they'd destroyed Tharm. Shannon hiccoughed a little laugh. She didn't dare join in a new battle with an alien any time soon. Shannon's human gas tank had run low. Almost empty.

A clean kill shot by the police could alone save Juneau, Essi, and her, for the moment. Maybe for always.

And so she waited. And hoped.

* * *

Shannon looked at her watch. Wednesday had leaked into Thursday.

And still she waited.

Torture.

A canine unit arrived and took up the hunt.

Minutes ticked by. Nothing. More nothing.

At last Shannon exhaled a long wobbly sigh. With any luck, Drom had flown the coop. A fit-looking guy with an alien driving him: they wouldn't catch him now.

"What do you think, Essi? Is Drom gone?"

en drrrmm. The child imaged him running, disappearing into the distance.

Right, gone.

Good news but bad news. Now the terrible responsibility of taking Drom down rested solely on her incapable shoulders.

She'd never in her life faced such an impossible task.

If she failed, he'd destroy her world. *Destroy her world.* Bizarre yet true. Tears dripped down her cheeks.

Uh oh. Here comes Quintana. She wiped her face.

He opened the car door and leaned in. If he witnessed the tears, he didn't mention them. Two of his fingers went to the midnight shadow on his chin and rubbed.

"Your car's totaled," he said in a formal, stiff voice, but added, 'You've already been checked out by the paramedics, right?" He tipped his head toward a medic unit.

"Uh, yes. Already checked out. Sure. Shook up but a clean bill of health." *Lie, lie, lie.*

"We need to get into your car to have a look at your cat and dog. They're locked in there. Where're your keys?" He sounded reproachful, as if he'd just added animal cruelty to the list of black marks against her.

She grabbed her keys from her jeans pocket. "I thought Dro— that guy might hurt them. That's why I locked them in." Sounded lame to her, and, she suspected, to him. Strands of hair had slipped loose from her braid. She wiped a few strays from her face.

"I called a vet friend of mine. She's heading here now. You warmed up yet?" He climbed into the front seat.

Shannon nodded her thanks when he turned on the heater without waiting for her answer. The heat drifted like a puff of talcum powder from her face to her toes. Better.

She sniffed. The heat brought forth the smells of old gym clothes mingled with hamburger and fries. Shannon peered down. A McDonalds sack lay on the floor at her feet. Her 9-1-1 call had caught the officers in the middle of a fast food dining experience. A few fries poked out of the top of the sack in a friendly way.

She leaned down and plucked up a fry. Just a little cool to the touch. Still smelled French fry-like. Shannon considered. This fry hadn't touched ground. Still, she hadn't fallen so low she'd eat someone else's cold fries off the floor. She inhaled the smell, licked salt off her fingers. Yes, she'd fallen that low. Just a tiny bite. *Mmm. Good.* She stuffed the rest of the fry into her mouth, picked up the sack, and rummaged for the rest. Quintana watched her through the rear view mirror.

"Do you mind if I finish these off?" she asked through a full mouth.

"Help yourself," Quintana said, "Don't choke, now." He grinned.

She ignored him and finished off the fries in short order. After that, she stared out the window with growing weariness. The red/blue lights flashed like a hypnotist's watch…

*   *   *

…. Shannon jerked awake. She lifted her head from the back seat of the police car and wiped sleep-drool from her face. She squinted out the window at a scene too bright for—she glanced at her watch—four in the morning. They'd set up tall poles topped with rectangular artificial lights. Uniformed men and women bustled about with reports for the brass. Four police vehicles and two unmarked cars lined the curb. Barricades blocked both ends of the street. Sounds of voices, vehicles, crackling radios fought their muffled way to her ears through the closed car windows and the wooly thickness inside her mind. Shannon watched in numb disinterest, as if the lights, the distant sounds came from a movie set. For a movie thriller no doubt. So unreal.

She looked around. A gang of reporters wandered about behind the barricade, looking for any news-worthy tidbits they could cajole out of the police.

Quintana had left the front seat. He stood in a small huddle of officers near the command post. They clutched cups of brew and a few of them snatched quick bites of unidentifiable foodstuff as they talked. He glanced over and caught her staring at him. Swell.

He returned to the car.

"You're awake, I see. Feel better?"

Quintana's voice, deep and kind despite his standoffish demeanor, washed over Shannon like a Hawaiian rain shower.

"Yes." *No.*

"You want coffee?" He leaned through the front window and reached toward her with a steaming lidded cup.

She took it with thanks and drank.

"They see any trace of Dro—the intruder?"

"No, sorry to say. He may have holed up in one of these houses, but I think he slipped through." He opened the front door and sat with his legs and feet outside.

Slipped through. *Good.*

"Did I hear you say his name? You know who he is then?"

"Uh, no. No idea who he is. Not a clue, no," Shannon said. "I...I nodded off for a while. Brain's not working too well yet."

"Ah." Quintana turned his gaze from her and stared out the door.

The two sat a few minutes in companionable silence, sipping coffee.

"Has your vet friend come to see Indy and Narci yet?"

"She's at the car looking them over now. Want to talk to her?" He stood and opened her back door. "Whoa. What happened to your foot? You can't walk anywhere on that. Let me have a look."

Shannon's eye fell to the floor. She'd forgotten that she'd stepped on a rock and dripped a trail of blood from her car to this one. The seat where she'd lifted her feet to sleep, gym shoes, a sweat shirt on the car floor, a work file—her foot had dotted them all with red-fading-to-brown. Drool dried on another file resting on the seat where she'd laid her head. To block Quintana's view of the car interior, she swung the offending foot out the door.

"I ran out of my house tonight without my sandals. I'm okay. I think I have some band aids in my car."

Quintana gave his head a small, curt and dismissive shake, walked around to his trunk, and returned with a small first aid kit. He broke open some alcohol-soaked cloths, and knelt by Shannon.

Gently holding her foot in one hand, he dabbed the blood and pebbles off the heel.

Oh for the love of Thor. Must she writhe in total humiliation every moment with this man? She hadn't clipped her toenails in weeks, a pair of blisters still decorated her heel from a 5K she'd run the week before, and here knelt Quintana, up close and personal with her bunions.

Quintana took a dry cloth from the kit and pressed it. He looked over at her. "That hurt?"

"Not much."

"Uh huh." He smoothed some ointment on the wound and laid a thick padding of gauze on top. Then he wound a strip of medical tape around and over her foot again and again until the bandaging gave the impression some madman had sliced off half her foot.

"Don't think it'll need stitches, but you might want to get it seen."

Quintana knelt there a moment with his hand around her foot. And another moment. His nostrils flared. Ah, her newly-acquired natural perfume. Her feet smelled of her special scent too? Bonus.

"Heavy socks would be better than nothing. You have any in your car? A gym bag?" he asked. Quintana laid her foot back on the car floor, as if it were made of precious crystal that could shatter at the slightest bump.

Shannon rolled her eyes. *Lord all mighty.* She watched his face and caught his slight wince when his gaze fell on his blooded belongings.

"No, no footwear I'm afraid. Um, sorry about this," she said, gesturing at the car floor.

He waved off her apology, reached over her, and lifted out a gym bag from the other side of the squad car. He fished around and pulled out a heavy pair of socks, which smelled like they'd percolated in the bag for some months. Clearly Ocean City officers were among those who drove their squad cars home each night. After they worked out.

Shannon eyed the socks. If they didn't give her athlete's foot they *would* help her back along the street to the car. She gulped, held out her hand, and smiled. "Great. Thanks."

When she'd socked up, she climbed out of the squad car and breathed deeply. The wind had calmed. The air smelled fresh. And the baseball bump on her head from the crash hurt like hell.

She could add a concussion to her current list of ailments. Not that she would point this out to anyone.

When they reached her car, she eyed the perky young woman who now moved gentle, skilled hands along Indy's head, ribcage, legs and back. Indy wagged her her tail as if she and the vet were old pals. Traitor. Narci peered from her kennel on the pavement next to a roomy silver SUV.

Shannon rubbed the mastiff's muzzle and accepted a big slobbery kiss, then bent down to coo to Narci. The movement sent her balance haywire, her head pain skyrocketed. *Keep it together.* She moved back to her poor crumpled car and pulled her cooler onto the hood. When the vet finished her hands-on exam of Indy's body, Quintana gave the dog a back rub in the exact place she loved best, while he accepted a raspberry-filled doughnut from Shannon's box. The vet declined one, shining a light into Indy's eyes and peering into them. Shannon chose a frosted pastry, inhaled its chocolatey fragrance, and gulped it down.

They ate in silence until Quintana wiped a few crumbs from his shirt front and said, "I do need to take your statement."

"Ask away."

As the officer lifted his pad and pen, a voice called out, "Officer Quintana, Miss Kendricks." The two turned toward the sound. Detective Yuk Chen strode toward them. Shannon had met him a number of times in the course of her work. A little rough around the edges, but a good fellow. Chen waved Quintana off with a curt, harried nod. "I'll take the statement, Luke, thanks. With one gesture and a turn of his shoulder, he dismissed his patrol officer.

Quintana snapped his notebook closed, his thick black eyelashes covered his eyes and his thick black mustache twitched. "All yours."

"Just a minute, Detective Chen," said the veterinarian, rising to her feet. She offered her hand. As Chen shook it, she said, "I'm Margie Wright, a vet friend of Luke's. I need to have a quick word with Ms. Kendricks and get back to bed, if I may."

Chen swept out his hand with a slight nod, as if to say, "Be my guest."

The woman offered her hand to Shannon. "Ms. Kendricks, Margie Wright. Remarkably, given the condition of your car, both animals look okay to me. I carry some mild pain relievers that I recommend for the mastiff. She took a beating in the back seat during the crash. I expect her to be sore for a while. No cuts, no breaks, no swelling inside her torso…" Margie walked toward the back of her SUV so Shannon limped along behind her as the vet ticked off the symptoms Shannon should watch for that might indicate an injury that the vet couldn't detect without her diagnostic equipment. Handing Shannon the pills from a case, she continued, "Take them both to your own vet in the next couple of days for a recheck. Your vet may want to do an MRI. And that's it for me." She slammed the SUV's back door closed and shook Shannon's hand again.

"It was kind of you to come out here in the wee hours of the morning," Shannon forced herself to say. "What do I owe you?"

"For a friend of Luke's, nothing." She smiled for the first time, dropping her professional manner. She went around the front to talk to Luke, and Shannon, with a slight frown, had no choice but to limp back over to Chen.

As she spoke with Chen, Shannon kept an eye on Quintana and Ms. Wright. His eyelashes gave off enough heat to melt an ice cream cone at fifty paces. And thanks to her weird behavior, she'd_lost any chance with him. She gulped. Ah well. Juneau's freedom was worth it.

When the SUV pulled out, Quintana headed over to a group of officers. Shannon turned her full attention Chen's way and wiped her doughnut-frosted mouth with her sleeve. Chen watched, his lips pursed. *You're right, Chen,* she didn't say, *no time to stop for the good linen while fleeing from a killer.*

Chen led her through the incident and as he finished the interview, he said, "If you think of more details later, call the Hillside Precinct and ask for Luke Quintana."

Gracefully done, Detective.

"Hillside. Got it." Shannon fished a sardine sandwich out of her cooler.

The detective, lips still tight in frown formation, watched her eat.

"Were you on your way to a picnic when your attacker arrived?" he asked.

Ha ha. Shannon would not dignify that question with an answer.

Gesturing at her crumpled car, she said, "I have a problem. Can you do me a favor? I need to pick up some paperwork my paralegal left at the office for me. Can you take me there and then to my house?" Lie. She needed to print out her resignation letter and put it on Portman's desk. Too ashamed to tell Chen the truth, and she didn't know him well. How could she tell her friends?

"Let's get it done."

"And my dog and cat?"

Chen looked at Indy, looked at his little sports car, looked at Indy again. He frowned, but said, "With your intruder still out there, I want you close to the police for a while. I'm low on officers, you're low on cars, so I guess the answer is yes." His briefcase and dry cleaning dispatched to the trunk, he patted the back seat and Indy cramped herself in. Then he jammed Narci's kennel on Shannon's lap.

*　*　*

At her office, Shannon typed the words she never dreamed her boss would one day compel her to sign. Her face, her fingers, her heart seemed made of wood. She printed the resignation. She signed it. She left Chen in her office and walked it down to Portman's office. The resignation lay heavy and cold in her hand, like a large river stone.

By morning all her friends and colleagues would know. If the lightning, the car accident hadn't already numbed her, she'd drown in the hurt of this moment.

The beluga stirred, responding to Shannon's grief.

Never mind, Juneau. You are worth the price.

Shannon signed paperwork that Jane had left in her inbox and took it down to the paralegal's desk. Her hand moved across Jane's name plate. Her friend shouldn't have to learn about the resignation from someone else on Monday morning. Shannon picked up Jane's desk phone and dialed.

Jane picked up.

"What? You're awake? I'm sorry. I expected your answering machine. Are you guys already up to leave for your sheep shearing trip?"

"Don't worry any on my account. Picker and I decided to have pickles and milk after our own little rodeo event, if you know what I mean." Wink and a nudge. "We never went to bed. You sound a little shaky there. What's up?"

Pickles *and milk?*

Shannon hadn't meant to tell anyone, but she opened her mouth and the whole intruder-car chase-crash misadventure poured out. Except the part about the aliens.

"Bless your heart, you get home and get some rest. And don't come in tomorrow."

"Um, Jane, I wouldn't come in tomorrow anyway. Portman fired me. But don't tell anybody. He's letting me hand in my resignation. That's what I'm doing at the office."

"He *what*? That polecat. We've got to do something. You want me to send Picker down there to give him what for?"

"Oh well, thanks, but no. Look, I didn't mean to spoil your post-rodeo event or your long weekend. We'll talk when you get back. Everything will work out all right."

Shannon hung up. She'd thought her spirits had hit bottom earlier, *but nope*, they sank even lower. Matters could sink no further; she'd hit bottom.

*   *   *

Shannon and Chen retraced their way from office to lobby. Shannon pushed through the revolving door of the Mannheim Building to the street, Chen a few steps behind her.

Just as the revolving door spilled Shannon onto the sidewalk, a large raven swooped toward her, inches above her head. A great whoosh filled her ears as the bird clawed her hair.

Clawed her hair? What the hell? Flapping her arms above her head, she jumped back and stumbled into a compartment of the revolving door. The bird followed, fanning the air above her with its wings.

Shannon's feet tangled, as the bird maneuvered its beak to reach her waving arms. The creature meant to bite her.

If she fell, the revolving door would ram her. When she stumbled, Chen pushed hard against the back of his moving compartment to slow its motion. She scrabbled for a handhold, grasped at the cross bar and found her grip, then burst out onto the sidewalk. Chen pushed through and joined her.

The bird, unwise in the ways of revolving doors, trapped itself, missed the exit, and found itself in the lobby. Its wings battered against the nearest wall. It flew back and forth, circled the lobby, smashed itself against the glass front wall.

Shannon peered into the building. The dim lights over the security guard's desk drew her eye to the man sitting in the large, shadowy lobby. Mr. Sanchez-Mendoza looked up from his book, first at the bird, and then at Shannon, and signaled for her to go on with a reassuring wave.

Happy to oblige. She desired no part of that bird. She picked her way forward, hand on the side of the building, determined to make it to Chen's car before Mr. Sanchez-Mendoza managed to shoo the black bird out.

The bird. Its spirit had brushed hers at the moment its claws brushed her hair, something as light as a…well, as light as a feather. Had Drom invaded the raven? No. She'd sensed none of the force and ugliness of his partner Tharm. A spirit much more free, more…innocent.

And it hadn't smelled rotten like Tharm. Like poor Andy. No, the momentary hint of its scent lifted her spirits, cleared her mind, filled her with peace, as if infused with sunshine itself, the smell of spring, of the high mountains, of something beyond her ability to name. And the spices of the Selador. The smell of a creature from Essi's world.

Essi?

Shannon imaged the bird; Essi erased it. The bird hadn't touched Shannon long enough for the little girl to tell who or what had invaded the bird.

Shannon glanced back—the bird beat its wings hard against the glass, frantic to escape.

Chen caught up with Shannon and touched her arm.

"You okay?" he asked.

"Just tired. As I'm sure you are. Sorry you had to act as my chauffeur." Shannon said. She meant it. Well, sorry that he was tired. Not sorry that she kept him and his gun close by. She lifted Narci's kennel and handed it to Chen while she folded herself into the front seat.

"You ever shoot a bird?" she asked Chen.

"What, that bird back at the Mannheim? He's harmless. But if I had too, yeah, I could nail him. Why?" he asked as he shoved the kennel right back into her lap.

"Just wondering," Shannon said. Maybe harmless. Maybe not.

Chen and Shannon arrived at her house without further incident.

Indy climbed out and Chen said, "What do you feed him? Small children?"

Humor at that hour.

Shannon leaned down and wrapped her arm around Indy's neck. "It's a 'her.' I've been letting her free range for meter maids."

Chen smiled.

"Hey, thanks for the ride. I'm good to go now."

Just let her get to the refrigerator and her bed. In that order.

"Would you rather go to a motel?" Chen said.

"No." She gestured at the dog. "Not with this big beastie about."

Chen said, "Now, I'm sure I don't have to tell you the rules, but I will. Number One, you stay in the house and keep the dog at your side and your cell phone charged and in your pocket. You eat in the house, you avoid crowded places, including your office. You need groceries——" and here he paused and lifted his eyebrows in a knowing way.

"—you have a friend bring them…."

He droned on, Shannon nodded without listening. Nothing she didn't already know. Nothing she wanted to hear. If Drom came back, she'd be ready. But she didn't plan to sit around and wait for him, or for any of her other problems to solve themselves.

In due course, Chen departed.

Shannon sat down at her kitchen table with a chocolate pound cake and a gallon of chocolate milk. When she'd nodded, as if implying repeated agreement with Chen's ultimatums, she had liked the idea of staying behind a locked door, safe and sound. So she hadn't been lying there. For a fleeting moment or two she did intend to stay put. She did. After a few moments reflection, she'd decided to *try* to stay put. Well, she *didn't* intend to try to stay put but she did intend to try to stay put *until* she went out. Okay, by the time Chen had left, her nods might have misled Chen just a touch, because nothing crystalized a girl's thinking like a night of terror. And this night had taught her one thing; Odin be damned if she'd sit at home and wait for trouble to come to her again.

She would go out. She had problems to solve.

So. First problem: the stolen casino check that the White Wolf wouldn't re-issue. Juneau wouldn't make it back to sea without it.

After she'd reflected on her meeting with Moon and the others, she'd decided that the Dickson Director wouldn't let Tremaine bankrupt her, but she suspected Moon *did* want to test her, to make sure she'd committed to the project. Logical. Shrewd. If the meeting hadn't left her so shell-shocked, she'd have taken a peep inside his mind. Too late now. So. She'd won the million and a chunk more; she'd lost the million and the chunk; now she'd win it again.

She pulled out her cell and called the White Wolf Casino.

Shannon glanced at the clock. Just after six a.m. She asked to speak to the manager on duty. When a Ms. Thompson came on the line, Shannon set forth the facts and asked again for the check.

Ms. Thompson said in a friendly but regretful way, "Look, I would reissue for you if I could, but I haven't received the okay from headquarters. I'll let you know as soon as I hear."

Shannon said, "Well, you know, I feel lucky again today. I think I'll come back in and see what I can win."

*   *   *

An hour later, Shannon paid her taxi driver and walked into the loud, smoky casino, in her jeans and tee shirt this time, holding the empty carton of fudge-lover's ice cream she'd downed on the way, pitched it in the trash, and headed straight for the roulette wheel.

Help me out here, Essi. Show me the numbers. Shannon imaged her plan. Essi's hum turned into a squeak. Good to hear the child laugh.

For a solid hour Shannon placed bets. Essi sent her lavender haze over a number and Shannon played it. At first she bet on even or odd. Then she ramped it up. Essi never missed a prediction. Shannon's winnings rose.

Thompson had been summoned at Shannon's request not long after she arrived. Several house detectives who had been summoned at Thompson's request arrived not long after the woman observed Shannon's success rate. Thereafter Shannon took a break from the wheel to submit to a hand-held metal detector. Several other measuring devices appeared. Shannon had no idea what the gizmos did or how they worked, but whatever the house detectives sought, they didn't find it. *Big surprise.*

Shannon resumed play. Now she bet specific numbers, increasing her take. *Much better.* Before long, Thompson invited her to please come to the office to discuss her missing check. "Of course," Shannon responded, smiling with grace and good will.

After Shannon had settled into the same chair she'd occupied on her last visit,. Thompson cleared her throat and said, "We—"

Shannon interrupted, held her palm up toward Thompson's red and uneasy face, and said, "If I don't receive a re-issued check in the next hour, I will come in here every day and play the wheel until I break this place. Please cash in my winnings for the day." She rose. "And if I am holding my reissue check in my hand when I leave, I'll never come back here again. I don't care for the place. I expect you have some people to call, so I'll just go get something to eat at the buffet. You can join me there."

Twenty minutes later, Thompson appeared at her dining table with a fresh check for $3.5 million dollars, a second check for this morning's take, and a one page contract in which Shannon would agree never to darken the White Wolf's door again. For this concession on Shannon's part, the casino threw in another $200,000. *Not bad, not bad at all.*

She signed. An oily texture, a distasteful odor had tainted her adventures here; she didn't plan to return anyway, but of course she didn't tell Ms. Thompson that.

On the way home, Shannon measured the cost of the casino trip in terms of her energy. The outing had taken a devastating toll. Her head sagged against the cold plastic seat back of her taxi. A jagged rip poked into her scalp. She could scarcely bear it, yet she hadn't the energy to lift her head away. She eyed the cab driver. She expected he weighed in at about a hundred-twenty-five pounds in his heaviest fur parka, which he wasn't wearing today. He couldn't help her. Nope, she'd have to roll herself from the cab to the front door. She might make it by tomorrow afternoon.

Not good. Definitely not good.

Her thoughts wandered to Moon again. He and Tremaine wanted to confirm that her commitment would carry her through the Project. *Good point.* She needed to consider the deepest ramifications of commitment herself. How she could work with the Dickson at some Alaskan facility while continuing her legal career? *Could she drop her old life altogether and go?* Impossible. *Or was it?*

Money wasn't the issue. She could live on the casino winnings for a long time. The legal profession, though, presented a different problem. Her pride, her self esteem, her sense of her identity had long ago woven themselves into a tight pattern based on her profession. She'd never extract herself without serious damage.

The cab stopped at a red light. A stillness wrapped her mind, as if Essi and Juneau held their breath while Shannon worked through her doubts. The light turned green.

No. Her reliance on her legal status as proof of her worth had been wrong, wrong, wrong from the get-go. She was who she was whatever work she did. Well, anyway, she was no longer who she used to be, thanks to her visitors. What better time to explore the new her?

She'd leave Ocean City for Alaska. So long as Narci and Indy could go with her.

There. She'd committed. Her hands shook and she gulped hard, but Juneau's wild excitement and Essi's happy hum soon infected her with eager anticipation.

Shannon directed the taxi to her bank's drive-through window to deposit the checks. One problem solved. Relief covered her mind like a warm rain. She decided to hit the fast food drive through while she was at it.

Much better.

Home once more, she wandered through the living room and stared out the sliding glass doors to the back yard. The sun had climbed over the high hills off to the east, molten like a ball of bronze fire.

Shannon ran her fingers in circles on one of the glass panes. Drom in the City; an attack bird in the sky. Maybe she should take Juneau's lead. Buy herself a yellow submarine and head out to sea.

Her gaze dropped from the bright sky to her yard. She'd mowed her grass last week, picked up the dog messes, most of them, okay nothing since Saturday. Her manicured flower beds awaited summer blooms. All quiet and comforting. The yard revealed no trace of the intruder who'd crept around out there last night, who'd chased her halfway across town.

No bird either.

After the attack at her office building, she'd peered out the car window, watching for the raven. No sign. Foolish to think a raven would follow her home. Most ravens most days. But she wouldn't call the one who dive-bombed her normal, nor would she call these normal times.

Two birds flew down to the lawn. Alarmed, she squinted at them, then relaxed. Robins pecking for worms.

But that raven. Straight out of Edgar Allen Poe. Could she swear it hadn't given off any malevolent vibes, any hints of Tharm-like nastiness? It had acted panicked in the lobby, of course—she could sympathize with that; she often panicked in the Mannheim Building herself, knowing Portman prowled the halls. But, the bird *had* aimed for her head. If not to hurt her, then why?

Essi? Shannon pictured the raven, and with it a wisp, and in the wisp, another adult from Essi's world moving into the bird's head. She infused the image with her best imitation of the sunshine-peace-river spice-something smell. Could Essi recognize him? Toss maybe?

No image as to the identity of the invader, but Essi did image the bird falling over in a dead faint.

Made sense. Shannon couldn't support Juneau and Essi much longer; a raven could never carry an adult or even an adolescent boy from Essi's world for more than a few hours, if that.

"Anyway, I'm glad it didn't follow me," Shannon said to Narci, who'd wandered up to the sliding glass door. Shannon squatted on her heels to stroke the cat.

All at once, Narci arched her back and hissed. A loud thwap accompanied the appearance of a black object inches from Shannon's face on the other side of the glass. Shannon jerked her head up and founds herself a thin glass pane away from a yellow unblinking eye.

She and Essi yelped as one. Juneau emitted a squeak. Indy barked. Shannon lost her balance, and fell onto her tush.

Narci scrambled out of the way.

Shades of Alfred Hitchcock. The bird? Here?

The raven stared at her.

Shannon stared back.

"What next, Essi?" Shannon imaged opening the door, picking up the bird and petting it.

In a wink, Essi erased the image.

Right. Err on the safe side. "Okay, how about this?" Shannon pictured casting the lavender through the glass to the bird. "Can I read its images and emotions from here?" Essi left the image up.

Okay then. Read the bird.

Wait, though. Who said this bird was even the same one that attacked her down at the Mannheim Building?

Idiot. How many ravens had ever, ever, in Shannon's entire life, landed on her patio and stared at her eyeball to eyeball?

Right. Ok, then. Read its images.

Wait. A creature so foreign to her—could the bird's little avian mind drive her mad? Plausible.

Go in there.

Going in there would be fruity beyond imagination.

Come on. Step up.

Stepping up would be crazy beyond belief.

Okay, here goes.

Shannon stared hard at the bird. The bird stared back.

On the count of three.

Shannon could sense Essi waiting. Juneau too. Anticipating. Tense.

Wait. Shannon hesitated again.

Essi's vibration twanged. Juneau nosed her along.

"Okay, here I go." She concentrated on the bird, listened with her new sixth sense, sought its images.

But did so gingerly.

The bird hopped closer to the glass door and tapped with its beak. *It wanted to come in?* Like that would happen.

So tired. Hard to concentrate.

Her attention strayed to her blue-eyed cat. Narci stood on Shannon's left at the door, hair raised, motionless, except for a switching tail, an unblinking gaze on the bird. The cat emitted a low trill.

Shannon's mind wandered to Indy, who had taken up a sentry post on her right. The dog leaned forward, alert, watching.

Shannon listened to her own shallow breaths and Essi's anxious vibrations. Juneau waited, still, but alert.

Focus on the bird.

Listen to the bird.

Thrumming. Yep, something from Selador occupied this bird. She broke contact, clamored to her feet and pulled the curtains over the door.

Essi? Could you see? She imaged the bird, added a wisp with no color and waited for Essi to fill in the color, to paint someone's face. *Who copiloted the raven?*

Essi's little hum took on an unfamiliar vibe. Like…like what? Like when a child sees a kitten. Or when an audience experiences a warm and fuzzy moment dreamed up by a movie director. A long, drawn out "oh" moment.

A child's heart reaching out to something sweet. Well. Not what Shannon had expected from the little girl. No fear. Not Drom, then.

celessstii.

A salesti?

Essi colored the wisp a soft yellow and from the wisp emerges a tiny creature. The child opens her palm and the salesti settles there. A quite small thing.

Made sense; the poor raven couldn't maintain much more than a marble-sized invader.

How cute. Shannon stifled the urge to whisper a long, drawn-out "oh."

The midget Seladoran reminded Shannon of a hummingbird, with fast-beating wings, as Essi imaged it hovering and darting. But the head didn't appear birdlike. Shannon couldn't quite make out its features.

Make the image larger, Essi.

As the image grew, Shannon picked out a flat muzzle, like a Persian cat's, a plump and fuzzy little body, teensy, round ears, four stumpy, fuzzy legs and a long fuzzy tail.

What's its name?

celessstii.

Oh. Salesti, as in a name.

"Her or him?"

celessstii.

All right. "It," then.

What is it? A wild animal? A pet? Shannon imaged.

Essi imaged that no one understood the salesti. But the child made a stab at showing Shannon what she felt.

The little Seladoran showed Salesti as part of the flowers, part of Tharm and Drom, of the Selador, of the two suns in the sky, of the stars, on into dark space….

Salesti, part of all things? It looked rather small and cute for *that.* Shannon must've misunderstood.

Why had it come? Shannon imaged the little creature in that room full of portals. Another accident? Did hundreds of creatures a day get slung around the universe as they happened past that strange room?

Essi erased that image and replaced it with Salesti's story. Essi's friend, the silvery turquoise kid Toss, searches the swamp area where the river Selador once ran. He rounds a bend and discovers ten or so of these little creatures in a pastel palette of colors, buzzing about or darting down to pick at something on the green-brown plants growing along the marshes. They radiate a faint, red glow. Toss opens a delicate, net-like cloth under the flock—or herd or pride or whatever—and one of them settles onto it. Toss folds the cloth to hide the creature, careful not to harm it. He makes his way back through the huge arch of the—what had Essi called it?—the Rissa, and works his way down to the portal room. He presses a button outside the entrance, and proceeds through without trouble.

Ah. The button. A crucial step to avoid a portal vacuuming up the unsuspecting.

As Toss hummed to Salesti, Shannon caught words *inside* the humming. She picked out the word "Essi." *In the humming.*

Then Toss walks to the same portal Essi had pitched through, and he unfolds the cloth with the same care he'd taken when he caught it, and frees Salesti. It flies toward the portal, mists yellow with a rosy glow, and disappears, materializing in the head of a raven perched on a wire above the sea lion pools: the same raven standing outside Shannon's sliding glass door.

Why do all the salesti glow red even though they have their own colors?

Essi imaged the salesti connected to one another by that red glow.

Shannon still didn't get it. What do you call them?

celessstii.

Didn't compute.

In Essi's image, Shannon could tell that seeing Salesti had surprised and delighted her, the same pleasure that overcame Shannon when she happened upon a butterfly she'd never seen before, as if she'd never been close to one of the little creatures on her world; perhaps because Essi had spent most of her time in the Selador River—at least before Selador dried up and took her mother with it. Or maybe no one could locate the salesti unless they wished, as when Toss had discovered them and borrowed Salesti.

Now that Essi was imaging about the salesti and Salesti, Shannon sensed Essi's emotions. Essi lived in awe, total awe of the tiny creatures.

Total awe of those playful little winged fuzzballs? *Why?*

Essi ignored Shannon's question. The child's image continued with Salesti's story. The tiny creature searches for the child. It brings her a message from her friend Toss.

So, what did the message say?

Essi imaged that Salesti wanted to give Essi the message without the interference of the bird's mind.

But Shannon's group couldn't all go over to the raven's mind to hear Salesti; if they boarded that little bird body, they'd burn enough energy to turn it into an over-baked raisin in fifteen minutes.

Could Essi go alone? Shannon imaged

Essi's vibration squeaked her protest and imaged Juneau fading away to nothing as the child moves to the bird.

Ah. To keep Juneau's spirit alive, Essi must remain with her.

Can Essi and Juneau go together then? Shannon asked.

Essi imaged: the bird flops over; still too much for the raven to handle.

Essi imaged a new proposal in which—

Oh, no, no, nein, negatory, nix, nope, no way. Shannon could *not*, would not take on another spirit, even one as tiny as Salesti's. She couldn't afford to. None of them could afford for her to.

Essi imaged her little girl face, anxious, tears forming in her huge round peepers; thick, long, pale blond eyelashes bathing in the pools of water collecting below her eyes; her little lips quivering.

Not biting, little one. They already had a health crisis looming here. Salesti would make matters worse. Image: Shannon removes her hand, Salesti does *not* cross over.

tosss. The child's lonely, longing whisper echoes through Shannon's mind.

Oh, for the love of Odin. No.

Essi restored the image of her weeping face.

Shannon softened. The child had lost her mother, after all. No one but Toss remained on her world to comfort her.

Well.

Maybe.

Oh, all right. But Shannon put her foot down about the bird. No raven; just Salesti would come over. *Grab the message, and send Salesti back.* Do it in under a minute. She showed Essi the image: Essi zooms to Shannon's fingertips touching the bird, Salesti zooms over, Essi listens to Salesti, and zooms Salesti back to the edges of Shannon's fingertips so the little creature can flow back. *Emphasis on "zoom," little one.*

Essi's hum intensified, bounced. Image: Essi hugs Shannon.

Yeah, well.

Not waiting, lest Shannon change her mind, Essi rushed to Shannon's fingertips. Shannon opened the sliding door, and although the bird jumped back, it didn't fly away.

Shannon reached down and touched it. The bird fell to floor.

"Wait a minute. Why did the bird collapse? Do not tell me—"

Essi didn't have to tell her. She sensed the raven landing in her mind with Essi and Salesti.

A screech of panic filled Shannon's ears, a desperate, wing-beating desire to escape, as if a thousand eagles had invaded Shannon's head and now all of them beat against its edges, frantic to escape. The sound ripped through her mind like stainless steel razors. Shannon clutched at the sliding door curtains, sagged against the wall.

Tuck it away somewhere, Essi, calm it down. Shannon imaged the bird off, far off, in some hidden corner in her mind like the one where Juneau hung out.

Essi found a place. The noise, the panic reverberated like distant echoes far back in a cave. Like one of Andy's empty caverns. Bummer. Shannon had plenty of empty space in her head to spare.

Shannon imaged Essi: *why had the raven flowed over?* But then it struck her: *why waste time? Never mind, Essi, just hustle.* Shannon replayed the Essi-zooming-around image.

The raven had crumpled about a foot from the door when Essi had kidnapped its little spirit. Shannon planned to position the bird for instant take-off as soon as Essi finished her business, so she picked it up and smoothed the feathers along its black body. A bit boney already, but so black and oiled that Shannon could see iridescent whirls. Quite pretty.

Salesti and the bird had boarded mere moments ago, but Shannon already suffered from an extra tinge of dizziness; hunger spurted in her belly, and her muscles caved a fraction more. Shannon needed food. She shuffled through the living room toward the kitchen.

So tired. Shannon stopped, unable to take even one more step. She sank into the deep, soft seat cushions of her favorite armchair. She let her shoulders loosen, her neck tilt back. She hadn't realized how much she'd tensed.

And why wouldn't she tense? All that had happened? No wonder her nerves had coiled like a python on a hapless wild pig.

Tense but tired. So very tired. Weaker than she'd ever been.

She would just close her eyes and rest while Essi learned what news Toss had sent and then she'd eat another of her crucial meals. She'd rest, just for a second….

* * *

Shannon stirred. Her eyes refused to open. Somehow lead balls had fallen onto them. So dizzy. Hard to think. She would push those balls off her eyelids so she could open her eyes. She would lift—no, she couldn't lift her hand. Her hand—was it chained to a cannon ball? Concentrating all her energy on her hand, straining, a soft, involuntary moan escaping her lips, she touched her eyelids. Nothing there.

Shannon wiped an unsteady hand across her face. So tired. She—

Then she blacked out.

CHAPTER SIX

FRIDAY

HER EYES OPENED, as slow as a turtle walk. She'd slept deeply, so deeply she hadn't moved; she slumped in her soft cedar green armchair in the exact position she last remembered. She hadn't dreamed, hadn't registered hunger. She registered it now, though. A tyrannosaurus rex screaming for food.

Her head ached, as if that same giant dinosaur had laid on it for an hour. Her arms and legs burned as if that dinosaur breathed fire. A searing pain blazed through her brain as well. Her body couldn't take much more of this.

Tired. So damn tired. She tried to stand up. Couldn't.

Not good.

She imaged. *Essi? Juneau? You okay?*

Essi hummed but Shannon had to strain to hear it. No images.

Juneau brushed her mind, a touch more like a whisper of wind. They'd weakened along with her. She'd let them down. *Kitchen. Now.*

She could read her watch face by rolling it an inch to the right without raising her head from the pillowy back of her armchair...neck couldn't take the weight...there.... Nine o'clock. She'd fallen asleep mid-morning. Had she slept until nighttime? She rolled her head again...hurt so much all the time now...and peered through the window. No, the sky filled the frame with bright morning blue.

Sluggish and confused, her mind couldn't puzzle out how it could still be Thursday at nine a.m.. Maybe her watch had stopped? She stared at the second hand for a while. Still moved. She continued to stare a while longer. Her thick mind settled in to watch the watch....

Had anybody ever been staring at a watch when it quit? That would be cool. She watched. Today did not promise to be her day to see it stop....

Something bad was happening here; she should do something about it.... Right.

Shake off the weariness.... She continued to stare at the watch, but she no longer registered anything....

After some time her thoughts returned to the puzzle of how it could still be mid morning on Thursday. Oh. Her cell phone would give her the accurate time. Where had she left it? Ah. She'd tossed it on the table by her chair when she sank down. *Could she reach it?* She craned her neck and moved her hand. A pain shot through her like an ice pick in the eye.

Got it. Holy Odin. The day of the week. *Friday?* Today was Friday? She'd slept twenty-four hours and now *Friday* morning had arrived?

Poor Indy and Narci would need food too. She searched for them, moving only her eyes, her head as still as a statue; it perched atop her neck like an iron block on a thin wooden stick.

Indy slept at Shannon's feet, one long ear flopped across her ankle, but Shannon couldn't spot any sign of Narci. The cat might have slipped out to catch her own breakfast.

...She'd held something when she lost consciousness. What...oh yeah, a bird. For some reason a bird. A raven ....Ah. The little creature, couldn't remember its name, had flowed over from the bird to pass a message from the boy, Essi's friend. And the bird's spirit had come over to her as well. Yes. Her eyes sank to her lap. The raven had disappeared. That meant the little creature...Salesti, yes, named Salesti, and the bird had returned to the bird's body and flown off. *Not too far. Essi, please say it stayed close enough to show you the way home.* She waited. Essi hummed, her vibration weakening toward flatline. No sense asking about the boy's message.

...Shannon floated unaware—until contractions seized her gut, the sheer pain bending her over until her nose touched her lap. She hadn't eaten in over twenty-four hours. *Too long.* A miracle she hadn't wasted away to a long piece of sewing thread by now. She must get to the kitchen. Somehow.

She'd never pull herself up to walk. So she'd crawl. Gathering the one ounce of strength she could muster, she pushed forward off the armchair and flopped to the floor. She lay there unmoving.... Then, with a grunt and a heave, she rocked onto all fours, and listing against the wall, moved forward, one hand, one knee, one hand — she collapsed, then spasmed with dry heaves. She blacked out.

* * *

Shannon dreamed a wet snake slithered up her face — *ew* — in a darkness as black as the sky of far away galaxies. A rushing toward light and — Indy's great tongue licked her forehead, nose, gaping mouth, and chin, the dog's immense jowls collapsing against her neck. Shannon closed her mouth, but found no strength to return the dog's loving kiss.

Food. She'd never make it to the kitchen on her own. She had no energy reserves left. She had nothing.

Nothing.

Shannon, who never cried, cried now. Flat on her back, her Indy licking away the tears, she cried. She'd die here on the floor. Actually die.

Unless she could call for help.

Using Indy's sturdy chest to maneuver herself into a sitting position against the wall, crying, so tired, so weak, she looked for her cell phone. It had fallen from her lap to the floor when she'd tried to move out of the chair. She reached, reached. *Got it.* That flurry of activity brought her energy back to zero. She rested.

When she had regained enough strength, she tried Becky. Cell. Home. Work. No Becky. Andy. Nothing. Jane? Jane had gone off on her four-day so she and Picker could shear sheep.

9-1-1.

No, not yet. The medicos would take her to the hospital and she'd never get out in time to take Juneau back to her body, or to send Essi home. Shannon would not recover otherwise. Drom might pounce on her here, as helpless as fish to an eagle. No, not the hospital. it couldn't cure her. The doctors could keep her alive for a while, but in the end she'd die. Juneau would die. Essi would die. So. 9-1-1 as the last, last ditch option. Otherwise, no.

Essi, if I, uh if I don't make it, you and Juneau must flow to a new human before the end. Got that? Take Juneau and pick a nice, bright person. And fat.

Juneau clicked, agitated. Essi whimpered.

Call somebody. Who? Shannon scanned through her phone's contact list, rehearsing what she would say. Well. What *could* she say?

Uh, hello, Marianne? Long time no see. Listen, can you drop everything and hurry over here this moment to feed me? Now when you get here, don't panic. I'm not contagious in any way.

No good. Most people would look down at her emaciated body, scream, and call for an ambulance.

Who then?

Maybe Scott. She gathered her courage. Her braid had fallen onto her chest when she fell. She touched it. Deep in her bones a warning sounded; she'd regret this. *Hey, regret sounded better than death.*

She tried to punch in the number for his office. Couldn't depress the buttons.

Press harder.

Got it.

His paralegal answered and said he hadn't come in yet. Okay. Shannon still knew his home number by heart. She cursed him for making her dial again.

Scott's sleepy voice filled Shannon's ears.

"Hello, Scott? This is Shannon. You're home, that's great. Listen I have a really, really, *really* big favor to ask. Can you come over here right away? I—"

"Sorry, Shannon. I'm in court this afternoon. Up half the night with a motion to strike that the plaintiffs bushwhacked us with yesterday. No can do. Have you tried Jane and Picker? See you in the office later. Gotta go."

"Please listen—"

The phone went dead.

Shannon closed her eyes. Tears dripped in a slow rhythm down her cheeks. She couldn't even cry fast now. *What now?* Her best options hadn't panned out. She might as well give in.

Try one more time.

She thumbed through her contacts searching for anyone, *anyone* who could roll with this crisis and not freak out and not take her to the hospital and who would get here in time. *Right.*

Her thumb paused at O - P - Q.

Luke Quintana's number. She'd repulsed him, but he might come. Police officers, like fire fighters, helped people. He'd treated her well even after the casino.

She smoothed her braid.

Worth a shot.

She pressed in the number.

"Quintana's Tamale Restaurant. A little volcano in each tortilla. Can I help you?"

Shannon looked at the phone again. Had the world gone mad?

"Quintana?"

"I believe so, yes."

"This is Shannon Kendricks. Look, I haven't had a chance to apologize for the casino and thanks again for lending me your sock…."

"Shannon. Hey, I'd like to come by and pick up my sock if I may. It's a very special sock." Although he was joking, his voice remained cool. He planned to stay arm's length. But she still needed his help.

Shannon looked down at her foot, still encased in Quintana's bandages and sock.

"Uh. I fell asleep after Chen dropped me off and I just now woke up. It's still on my foot."

Why in Odin's name was she talking about his damn sock?

"I see. You slept for, what, twenty-four, twenty-five hours?" Quintana's voice grew more somber.

"Yes. And that's why I'm calling." Shannon stopped. *Spit it out. Come on.* Her hand touched her braid. It held tight. The tears started again. Talk about reaching the bottom of the barrel. She'd seeped through the cracks on the bottom and dripped through the floor boards into cold, dark dirt….

"You all right?" Quintana's deep, gentle voice brought Shannon back. She knew it; he couldn't help caring about another human being in trouble. A good trait in a man.

"No, I'm not all right. I need help," she blurted. "Please, can you come here now?"

Quintana remained quiet for a minute. He could hear her crying most likely, although she tried to muffle it.

"What happened? Do you think that jerk has come back?"

"Oh no, nothing like that. My dog would bark her head off if someone came into the yard. I…I'm not well. I can't get up off the floor. I tried crawling but I blacked out. I can't get anywhere. I'm in a lot of pain."

"I'll call an ambulance."

"No, please. That would cause the worst things. It's a long story. Too long. I don't want medical help; I want food, a ton of it. You know about my, my problem. I fell asleep and didn't eat for a day. A disaster. I can't get to the kitchen. I may not survive this, it's that bad, Quintana—"

"Luke."

"Okay. Luke."

"Let me ask who's patrolling nearby. They can get to you a lot faster than I can."

"No, please. Anyone else would take one look and call for an ambulance. I can't go to the hospital, I can't." More silence.

"All right. I'm on my way."

"Thank you. I can't tell you how much—um, if you have any ice cream, could you bring some?"

Shannon wanted to go back to sleep. Maybe being buried in a snowstorm worked the same way. A person in the snow, drifted off and never woke up.

No. Stay awake.

She imaged Essi and the little yellow, uh, what was the thing?

celessstii, Essi whispered faintly.

Salesti, right. Shannon imaged: the raven and Salesti flow back to the raven's body and they fly off to hang around somewhere nearly, right?

You're weak but try to image, Essi.

Essi stirred, gathered herself. She erased Shannon's images. She imaged nothing new.

Uh oh.

Shannon picked up reluctance in Essi's vibration—that didn't bode well. What else did Shannon sense? Guilt.

Essi had better not have kept the raven and Salesti in Shannon's mind after all. Shannon listened for the distant echoes of the raven's frantic spirit. Quiet. She listened for Salesti's tiny buzzing thrum. Didn't hear it. The raven and Salesti *had* gone. Then why had Essi erased the image of them leaving in the bird body?

Don't push the child. Not now.

What did Toss want to tell you?

Images: Salesti will take Essi home.

Good news, right? Salesti would take Essi home as soon as they'd returned Juneau to her body and all would be well.

Bet you're looking forward to seeing him soon, right?

Essi created no images in response. She fell silent. No, correct that; she settled into a low steady hum. Preoccupied. No room in her guilty little head for Toss.

Uh oh. Essi had left out something important. Hidden it. Bad news incoming.

Shannon didn't want to hear it…. She almost nodded off again….

Essi resumed the story of what had happened while Shannon slept. The little girl wanted to tell the truth, even if it made Shannon mad. Sweet baby.

Essi imaged: the child and Salesti finish Toss's message and the little creature flows down the sleeping Shannon's arm to her hands that cuddle the still raven. Juneau begins to make sharp clicks, rushing around Shannon's head as if swimming around her pool at a mad pace.—

Trying to awaken Shannon? It hadn't worked; she must have fallen into the deepest of sleeps.

—Narci has jumped into Shannon's lap for her own cuddle. Narci inspects the raven trespassing on the cat's accustomed spot. Narci reaches out her paw and pokes at the bird. And pokes again. And just then —

Uh oh. Deja vu with a new cast of characters.

—The bird stands and shakes himself. He grooms under his wing. He cocks his head at the cat, flies up, circles the room, and disappears around the corner into the kitchen.—

So. The bird spirit returned home and the bird revived. So far so good.

Essi built her images more and more slowly.

Why didn't Narci pounce on the raven before it flew off? Her cat could be quick when she wanted, and she wanted nothing so much as birds. Fortunately, she'd never caught one, but this time, the raven had stirred unaware of the cat. Any other time her little bird catcher would've pounced. Definitely. So why didn't she?

—Narci's attention does not fix on the bird. The sleek cat shakes her head, reels across Shannon's lap, jumps down and runs in circles.—

Panicked.

Shannon knew the feeling.

—Essi showed Salesti now occupying the cat.

Just great. So. Narci had poked at the raven just as Salesti flowed into it, and Salesti had flowed right on over to her poor cat, just as Essi had flowed right on over to Shannon when *she* had touched Juneau at the worst possible moment.

The bird spirit stayed with the bird at least?

Essi affirmed.

Salesti on board Narci. Shannon would've shaken her head at this new complication if she'd could have. Instead she mustered a slight downturn of the corners of her mouth.

Good thing this stowaway was so small; any larger alien on board and Narci wouldn't have survived more than a few hours.

But where had Narci gone? *Had* Shannon's cat survived?

Shannon imaged Narci running off and coming home.

Essi erased the part where Narci returns.

The cat remained out there somewhere, then, her energy ebbing because of Salesti. Shannon had to feed her, and fast. *But how?* She couldn't move a muscle.

Shannon looked at Indy. The big lug loved to play games with Shannon, and she carried a good-sized brain in that big thick skull. She'd learned the "find" command and "bring."

Shannon had never sent her after a cat, of course.

"Indy. Go find Narci. Go find her. Bring her to me. Bring Narci."

The dog sat up and looked at Shannon for a minute.

"Go on, sweetie, find the cat."

The dog padded off to the kitchen and the dog door clacked open and closed. A long shot, but the only shot available.

After that, Shannon laid back against the wall and started counting backward from one thousand. She made herself start over every time she lost her count....

...Shannon's mind drifted. Something nagged at her.... Why had Salesti insisted on connecting with Essi without the bird when it could have explained how it would take Essi home from the bird with Shannon touch? Had Salesti used Toss's message as an excuse to come over?.... Did it know about Drom? Want to help?.... Okay, that sounded crazy....

* * *

"Shannon, wake up, come on, cara, wake up."

Shannon smelled a cinnamon roll. Her eyes opened. Yes, a cinnamon roll. Luke tucked the pastry in her fingers. She couldn't lift it.

"Maybe some sips of this chocolate shake first." He brought a straw connected to a super-sized container to her lips.

"I have another one when you're ready."

She drank, nodding her thanks, and didn't stop until the shake cup slurped with the last drops of the drink. And the second one. Then she hefted the cinnamon roll again. Success. She bit a great chunk out of it, once again nodding her appreciation to Luke.

"Well at least you weren't jerking me around this time. When I came in and caught sight of you, I thought I might have to call the morgue. Scared the living daylights out of me." He pointed to the rapidly disappearing pastry. "We should pack those in our first aid kits instead of smelling salts. I tried salts on you, and not an eyelash fluttered. Here, let's get you off the floor."

Luke carried her over to the couch and laid her down as if she were a porcelain doll. If she didn't feel so rotten, she'd hate this attention so very much.

Luke pulled her afghan over her. "You still need food?"

Shannon nodded. "Bring as much as you can as fast as you can."

Luke frowned as he handed over the twelve pack of cinnamon rolls. "You need an ambulance, no question. I'm going to fix you one of your deluxe coolers of food and then either I am going to call the ambulance or you are going to give me a good reason why I shouldn't." He stalked off to the kitchen.

Shannon ate every crumb of every roll. *Marginally better.* She checked in with her two charges. More energy in Essi's pulse and Juneau's call. But not enough. Not nearly. She vowed not to leave a shred of food in the house uneaten. Just give her an hour.

No joke. This had been a close call. Very close.

Tomorrow she'd—wait, not tomorrow—today, Friday. She'd slept through Thursday. Friday. Moon's deadline for reaching an agreement with the SQ and the other backers. Had Juneau's body made it? She checked her cell for any sign Moon had called. Nothing. No calls from Becky. They'd have called if Juneau had…had…Moon might call Shannon any time now. Maybe she'd better clean out her food supply in *half* an hour.

Luke returned with the cooler, packed full, as promised. He also brought in several hot dishes, some reheated from Shannon's refrigerator, some she didn't recognize. Including tamales.

"You make these?"

"My grandmother. There's a raven in your kitchen."

"Yes."

Luke nodded in silence.

"Does he look okay?" Shannon asked after a moment.

The fingers went to his chin stubble as Luke considered this question. "Looks good, good. Nice color, has all his feathers. He's helped himself to a pie sitting on the kitchen counter. You want me to give him a tamale?" Luke said.

"Sure," she said. "The poor thing needs all the energy it can get."

"Mm hmm."

Shannon steered the conversation along less alarming paths, ate prodigious quantities of food. More of her strength returned. But she hadn't rebounded as fully, nor as quickly as she had earlier in the week. Another episode like this one and she wouldn't rebound at all.

When she asked about his grandmother, Luke launched into a description of his large family here in the city. As he talked, Shannon's mind floated away, a huge chasm widened between them. He had five siblings, lived in a huge extended family. She had no siblings, her parents now estranged from each other, from her. Different worlds.

She pulled her braid over her shoulder and smoothed the tip. Half her hair had come loose.

Unbraid it.

No. Leave it alone. In fact, tighten it up. She rebraided it.

Her mood plunged.

Luke stopped talking. Shannon could think of nothing to say. In the silence the dog door slapped open and slammed shut. Indy appeared and stood in the middle of the room with a limp figure dangling from her big mouth. It didn't move. Looked quite dead.

"Jesus, I'll get her outside with that—"

"No, wait, she's carrying my cat. I sent her out to fetch Narci. Indy, bring her here, baby, good girl."

Not dead, Narci, please, not dead. Essi's vibration hummed, tense and anxious. An image of Juneau appeared, hovering close, eyes intent on the cat.

"Come here, Narci, poor sweetie." Shannon lifted the limp cat from Indy's jaws. Luke half-stood, as if he didn't expect the dog to give up her prize, and then sat down again when Indy opened wide as soon as Shannon had secured the cat. Indy crowded in to examine the cat along with Shannon.

So did Essi and Juneau.

"Is she alive?" Luke asked in his quiet way.

Shannon felt for a pulse in the cat's neck. A weak throbbing under her fingers. Still warm. Narci's small chest lifted.

"Yes, but she needs food. She, she uh, has the same disorder I do. Can you bring me her cat food? The cans are in the cupboard by the sink. Bring lots. Never mind about a dish."

Luke returned with a pile of cat food cans and a spoon. Shannon held the lifeless-looking cat in her arms. Luke opened a can and dipped in the spoon, lifting it to touch Narci's nose. The cat's eyes opened.

He looked at Shannon. "That's it. I'm throwing away the smelling salts."

He sat down beside Shannon and fed Narci from the tip of the spoon. For a few minutes only her mouth moved, although it moved with enthusiasm, like she'd been starved for months. Bit by bit, signs of life returned to her. Her ears came up, her nose sniffed, then she sat, then she wriggled until Shannon plunked her down on the coffee table so she could stand on all fours and eat in earnest. Luke placed the can in front of her and opened a second.

Essi's humming danced in her head. The child had been petrified that the disaster would end in Narci's death. Shannon imaged her a hug. Juneau relaxed back into Shannon's brain shadows.

Wait. Shannon's head jerked. *Narci's body could live, propelled by Salesti, even if Narci's spirit had expired. Narci? You there?* Shannon placed her hand on the cat's back, searching for the cat's emotions and images. Her excitement over the food knew no bounds. The sole image—her cat food can and its content. What else? Yes, Shannon recognized the cat's familiar sauciness. Her fondness for her cat food and for Shannon. Recognized the wildness to her, akin to Juneau's, although softer, milder, as if the thousands of years that cats had lived as companions to humankind had smoothed the edges of her feral nature. Thank Odin.

Narci lived. And Shannon would keep her that way.

And Salesti? Shannon stroked the cat, searching for Salesti. There. The little creature had tucked itself into a far corner of Narci's mind to help calm the cat, humming in a soothing tone, much like a purr.

Salesti's hum reverberated up Shannon's hand. Essi halted her own hum, listened to Salesti, then resumed her own humming, even more relaxed than before.

Salesti's thrum sounded calm, satisfied, steady. Not weak, even though Narci hadn't recovered yet. A strong little thing; much stronger than Essi. Shannon focused on Salesti's hum.

Concentrate.

Shannon received the impression of a flame on a gas burner, set on low, but capable of much greater heat and force. Strange and unknowable.

Narci turned her big blue eyes to Shannon for just a moment before she returned to her salmon and whitefish can. No fear of her alien guest.

Her family, Narci, Indy and her. Safe. For now.

Shannon whispered her thanks to Indy for bringing the cat back—and for her great timing. Luke would forget all about—

"So," he said, as he rose from his place beside her, disappeared into the kitchen, and returned with a chair from the kitchen table. He slid the coffee table off to the side and set his chair eye to eye with Shannon. Narci didn't flinch. The food held her full attention.

Shannon noticed for the first time that he hadn't dressed in his blues. Jeans and a polo. Nice fit.

"You're off duty?"

"Yeah, I'm filling in, night shift right now. Midnight to 8 a.m. So, what's going on?"

"Oh, a long story, and boring. Don't want to put you to sleep. You want some of this cake? It's great with the whipped cream."

"I have plenty of time. Nothing bores me. And, yes, I'll eat some cake. With whipped cream." He pulled the cake out of the cooler and cut two pieces.

"I'm fine now, thanks to you. That's what counts, right?"

He looked at her and raised his eyebrows.

"Well, not so much 'fine,' as recovering well." He gazed, she squirmed. "Recovering. Okay, I will recover. Later. Thanks to you. All good. If you need to go, I'm strong enough to make it to the kitchen, which is all I need."

"Even if you could get to the kitchen, which I doubt, you wouldn't see much to eat. Someone will have to go to the grocery store." He smiled.

Blackmail. He would get the groceries if she would talk. And Luke an officer of the law.

Shannon searched his calm face, his incredible eyelashes. Quite incredible.

"Officer—"

"Luke."

"Luke. As you know, the bolt of lightning that struck me over at the SQ on Sunday left me with some…problems. And left Juneau in a coma. I tried earlier to tell you about it. I doubt you believed a word of it. I know it sounds crazy. So let's leave it like this: I'm not well. Let me get healthy and when this is all over, we can start over and go out and eat pizza like regular people. Yes?" There. That sounded perfectly sane.

"I'm not sure you've ever been 'regular people,'" he said.

Was that a compliment or—

"And the cat? Was she at the SQ too? Is that why she's also unwell?"

Man, hard work to get this guy off topic.

"Eh, no, that happened while I slept through yesterday."

"Just a coincidence that her—" he paused. "—eating disorder is just like yours?"

"Well, in a way, a coincidence, yes, or maybe not quite a coincidence, maybe more of an ironic parallel. An accident anyway. Sort of a logical accidental ironic coincidence thing."

Well played, cabbage head.

"You know, your perfume is quite distracting. Amazing stuff to cling to you through a car chase, a car wreck, a long sleep in my squad car, a bloody foot, blacking out here for an entire day, and waking up half dead. Maybe more than half."

He frowned, as if struck by misgiving.

Hey. Did he think, for Odinssake, that she'd run upstairs and refreshed her perfume before he came? Did he think she had faked her need for help? Anger reared up like a six-foot giant, followed by humiliation, an even bigger giant: he thought she'd *do* that?

"It doesn't fade," she said. Like he'd believe that. "Incredible stuff."

"Yes," he said, his voice sounding like "liar, liar, pants on fire," but saying, "Uh huh." Luke leaned forward. His breath caressed her cheek. She closed her eyes. His lips brushed hers. His breath smelled of peppermint.

Lavender haze filled her closed eyes.

Shannon looked down at her cell phone. Lavender. *Phooey.* Said "Excuse me just a second," and then waited. The seconds ticked.

Luke waited, drumming his fingers on his stubble, his head cocked a few degrees. Her grandfather clock marked off the silence a click at a time. Luke sat there.

Who knew? Her lavender haze could predict a call or visit longer and longer in advance. But as far as romance—bad move, bad, bad move.

After an interminable pause, the phone rang.

When Shannon answered, the caller had stopped to talk to people in the background, his voice muffled.

"Hello?" Shannon said. "Can you hear me?"

"Ah, Ms. Kendricks. Forgive me. This is Dr. Moon. The situation here makes phone talk difficult. Did you raise the sum Mr. Tremaine required of you?"

"Yes I did," Shannon said and couldn't help the pride that crept into her voice. "And then some."

"Excellent. In that case, we need you at the Research Center now. Important people are present at a reception here and want to meet you before they will agree to the Project. Your presence is critical. My office."

Oh no, no, no. Not now. She could summon no energy, no enthusiasm *now*. She could inspire no confidence. One look at her and the backers would back all right—back right out of the Project.

"Of course. I'll come as soon as I can."

PART THREE

PHOENIX RISING

CHAPTER SEVEN

TIME BECOMES CRITICAL

"AND YOU MUST BRING JUNEAU OUT OF HER COMA as well," Moon said, adding to his demand that Shannon come to the Dickson right away. "Some of the people who must sign the contract will not agree to sign until she returns to consciousness." Moon clicked off.

Juneau's body had survived. But what about her bluff? She'd said she wouldn't bring the whale back *until* the stakeholders sealed the deal to set Juneau free. *Think!* She must think of some way to safeguard Juneau's freedom even if she brought the whale back first. But the brain…thoughts moved like slugs fighting their way through frozen snow.

Her breathing became labored. Shallow breaths, too many of them. All the food she'd just shoved down her throat—what Essi hadn't already used up anyway—threatened to resurface. She gagged, paled, and stared at Luke staring at her. He reached out and with a gentle touch pressed her head down between her knees.

"Breathe," he said. "Take slow deep breaths. I'll get you something cool to put on your forehead. Just hold on."

She kept her head down. *Breath deep. Slow.* Her braid, firm and thick, dangled next to her eyes, stretching down and brushing the floor as she tried to outlast her stomach rebellion. *Deep. Slow.* She reached for the tip of her solid braid with one hand and held on.

She didn't have to time for this. She had to get to the Dickson. The whole Project depended on it. Although she wouldn't help Juneau's cause by showing up with her stomach contents all over her shirt. And if she stood up, she would shake like laundry on a wind-whipped line. Every time she became weak like this, her head hurt more and more. At the moment her head hurt so much her vision darkened. She couldn't think. All the banging it had taken didn't help either, of course.

Luke's legs reappeared in front of her lowered view; he sat back down, scooted his chair closer, reached around her head, and pressed a cool cloth to her face.

Better.

She waited a few moments more before she sat up, still grasping her braid in a tight fist.

"If you have time, I...can you stay a few more minutes?" Ye gods it killed her to say that. Old independent Shannon Kendricks.

"Not a problem. What is it? Who called?"

Shannon's mind leapt away. How had she managed to almost kill herself through her careless nap and energy deprivation just when Juneau needed her? Juneau needed her strength, but she had nothing left to give to the whale, no strength, no brain power. Correction: if push came to shove, she would summon whatever it took to return Juneau to her body with her last breath. *Promise you that, Juneau.* But as for making an impression on Moon's crowd? She might as well be an American minnow swimming to London. The SQ would take Juneau back to the tiny confines of the SQ and the whale would go mad. Juneau brushed against her, Essi hummed to sooth her.

"I have to think. But there's no time. Damn it, I'm so freaking muddled up, my brain is like oatmeal. I can't think." She did *not* add, Help me, Luke.

Anyway, he couldn't help. He didn't live in her bizarre universe.

Yet, as if she'd asked out aloud, he took her hand and said, "All right, we'll work it through. First, who called?"

"Dr. Moon. He's the Director of the Marine Mammal Research Center down at the U. You know it? The Dickson?"

"I've worked security there. Now, what did he say?"

"They took charge of Juneau, you know, the whale, after the lightning, to bring her out of her coma. But since then I've learned she hates it in her tiny pool. She needs to go free, Luke, or she'll die even if she recovers from the coma. So I proposed a Project to Dr. Moon that would free her. He needs me there now to convince some people to take on the Project. If I were my normal self, well, as normal as I get, I *could* convince them. But I'm not. I can't think. I can't move, I'm so very tired. I may never get well. Just look at me."

"You'll get better in a few days. For now, let me drive you over there. I'll hold you up. We'll pack up everything we can grab for the cooler and you can eat all the way. Better get some shoes, kid."

Shannon looked down. Luke's socks. Oh right.

"But Narci."

"You have a kennel? We'll load her up and take her and her food so she can eat too. What else?"

Think, bird brain. Oh, bad choice for the selfie insult. "Um. The kennel is still in the hallway. I dropped it there after we escaped from Drom."

Luke threw a sharp glance her way, but said nothing. He hauled the cooler back to the kitchen, and when he finished filling it, he set it in the hall. Then he came back and slid Narci through the kennel door.

Shannon watched with fascination as the cat padded in without a fight. Mother of Odin. By rights, Luke should be lying in shreds on the living room floor. Maybe Salesti calmed the cat, just as Essi calmed Shannon. *In that case, feel free to leave a lot of calming powder with her, Salesti.* Shannon imaged the little creature shaking powder off like a dog shaking off water.

Salesti buzzed in delight and commenced to wiggle.

Shannon watched in fatigued amusement. She'd grabbed a sandwich before Luke whisked the cooler off to the kitchen and while she waited for him, she gobbled down her peanut butter/tuna on rye.

After Luke had loaded the cat kennel, the cooler and four of her oversized fabric bags packed full of food into his car, she asked if he would help her upstairs to change out of her rank clothes.

"Sure." He picked her up and moved off.

"Put me down. I just need a hand. I can walk."

"No you can't," he said, and that ended that discussion. He deposited her in her bedroom to accomplish what she could in a few quick minutes. Mortifying. She rifled through her closet, then wobbled into the bathroom and closed the door.

There, she drew a deep breath and threw on an upscale pale green dress, washed her face, and peeled the bandages off her foot. The wound had closed. Good. She slapped a couple of band aids on it and slipped on her sandals. Ooch. Each step made her wince. No time to make a new bandage now.

Even so, when she limped back into bedroom, hugging the wall, she waved Luke off. She could stand on her own two feet. Well maybe she couldn't. But she wouldn't tell him. Hah.

She did her best to ignore her unmade bed. If she didn't look at it, maybe he wouldn't. Because if he looked at her bed, her discomfort would know no bounds. She glanced at him from the corner of her eye. He was looking at her bed. Color her scarlet. Watch her die a thousand deaths.

She struggled down the stairs, propping herself up by gripping the banister, Luke close behind her. Although she buckled a couple times, Luke braced her, and prevented her from falling head first to the bottom.

By the time she'd made it down, she'd spent all her energy. Luke placed his arm around her waist. Since he stood about six inches taller than she, this arrangement lifted her off the ground and allowed him to carry her anyway, vertically instead of horizontally. Yep, mortifying.

Shannon sat in the back seat of the car with the kennel and the cooler to feed Narci and to shovel in as much food as she could as fast as she could to further rebuild her energy and clear her mind. *What a coincidence.* She couldn't answer Luke's questions because her mouth remained full at all times.

What if the Project fell through? What would Juneau do then? Or, what if Juneau's body succumbed before she arrived? What then? Juneau couldn't survive in Shannon's head without Essi, and Essi couldn't stay if Shannon was to survive.

Essi, her hum loud and shrill, interrupted Shannon's unanswerable questions.

Essi showed her the man harboring Drom, as they remembered him, a guy in black with a ski mask. The man stands by the pool where Juneau floats next to the Darth Vader machine.

Holy Odin. Essi feared that Drom would come for them at the Dickson, and the thought terrified the child. Poor kid. Shannon imaged herself with her arm around the child. She'd take care of Essi.

But how could Drom know about Juneau?

The answer came to her like a slap in the head. The same way he knew where Shannon lived: Drom had come through the portal somewhere at the SQ, just like Salesti, Tharm, and Essi. He'd commandeered the head of someone *who worked at the SQ,* and everyone there knew SQ had sent Juneau to the Dickson. If they knew about the reception, they'd figure that Shannon, her fondness for the whale well known, would of course attend.

Drom *would* come for her at the Dickson. The thought terrified Shannon too.

She whipped out her phone and called Becky. The same muffled crowd noises of Moon's call filled the background when Becky picked up. *So.* Becky had been summoned to the Research Center too.

"Where are you, girl?"

"I'm close. But I need to know something important. Since Sunday when Juneau and I got into this mess, who besides you and Andy has worked or dropped in at the Marine Mammal Center? Staff, I mean."

"Are you crazy? I haven't got time for that now."

"Yeah, forever crazy. Listen to me. Shut out all that noise down there just for a minute."

Becky uttered an oath and said "I'm listening."

"Someone who works or volunteers in our area attacked me last night."

"No way. The people—"

"Listen. Another creature just like the one who tried to take Andy may have invaded or even evicted someone we know."

Shannon looked up. Luke's eyes watched her in the rearview mirror.

"My God." One thing about Becky, she caught on as quick as sun-dried grass in wildfire.

"Right."

Essi interrupted with a burst of humming and imaged to remind Shannon that Salesti had landed at the sea lion enclosure. The portal *moved.* So Shannon had no idea where Drom had come down.

"What?" Shannon's high-pitched cry caught Luke's attention.

"What?" he asked her.

"What do you mean, 'what'?" Becky asked her.

"Hold a sec." She put her hand on the receiver. "Nothing, Luke, sorry." She tried to think. Couldn't think. But of course the portal moved. Shannon knew that; it had moved from the whale pool to the walrus pool before Tharm landed. Salesti must know where portal would hover at the crucial moment when Shannon sent Essi home. That's why Toss had sent her. And why she must stay. And it also meant that the unlucky invaded person might never have visited the Marine Mammal Center at all.

"Never mind, Becky. I'll explain later," Shannon said.

"What? Sweet Jesus, you'd better explain later. Listen, I can't stay on the phone." Becky hung up.

"We're here," Luke said. He parked right at the curb on the edge of campus nearest the Dickson and tossed a sign in his windshield. Shannon slipped more open cans of food into the kennel to keep Narci and Salesti alive, clambered out, and hobbled off. Luke kept her upright and steady, one arm around her waist.

As she passed into the towering atrium and headed for the elevator, her body shuddered. Would she and her friends face down Drom today, as they'd faced Tharm? Shannon couldn't do it. Not a chance.

Distressed squeaks and clicks filled Shannon's mind.

Juneau?

Essi imaged. The whale balked at viewing her body again.

No worries, Juneau; we're not going down there yet. When we do, you'll go home.

As they stepped out of the elevator, Shannon spotted Moon entertaining a crowd of people. It looked as if the reception had overflowed into the hall.

Moon spotted her at the same time. "Shannon," he called, and excused himself from his fans. He glided to her side and took her arm. "Come. I want to introduce you."

Shannon eased her arm back. "I'm sorry. I'm not at all well. I need to eat something before I do anything else."

"Perfect. We have a buffet inside. You can eat to your heart's content."

Shannon didn't have the energy to argue. Luke turned her loose and she leaned on Moon instead. Leaned *into* him. Draped herself on him. They weaved their way forward. If he wanted her at his reception, he would damn well carry her there. She peered back one more time at Luke, who had walked up to the group Moon had abandoned and greeted a tall, salt and pepper-haired man with broad, thin shoulders and long bony hands. Luke knew everybody. Once again that sense of distance between Shannon and Luke rolled over her. His connected life; her solitary one. Tears formed.

Just inside Moon's door, Shannon caught sight of Becky. She stood near the buffet table, a plate in her hand, chatting with Christian Kaiser, the Director of the SQ. As Shannon watched, Andy joined her. Something struck Shannon as not quite right about Andy; too stiff, too edgy.

"Just one sec," she said to Moon, and leaned on a chair, resting but taking the opportunity to watch her friends.

Andy grabbed Becky's arm and jerked on it. He barked something at her. Shannon couldn't quite catch it. Becky froze. Kaiser looked anywhere but at Becky. Then the Director tipped his head and rushed away, his back stiff. Andy had insulted him. Becky pulled her arm from Andy's grasp, said something quiet but sharp, headed for the exit, and brushed past Shannon as if she were invisible.

Oh, Andy. Tharm continued to destroy his life even after her death. Shannon blinked back tears, turned back to Moon and allowed him to half-carry her further into the room.

To give the Director credit, he did ease her into a seat within minutes, went off in search of "her partners," whatever that meant, and promised to bring her a plate from the buffet.

As Shannon rested, Essi formed images. Shannon could tell from her hum that something puzzled the child. Something important.

Essi imaged: Shannon loves Juneau. Shannon lets Juneau go back to her body. Then maybe a question: does Shannon stop loving Juneau? Does Juneau stop loving Shannon?

Shannon imaged back. Yes, Shannon loves Juneau very much. But Juneau needs her freedom. Letting her go makes Shannon sad but also very happy because Juneau will go free. She will always love the whale, if they're together or apart.

Sad but happy, Essi imaged.

Yes.

Essi turned inward, humming to herself.

Through a haze, not lavender, but her thick mind fog, Shannon's eyes roved the room. The table and its chairs, the couch, the high backed easy chairs, even Moon's desk had disappeared. Chattering, glistening, wealthy people crammed the office, trampled Moon's plush burgundy carpet, dropped dirty plates in the large ceramic urns holding towering ceiling-high palm trees, talked over one another, plucked food from waiters' trays.

Food. Her hand went into the air, waving to catch the notice of a smart young man in his white short jacket. No luck. Her arm, soon too tired to hold up, fell back to her lap.

Continuing her idle survey of the room, she spotted Ambika, in a spectacular gold sari and red bracelets, Tremaine, the Mayor, a few other movers and shakers. The Bigs from SQ.

The mega-rich and powerful had come to celebrate Juneau's promised recovery and proposed freedom, sure; but others as well: the white lab coats of researchers, the tee shirts and jeans of students, and the logos of the SQ staff mingled with the formal wear and tuxedos.

At the far end of the room, Moon approached Todd and spoke in his ear, nodding toward Shannon. *Good man.*

To Shannon's dismay, even before the refreshments arrived, the Director shepherded the first of visitors over to meet her. Shannon didn't, couldn't, rise.

"Shannon, I'd like you to meet Mr. and Mrs. John Montague. John is the CEO of the Telecom Corporation in Sacramento and one of our strongest supporters."

He smiled down at her, a politician's smile. A clean-shaven Abraham Lincoln. His wife took Shannon's hand in both of hers, her bracelets, bands of sapphires and diamonds, their sparkle dark in the dimmed lighting, slipping toward Shannon's fingers.

"Call me Sheila," she said, a slight New England accent clinging to her words, tanned but wrinkled face and arms speaking to more recent years in the west coast sun.

"Thanks. I mean for coming. I, uh, I contracted the flu, sorry. Not at my best. A bit too dizzy to stand up. I…." Words failed her.

John and Sheila Telecom Montague, who'd leaned down toward her to hear her faint words, their plump round heads first dipping like two minor suns, then floating back at the word "flu," took their leave.

Moon tried two times more with the same unhappy results.

With a stiff face and a stiffer voice, he said, "Perhaps I'll give you a moment or two to eat before continuing my introductions."

Shannon slumped. A hurricane roared in her head. She would faint soon. No lie. She hadn't made a very good showing so far. *So sorry, Juneau. So sorry.*

At last Todd arrived with two full dinner plates. Both for her.

"You're my pal for life. I'll need more, though, I'm feeding a fever."

Todd's initial grin, pale and shy in that great mass of red beard, faded into puzzlement. "'Starve a fever.'" Even so, off he went to the dessert table.

She ate. Her surroundings sharpened into focus. *Where had Luke gone?* No sign of him anywhere.

The noise of dozens of chattering guests continued to jam Shannon's ears. Shannon avoided these gatherings because she hated this heavy, deafening, fragmented noise.

Time to round on the subject she'd rather ignore. *Drom.* Could she locate him? Shannon imaged to Essi.

Essi hummed, an urgent high vibration and imaged: Shannon looks out at the crowd. She throws her lavender haze over the well-coiffed heads. A small image of Drom rises from a blank face in the crowd above the fog.

Essi thought Shannon could throw out her lavender haze, focus on the alien and, just like that, his location would reveal itself. What—her haze worked like a divining rod?

But facing Drom? In her condition? Ugly thought.

She chewed on her plates of finger foods for a while, working up to casting the lavender. Mmmm, salmon pastry…good, Juneau, yes?

Juneau, attuned to Shannon's sense of taste, rubbed along her mind.

…Where *was* Luke, anyway?…Lavender haze on the office door, someone coming—and, as if conjured by her thoughts, Luke entered. Not far behind him, Becky.

Becky and Andy had become so close that no one thought of one without thinking of the other. *Andy.* The way he'd barked at Becky. How does a person tell her best friend—well, maybe not her best friend what with the necklace and trying to free Juneau, anyway the person whose grief wouldn't overshadow their friendship as soon as Shannon retrieved that emerald necklace—how do you tell her that the man she loves will never recover from his terrible nightmare invasion because it's still happening? That Tharm left her accursed powder behind and it would influence him? Shannon pushed that conversation away. Her head throbbed worse and worse, Thor and his hammer in there beating on her skull. Add stress to the list of reasons her poor noggin would never stop pounding.

Stalling once again, when she ought to search people's minds for a vile other-worldly killer. Go figure.

Do it. Throw the lavender haze. If she could.

She imaged Drom, but instead of imaging in her mind, she imaged outward. To her surprise, the lavender haze rolled from her lips like mist and hovered over the entire room. A quick, furtive check of the room told her nobody had run screaming for the exit; nobody had even twitched. So far so good.

While the lavender haze drifted above the crowd, Shannon scanned for SQ staff and volunteers. She'd spent many hours off duty from her volunteer work wandering the SQ, reading information boards, watching the various creatures in their exhibits, talking to staff. She would recognize most of the staff members who'd come. And one of them carried Drom.

She watched the haze. Nothing yet. Maybe Drom hadn't shown up. Maybe he'd taken his stolen body back to some safe, dark place. That move might make sense. He would need to regroup. To eat. After all, it must take a ton to feed him. No, it took a ton to feed Essi and Juneau, so it must take two tons to—

And then she found him.

Drom. Floating above the head of David Fielding, the SQ volunteer Andy and Becky had left behind to care for the walrus, Wally, after she and her internal friends saved Andy from Tharm's attack.

Poor David. A good kid. Once.

Drom must've landed in David's mind, maybe the same day Essi and Juneau came to Shannon, calculated that the portal would spill out Essi at the whale pools and sweet-talked his way into Becky's area to seek out who sheltered the child.

Essi retreated far into Shannon's mind, so deep Shannon heard nothing but the softest thrum. Terrified.

He can't hurt you, Essi. He'll never reach you.

The sound of Juneau's jaws clicking in aggressive snaps echoed Shannon's sentiments.

Shannon shifted, hugging her arms close to her. *Maybe she should just let sleeping aliens lie.*

David, a nice-looking young student, blond, lean, friendly, bright, now exuded dull fatigue in his every move. He stooped, as if too tired to hold his shoulders up. Black half moons smudged the skin under his eyes. In his hand, a large plate filled to overflowing with little sausages. *Been there done that.* Shannon popped her own sausage-in-pastry into her mouth.

Shannon wanted to cry for the guy. Drom on board. So awful for him. *By Odin's eye, we'll rescue you.*

She stuffed a ham and cheese roll into her mouth and swallowed it down.

But now that she'd identified Drom's carrier, she needed to disappear. Fast. This crowded room presented a damn poor setting for a showdown. *She* presented a damn poor specimen to take Drom down, too. She'd ask Luke to take her home, where she could make her plans.

As if David sensed her eyes on him, he turned from the short blond-haired woman he'd been talking to, and stared straight at her. He excused himself and threaded his way toward her.

Goosebumps appeared over her body.

Don't panic. Or panic but don't show it. Or show it and run.

Run. Okay, walk. Okay, stumble away—to the nearest person with a gun. Luke.

Hold up. What did the wise ones say? *Know thine enemy.* Shannon set her jaw and focused on David, focused lavender. Listened.

Drom's deep, slow drum beat struck her first, unpleasant, impatient and powerful, much deeper and darker even than Tharm's. The thrums reverberated into Shannon's subconscious, to places where every person understood utter fear and complete horror, to places where no one except monsters spent time. A place Shannon had never known about, and now struggled to escape.

Essi's hum had become so quiet Shannon couldn't sense it. The child didn't want Drom to hear her. She imaged standing in front of Essi, the child hidden.

The black and burgundy-shrouded creature made no attempt to contact her, sent no images. Drom hadn't detected her probe yet.

Shannon reached for Drom's emotions, and when she found them, they repelled her, disgusted her, sent sheets of terror, as cold as horizontal freezing rain in tornado-force wind.

Arrogance. Cruelty. Perversion. Corruption, stronger and filthier than Tharm's, a soul damaged beyond imagination. He must smell like a rotting sewer, like Tharm, but ten times worse, and David would too.

Yeah, Shannon didn't care whether Drom had her pegged yet, she wanted no part of sewer boy. As she withdrew from David's mind, she caught a slight hint desperation—Drom's. A despair borne of imprisonment and fear, just as she'd sensed in Tharm. Him too? Who or what could hold such powerful beings in its control? Shannon would have to learn about that being if she wanted to end this nightmare.

Essi, any idea? Hmm, hard to image—she tried to capture the sense of Drom's pain—and then imaged Essi looking.

Essi added nothing. Such a dominator puzzled her.

At that moment Shannon caught a whiff, a mere stir in the air inside David's mind of a…a *thing* lurking far back in David's brain. Strong, primeval, powerful. A creature of pure instinct. Full of dark will and little else. *Kill. Eat. Breed. Kill.* Single-minded, destructive. Like a pool of molten lava that would, if stirred, flow over every living thing, consume it, and flow on. Powerful, implacable. Like a glacier grinding its path to the sea. Fire and ice.

And it would not turn Drom loose.

What is that thing? Shannon imaged.

Shannon read Essi's emotions: *puzzle. mystery. new.*

Thor's hammer, that creature could make a stone cringe. No wonder even the repulsive Drom and Tharm longed to escape it.

The reeking creature could make Shannon its slave too, of course. So far, it hadn't detected her. Not wise to press her luck.

Time to beat a hasty retreat. *But wait.* As her probing mind moved from Drom and the other thing and prepared to depart, she noticed one more set of emotions. Human.

So they hadn't turned David out into eternity. Thank Odin. They held him there, in some tiny tucked-away place. His grief, his overwhelming pain and fatigue, horror, insanity, hunger, his desire to die—all this suffering engulfed Shannon like a ten foot wall of water.

Hot tears hit her cheeks. David suffered, deeply suffered.

Shannon snapped back to her own mind, confused, her thoughts disjointed. She'd traveled to David's mind, and now where was she? She blinked and focused on the crowd. Oh. Moon's reception. Right. The shaking began again. The casting had consumed precious energy. She downed the remaining pastries on her plate.

The partiers continued their good-humored hobnobbing, oblivious to the black inky stain of malice in their midst. She peeped in David's vicinity. He advanced toward her. People gave him plenty of clearance—not from a sense of Drom's darkness, but from the smell.

The David-thing pushed his slow, shaky way toward her. She'd have sworn that she lingered long, long minutes in its mind, but judging by the David-thing's still-distant approach, she'd visited his mind ten or fifteen seconds.

By now David would've guessed that Shannon housed Essi, and so Drom knew that, yet he hadn't guarded against Shannon's probe, hadn't sensed her there. If Drom believed Shannon didn't know he'd taken David, he meant to catch her unawares. And snatch Essi back. Maybe her too.

The David-thing inched closer. Ten feet away now.

Too close! Why hadn't she made her way to Luke right away? *Get going.*

Shannon swayed to her feet. She stepped to the wall and, using it to keep her upright, she hurried, in the loosest sense of the word, toward Luke, pushing on through knots of guests.

That third entity—what *was* it? Odds on, one of the SQ creatures had received that unfortunate honor. Maybe Drom had carried it aboard David, in the same way Juneau had arrived with Essi. David had come from the Brackish Water Center. One of its denizens?

Just then, Todd returned to her abandoned chair with an overflowing dessert tray. Bless him. She motioned him over.

When he arrived, Shannon grabbed some small, round chocolate covered cakes from the tray and stuffed them into her mouth. "I need to get over there to Luke. Can you help me?" Shannon, asking for help again. Her whole Amazon Woman persona crashing down around her ears. She ran her hand along her braid; it hung straight, neat, and true.

"Sure. I'll leave the tray."

"So long as you go back for it," Shannon said, and watched him with regret perch it on a nearby table.

As they approached, powered by Todd, Luke turned to her.

"I need to talk to you," she said.

"Why?"

"The guy who chased me the other night followed me *here*. Can you sort of scare him off?"

He regarded her for a moment with an expression she couldn't decipher. Then he turned his back to her and spoke with a white-haired couple standing at his side opposite Shannon. The woman kissed Luke on the cheek and the couple drifted away.

He pulled out his cell phone and said, "I'm calling Chen."

"No wait," Shannon said, her hand on his phone. "Don't."

Luke lifted her hand from his phone, his grip strong and insisting. Still, he didn't impart so much as a thumbprint.

"No—" she protested

"Officer Luke Quintana here, Hillside. I'm with Shannon Kendricks at the Dickson Marine Mammal Research Center, the Director's office. Big party going on. Ms. Kendricks believes she's spotted the man who chased her the other night." He listened.

"She says she's positive…. All right." He handed the phone to Shannon.

"You've made a positive ID?" Detective Chen's voice cracked across the air waves.

"Yes, it's him. But you don't need to come. There's, um, no problem. And if you show up, someone could get hurt so...." *Confusing. No way to clarify.*

Luke listened, his face unreadable, and waited for Shannon to return his phone.

A pause on the other end lasted so long that Shannon took the phone from her ear to see if he'd disconnected. No. Chen had placed her on hold without saying a word.

Hey, Essi. Can I cast the lavender through the phone? Shannon imaged.

Essi imaged herself, shrugging.

Funny, smart child.

Shannon concentrated.

Chen, on the phone at the other end, fumed. Shannon could watch the numbers as he counted to ten. Finding ten wasn't enough, he counted on. Shannon could imagine him going on, to a hundred, five hundred—

"Ms. Kendricks?"

Shannon, startled, blinked, back inside her own head. She said she was still on the line and Chen said, voice like iron bars, "I hope you realize you sound completely unhinged. The perp's standing a few feet away, but don't bother to come arrest him? Take me fifteen minutes to get there. Don't approach him. Let me talk to Luke."

Luke listened, uttered several affirmatives, and rang off. The David-thing had stopped well away from her, alone now. He gazed out the window while he ate a handful of nuts, but Shannon saw that he struggled to spy on her from the corner of his eye.

Don't panic. Okay, too late on the panic. Do not *act* panicked.

She resumed her appeal to Luke. "Listen. Call Chen back and tell him we're okay. If you can just make sure that he doesn't come near us—"

Luke shook his head back and forth and kept on shaking it. "If this is the guy who chased you, we'll arrest him here and now. You and I are going to keep an eye on him and let Chen and his men handle it. Don't worry, I won't let him hurt you."

Shannon grabbed her upper lip with her thumb and forefinger, touched by his words, but not convinced. *Yeah, and who is going to keep him from hurting you?*

Shannon noticed that Todd had remained at her elbow, listening with sparkling eyes to this conversation. The fewer noses in this ugly business the better. She turned to him.

"Todd, after you bring me that dessert tray, could you go down to the front entrance and show the police where to come? That should save a lot of time."

"On it." Todd hustled off.

"Point the guy out," Luke said.

Shannon considered refusing to point him out. No, she'd end up in the slammer for obstruction when Chen showed up, a place Drom could attack her without trouble. Enter a police body, and walk right in. A place from which she could not run. She relented. "Over by the window, alone. Alone because he smells like a sewer. Blond hair, sick looking. SQ tee shirt and black jeans."

"Got him. Who is he?"

"David Fielding. Student here at the U and a volunteer at SQ."

Luke whipped his phone out again and called in the information.

"But here's the thing. I don't want you to arrest him. He's too dangerous. Just scare him off." Do not touch him, she wanted to add, because if you do, you'll end up carrying a nasty alien and something even nastier. But she couldn't say that. If she did, Luke wouldn't believe it.

Todd arrived with the food tray.

Her legs felt as if they weighed tons, her muscles trembled from the effort of keeping her upright. She needed to sleep. And before she slept, she needed to eat.

Luke gave her a cool look, removed the tray from her hands, took her by the arm and led her none too gently and much too quickly out of Moon's office.

"Hey," she said, "I need that food."

"In a minute," he said. "You said we needed to talk. So we'll talk."

Partiers had drifted to the outer administrative office to escape the packed inner room. Luke hauled her past them into the hallway, past the thinning groups of guests, down to the shadowier recesses where, during the day, professors plied their craft in crowded offices.

"Look. You told us you didn't recognize your attacker. But you lied. You *do* know him. And whatever his real name, he goes by Drom. You call him that at your house when you were even loopier than now."

"I wasn't loopy. Am not."

"Beyond question loopy. And you know this guy, you know he chased you half way across town, you believe he wants to kill you. Yet you hid his identity before and now you don't want him arrested. Why protect him?" Luke's voice held the sound of black fury.

Protect *him*? Well. How different this bizarre situation looked to people who lived in the normal world.

Shannon leaned her back against the wall and she slid down the smooth surface to the floor, where she huddled, her knees hugged to her chest, the folds of her dress tucked against her thighs, her head propped against the painted plaster. Luke remained standing, his arms across his chest.

Shannon sighed. She'd have to spill the beans. "I don't want to protect *him*," she said. "I want to protect *you*. And any other officers who might touch him."

"Why? Has he contracted some disease? Have you?" Quintana asked, his face turning pale. Was he counting how many times he'd touched her?

"Yes, he's sick. And yes, like me." Shannon looked around. The few souls in the vicinity paid them no heed, their body posture conveying the message: just a couple engaging in a fight; how uncouth and embarrassing.

Keep it simple. She took a deep breath and spoke in a quiet voice. "But not the way you think. Not contagious, well, it is, in a way, but not from me to you—well, forget that, but remember how I tried to tell you before, a little girl from another world blundered through a portal and streamed into my mind, and brought Juneau's consciousness with her on Sunday when the lightning struck us and Juneau fell into a coma because her spirit had left her body, so when I return Juneau to her body, people will think she's recovered from the coma and the point is, the little girl alien can move spirits around and so can the alien Drom, who's invaded David's head, so if you arrest David, you'll touch him, at which point Drom could stream to your head and either take you prisoner or kill you. You see?"

She craned her neck to look at him. He rubbed his stubble and puzzled over her bizarre words. His expression never changed. In his eyes, though, Shannon detected an emotion that she hadn't sensed from him before. Pity?

Now *that* infuriated her. *Pity?*

"So," he said, his voice low, "Drom is an alien?"

"Yes, but not one from Essi's world—Essi's the little girl alien I carry—and he pretty much sucked Essi's world dry and now he wants to do the same here and Drom also pulled some SQ animal into David's mind, but I don't know what animal, in the same way Essi and Juneau entered mine, but while Essi's a sweet child, David's creature's perverted and evil and while Juneau is wild but magnificent, the SQ creature in David is a primitive, unrelenting killer."

Quintana contemplated this information. He unfolded his arms from his chest and said, "Looks to me like the…the *aliens* already *are* killing you. Minute by minute."

"True," she said. She couldn't deny it, weary in every muscle, every bone. "They need a massive amount of energy to stay alive in humans. More than we can deliver. I'm losing ground. But I can't get well until I can send Essi home and I can't help her get home until she and I send Juneau home and I can't send Juneau home until the Dickson agrees to the Project."

"The project?"

"To set Juneau free in the ocean. Essi and Juneau want to help me defeat Drom. So I have to take care of Drom as soon as I can. "

Quintana stood there looking down at her.

"A lot to take in," Shannon said.

"I would say so."

The two remained silent. The minutes ticked by.

"The cat?" Quintana asked.

Shannon hiccoughed a little laugh. "I forgot about Narci. Yes, she's got one too."

"Some murderous alien has taken over the *cat? The cat?*"

Yes, well. A lot to take in at one time indeed.

She said, "Not a murderous alien. A tiny creature named Salesti. A funny, happy alien. It landed in a bird, and I took it onboard for a time so Essi could pick its brain for a message from Toss, and then Essi tried to put Salesti back in the bird but Narci got in the way and Salesti landed in the cat. An interesting little creature. I can't quite get a bead on it."

"Toss?"

"A friend of Essi's back on her world."

"Sure."

Too much information.

"A bird? That would be the raven in your kitchen?"

"That's the one."

"And you want what? To deal with this Drom by yourself so he doesn't touch anybody else? What makes you think you can?"

"Another alien came down, named Tharm."

"Another alien." Luke's hand went to his forehead and rubbed, back and forth. He squeezed his eyes closed.

"Yes, and Tharm invaded the SQ vet Andy and tried to push his consciousness out of his head, which would kill him, so Essi took our spirits over to Andy's mind and we teamed up, Andy, Juneau, Essi, and I, and pushed the alien out instead, so now I have to push Drom out too."

"In the shape you're in? You couldn't fight a fly."

"It's a mental fight. I'd have a shot."

"Not right now, you wouldn't."

"Which is why we have to just scare him away for now."

More time ticked away in silence.

Shannon's mind drifted. She shook herself to stay alert. She noticed her braid had begun to unravel.

"So will you call Chen off?"

"No. Even if I wanted to, which I don't, I couldn't. He knows this is our perp. He's en route. He won't turn around now."

Shannon rubbed one wrist with the other. All right then, she'd have to scare David off herself.

"Well, I don't like it but let's go back inside until Chen comes then."

Shannon looked up at Luke. Did he accept her story? She could read most people with ease. But him? A closed book. Sure, she sounded like so much Alice in Wonderland Queen of Hearts. Like she'd downed a few too many New Mexican mushrooms. But Luke would believe her. Could believe her. Might. Okay, so he wouldn't believe her. Was he humoring her, then? Patronizing her? Something low in her gut twinged at the notion, but she let it go. At this exact moment, nothing mattered but Drom and that primitive thing in the next room. She'd deal with twinges in the gut later.

As soon as Quintana helped her back into Moon's office, she spotted the blond girl—with the David-thing. He must've returned to her the minute Shannon and Quintana left. The girl smiled up at him, touched his arm.

"Chen's getting close," Luke told her, checking a text message on his cell phone.

Shannon, resigned, frightened by what could happen when the police arrived, picked her way to the far end of the room with Quintana's support, and collapsed onto a chair. When Chen made his way to her here, far from the door, the David-thing would at least have a shot at escaping. On the way, she retrieved her dessert tray.

Quintana stood by her chair, still silent, studying the David-thing, concentrating on his every move.

She had just started on her second piece of lemon cheesecake when Todd returned, Chen and two uniformed officers in tow. He searched the room for her and once he spotted her, he guided them over.

Before Chen could speak, Shannon stood, grabbed his arm, and pointed across the room. She made as big a production out of it as she could, as if she'd yelled across the room, "You see who this is, Drom? You'd better get out of here."

"See that blond-haired guy in the teal blue SQ volunteer shirt?" She pointed him out to Chen, her arm extended, accusing index finger held rigid. She kept it there. "Tall, tired-looking, talking to a short girl also blond."

"Keep your voice down," Chen said, pulling her arm down.

Shannon said, "No doubt in my mind, he's the one who chased me and escaped the police." *Escaped the police, Chen. Chew on that and not on me.* "I'm worried about that girl with him."

Attracted by Shannon's exaggerated movements, the David-thing turned their way. Once he caught sight of the uniforms, David's eyes opened wider and his jaw tightened, his companion forgotten. He stuffed the last of the cake into his mouth, ducked low, and launched into the crowd.

Shannon wished him luck. *How ironic was that?*

"Keep the girl here," Chen ordered, as he launched into the packed assemblage and steered a path to intercept David. Chen had approached to within ten feet when David glanced back and spotted him. David's face darkened; his arms flashed forward; he seized a tiny silver-haired socialite, a frail seventy-five-year-old in silk and diamonds. With his forearm locked around her neck, he dragged her with him. She tried to scream but emitted instead a choking sob; her diminutive fingers clawed at his arm. David acted as if he didn't feel a thing.

Chen shouted for David to halt, but he pushed his captive toward the entryway, where officers eased back at Chen's signal.

"Stay where you are. If anyone comes through this door, I'll kill her," the David-thing said. He disappeared through the door and kicked it closed behind him.

Guests, panicked, pushed toward Shannon's end of the room, slowing Chen's progress. He pulled his radio to his mouth and barked instructions to officers outside. An age-spotted man in black tails and tie, whose arm had encircled the kidnapped woman moments ago, shoved his way toward the door.

"You," Chen shouted and pointed at the man, "Stay where you are."

When David disappeared, Shannon grabbed a spinach canapé along with Quintana's arm as he headed for the young woman who'd stood talking with David, and who now remained glued to the spot where David had left her.

"Hi. My name's Shannon. Detective Chen there, the guy with the gun and radio," Shannon said, waving in Chen's direction, "told me to ask you to wait here."

"Told *me*, you mean," Quintana said. "Sit down, Shannon."

The girl turned a pair of huge green eyes to Shannon. "You know David?" she asked, still stunned by David's flight.

"I'm a volunteer at the SQ," Shannon said. "That's how I know him."

"Oh," the girl said. She blinked twice, Shannon's fifteen minutes of fame sinking in, "you're the one who's going to save Juneau. I'm Jessica, David's sister. Fantastic, what you're doing." Without missing a beat, she added, "I don't know why David would kidnap that lady. That voice didn't even sound like his." She gave her head a small shake. "This is all so confusing."

David's *sister*. Shannon shoulders dropped five pounds of tension. She sank into a chair, just as Quintana was about to tell her to sit down again. *The David-thing wouldn't go after David's own sister, would he?* But Shannon's memory of David's suicidal desperation lingered, along with the sense of a cold killing drive impressed upon her by the unidentified invader, a drive untempered by any trace of compassion. Add Drom, twisted, corrupt, and, on second thought, yes, the David-thing would murder David's sister in the blink of an eye.

It would show no mercy to Shannon either. Ice replaced blood in her veins. She might never warm up again.

As Quintana questioned the girl—*Where did David live?…Did she live with him?*—Shannon pulled up a chair and attacked a pile of powdered drop cookies. *A hostage.* Something Shannon hadn't anticipated. *Shannon's fault.*

Leave the old lady alone, Drom. Stick with David. Just go away.

The police permitted no one to leave while David and his hostage remained at large in the Dickson building. His questions answered, Quintana moved off to convey the new information to uniformed officers who appeared at the door. Shannon watched him speak into his radio, passing the information on to dispatch as well.

She patted the chair next to hers.

"Have a seat. Terrible thing isn't it? For the record, I don't believe David's a criminal."

Jessica watched Quintana's departing back, still stunned. Then she registered Shannon's words and sank down.

"Thanks. The police think he tried to invade your house. Why would he do that? David wouldn't hurt a fly." The girl turned wounded eyes on Shannon. "And Officer Quintana said you're the one who accused him."

Awkward.

Shannon needed information to reach David before the police did—and needed this girl to spill it. If Shannon didn't get to him first, somebody would die. And it wouldn't be Drom.

"Look. I'll tell you the truth." Part of it. A proximity of it. Well, not all lies. "I believe someone forced David to come after me. He didn't want to. But he's the key to the real criminal. I hope the police never get their hands on your brother." True; no hands on David, no touching, no invading, no dying. "The important thing is to smoke out the real criminal. Can you tell me anything, anything at all, that you didn't tell the officer that would help me locate your brother and the other guy before the cops do?"

"You'll save Juneau's life. Everybody's talking about it," Jessica said.

True, but what did that have to do with price of tea in Tanzania?

"David told me once he wished one of the whales down there, any of them, would adopt him the way Juneau adopted you."

Ah. Shannon had earned her creds with Jessica.

David's sister kept those big green eyes on Shannon for another beat. "Do you think that other guy will hurt David?"

Odin have mercy. Why didn't the girl just hold out her hand and ask Shannon to cut it off? "He's in big trouble, for sure. Through no fault of his own, David's mixed up with a vicious man. Very vicious." No lie.

Jessica's cheeks reddened in blotches. The tears welled up in her eyes. "Maybe you can save him. Like with Juneau."

Or maybe not. Drom had occupied the kid for a long time already. Even if Shannon removed the alien, he'd leave lots of ugly Drom-powder, living stuff, behind to contaminate David. As would the other invader thing.

Jessica looked off toward the door, her eyes unfocused, her forehead wrinkled, as she racked her memory for information. Then she lifted those huge eyes to Shannon.

"The officer didn't ask me about the Maintenance Center."

"What maintenance center?"

"He asked me where else David had worked or volunteered *besides* the SQ. So I told him. But he never asked me if David worked any place other than the main campus *at* the SQ."

"Oh. You mean the SQ maintenance warehouse out on Otter Bay?" Shannon asked.

"Yes, way out there." Jessica explained he'd started working weekends there while still in high school, helping the maintenance crew—anything to get a foot in at the SQ.

"Thank you," Shannon said, throwing an arm around Jessica's shoulder and giving her a quick hug. "And it's okay with me if you don't rush over to the nearest police officer and fill him in."

"I'm half in shock here," Jessica said. "I can't remember my own name, let alone what we just talked about. What did we just talk about?"

This kid rocked.

Shannon cleared her throat. "Say, did you notice that you and I look a bit alike? Funny coincidence, hey? I, uh, went with the light hair on, oh, Sunday night. How about you?" Shannon kept a close eye on the girl for any sign that an alien had bestowed a new hair color on her, as Essi had refashioned Shannon's. She'd already checked out Jessica's eyes. Green.

"No, David and I both. Towheads from birth," Jessica said. "I'm glad to hear you just changed your color," she said with a nervous laugh. "I was afraid for a minute you might be a long-lost sister."

Shannon relaxed. Jessica struck her as genuine. No alien on board. But coincidence didn't explain the eery likeness between her, Essi, and David's sister. Something accounted for it. But what?

Essi? Why does she look like us? She imaged the three of them all staring at one another with puzzled faces. *Wait a minute;* four of them: Essi's mother could pass for Jessica's mother too.

Essi remained quiet. An uneasy quiet. The child didn't know—or wouldn't tell.

The two remained quiet for a time, then Jessica asked, "Do you think they caught him yet?"

No shots had echoed through the campus. Perhaps the David-thing had eluded the police again.

"I hope not," Shannon said. She spotted a uniform speaking with Moon, and after a short conversation, Moon pointed Shannon's way.

The officer joined them and sent Jessica, still dazed, off with a policewoman who would act as the girl's bodyguard until the OCPD captured her brother. They'd received no further news about David or his captive.

Moon now stood with a group of men and women away from the main crowd.

The Project depended on Shannon.

But the world depended on her, too; the world just didn't know it.

Juneau? Go home now or stay with me? Shannon imaged.

A frustrated, fearful set of squeaks echoed in Shannon's mind. The whale brushed her mind once, then again, and again, as if Juneau were circling her pool in agitation, as a tiger would pace his cage.

A terrible choice, sweetheart: go home now and save the body while you still can; or stay with us to help with this mess, but risk losing the body. Either way works, Juneau. We support you either way.

Essi hummed her agreement and wrapped her little arms as far around the whale as she could.

All at once the sense of Juneau's pacing ceased. The beluga let loose a clicking, squeaking scream, a feral sound like nothing Shannon had ever known. A high-pitched battle cry. Defiant. Angry. Wild.

You sure?

She stumbled a step forward as the whale nudged her.

Right then. Shannon picked her way toward Moon's group, leaning on chairs, tables, stranger's arms, shoulders and backs, mumbling "sorry" and "excuse me."

When she'd struggled to Moon's side, he said, "Ah. Shannon," his voice stiff, cool, unforgiving of her performance debacle. "The whale awaits. My colleagues have asked to watch while you pull Juneau from her unconscious state and restore her to us."

"Um, can I have a word?" Moon spoke a few words to his guests, then turned to her and guided her toward one of the windows.

"I have been called away, but it won't take long. A true and profound crisis, otherwise I'd never leave here, I promise you. Will Juneau make it for a few more hours?"

Moon's face took on a red tinge. "Shannon, you must not ruin our chances with these people. We need them if the project is to have any chance of success."

Tears pooled in Shannon's eyes.

More tears. Ye gods. Well, she might as well get the most out them. She allowed them to roll down her cheeks.

"I understand. I'm the one who started this whole thing. Nobody wants it to succeed more than I do. You have my word that I have no other choice." And, she didn't say out loud, she *would* stay strong enough to save Juneau when the opportunity came.

Moon's toe tapped the thick carpet without sound. Then he said, "Very well. Yes, Juneau still holds on. But not for long. You will come back as soon as you can?"

"Of course. Promise me you'll let your guests know that I'm coming back, even if it's late, uh maybe even very late, and then I guarantee Juneau will regain consciousness. Don't let them leave. Just make sure that they give their word they'll sign on the dotted line the moment she comes around, that nothing else will stand in the way of their full commitment. Oh, and tell Tremaine that my check will not bounce."

Shannon didn't need her new skill set to read Moon's emotions. Rage and astonishment, in that order. Yet in a blink his face recomposed itself into its usual calm. Moon regarded her without a word for a long moment. Then he nodded and moved back to his guests.

As Shannon made her way toward the door, she heard him say, without missing a beat, "Well, as Ms. Kendricks has been called away, and must delay her work with Juneau, perhaps I can talk you into drinks and dinner at the Indochine on the Sea. The chef is a personal friend...."

Nice recovery, Moon. She'd do everything in her power to make it up to him when she came back. If she ever made it back.

A police officer let Shannon know that Quintana had volunteered to report to his shift early to assist in the search for David. But he'd arranged for a squad car to reunite her with her cat and her cooler, and cart them all home.

A few minutes later, the police unit pulled to Shannon's curb. Two officers assisted her and her belongings to the door, then returned to their car and settled in. Chen had assigned them to protect her after David's successful kidnap attempt.

Shannon stood and watched them through the open door for a moment, her eyes troubled. More people to worry about.

She slid the cooler along the floor to the living room. Outside her living room sliding glass door another officer made himself comfortable on a lawn chair. Yet a fourth officer lounged at Shannon's patio table reading the paper.

Narci meowed.

"Oh; sorry, baby." Shannon retraced her steps to flip open the kennel door and free the cat. Narci wiggled her butt, her eyes on the couch, and set herself for an easy jump. She leaped; the back legs failed to hit level; and she fell without grace to the floor. "Aw, still weak, kitten? No surprise." Shannon gentled the cat onto the couch pillows and used the wall to limp her way into the kitchen for more cat food. When she returned, she placed her palm on Narci—so much easier than the long-distance way, so little concentration required—and listened to little Salesti hum. A quite contented hum.

"What *are* you, Salesti?" Shannon murmured.

…As if in response, Shannon caught the image of a flash. Not so much an image as a *presence*. A looming intelligence. An incredible gentleness. An inexhaustible playfulness. An infinite *power*….

Shannon jerked her hand from Narci's back. Had she just experienced what she thought she had? *No way*. Already uncertainty clouded her memory of it.

She shook it off.

"You eat, Narci, eat all you can. I ought to pull Salesti back over here, baby," Shannon said to the cat as she ate. "But I just can't bear the thought of taking even that teensy tiny creature on board right now. Can you keep it just a little longer?"

By way of answer, Narci scooped a scattering of chicken-flavored cat treats into a pile, crunched them into bits, curled up, and dropped off to sleep.

Shannon's exhausted mind and aching bones screamed to do the same. She could grab the soft quilt from her hall closet and settle back on her couch…

No.

She couldn't sleep yet. The David-thing might have fled to the maintenance warehouse to hide. She'd vowed to beat the police there. Shannon drooped at the thought. So tired. So drained. She yearned for this nightmare to end. She freed her hair from her long braid.

Think about something, anything to stay awake. So, now she knew that David housed Drom and whatever held him enslaved. David came down from the Brackish Water Center. So….

The doorbell rang. Shannon struggled to her feet and stumbled to the door. When she answered a delivery driver announced his arrival from the local grocery store. A police officer stood by his side.

"I didn't order anything," Shannon said. "Maybe the neighbors ordered it."

"Your name's on the paperwork, hon," said the officer. "Says here Luke Quintana ordered it. You know him, my sometimes partner, right?"

"Oh, Officer Taney. Sorry, I wasn't paying attention. How're you? How come you're not with Quintana?"

"We both volunteered to come in early. Chen assigned him to the hunt. I got assigned to you." She shifted her shoulders, as if to say, "Luck of the draw."

"Oh. I expect you'd rather Chen sent you on the man hunt." She hesitated. "But maybe you're the lucky one. David is dangerous. I mean more than your usual kidnapper."

Taney didn't look impressed. "Maybe. But what I meant is, I got the distinct impression Luke would rather guard you." She waited, as if expecting an answer. Shannon remained silent. "Anyway, the groceries came from him. I'm just outside. Call if you need me, honey."

Shannon thanked her. Nice of Quintana to order groceries, thoughtful. He must've arranged it before matters had gone south at the Dickson. Now she could see him arranging a mental health evaluation.

Well, if she couldn't sleep, at least she could eat.

The delivery driver hauled the containers into the kitchen while Shannon and Taney chatted.

"Having a party?" the middle-aged man, navy blue slacks and white shirt crisp and wrinkle free, asked as he placed groceries on the kitchen table.

Shannon smiled, the skin around the edges of her eyes tightening. She shook her hair free of its pony tail holder. "A party of one." She gave him a tip and sent him on his way.

She locked the door, pulled the nearest grocery bags to the table, and grabbed whatever came to hand that she could eat right out of the container. Which meant about everything. Quintana had ordered well. No prep time involved. Her stomach quieted but her mind refused to clear. Shannon stared, unseeing, exhausted. Odin's thunder bolts, as ever, smashing against her skull.

Another knock at the door. She blinked and looked around with confused and drowsy eyes.

What now?

"Just a minute," Shannon said through the door. She noticed a chicken leg in her hand and took a bite. She placed it back on the plate, wiped her hands, smoothed her dress. She glanced out the window and returned to the door.

"Detective Chen, welcome." *Welcome like an outbreak of shingles.*

This would not go well.

Chen entered, looking fresh and relaxed. In fact he looked downright cheerful. *How irritating.*

"I'm not quite done eating; you want something?" She didn't sound quite as gracious as she meant to pretend. "Have a seat."

Chen did a double take at the empty packages and cartons amassed on the table and. said, "Someone here with you?"

"No, I ate all this all by myself." *So what?* To demonstrate, she resumed her seat and munched from a sack of sweet potato chips. "Want some?"

Chen started to say something, but gave it up and slid onto a chair. He leaned back and smiled again.

"So, did you catch him?" Shannon asked. *Please say no.*

Chen's mouth drooped a fraction of an inch. "No. He slipped away. But it's just a matter of time. We're watching his place, monitoring his credit cards and bank accounts, covering the airport, bus station, boats, rental agencies, you name it."

Tread carefully. "Anywhere else he could be?" Shannon asked, as if in idle conversation.

"We're keeping an eye on his apartment, the university, the SQ. A couple of former employers. Cruising the city. Don't worry. I've placed extra people on watch here, too." Chen grinned. "We owe him one thing: taking the former Lieutenant Governor's wife hostage loosened the Department's purse strings."

"Is she all right?"

"He let her go. No thanks to us. If one of my officers could've taken a safe head shot, Fielding would be dead. But we couldn't risk a shot."

"She, uh, anything unusual about the way she acted when you found her?" The Drom she'd come to know would scorn such a weak body, but better to ask.

"Funny you should ask. Quintana asked the same thing—he wanted to see if she'd started acting strange. Suspected a drug injection or some such. In fact, Quintana shoved another officer aside to reach her first. Pulled his gun out. The gun might've gone off. He could've shot her—the former Lieutenant Governor's wife, for crissakes—or even himself, the way he bulled in there." Chen wagged his head. "Unlike him to ignore protocol. He's one of the best in the City. So why're you and Quintana so worried about the woman?"

"Oh," Shannon said, "you know, just worried about her." *Way to go. Sharp response.*

Chen scowled.

So Quintana planned to shoot the woman if he discovered Drom on board, or to shoot himself, if Drom invaded him. Shannon shivered. So maybe he did believe her. Or at least wondered about it enough to hedge his bets. They'd have charged him with murder if he'd killed her. And if Drom took him—Shannon's chest twisted inside at the thought.

Anyway, Quintana hadn't hurt anyone and Drom still occupied David. Shannon still needed to know if Chen had discovered David's knowledge of the maintenance facility. "The SQ's a big place."

"Yeah, I know. But just five gates and no other way to enter, since a solid wall surrounds the whole shebang. We're sweeping every inch of it inside just in case."

Didn't sound like they'd discovered his connection to the Otter Bay facility yet.

"Well, anyway, I don't want police protection. Thanks all the same."

Chen ignored that remark. His mind had wandered elsewhere. He picked up a shrimp on a toothpick, and twirled it. "Fielding shoved her down, told her to stay put and not make a sound or he'd break her neck. We found her behind a potted plant, curled in a ball, quiet as a church mouse. He exited a side door that led out onto the campus. Students everywhere. By the time I hit the campus grounds, he'd put a hundred educated heads between him and me."

Why hadn't Drom killed the woman? He enjoyed killing. Maybe he had no time, with the police hot on his heels. Lucky Mrs. Lieutenant Governor indeed.

"Learn anything else?" she asked.

"He's a full-time student here. Majoring in oceanography. Good grades. For a couple days, though, he's been AWOL from classes. His sister hasn't seen him either until today."

"Any evidence he'd come here?"

"Found his DNA and fingerprints on your car; his shoes left the prints in your yard. Not a doubt in my mind he's your attacker."

"Anything in his apartment?"

Chen grinned. "Oh yes. And the place reeked like a swamp."

No surprise there.

"The apartment looked like a hurricane had torn through. Dirty dishes. Trash. Classic case of a mind gone bye bye. The weirdest thing, though, he had a freezer and a refrigerator full of meat. I mean packed full. The cupboards? The same, meat in cans. Not a radish or a strawberry anywhere. No beer, no milk, no cereal, no top ramen."

Meat. Juneau's urges had translated into Shannon scarfing down sea food; the unknown animal, maybe from the Brackish Water Center, wanted meat. Add Drom the psycho; what would he have craved? To kill—

My god.

Shannon coughed into her fist. "Uh, I think you might want to check the meat. Some of it could be, uh, but probably isn't, but, um, there's a small chance it might be, well, human."

Chen's head jerked forward. He leaned in toward Shannon. "You're not serious. Jesus. Why would you think that?"

Why? Because David's unidentified primeval thing thinks like a meat-eating predator, and his master, Drom, thinks like a murderer, that's why. Shannon ignored the question and rushed on. "So did you learn anything else?"

"Why would you think that?" Chen repeated, in a louder voice.

Like a dachshund with a tight grip on a pant leg.

"Just check it, okay?" Shannon's lungs took in a big gulp air and held it. *Please, Chen, no follow up, no follow up.*

Chen squinted at her. But he sighed and let it go.

Shannon exhaled soft breaths from her lungs, so Chen wouldn't hear her immense relief.

"His sister, the girl at the pool who looks just like him, Jessica Caslin, swears he's a decent kid, no trouble with the parents, no mysterious tortured dogs or cats with arrows in their eyes in his early years. Honor student in high school. On a football team that made it to State finals. Jessica says he always wanted to be a marine mammal researcher."

"Doesn't sound like a killer."

"No, and if he hadn't run, dragging a well-to-do, silver-haired rag doll with him, I wouldn't have believed you. Now…now I do."

Shannon clung to the subject of David.

"So what does his sister think happened to him?"

"Said she didn't understand it. Jessica married her high school sweetheart, who's in the military, serving in Afghanistan. Jessica and David have always been tight, so when she feels lonely, she and her brother go somewhere and hang out. Until this week."

"I feel sorry for her."

Chen agreed, but his face remained untroubled. "Anyway," he said, "this week everything changed. He turned her down when she wanted to go to a movie or their favorite pizza parlor. She learned from one of his buddies that he cut everybody off. Didn't answer his phone or his door. That's why she wanted to collar him at the whale's party." He puffed a soft cynical chuff through his nose. "The whale. And *you're* the one who's going to bring him around? How's *that* work?"

"Juneau's a 'her.'" Shannon said, then looked him in the eye. "I know her well. I volunteer down at the SQ. Have done for years." Two could play at doggedness. "So what do you think happened? What changed him?"

"If I knew that, I'd go apply to the university for an honorary Ph.D. We'll have to catch him and ask him. My guess, though? Drugs. The usual."

Shannon ate in silence for a few minutes. Chen studied her. Shannon pretended she didn't notice.

"So. How'd you peg him as your attacker?" he asked.

Shannon stopped chewing a chunk of strawberry cheesecake energy bar.

And now they'd come to the nub of it.

He'd been free with the details of the case and he expected quid pro quo. While she appreciated his quo, she could give him squat for quid. She stared at her plate.

"Don't think I'm not grateful that you handed me the guy on a silver platter," Chen said. His fierce gaze burned her face. "But also don't think that gratitude buys you much. I'll book you and take you in for impeding a police investigation if I have to."

Shannon wriggled like a worm on a hook. *Try playing it straight. Straightish. Try playing it not too crooked.*

"That's a hard one," Shannon said. She swallowed her current mouthful but it stuck in her throat.

"No, it isn't hard," Chen said. "You identified the right man. How'd you recognize him?"

Like a labrador retriever gripping a pull toy.

"Well, you know I had a look at him at my house that night. Did I tell you thank you, by the way, for a job well done on that?"

"Yes you did. And I'm not buying the ID. The description you gave my officers fit half the men in the city. If we'd pulled this guy in based on your account, any decent lawyer would've had him back on the street before the ink dried on his fingerprint card. Try something else."

Like a Great Dane with his paw on your neck.

"Well, here it is then, and I know you won't believe it, which is why I'm reluctant to say it." Shannon paused. "I have some modest psychic powers."

Surprise washed across Chen's face like the incoming tide, followed by the slow ebb of disbelief.

Shannon looked off, as if remembering in vivid detail. "David came up to me at the reception. He shook my hand and images flashed in my mind. I knew."

"That is bullshit."

Correct. "I'm seriously gypsy." Oh right, she looked the Roma for sure, with her blond hair and green eyes. "Give me your hand and I'll show you." She didn't need his hand, of course, to toss the lavender at him, but she'd warmed to the notion of a palm reader persona.

Chen's frowning face turned blank. "You're serious. You've gone round the bend, you know that?"

Possible.

Bewilderment, illness and frustration had churned in her stomach all week. She erupted. *No one believed anything she said anymore.* It ticked her off. Chen leaned forward and held out his hand.

Steaming inside, Shannon closed her eyes and ran her finger along Chen's palm.

Now, what would a gypsy say? "I see a scene from your childhood." She paused, hoping her prompting would stir Chen into some memory-filled images. "I see your father." *Come on Chen, picture something.* "And you."

There. "I see you, about seven years old, kneeling, crying over a little bunch of wild flowers that you've planted. Your father's just trampled them with his boot and he takes his belt strap—" Shannon's eyes shot up to Chen's milk-white face. *Odin's eye.* She'd stumbled onto Chen's childhood from hell.

Chen jumped from his chair, tipping it over backwards. His face hardened to stone and remained that way for several long seconds as he struggled to compose himself.

What a disaster. Temper and psychic powers did not mix. Her hair, now hanging straight, tangled under the touch.

"Well, talk about stupid. I'm sorry," she said, eyes fixed on her hands.

Chen didn't reply. He paced to the door. Turned. Paced back. Resumed his seat across from her. Propping his elbows on the table and lacing his fingers under his chin, he stared at her.

She assumed a knowing look. "Stranger things Horatio…"

"You're misquoting *Hamlet* now? That's gonna explain things?"

"I'm sorry," Shannon said again. She finished off the remnants of a pie she'd started earlier and poked for remaining edibles through the sacks, paper, cardboard and plastic littering her table.

Not always a good thing, peering into someone's mind. If she lived through this nightmare, by Odin's eye, once she learned to control this new "skill," she'd never cast the lavender except to save somebody or herself.

Chen spoke after a few awkward minutes. "The City uses a psychic guy on occasion. He's full of bunk. You want a job? Moonlight a little?"

"Oh, no thank you. Nope, no interest. Plus, I, uh, I go through long periods when I can't sense anything. Then, once in a while, I'm cursed with a couple days of these strong sensations. So you couldn't count on me." No wonder nobody believed her anymore. These days she lied as often as baseball players spit. "Anyway, that's how I pegged David." The holes in her story could swallow Lake Okeechobee.

"I suppose you didn't get any read on where he would go hole up?"

"No. I panicked. I didn't stick with his thoughts."

Chen fished in his jacket pocket and pulled out his car keys. Excellent. Shannon could climb off the hot seat. She relaxed—until his hand with the keys slammed down on the table's copper tiles, making her jump.

Chen said, "You said you didn't know your attacker. Why would he want to attack *you* then?"

Er. Think. Think. Shannon shifted in her chair and played with a bite of crust she'd left on one of her plates. "Well," she said, drawing the word out with a lift in her voice, as if considering this fascinating question for the first time.

"Well?" he repeated.

Drom wanted Essi. He'd invaded David who knew what had happened to Juneau; Drom figured out that Essi and Juneau had landed with Shannon. Simple.

That explanation, though true, would never fly. She needed some sane-sounding nonsense.

"My guess? He had some sort of sister fixation. Maybe he desired her but couldn't have her so he hated her. But he also loved her since they were siblings so he couldn't hurt her. He needed a surrogate. So since I have the same coloring—you noticed the similarity?—he came after me instead." *What a bunch of baloney. Sorry, David.*

Chen's eyebrows lifted. "Did you read his mind, pull out that little concoction from there?"

No.

"Uh, yes. Yes I did."

"It's possible, I suppose." Chen sounded unenthusiastic.

The next question veered right. "What else did you read in *my* mind." The words shot out, sharp and aggressive.

See? The ability to read images and emotions, an inky advantage at best.

"Oh nothing, no, nothing. Zip. Girl Scout's promise. Cross my heart and hope to cry." She raised two fingers, thumb tucked. *Not that she ever took up scouting.* "Not a thing."

Except for that scene when you got revenge on your father. Chen, Chen, Chen. And you grew up to be a police officer.

Chen's deep brown eyes took on the color of slate.

Chilly.

Chen grabbed his keys and stood. "Don't keep anything back from me on this case. Your life could depend on keeping me informed, leaving out nothing. Do you understand that?"

"Yes, of course, and I will tell you everything I can." Omitting the things she couldn't tell him—the other-world creatures hosted by her, her cat, and David, and the quest for world domination.

Chen instructed her to call him if she thought of anything else and took his leave by way of her back door. Shannon followed his voice as he chatted with an officer on the back patio, and then one on the front step.

She'd forgotten the police protection. She'd said she didn't want it. He'd ignored her. Well, too bad; she didn't plan to issue invitations when she took off in a few minutes.

Shannon assessed her body. Better than when she'd awakened this morning from her inadvertent long sleep, but a far cry from the Shannon of a day ago, and a million miles worse than a week ago, before all this began.

Returning to the couch, she sank against the cushions. She'd call Becky to get some information. Besides, she'd love to patch the rift with her friend.

"Hey, Beck. How are you?"

Becky remained silent a beat too long, then said, "It's been a helluva week, and now this thing happened to David at the Dickson. People said you accused him of attempting to assault you. Did you?"

Happened *to* David?

"He's the guy who kidnapped somebody's great grandmother at the Dickson, Beck."

"Because the police panicked him," Becky shot back.

Shannon rubbed one hand up and down her cheek, settled further into her cushions and explained how David had come after her, and the police now had evidence to prove it.

"No way. David's just a kid, a sweetheart. A softy. He'd never attack anyone. How could you think that?"

"The evidence. He may have been a gentle guy once, but something happened to him. He's sick."

Becky didn't answer.

Great. The list of things her friend held against her grew again. The emerald, Tharm's attack on Andy, Juneau's proposed release, and now David. *Be fair, Becky, don't shoot an innocent bystander.* Well, not innocent. A reluctant by-stander. Well, not a by-stander…. Oh forget it.

"You mean sick like Andy's sick? You're saying he has an alien on board too, right? And it's making David angry and aggressive just like Andy? So are you saying Andy will attack someone, like David did?"

Holy Odin. Give Becky A, she'd give you B through E right back. *Quick, think.* "Oh no. Well, yes sick like Andy, yes an alien on board, yes the alien's making David aggressive, but I don't know if Andy's going to attack anyone. No one knows."

"I meant that remark as sarcastic. Are you telling me Andy *might* go that wacko?" Becky's voice rose note by note up the musical scale.

"I mean an alien boarded David, just as Tharm boarded Andy, yes, but we, um, got rid of Andy's alien. David's alien hasn't left and the alien's the one with sick instincts. Plus another Earth creature boarded David, which didn't happen to Andy, and David's Earth creature's a stone-cold killer. So David's in a world of hurt."

"Oh, you think Andy's not in a world of hurt?"

Could this conversation sink any lower? "No, I didn't mean that." Shannon put her phone on speaker and rubbed her face with both hands. "I'm hurting some myself, remember. I'm not thinking straight. I'm hardly thinking at all. I'm sorry. I just meant that David's alien has lived with him a week or so, along with this other creature, and they're still in complete control. We ousted Tharm in, what? Less than an hour? So, however bad Andy has it, David has that in spades."

Becky relented. "Yeah, I know what you meant. But Andy's not doing well. He's touchy and mean spirited. I've never seen him like this. Worse for David maybe, God help him, but Andy's in bad trouble." She stopped a moment.

And now she is thinking her way from F to F….

"Andy told me how much his alien wanted your alien. Did David come after you because his alien wants her too?"

And Becky arrives at F. "Right."

"Can't you just give her to him?

"No," Shannon said. Her voice did not invite further discussion.

Becky burst out crying. "I can't take this anymore. I'm going to suffer from nightmares until I'm a hundred years old."

Shannon ached for Becky. So little she could do.

"You want to hook up? The three of us or just you and me, whatever you want."

"We don't much feel like hooking up. Why don't you stay home and rest?"

The cold of her tone stuck to Shannon's mind like ice to a tongue. Shannon's tears welled up. *Please Beck. Not you. Don't quit on me yet.* Shannon would've spoken, but didn't trust her voice.

"Juneau doing okay?" Shannon asked when she could manage it.

"The same, no thanks to you. What happened to the big finale to the party today, where you said you'd use your magic powers to pull Juneau out of her coma?" Becky said, bitterness icing her words. "Pull her out so you could free her into the wild. Where she'd die."

Shannon couldn't cope with an argument over the wisdom of the free-Juneau plan now. Or the sarcasm. She didn't answer.

Yet another battle to fight. To get Juneau to sea *and* win back her friend. However, the battle of the moment involved David, and Shannon needed information on the creature riding the poor kid.

"Listen, I mentioned that another zoo animal flowed over to David when his alien boarded. I think it happened at the Brackish Water Center. I need your help figuring out what SQ creature from there might have been sucked into a three-way mind meld with David."

"You sure this time?" Becky asked.

Yeah, okay, before she'd told Becky to think of visitors to the Marine Mammal Center. But that didn't justify the sharp bite of her friend's words. "Yes, I'm sure. Now that we know the alien invaded David—"

"And David came from the Brack. I get it. So you mean, have any of the critters up at the Brack gone into a coma?"

"Right. Or died."

"Died and left the animal trapped in David's mind? Oh my lord in heaven. I wouldn't call anything they house up at the Brack a cozy companion, I guarantee you that. I swear, girl, hosting one of the Brack's creatures would turn Shirley Temple into a serial killer. If David's taken on a Brack beast, maybe you got it right after all."

"So, any unexplained comas or deaths?"

"Not that I know of, but I don't hear all the news from the Brack. I'll make some calls and get back."

Shannon clicked off. Next step: the SQ maintenance facility on Otter Bay, but she still needed a car since a wrecker had towed hers to the junk yard.

Taxi? No, this mission must remain under the radar. No taxi records that Chen could check. Plus, she didn't want to involve some poor innocent cab driver in all this. Anything could happen out there, and ninety-nine percent of the possibilities would end very, very badly.

Should she try Quintana? Negatory. As with Becky, his list of disappointments with Shannon grew by the hour. At this point, he either thought Shannon had gone insane, or that she'd told him the truth, in which case he'd need some days or months or years to digest what she'd told him. Under any of those scenarios, who'd blame him if he'd rather get thrown into a pit of snot than take a call from her. Ever.

No, not Quintana.

And not Scott, ever again in three million years.

Jane and Picker had gone on their vacation.

Shannon's hands balled in frustration. Back to Becky and Andy then. Shannon would ask for a lift, no more than a lift, and hope Becky would still give her one. But no way would Shannon involve her friend in what would go down at the SQ. She'd insist that Becky stay well back.

The maintenance facility. Shannon and Essi versus the unknown beast, Drom, and David. The Biblical David and Goliath? More like sickly David and David's tiny brother against Goliath, Goliath's Daddy and his sickly little brother.

But. The bottom line? Drom, the sick bastard, meant to kill and enslave people. Someone had to stop him. And all fingers pointed to Shannon.

Face it. She wouldn't survive. The thought hollowed out her insides, dragged her spirit lower than it had ever gone, into darkness she had never known.

Well, so be it. *But by Odin and Thor, by all the gods of all the heavens and hell and hades too, Shannon would take Drom and the beast down with her. And get Essi and Juneau out before she sank. Now how….*

When the phone rang, Shannon opened the line but didn't speak. Her mind hadn't returned from deep and furious planning—forming and rejecting ideas to keep Juneau, Essi, and Salesti alive when…when Shannon died.

"Shannon? You there?" Becky asked when Shannon still didn't speak into the phone.

"Sorry. Off brooding in my own little world. What did you say?"

"You guessed it. One of the most valuable animals in the Brack's collection, their salt water crocodile, Old Salty, died two days ago."

Two days ago. When David's behavior changed. When he came down to the Marine Mammal Center.

"How'd he die?" Shannon asked.

"He acted fine, and then one day, wham, they came in and found him dead. Ann runs the operation up there. She said they estimated the croc's age at seventy, just about as old as this species gets in the wild. So, she attributed his death to old age. Salty was huge, by the way, near record size, twenty-two feet long, four thousand pounds. My sweet Jesus. A salt water crocodile ranks right up there near the top of the man-killer list. Those crocs consider humans in their territory just so much meat: they attack and eat them. And they're aggressive if you push them."

A predatory crocodile. If it weren't so chilling, Shannon would appreciate the irony that one of the most primitive creatures on Earth was the first to overpower Drom and Tharm, ancient conquerors of the universe. Just as they attacked without warning with their formidable mental powers, Old Salty had overpowered them with instincts more formidable than intellect.

And now, the predatory crocodile and a warped Drom had combined in David's mind. No wonder the kid yearned to end it. Shannon's eyes filled with the wet again.

"What else do we know?" Shannon asked, reaching for a box of tissue.

"Not much. A zoo supplier captured Old Salty in Australia, sent him to the SQ. The croc lived here fifteen years. They fed him live prey as part of their realistic exhibiting, although we're not talking the larger stuff that the big boy used to catch in the wild—horses, even water buffalo."

"So, you think SQ-goers would've protested if you threw a Shetland pony to him?"

"Seriously. Anyway, his life went on much as it had in the wild. He ate live crabs, rats, crows, and so forth, and also zoo meat. I watched him a few times. He'd wait below the water surface for some unsuspecting creature to come to drink, then he'd move on it fast, grab it, and drown it by holding on with those stupendous jaws and rolling."

"Where would a croc hide out around here?"

"Around here? Crocs don't live in this area, thank God, so it's hard to say. Near water maybe. In the wild, these guys live in swamps and river estuaries, but they can travel a long way in the ocean. Somebody found one all the way up in the Sea of Japan once."

"Say Salty's instincts influenced Drom. Top of the food chain. Maybe he wouldn't even bother to hide?" Shannon asked.

"Good prediction. If Old Salty has anything to say about it, he'll stand his ground and take down anybody who comes after him. And if anybody does go for him, he should arm himself with an elephant gun."

"Well, he lives in a man's body now. A regular gun should take him out, right?"

"Girl, it sometimes takes a barrage of bullets to stop a man *without* any extra guests. Somebody on drugs or whatever. If they're crazy enough to think they're invincible, they don't go down like any old fool. Translate that into a man run by a king-of-the-hill primitive predator. The shooter better empty the entire chamber into David before the kid reaches him. Or her. *Shannon*," Becky said.

So. If Drom survived long enough on Old Salty's rage to reach a fresh body, he'd touch, flow, and voila. Dead David, new host.

"You got a gun?" Shannon asked Becky.

"You bet your sweet Smith and Wesson." Beck said. "Please tell me you do too."

"Uuuuhhhh, no," Shannon said. "Not my thing."

"Better get one. The sooner the better."

Shannon rejected the thought of killing David to get at Drom and Salty. David didn't deserve to die. She meant to send the unwelcome guests off to eternity but not David.

"I need a favor," Shannon said. "I need to a ride over to the SQ maintenance center on Otter Bay. David might've retreated there. Can you take me? Just a ride. I don't need any help once I get there."

"Hang on, let me ask Andy."

Muffled voices engaged in animated conversation.

While they talked, Shannon reviewed her options. Her heart wouldn't break over the need to take out Drom because he'd already destroyed Essi's world and wanted to destroy hers. Old Salty—sad; he didn't ask for this mess—but now that he had been trapped, he'd fight to the death too. Innocent in his own stone-cold killer way.

Becky came back on the line.

"You can't stop that thing by yourself. Andy wants us to help."

"No way. Too dangerous. He could take Andy's mind like Tharm did, make Andy even worse. Forever. Or yours. Not happening."

"What about you? What if it takes over your mind?"

"I have a contingency plan."

The sounds of Andy's and Becky's conversation half-smothered by Becky's hand on the speaker floated over the line again.

"All right, we're coming."

She grabbed her braid in one hand. "Thanks, I owe—"

"On one condition."

Shannon's voice turned to stone; she threw her braid back over her shoulder. "What condition?"

"Andy wants us to stay nearby. We won't come within touching distance of David. But Andy wants to help in any way he can."

"No."

"We're big kids. You are not the boss of us. Andy also has personal reasons for wanting to stop the alien."

Yes he does. Poor Andy.

Shannon looked out at the neighbors' houses. All looked calm and peaceful, as if their occupants carried no burdens on their shoulders, knew nothing of bone-chilling fear. *False impression, of course.* Her neighbors carried their own worries and fears. But none of them would foray out today to do battle with a crocodile-alien-messed-up-guy-thing. Becky should stay among the safe, like her neighbors.

Shannon played with her braid, took off the ponytail holder, stretched it back on. She should finish this alone. She'd always gone it alone. Ever since one tiny peanut hidden in a little cookie shared with her best friend had killed him right in front of her eyes. From that day, the child Shannon's logic governed her heart and mind: if you don't ever want to hurt another friend, don't let anyone become a friend.

But Becky, bless her dogged heart, had ignored Shannon's walls, acted as if the walls didn't exist. And Becky had become her best buddy. Now Shannon had lost a friend again on account of the emerald, on account of Andy, on account of Juneau. But no matter what Becky thought of her, Shannon still loved Becky and had no intention of letting her get hurt. Shannon placed her palms under her chin and pushed her fingers into her temples, hard.

"You still there?" Becky asked.

Shannon held her braid in one tight fist. "I"m looking at horrible, rotten stuff here," Shannon said. "You keep your distance. Promise?"

"Promise."

"And Becky? Bring me your gun."

Shannon hung up, packed food, fixed her foot as best she could, and kenneled Narci because she needed to bring Salesti along. All these tasks took her a while, but she'd managed it by herself, at least. Who needed a muscular police officer to carry her around? Hah.

She opened the front door. Indy looked up at her, tongue hanging out, eyes full of light, a big square face hoping for a ride.

"Sorry, baby. Can't have Drom pushing his fetid way into *your* mind. You stay here and stay safe." Shannon squeezed her eyes tight. Who would love her big sweetie if Shannon never came home?

At the curb, the officers slouched in the car, heads back, listening to a baseball game on the radio. She leaned in the window.

"Hi, Officer Taney. Long time no see. How's it going out here?"

The officer tapped the steering wheel as if in deep thought. "Oh, I dunno. About as fun as scraping fungus off my toenails. How's it going in there?"

"Just wanted to let you know that a couple friends will come in a minute to take me on an errand, so if you wanted to take a break or anything, you can do that while I'm gone. You can sweep the house for intruders when you come back, right?"

Taney's eyebrows dipped. "I thought Detective Chen told you to stay put."

"He did. And I will. But Detective Chen okayed this one trip. You can check with him. Oh, here come my friends. Catch you later." Shannon moved off before Taney could respond. Odin's eye, she lied with such ease now, pretty soon she'd start believing her whoppers herself.

They loaded Shannon's cat and food into Andy's jungle green jeep and took off. "We need to lose the police car without being obvious. Take this next street through the Pine Ridge subdivision. I learned all about this area during a big lawsuit I handled. Confusing as Byzantium back in here. I'll tell you where to go."

Shannon and the cat ate while she kept an eye out the back window. Didn't appear that any police units had kept up with them. When they reached the outskirts of town, she relaxed.

"Becky said we're going to the SQ maintenance warehouse out on Otter Bay?" Andy asked.

"Right. We think David's hiding out there."

"We?" Andy asked. Shannon didn't miss the knife-edge that slid along the one word.

"Yes, 'we,'" Shannon replied in a light and casual voice. Andy had become fragile. He didn't need any lip from her.

A memory settled on Shannon. One brutal day last winter, one of the coldest, rainiest, windiest ones, she'd stood in front of the sink washing a fish bucket and Becky sat bent over a broken fish net handle, wrapping it with duct tape. Andy had walked in, clip board in hand, and chatted about the rash on one of the harbor seals. Becky listened to him without looking up but Shannon had turned when he came in. He wore a hat made of long thin balloons shaped into a giraffe. The knucklehead walked over to the medicine cabinet for some ointment as if nothing were out of the ordinary. Becky glanced at him to say something and let out the whoop he'd been waiting for. "What?" he'd asked.

Odds on, he'd never pull those goofy jokes again. Too much grim Tharm for that, too much anger. Shannon felt so bad for him.

"'We' meaning Becky, me, Juneau of course," Shannon said. "And Essi. Did you get a feel for her when we came over to help?"

Andy drove for a few blocks without replying. Then he answered. "Yes, I remember her. Nothing like mine."

Resentment radiated from his words. "Right," she said.

"Lucky you."

Poor Andy. Tharm had put the queenly screws to him. Shannon wouldn't jab another knife in his wound by mentioning sweet, mysterious little Salesti.

With the public beaches well behind them, they entered an undeveloped area of tall brush and protected wetlands. A few dirt roads cut through small hummocks and low impenetrable ravines.

"You know that big hill you climb right before you drive down to the warehouse? Stop before you get to the top. You guys can watch from there in case I need help."

As he turned onto Bay Road, Andy said, "I don't know. I think I should—" His voice sounded edgy, strung tight, a guitar out of tune. He stopped when Becky put her hand on his arm. He glanced at her and sighed. "All right. We'll wait there."

Becky nodded. "Yes we will."

Shannon pointed to the next rise, where a band of pines grew. "There. Nobody can see you if you stay close to those trees."

"You have a plan?" Becky asked.

"Grab David and kick his aliens into molecular bits."

As she opened the door to climb out, Essi hummed to attract her attention and imaged Shannon opening the kennel to let Narci out. Salesti's request. The image showed Narci leaping out, walking down the hill, Salesti in her head.

Keep Narci out of harm's way, Salesti.

She opened the kennel and Narci jumped down. The cat fell in with Shannon as she walked. Look at that: free-roaming Narci in tight formation. *Will you stay and keep her in line, Salesti? Like forever?*

Salesti's tiny laughter tinkled like a dormouse's piano.

Narci. Did her little muffin carry enough fat reserves to take on Juneau and Essi for a short time if need be? So long as the cat stayed close, Shannon could pass them over to her if Shannon's luck, and, life, came to an end. Narci could take Juneau, Essi and Salesti to safety. But she wouldn't survive long with all three aboard.

Shannon studied the area, intent on anything out of the ordinary. The wind had chased a thick herd of gray clouds from the ocean onto the hills. The moist air stuck to her, like cotton candy.

Shannon strapped on her backpack and set off down the hill with a mallet Andy had given her for the purpose of breaking and entering. In the end, she'd decided to leave the Smith and Wesson with them, for use if Drom and Old Salty took her body.

Thoughts of her death led her to seek out Essi; she imaged her arms around the child, kissing her forehead, kissing her cheek. Imaged the child flowing over to Narci if she even suspected that Shannon might…die.

Essi's worried hum filled Shannon's ears.

Shannon imaged over to Salesti. *Board someone stronger than Narci as soon as you can. Someone to take Juneau to her body and get you and Essi to the portal. That's all that matters. It…it will have to be Becky or Andy.* Odin's eye, how she hated to involve them any more than she already had, but they'd agree to it. She trusted them.

Shannon visited Juneau, too. She savored the whale's splendid wildness, and the feel of shooting through the ocean with her, the sun on their backs, the salt air, the waves. Juneau brushed against her. Her spirits lifted.

She approached the facility.

Although the primary SQ maintenance facility adjoined the park, SQ had constructed the compound here on Otter Bay to house the pumps that circulated salt water to the pools and tanks via underground pipes, and then recycled the water back to the ocean. Outdoor equipment also came here for repairs.

Shannon surveyed the large gray warehouse squatting on a concrete lot. A few trucks, bulldozers, and other vehicles lined up in neat rows along one side of the building, like an army squad saluting a general. A twelve-foot fence surrounded the entire lot, crowned by three rows of barbed wire that tipped outward. No way would she succeed in breaking in by climbing over that bad boy.

Shannon had once ridden out here with Fred Delaney, the SQ Maintenance Chief, to see why the beluga pool had clouded up. Freddie had undone a heavy chain at the gate secured by a huge padlock. She didn't have a key to the lock, so she hoped Andy's mallet would do the job.

She needn't have worried. The padlock had disappeared and the heavy chain lay in a coil off the road.

Well, well. Somebody had gone in.

And hadn't left.

She glanced at her watch. After six now. Any SQ staff that might have been here should've departed hours ago. Nothing moved on the front or side lots.

She scanned for any car that looked out of place, but all the vehicles sported the regulation pale teal coloring and the familiar leaping orca logo. Still, someone could hide a car out of view behind the warehouse.

Shannon pushed open the gate and walked in.

She leaned down, stroked Narci and imaged to Salesti: Narci goes around to the back, comes back and Salesti images to Shannon the details of the scene.

Salesti understood. Narci trotted off, stopped to sniff the corner of the building, then disappeared.

Careful, kitten. Shannon shifted from one foot to the other as she waited. *Come on, hurry up, baby.*

A moment later, the sleek little cat reappeared. Shannon gave her a whisker rub. Salesti imaged: more SQ vehicles. And an old black sedan.

Shannon remembered an old black sedan in the SQ volunteer parking lot. David's, then.

She pulled out her cell phone as she walked toward the door, digging in her backpack for chocolate. She stifled the urge to turn and wave toward the stand of trees at the top of the ridge where Becky and Andy hid—the David-thing could be watching her. Shannon lowered her voice, told Becky about the car, and promised she'd stay on the phone when she entered the building.

The one door on the facility's front side opened with ease. Whoever'd gone in wouldn't lock it until they left. The heft of the mallet felt solid in her hand. The last few candy bars had given her enough strength to carry it.

"Hold up," Becky said.

"What?" Shannon asked.

"Andy says this is too easy. Front gate unlocked, front door unlocked. What if David's laid a trap?"

Shannon considered. "I think it's carelessness. The David-thing assumes workers won't come out here on a gorgeous summer night. It doesn't know that I know of David's connection with this place. So why would it bother? Easier for it to come and go this way."

"But should you gamble on that?" Becky asked.

Shannon's lips and jaw tightened. Even if the David-thing had anticipated that Shannon would come, she still must face it.

"I'm ready for it, if it's a trap," Shannon said. *Liar.* She opened the warehouse door. She and Narci peered down a dark hallway and stepped inside.

Dark offices lined each side of the hallway here. They housed the machinery farther along.

She crept a few steps at a time down the hall, using the wall for extra support, stopping to check each office door. All locked. The individual offices used key cards for access, which David, a volunteer at the SQ exhibits, wouldn't carry, so he couldn't hide along the way. Even so, she looked backward every few feet, just in case. *So far so good.* Her nerves brittle, she suspected she'd shatter like glass at the first noise, even if *she* made it.

About half way down the entry hall, another corridor joined hers at a right angle. She could go straight toward the back of building, or turn right.

Narci skittered down the side hall, then back. Shannon cast the lavender. Salesti imaged: someone in one of the rooms on the left side, last door.

Shannon listened.

There. A slight clinking.

Salesti confirmed the occupant: the David-thing.

Tingling fear started at Shannon's fingertips, ran through her veins, vibrated her bones.

She stumbled back toward the front door, until she could whisper into her phone without fear of being overheard.

"I think I found him, but I haven't reached the room yet."

"Jesus, get out. Call the cops."

"No, no cops. The alien could take one over when they try to cuff him. I have to do this myself."

"Then we should come in."

"No, you shouldn't. Here is the critical thing—" Shannon tried to swallow and couldn't, as her fear had grown to the size and shape of an orange in her throat. "If I can't push the alien out of David's body, then the thing may come over to me. You'll need to figure out in the blink of an eye what's happening through the cell phone. I'll try to keep talking. You'll have to do whatever needs to be done."

Becky jumped ahead to the point, of course. "Oh no. No and no. If that thing jumps into your body, are you saying we're supposed to shoot you?"

"Yes, that's exactly what I'm saying. Stay up there and shoot anything that comes out unless you know from the cell phone that it's me and me alone. Ignore my voice. If they've taken over, it won't be me anymore. It'll just be one bastard alien who's murdered me but speaking with my vocal cords. Andy knew Tharm. Tell him this one's worse. He'll do it."

"But if it can use your voice, how can I tell if it's you?"

"I can't use a code, because Drom can steal it. But—talk about something from our deep past. I'll say something back. If the David-thing controls me, it'll have to search. Any pause means I'm gone. Oh, and if worse comes to worst, Narci will carry out Juneau and Essi, my child creature, so take care of them. Salesti will tell you what to do."

"Salesti?"

"Don't worry about it. Just take care of them."

"There's got to be some other way."

"Maybe. But this way presents itself. All I've got." Shannon thought for a minute. "And remember, above all else, Do. Not. Touch whoever comes out. Capisce?"

"I understand. But I hate this. Come get the gun. Just shoot the mother."

"No. I'm going to try to get David out of this."

Becky said something to Andy.

When she didn't get back on the line, Shannon crept back to the hallway intersection and listened for noises down the hall again.

Getting dizzy. She tossed some sugar cubes into her mouth. And some more.

Two minutes and twenty-seven seconds later a chair scraped in the last room, left.

Essi's hum increased. And there, Juneau, stirring, wildness ready to surge, her energy and power with Shannon.

Shannon touched Narci and imaged her plan to Salesti.

Salesti's tiny high buzz responded. Ready and willing.

The tiny creature zipped into her mind. Narci slumped to the floor, exhausted.

Shannon slid off her pack, and flip-tabbed open several cans of cat treats in case the cat awoke.

"I'm going in now," she said into her cell.

Shannon stumbled down the hall. She'd lose her last remaining shred of courage if she stopped.

The open entrance to the room loomed. Another step and she reached it. She breathed deep.

Stepped out.

Turned.

Scanned the room.

The David-thing stood at the sink, dipping a plate into sudsy water. David looked terrible, much worse than the last time Shannon had seen him. Worse than she did.

He'd lost more and more energy to the alien. Bastard Drom. She closed her eyes. The darkness blazed red. Sorrow. Outrage. Fury.

She pushed past the chair the David-thing had vacated; maybe she yelled; she couldn't tell; a rushing sound flooded her hearing.

The David-thing turned. David, the real David, uttered a strange guttural cry. But Drom smiled and pushed the David-thing toward her. He advanced on slow, wobbly legs.

Just before they collided, Shannon brought the mallet around, swung it hard at David's arm and connected. The body's pain would distract them. Smile at that, Drom, you cud bucket.

She flashed images: once David falls and Shannon flows over, Essi stays in Shannon at the point where she'd touched him to keep contact for their quick retreat. Salesti and Juneau would come with Shannon.

Shannon tucked her cell phone into her jacket top, so Becky and Andy could hear everything that happened.

The David-thing kept coming. Shannon threw herself at him.

They crashed back to the sink.

David—so thin!—fell like an anvil. Hit his head.

Unconscious. Shannon pounced on him, rolled her back against a cupboard, and grabbed tight to his wrist.

"We're going over," she said into her phone, and touched her braid once for luck.

Essi ferried Shannon to the tip of her finger, and sent her on. Juneau flowed with her, and little Salesti buzzed into the young man's body.

David's unused brain appeared to her interpreting spirit much the same as Andy's empty cavern.

David's consciousness flickered. Drom, awake and watching, readied himself for attack.

His arrogance hit Shannon first. He expected Shannon, another puny human, and Essi, a child. He intended to kill them without much exertion.

Juneau, the wild fighter, roared.

Drom's first surprise.

Even Shannon didn't expect what came next. Salesti, that tiny creature, *grew*—no better way to describe it. It loomed, a far bigger presence than Shannon or Juneau, full of...of flame. Beautiful, luminescent, terrible in its fierceness.

Shannon, forewarned and forearmed with rage for David, bolstered by Juneau's fierce fighting instinct, and Salesti's giant heat, met Drom head on.

Not what he expected either. Surprise gave them the edge.

Salesti's fire burned Drom; he gave ground.

They pushed him inch by inch toward the edge of oblivion.

When he blocked Salesti's flame, Juneau's wild force rolled him like a crumpled paper in a gust of wind.

When he held the Juneau's force with his own, Shannon's extra rage overpowered him.

Another few inches.

Almost to the edge.

Burn, push, rage.

Drom's arrogance had abandoned him. His desperation palpable, his bewilderment, his disbelief.

All at once another cold force hit Shannon. Blood lust. Chilling, terrifying, merciless. Death stalking, rising from a black abyss.

Salty had awakened.

Shannon and her friends faltered at the first sense of Salty. Drom, shaken, fled to some chamber of David's mind beyond the crocodile. Coward.

To stay meant to die and Salty meant for Shannon to stay. He advanced. Shannon had once seen a croc on TV grasping a zebra in its great jaws and rolling it over and over in a death spiral. Salty would take her just like that.

Salesti surged to Shannon's aid, flame against ice, and held the croc at bay. Juneau blitzed into the reptile's implacable advance.

Not enough.

A terrible pain gripped Shannon and roared through her thoughts. The croc.

"All of you," she said to her team, "Go, get out, take David."

Shannon would stay here. "Get the mallet. Kill it."

She could keep the croc occupied long enough for them to escape.

"Go," she screamed.

But they refused to leave her.

"Please."

They held fast.

The fight left her.

"All right. We'll go together."

Shannon fought the terror that threatened to freeze her in the fatal crocodile lock. She searched for Juneau and, bolstered by those blazing black eyes, she summoned the will to move.

"David," she said, screaming into his mind. "Where are you?"

A weak voice croaked out. "Here."

"Come on, hurry," Shannon said, her voice urgent.

Drom, the rear guard restored, roared; Salty's savage desire blasted the air around her.

She squinted, found the spirit of David, reached out, and grasped him.

She flashed a momentary image of herself retreating and fleeing to her office, as if she still hadn't learned how to keep her thoughts to herself.

She'd planted this image in case the David-thing survived.

"Now."

She, Juneau, and Salesti flowed back to Shannon's body, supporting David, shouting to Essi to let go before Drom and Salty could follow.

Essi turned David's hand loose the moment Salesti crossed over.

Shannon, back in her own body, picked up the mallet, her hands trembling. Smash its head in, do it. *Do it.*

"No, not my body." David's voice rang with anguish. "Let me go back and die if you're going to kill my body."

Hell. She didn't dare touch David's body again to send David back, not with Drom over there seething to get at her. And anyway, she never send him back and *then* take a mallet to him.

She gazed at the body. She couldn't crumple him like a pumpkin as he watched through *her* eyes either.

What should she do? What if she retreated to Narci, sent everyone over to the cat, and let Drom and Salty take her. Andy could shoot her and David could get home to his body later.

Right.

Not right, came the group response.

She pushed the David-thing in the shoulder with the mallet and it fell back, giving Shannon time to struggle to her feet, away from its grasping hands, and out the door. Drom manipulated David's body up a few seconds later and it came stumbling after her.

"Trying to get to the front door," Shannon said, each word panted into her cell phone. "I have David's spirit with me. Drom's chasing us…shoot it…. Hey, remember that time in eighth grade we tried to run away and got lost up in the hills?"

The David-thing's shuffling footsteps sounded behind her, but he moved no faster than she did. A couple of zombies. Not daring to look back, she strained to gauge the thing's progress. Its footsteps sounded closer. *They're pushing his body to its absolute limits. They don't care if they kill him, so long as they reach a fresher body—Shannon's.*

"You sons of bitches," said David, cursing them in her mind.

"Yes I remember when we ran away," Becky said into the phone, her excitement—or was it fear?—evident in her wavering voice. "What did we see up there?"

"Elephants. I'm still in control."

Keep going.

Shannon would shut down soon. Her body's fatigue from the battle weighed on her like the improbable circus elephants they'd run into up in the hills that night so long ago.

Come on. Reach Narci, send these friends to her.

Salesti, look out for them.

She made it to the hall turn. *Yes!*

But Narci's sleeping form had disappeared.

A few cat food cans rolled at her feet as Shannon limped through. The cat had awakened, eaten, and fled.

She reached the door and lurched out into the parking lot, screaming. "It's right behind me." Her weary steps propelled her forward away from the building—and she came to a dead stop.

Andy's jeep sat six feet in front of her. No one in it.

The jeep down here? But Andy—

Shannon spun around.

Andy hugged the building, two feet right of the door, his back to the wall, his head turned toward the entrance. He held his gun pointed upward in his right hand, waiting for the David-thing to come out. Becky stood right behind him, her hands clutching his left arm.

Shannon opened her mouth to say, Are you crazy? Get away.

Too late. She could just make out the David-thing stumbling down the hall from the dark interior.

If the David-thing erupted from the building and caught her staring at Andy, Drom would kill the vet.

Look up the hill, as if they still hid there.

She turned. Detected the David-thing's footsteps clatter along the last few feet of the hallway and burst from the door. Pointed backward toward the door with one hand as she struggled to take another step toward the hill and away from her friends. "Down here, down here, shoot it," she screamed toward the hill. She expected David's frail fingers to clench her shoulder, Drom and Salty to seize her body, and when it happened she would know that she'd failed Essi and Juneau, but not the world, as Andy poured a stream of bullets into her. *Don't look back.* "Shoot them," she screamed again.

Andy howled, full of torment and hate; full of the memory—and the poisonous powder—of Tharm. Shannon spun once more.

The David-thing had taken a step toward Shannon, but at the howl, he turned on Andy like a wolverine cornered.

"Move back," Shannon said. *Didn't he understand the danger?*

Andy stood his ground. But before he could aim and shoot, the David-thing's arm shot forward and grabbed Andy by the gun hand.

"No!" Shannon screamed.

The mallet—still in her hand. She stumbled toward the David-thing, swung the mallet out, up, over, desperate to make him let go of Andy. She hauled the mallet down with both hands.

The David-thing leaned to the side at the last moment. The mallet landed on its shoulder. Mallet and shoulder bone broke with a crack.

As the David-thing fell, Shannon's eyes moved to Andy.

A grin spread across Andy's face.

Drom's grin.

Shannon had reached them a second too late.

She struggled to summon the courage to swing again, this time to kill her friend Andy, caring, goofy, gentle Andy, Becky's Andy.

But before she could move, Andy, shaking, jerking, grunting, pulled the gun to his temple and fired.

He crumpled to the ground next to David.

"No!" This time Shannon and Becky screamed together.

Oh Odin, not Andy. He'd had enough willpower in him to fight that bastard, just like at the fish house. Andy knew Drom would soon push him out of his own head, and struggled with all his might to take Drom down with him. To stop Drom and Salty. To end his own torment.

Shannon knelt and touched David. Coma. Nobody home. Drom and Old Salty hadn't fled back to him. She stared at Andy's ruined head.

Andy dead by his own hand, those awful creatures tormenting him in his last minutes. Becky would never recover from witnessing it. Shannon's heart broke for her. She stumbled toward her friend.

Then she registered the look on Becky's face.

No no no no no. Just as Shannon had taken out David to save Andy a second too late, Andy had shot himself a split-second too late to save Becky.

Shannon reran those last few seconds once more. Andy had put the gun to his head. Becky had grabbed his arm to stop him—and Drom and Salty had fled right on through to her the instant before Andy shot himself.

The Becky-thing stood staring down at Andy. Then she turned to Shannon and laughed.

"Come on, you bastard." Shannon said, wielding the mallet. "Come on over here. Let me beat you to a bloody pulp. I'm begging you."

As if she could bash in her best friend's skull. Not Becky. She couldn't.

And yet everything depended on her. She must do it. She took a step toward Becky and couldn't help looking down at Andy. *Dead. The bullet hole, the blood pooling under him, bits of....* She squeezed her eyes shut. Her grip on the mallet tightened. She had to stop Drom. No matter what it took.

All at once Becky turned and sprinted toward the jeep. Shannon stared after her. *Get Andy's gun. Shoot her.* Drom will make Becky kill, contaminate dozens with his living powder, hundreds, maybe. Enslave them. Suck them dry.

Shoot her.

Shoot.

Shannon grabbed for the gun that had fallen to the pavement next to Andy's body.

No.

She pulled her hand back. Drom might keep Becky as he'd kept David. She couldn't shoot the body if any chance remained that the essence of Becky remained there. Not yet.

Becky jumped in the open door of the jeep, backed up, swung around, floored the gas pedal, fish-tailed, and slammed out of the parking lot.

Shannon's chance had passed.

She should've done it. Of course she should have. Even Becky would've wanted her to.

Shannon's strength deserted her. Once again the battle with an alien had depleted her. She sank to the step beside Andy. Her whole body shook with her sobs.

Andy and Becky. Lost because of her.

Essi?

Essi imaged herself pale and shaking, but nodding and standing by Shannon.

Good job you did there. I knew I could count on you. You too Salesti.

Shannon sent her love to Juneau, who rubbed her in return, a weak rub now, without moving.

Narci rounded the side of the building and padded across the concrete to rub against Shannon as well.

Good to see you, baby.

Salesti imaged its desire to return to Narci. Shannon obliged.

Salesti. Shannon couldn't shake a sense that the tiny alien held more power in reserve. In reserve for what? Why would it hold back?

Salesti?

Silence.

"Shannon, can you hear me? Let me go back to my body," David said into the quiet of her mind.

Shannon looked at David's broken arm, his frail body. He needed a doctor.

"Wait a bit, David. If you go back now, it will hurt like holy hades. I'll get you there before the ambulance leaves."

Shannon felt around in her pocket. At some point she'd dropped her cell phone. She looked around and spotted it a few feet away.

Fortunate. Any farther, forget it.

She gathered some small bits of energy and leaned forward to pick it up. Dialed 9-1-1.

"Hello, this is Shannon Kendricks. I need an ambulance for a badly wounded man here. And I need Detective Chen for a…suicide."

The dispatcher patched her through to Chen.

In a wooden voice she said, "You need to get someone out to the SQ maintenance facility on Otter Bay. Andy Fernando, the SQ vet, has killed himself. David Fielding is here, serious injuries, unconscious, but it turns out he's not the attacker…that's right, not David." She hung up on Chen's questions. He'd sounded furious. *Too bad.*

She dropped the phone and took Andy's lifeless hand. She rocked. Forward…Backward….

…Narci curled in her lap, Shannon stroked her…*Essi.* She hugged the child close…Essi curled up in her lap too….

"Shannon?"

A male voice. Confused, Shannon lifted dull eyes and wondered where…. Oh right. David.

"Hang on. Your body's pretty broken. You don't want that much pain yet." David lapsed back into silence.

…*Andy dead. Becky taken…*

Tears covered Shannon's face like a lace veil. Her hair had come out of its braid and hung in limp strands.

…She rocked…David spoke.

"You know what Drom told me? The sick SOB said he didn't kill me because he…I don't know, he loved me like a son. He told me I reminded him of a woman and child he knew on the cellar door."

"The Selador." Shannon's voice, flat, hollow, corrected him like a robot.

"Right, from a cellar door. My god, I can't even think about it, it makes me so sick."

Great Odin. Shannon imaged, "Drom loved your mother, *Essi?*"

Essi didn't erase the image. Her hum stayed low, quivering, so sad. Shannon could not bear it. She imaged, wrapping the child in her arms, then closed her mind to all sounds. She pulled her pack off her back and ate the last of her candy bars. And rocked….

…. What? Oh. Police sirens. Ambulance coming. She sent David home. His eyes blinked wide for a minute, then rolled up in his head. He'd fainted from the pain….

David had accumulated a raft of living powder from Drom during the alien's long stay with the student. Poor David. That experience would twist him, for sure. Because of the living powder, odds on, he'd never recover. Something else to deal with….

She rocked and rocked.

A pair of strong arms lifted her.

Quintana? She opened her eyes. Not Quintana. A paramedic.

"Please don't let them take me to the hospital," she said in a hoarse whisper, and then she blacked out.

CHAPTER EIGHT

TIME SLIPS AWAY

WHEN SHE CAME TO, she lay in a hospital bed.

Not again.

Dizzy. She waited for her mind to clear. It didn't. Her gaze floated here and there.

Lights in the room dim. Out the window, black velvet.

Walls the color of California sand.

The door stood open. In the hall, the edge of a chair faced away, the edge of a woman sitting in it. Police uniform.

Connected to Shannon's arm, needles and tubes. Glucose drip.

Good thing, the drip, or she'd have gone on to the Big Sleep by now. And Essi and Juneau would've gone with her.

Essi? Juneau?

Essi imaged herself, tired, haunted, still curled in Shannon's lap. Juneau floated beside her.

Shannon hugged them tight.

Shannon's mind raced. *Essi, Narci, the battle, the bodies, Shannon heart-sick, depleted....*

Narci! Shannon struggled into a sitting position. Had anybody noticed her at the SQ warehouse? She pulled her covers away and groped for the call buzzer. *Where had they hidden the thing?*

Her fingers closed on it. She buzzed. And buzzed. With Salesti on board, Narci needed food. If no one had noticed her, she'd die out there. They both would.

The police officer stopped patting the chair arm with her palm to the beat of unknown music, took off her headphones, and leaned into the doorway, still in her chair. She twisted her head to look at Shannon.

"Thought I heard something."

Officer Taney.

The woman stood up and stretched, ambled into the room.

"You're awake. How're you, honey?"

"Please, my cat. I took her out to the SQ warehouse where…where everything happened. She suffers from the, uh, same condition I do. If she doesn't eat, she'll die. Someone has to go get her."

Officer Taney patted Shannon's arm. "Take it easy, honey pie. The cat's fine. Luke Quintana stopped by to see if you'd come around. He told me to tell you he went out to look around at the warehouse and he found the cat and took him home with a 32-pack of turkey and chicken medley cat food. And he stopped by your place to feed your dog."

"Narci's a her," Shannon said, out of habit. "I don't remember Luke coming here."

"Don't you worry about being confused, sugar. You've been through hell, far as I can tell." Taney hesitated. "You know I gotta call Detective Chen now."

Chen. The last person Shannon wanted to see.

Chen would drill her for answers, but he'd refuse to tell her anything about anything. Maybe Taney would spill.

"Do you know how David Fielding's doing? He's here, right?"

"Still in surgery. Arm and shoulder crunched into teeny tiny bits. Said you did it." Taney beamed her approval. "Detective Chen will want to talk to you about that, too, I expect."

Taney must've caught the dismay in Shannon's face, because she added, "But don't worry about it, honey. Fielding refused to press charges. Said you didn't mean anything by it. Uh huh." Taney folded her arms across her chest.

"And you didn't get that from me."

A nurse poked her head in. "Was that you with a heavy finger on the call button?"

Officer Taney answered for Shannon. "Uh huh, I been timing how long it would take you to get here." She tapped her watch with a frown. "Uh huh."

Way to go, Officer Taney.

The nurse bustled to the bed and forced herself between the officer and Shannon. She proceeded to check this and that, ask pertinent and impertinent questions.

Shannon endured.

Taney eased back into the hall to make a call, keeping her voice low.

Shannon had to get out of here, go after Drom. But in her weak condition she'd never escape without help. But who?

Stay awake. Devise an escape plan.... she dozed off. Some time later she awoke, startled. A movement had caught her attention.

Becky?

No, not Becky.

Chen sat by her bed, staring at her.

The detective took out his cell phone, and started working his thumbs, setting up a file, ready to take notes.

"You're awake. What happened out there?"

"Don't beat around the bush, now, Detective. Enough with the niceties. And no, I'm not feeling better. I'm not well at all. Thanks for asking. Oh wait. You didn't."

Chen ignored that. He raised his index finger in the air. "One, we find a dead man, preliminary ruling, suicide—nobody else's prints on the gun, and the angle of the shot looked right. But a damn strange time and place to do it. And you witnessed it."

Two fingers up. "Two, we find David Fielding, his shoulder smashed, by you, he says, but doesn't elaborate. And he insists he didn't kill anybody, despite the fact that we found human remains in his refrigerator. Which you alerted us to."

So. She'd guessed right about Drom's murderous heart. Her stomach lurched.

Three fingers. "And three, we find you out there with the suicide and the murderer, deep in shock. And you also tell me Fielding, who we know did once attack you, and whom you did attack, isn't involved after all. Tell me why I shouldn't book you on charges of murder, accessory to murder, felonious assault and aiding and abetting."

"*Me?* I didn't murder any one. You know that." He knew that. Didn't he?

"I can't assume that," he said. "A week ago if anyone told me I'd suspect you of any crime, I'd have laughed my head off. Not now.

You're mixed up in this somehow, you're in trouble, and you'd better tell me what you know."

Shannon took a quick peek into his images and emotions, to see if he meant to bluff her into talking. *Uh oh.* Not bluffing. Well, she could see his point; she *had* smeared her handprints all over this mess.

Chen leaned toward her. "So, what happened? Why did you all go out there? Why did Fernando off himself? Or did he? Why did you beat Fielding to a bloody pulp? Why did you lie and say he didn't attack you?"

"Back off. One question at a time. Please. And Andy Fernando was my friend. Give him some respect."

He sat back. "Sorry. You're right."

He didn't sound sorry.

"Just tell me what you know," he said.

Shannon assumed a deep-thinking pose for Chen's benefit, but what could she say, since he'd never believe the truth? She couldn't think. Her quick wit had frozen, silent and barren as tundra.

When Chen started to speak again, she stopped him and said, "I knew that David once worked at the SQ warehouse, so I went out there to look for him, and Andy went with me."

"It didn't occur to you to let *the police* check out the warehouse?"

"You'd been questioning everybody. I assumed you already knew about the place. I thought you might already be out there." Shannon said, pleased when Chen flinched at that little barb.

"Anyway, Andy hadn't been himself this week. Ask anybody who works with him. Something had happened to him. So, out there, he tried to shoot David because David came after me. Then he realized that the *stranger* had made David do it, and, um," skipping a tiny bit here, "I, well, almost shooting somebody innocent like that, Andy thought he might endanger to other people."

Andy had tried so hard. The tears huddled at the tips of her eyes. If the gods possessed hearts, Andy had died believing he'd killed Drom and saved his sweetheart.

Chen said, "Is Fielding telling the truth? Did you pound him with a mallet?"

Uh oh. Shannon lowered her eyes and issued a dramatic sigh. "Yes. I thought he meant to kill me."

"Why?"

"Because he ran at me."

"He ran at you? Attacked you? *Again*?"

"Well, yes. But the stranger made him."

Chen through up his hands. "You keep mentioning some stranger. Who the hell are you talking about?"

"Right. After Andy—after everything happened at the warehouse, the stranger ran away." Sketchy but true. Missing some details. Okay, misleading.

Chen lowered his phone onto his lap. "You're saying some stranger kidnapped David and took him out to the Otter Bay facility? The same person who attacked you?"

"I am." Although Drom qualified as a "person" only in the loosest sense.

"Responsible for the human remains we found in Fielding's freezer?"

"I expect so."

"Do you know him? Description?" Chen asked, lifting his cell again, to type in her answer.

"Tall, thin, sick-looking. Long, dark hair, but scraggly. That's the best I can do."

Dr. Bennett breezed in the door.

"I think that's enough for now, Sergeant," the doctor said, holding out her hand. "I'm Doctor Bennett and you are?"

"*Detective* Chen. I have a few more questions for Ms. Kendricks and then I'll go."

"I'm sorry, but the questions will have to wait." Dr. Bennett flicked her hands at him and shooed as if sending off an aggressive goose.

Chen scowled and said to Shannon, "All right, but I'll come back as soon as the doc says it's okay."

"Detective Chen?" Shannon said as he stamped across the room. "Keep a close eye on David. Being forced to do the dirty work for that killer, he's messed up. *Very* messed up. He'll need some serious help."

Chen's lips tightened. "I'll take care of it."

Shannon watched his stiff back depart. Straight-arrow, super lawyer Shannon Kendricks, now a murder suspect.

Essi picked up Shannon's humiliation and resulting distress, and Shannon soon sensed the little girl's own distress.

Never mind, Essi. Protecting you and this whole damn planet are plenty worth a smudge on the old reputation.

"How do you feel?" Dr. Bennett asked, pointing a light into Shannon's eyes.

"Good enough to go home," she said. *Lie.*

"You're in police custody, as I understand it," Dr. Bennett said. "Might as well stay here, where staff can take care of you."

While Dr. B. checked her over, Shannon eyed the physician. *She could help Shannon get out of here. Time to tell her the whole story.*

So Shannon did.

Dr. Bennett laid her hand on Shannon's shoulder. "I know what you're telling me seems real to you. You've experienced it. All vivid and solid. But these are side effects of the condition you've contracted, I'm afraid. Hallucinations of the most convincing kind. But nevertheless hallucinations."

Shannon folded her arms across her chest.

Careful now. No more strolling down memory lane like the fiasco with Chen. "Think of an animal, any animal and picture it," Shannon said, and watched as Dr. Bennett pictured and discarded several before she settled on a giraffe.

"Ok I—" Dr. Bennett began.

"Giraffe. You rejected a horse, dog, cow and elephant before you settled on the giraffe."

Dr. Bennett showed no outward sign, but Shannon felt the cold edge of uncertainty and unease that sliced along the doctor's neck.

"Good guess," she said.

"Not a guess," Shannon said. "Try something harder."

A microscopic thingy appeared in Dr. B's mind.

"Good lord, you don't think I know what *that* is, do you? I dropped out of Microbiology to take a Pre-Law Tort Class." Shannon looked it over. "Let's see. It's shaped like a 3-D triangle, purselike, it has three or four tentacles coming out of the middle of it, it's transparent and something is going on in the center there but I can't quite make it out."

"Yes," Dr. Bennett said in a voice so soft and unsteady that Shannon strained to hear it, "Very good. Giardia lamblia, a flagellated protozoan parasite."

And just like that, Dr. Bennett believed her; Shannon could see it in the physician's bright eyes, the pink flush of her cheeks, the way her hands fiddled with the hem of her white coat. *Quite a surprise.* Rational, logical, no nonsense Dr. Bennett, so quick to accept an alien child and a whale inside a human mind, aliens here to conquer the world.

Shannon's story would at least help the doc understand Shannon's mysterious rapid deterioration and how to fix it. Perhaps Dr. Bennett had been eager to accept any explanation for the inexplicable.

"I understand your desire to track this alien down. But first things first. I'm going to give you a shot and medication to boost your system."

Shannon downed the prescribed pills and endured the shot. Afterward, the doctor pulled up a chair, sat on the edge of her seat, and came around to the elephant in the room—the doc's overwhelming desire to confirm Essi's existence.

"Just give me a tiny glimpse of it," Dr. Bennet said, her eyes pleading. "A chance to know for certain that other sentient species exist in the universe. Just think of it!"

Oh yeah, Shannon thought of it, all right. All the time.

What do you think, Essi? A brief foray into her head?

Essi left Shannon's image standing.

"Take my hand," Shannon said. "Essi wants to meet you, and I want to talk with you about a jail bust."

* * *

Dr. Bennet grappled for a minute or two with her obligations as a law-abiding citizen and her worry over Shannon, but scientific curiosity and her duty to the world won out. While Shannon changed into her clothes, Essi and Juneau spent time in Dr. B.'s mind.

When they'd prepared for Shannon's needs, Shannon shuffled into the hall, leaning on Dr. B.'s arm, still attached to the glucose drip. Or so it seemed.

Officer Taney stood up and threw her newspaper on her chair.

"Now where do you think you're going?" Her hands went to her hips.

Dr. Bennett smiled at her, but her voice rippled with authority.

"Shannon must get up and walk, so her strength will return and her mind will clear. I insist."

Officer Taney hesitated but, eyeing the pole and glucose drip line that tethered Shannon, she let them pass, sat down, and watched them from her chair, her palm patting out a staccato beat on the chair.

They made their way, unhurried, to the end of the hall and turned left toward the elevators, and out of Taney's sight.

Then they flew into action.

Dr. Bennett grabbed Shannon's sandals out from under her white coat and removed the needle of the drip line from her shirt sleeve, where Dr. Bennett had taped it after removing it from Shannon's arm earlier. Shannon pulled off her hospital socks, stripped off the hospital gown and strapped on the shoes. They'd hung her backpack on a bar on the drip rack. She grabbed it, flipped her braid to her back, and turned to give Dr. Bennett a hug.

Dr. Bennett's face lit up in surprise.

"You're the best," Shannon said. "I'll insist on my deathbed that you knew nothing. Thanks so much."

"I experienced Essi, that's enough. Now go."

Shannon stepped into the elevator and pushed the down button. Still weak, woozy, she sagged against the elevator wall.

"Good luck," Dr. Bennett said as the elevator doors closed. The doc would give Shannon five minutes, amble back to Shannon's room, tell Taney that her patient needed kleenex, amble back, then shout for the officer from the elevator lobby, kleenex gripped to her heart.

Taney would go wild, and so would Chen, when they discovered Shannon had slipped away again. But Chen would never succeed in browbeating Dr. B. into changing her story she'd been duped and horrified, just like Taney.

Shannon moved from the elevator to the lobby, and out into the harsh light of the parking lot.

Now for the tricky part.

Chen would figure she couldn't get far on foot; he'd seen her thin arms, listened to her weak voice. He might waste some time calling her friends. But he wouldn't expect her to know the bus routes, and he'd be right about this area around St. James—she didn't know it well. However, she'd long ago downloaded the local transit app onto her cell phone, and she pulled up the information as she moved into the shadows.

The detective might figure she'd aim for home or the Dickson. So instead, she hiked two blocks north and boarded a bus traveling up the coast, headed for Bay City, twenty miles up the highway.

Picking a stop in Bay City at random, she climbed down, sat in a bramble of bushes, and dialed Quintana. Squeezed her braid with her free hand, curled her knees to her chest, waited for him to answer.

When David had first come after her with Drom and Salty on board, she'd run to the police, at a terrible risk to them. Today, she'd tried to face Drom again, and Andy had died and Becky had landed in terrible trouble. Next time she'd get it done or die trying.

*   *   *

Luke had been kind to rescue Narci out at Otter Bay and take care of Indy. But what she had in mind now? Odds on, he'd run screaming when she told him. Still, she could think of no one else.

His voice came on the line. "Quintana's Pizzeria," he said. "Today's feature, cheesy jalapeño crust. Refried beans on every slice."

She gulped, then her words raced out of her mouth like hounds to the fox. "It's Shannon. I know I'm still not high on your list and I expect you know what happened at the SQ warehouse and yes, Chen wants to question me, but I…I need your help. I've got to stop Drom and Old Salty, and I've got to do it tonight while I still can." She gripped the phone as if she had his arm and didn't plan to let go until he agreed. She stopped breathing. Her muscles clenched her arms and legs close to her body, like an unborn baby.

Everything depended on his help.

Everything. It had come to that.

And worse, she needed help from others, too. For the first time in her life, she faced something she couldn't do alone. She needed a team: Salesti, Narci, Essi, Juneau, Luke, and Indy. She held the tip of her tight braid in the palm of her hand. *A beautiful, firm braid. It had grown longer and thicker by the hour.*

Silence on the line.

Then Luke said, "Chen wants to question you?"

She shouldn't have told him. "Well, I may have misunderstood Chen. In fact I think I did." *Bad, bad Shannon.*

"Shannon."

"Or maybe he said he planned to arrest me on suspicion of murder, accessory and other crimes," Shannon said in a rush.

"Drom's the alien, right? And Salty is who?"

"Oh, sorry. He came from the Brackish Water Center at SQ. Old Salty. A salt water crocodile. Frightening thing."

"A crocodile is running around loose?"

"No, he's in Becky's mind with Drom."

"In *Becky's* mind? You said David before."

"Right. Out at the warehouse, they moved from David to Andy to her."

"I'm sorry about Andy. I caught it on the police radio." As if his mind had just now caught up, he said, "You say the croc's in Becky's head?"

"Yes, its spirit. Like Juneau and Essi in mine."

"Essi, the child alien." Silence. "Listen, how did it go down at the warehouse? A man died out there, and someone beat the hell out of another guy. You need to tell me what kind of trouble you're in. The truth. Does this have something to do with the gambling debt? Loan sharks?" He hesitated for a moment. "Drugs?"

Eye of Odin. Shannon the drug addict, gambling to support her habit. Shannon grasped her face with her free hand. Of course he'd think that—her confusion, apparent delusions, weight loss, hunger. Murder and mayhem. It made perfect sense.

Shannon described the terrible events at the warehouse, but held out little hope he'd buy her story.

"The, uh, version I gave Chen may've led him to think something slightly different happened, and I, um, I may not have mentioned Becky to him. I've got to get Drom and Salty out of Becky's mind so no one shoots her. And so Drom doesn't force her to kill." Shannon's voice quavered.

An image from Essi: the child flows through Shannon's hand to Luke's hand, and to his mind for a visit, just as she visited Dr. Bennett.

Well. On the one hand, that would prove her story all right. *Should she offer?* On the other hand, if Essi visited Luke, he'd become vulnerable to Drom while she stayed there. Shannon had not worried about Essi's quick trip to Dr. Bennett, with her door guarded and the Becky-thing in hiding, planning its next move. The more time that elapsed now, though, the higher the danger that Drom would come looking for her.

"So, you're telling me I should watch what I say to Chen?" Luke's voice sounded more and more tense. He didn't like this business. And who could blame him? He could lose his job if he stuck with Shannon long enough. *And right there, another reason to avoid entangling him more.* She wouldn't do it.

"Uh. I feel like you don't believe anything I'm telling you. What if I send Essi to see you when you come pick me up?" And there lay the crux of the matter. She longed for him to believe her, to have faith in her, no matter what. *Bad move.*

A sigh whispered through the airwaves.

"No, I think not. Thanks anyway."

So, did he turn her down because he didn't believe her and didn't want to tell her that no little aliens had come for a visit? Or because he did believe her and didn't want proof that he shouldn't believe her? Or he didn't want an alien creeping around in his skull? Or…. Once again, all bad options.

"Aren't you supposed to be in the hospital?"

"Well, yes, but I left. Well, escaped, you might say. Chen will say."

More silence. A lot of gaps in this conversation.

"What's your plan?"

She explained that too.

"Shannon," he said. Then stopped. "Chen…I can't…I don't…oh hell. I'll pick you up in thirty minutes. Give me your location."

Shannon read Luke the cross streets. While she waited for him, she cast the lavender back to the hospital to David so she could make sure their stories would line up. Could she reach that far? Communicate with someone in surgery?

Just as she turned her attention to David, she spotted a police car cruising the street. She tucked further into the shadows.

Be the bush.

Be the bush.

Ye gods, they drove in slow motion.

The light turned red and they idled not fifty feet from her for two excruciating minutes. Shannon held her breath, struggling to remain motionless.

The light changed and they moved on.

Okay. *Concentrate. David…Yes, there.* He'd come out of surgery but hadn't recovered from the anesthetic.

She watched his images—or rather nightmares. *Drom invades. Killings. The warehouse. Their fight. Shannon whacks him with the mallet. Andy. The police. Drom. Salty. Shannon takes him to her mind.* Faster and faster the images came. *He returns to his body—*

Then his shriek.

CHAPTER NINE

OUT OF TIME

DAVID'S PAIN, unbearable and searing-hot, struck her like a flaming spear.

Shannon yanked the lavender back, covered her ears, her eyes closed tight.

But after a time, she tried again.

All quiet.

She told David the story she'd told Chen. *Remember all this, David, when you wake up and Chen pounces on you.*

Debris on the ground where she huddled chafed her. She shifted about in the bushes.

Hurry up, Luke.

* * *

He came bearing groceries, Indy, and Narci.

Shannon struggled out from under the bush and into the car, hugged Indy, and wiggled her fingers into Narci's kennel. She caught Salesti's happy buzz. Narci purred. Indy slurped her face.

Luke had taken good care of them. She turned to thank him, but swallowed her words. His face looked hard and stiff. Grim.

Without taking his eyes off the road, and without a word, he handed over an ice cream cone. Chocoholic Double Diablo. Her favorite.

He sniffed. "Just checking."

Ah, the perfume.

Neither of them spoke.

Awkward.

All the way to her office, Shannon stuffed herself with high energy food that Luke had packed in a hurry.

A shower of doubt drenched her *She should go home. Think of some other way.* Because if she proceeded, her plan would add Indy to the group already in a world of danger. She cried. Again. She hugged her big mastiff hard. "I love you, baby. I'd never ask you to do this if I could think of any other way."

Indy slurped away her tears.

They arrived downtown, drove past the Mannheim Building to check for police cars, then parked several blocks away. Luke crept closer to see if the police had staked out the building or if Becky hid nearby. Shannon had dropped the thought of her office in Drom's presence at the warehouse so he would expect Shannon to go there tonight. The Becky-thing would come.

She caught a flash of silver yellow out of the corner of her eye, leaned sideways out the window, and looked into the sky. The wind had brought dark clouds, but the clouds hadn't brought rain. Instead streaks of lightning flashed cloud to cloud, one after another. On another day, Shannon would've watched for hours, fascinated, delighted. But not tonight. *Maybe never again.* She drew back in the car.

When they'd driven by her building before, a homeless guy lying on a bench at the bus stop one door down from the Mannheim had caught her attention. He slept, or pretended to, within easy view of the Mannheim lobby entrance. The homeless didn't hang out on this block. The police moved them along; the current City Council didn't care to view the persistent, as-yet unsolved issue of homelessness on its own doorstep.

Luke returned and hopped in. "Undercover cop decked out as a homeless guy on the bench in front of the Mannheim Building," he said. "Nobody else."

They'd go around the block to the Mannheim Parking Garage, then. Shannon directed Luke there and pulled her gate card from the glove box. The big metal door rumbled up, and they drove down the ramp to Level C.

No cars remained parked here in the earliest hours of Saturday morning. But if Chen had stationed someone outside, he might've assigned someone to watch the security cameras that guarded the parking garage.

Shannon could not let the police catch her here. It would ruin everything.

She pointed the cameras out to Luke, who studied the lens angles.

Shannon's eyes strained to see into the shadows. Becky had no way to gain access to the garage. Still….

"We're good," he said, and climbed out of the car. "Come with me." Shannon opened the back door for Indy to jump out and pulled out Narci's kennel. They stayed close to the wall that formed the outside of the elevator bank and moved forward.

"We're good?"

"The camera above the elevator door faces too far outward. They'll catch most people, because they stand a bit back from the elevator to avoid being run down by the crowd getting off. But if we hug the wall next to the elevator doors and slip in, the camera won't record us."

He turned, faced the wall, and inched over to punch the up button. They waited.

In the name of Odin, could the blasted elevator move any slower?

A motor creaked, a bell dinged, and the elevator door slid open. Luke slipped across and in, inches from the wall all the way. He held the door with his foot, and reached for Indy's collar as Shannon guided the dog's back end along the wall. Shannon edged her way back for the cat and stepped forward. Sweat dripped down her back.

She must not get caught now.

"No good," Luke said, thrusting his arm back to stop Shannon's advance. She froze.

"The kennel's too wide. Leave it."

Shannon lifted Narci and held her close as they inched along to the elevator.

They'd made it. Shannon slid her office card into the slot and the elevator jerked upward.

She relaxed.

"This should take us to my floor without stopping," she said.

The elevator jerked again, and came to an abrupt stop. They looked at the digital read-out. The lobby. The doors slid open.

Was Becky waiting on the other side, a huge axe in her hand, ready to chop her former friend into small pieces of otter food?

Before Shannon could cast the lavender, the doors swung wide. No Becky. Shannon could see a side view of the night security guard at the information desk straight in front of them. Mr. Sanchez-Mendoza. His monitors glowed, ten or so bright little television windows. But, like night guards everywhere, he ignored the monitors. A book lay open on his lap, he kept his eyes on the pages, reaching now and then for a potato chip in a large red bowl and sipping from a diet ginger ale.

Chen might've given Mr. Sanchez-Mendoza orders to call if he spotted Shannon. And if Chen caught Luke here.... The cat lay still in Shannon's arms, Indy closed her panting mouth. No one moved an inch, as still as a photograph.

When no one departed from the elevator, Sanchez-Mendoza glanced up. Luke leaned out and gave the guard a confident wave and flipped open his badge.

"Ocean City Police. Have you seen a Ms. Shannon Kendricks in the building tonight?"

Sanchez-Mendoza took a good look at the badge and, satisfied, shook his head. "No, but I don't always see her come in. You want to check upstairs? You know where her office is?"

"Sure do. Thanks."

No one had clued Mr. Sanchez-Mendoza in. *Good.*

Luke shot his hand out for the button that shut the door again.

The door closed and the elevator resumed its upward journey. Everyone let out a breath. Luke raised his eyebrows.

"Not sure why it opened," Shannon said in a whisper. "I haven't come in to the office this late in a while; maybe it always opens at the Lobby now."

At last the chimes signaled Shannon's floor, the main level dedicated to the County Legal Office. They moved in a tight group into the unlit hall. She groped along the wall to the end of the hall, used her card key to open the office door, and flicked the light switches. Lights would go unnoticed at this end of the building, which looked out onto an alley.

Shannon plunged into the cooler for another snack and thought about the security guard. If Chen had alerted him to report Shannon's appearance, he would have looked up at the chime of the elevator doors opening. Good. The security guard didn't know Shannon was on the lam. She could continue with her plan. Still, good thing Mr. Sanchez-Mendoza hadn't spotted her.

She picked up the receptionist's phone and called the security desk.

"Hello? Mr. Sanchez-Mendoza? Shannon Kendricks. I'm expecting a…a notary any minute. Could you let her in? I'd appreciate not having to come all the way down there to get her."

"Ms. Kendricks. What're you doing here at this hour on a Friday night? That's crazy," Sanchez-Mendoza said.

Shannon cleared her throat. "You're telling me. In fact, don't tell me, tell Matt Portman. I'm preparing for *his* meeting tomorrow morning." Shannon wished she could see the stink-eye Mr. Sanchez-Mendoza laid on Portman on Monday.

"I'll let the notary in, Ms. Kendricks. Hope you get outta here soon. Oh, and did you see that policeman who was looking for you?"

"Yes, yes I did. Thanks, Mr. Sanchez-Mendoza." Shannon hung up the phone.

"A notary?" Luke asked, smiling.

Shannon crinkled her eyes in mock anger and perched on the receptionist's desk.

So far so good. She opened a bag of frozen burritos. Frozen, cooked, all the same to her. She started to unwrap one. Luke set down a peanut butter jar he'd just opened and took the burrito bag.

"Microwave?"

Shannon pointed to the lunch room, down to the left, then dipped into the peanut butter with a knife.

The Becky-thing should arrive any minute. *Please Odin, tell her Drom hadn't pushed Becky out.* Shannon closed her eyes and rubbed her forehead. The Becky-thing would attack Shannon. Could she fight a monster with Becky's familiar smile, her eyes, her voice?

Luke returned with the burritos.

"I won't fight Becky," she said, picking up a burrito with a napkin. "I will not, unless Drom's already killed her spirit. And even then, it still looks like her. Not sure I could hurt it."

Luke's face grew hard, his mouth grim. "You shouldn't have to fight your friend. Let me do it, if it comes to that. Whatever happens, don't question yourself, Shannon, and don't question me. If we hesitate, we'll die. Your dog and cat. The little girl in your head. A lot of other people. And if Becky's not gone already, and we hesitate, she'll die anyway. And you know she'll suffer hell first."

"But, I have to take care with her body. Respect her life. Look for the best choice, or the kindest of the bad choices." She believed what she'd said, solid as a stone. A round smooth stone to touch in the dark.

He gave her a tired, sad smile. "I like that about you. But at some point, the time for deliberation, taking care, as you say, passes. A split-second of delay could mean more murder, further spread of—what did you call it?—that destructive powder from Drom and the croc. We can't risk it."

"All right," Shannon said, her voice louder than she'd intended, "I don't need you to remind me. But I won't throw Becky away unless I can't think of any other way."

Luke didn't respond.

They reviewed the plan again.

A long, long long-shot.

"You realize," she said, "that if we can't push Drom and Old Salty out of Becky's head, and some of us can't get out of the Becky-thing's mind, you'll have to kill it anyway."

He said nothing. He didn't nod.

She ate in silence, he fed sandwiches to the dog.

"Why here?" Luke asked after a minute, leaning on the reception desk. "Why here for the showdown?

Shannon paused. "I guess because I wouldn't endanger anybody else. I know the layout. Becky doesn't. Other stuff." Shannon hadn't taken time to wonder about her choice. Why *had* she chosen her office—her former office? *Some sort of bitter subconscious revenge against Portman?*

No. In some unstated, hazy way, she'd figured that since her career had ended in this office already, her life might as well also end in the place. Fitting somehow. Loki be damned. *How had her unhappy career in this office come to equal her life?*

She glanced down to the right toward Jane's cubicle. Shannon might never see her paralegal again. What had she said to Jane the last time she talked to her? Something mundane.

Shannon pulled a yellow legal pad off a stack on the receptionist's back file cabinet, a pen from the tin of writing implements, and settled down at the front desk to write a note to Jane and to watch for any sign of the Becky-thing.

Motion caught her eye. Narci barreled down the right-hand hallway. No doubt her little blue-eyed feline wanted the cat food that sat at Shannon's feet. Shannon bent to her note again, but Narci jumped right onto the desk, pattered across to Shannon, leaped onto her shoulder, and sunk her long claws into the thin fabric of Shannon's T-shirt.

"Ow," Shannon said. "What's the matter with—"

She looked to Luke with wide eyes. He understood.

With the cat connected to Shannon's shoulder, Shannon saw Salesti's image without difficulty: the Becky-thing had arrived.

So, Mr. Sanchez-Mendoza had waived Becky through, as planned. The Becky-thing might suspect a trap now, but its Drom-fed arrogance and Old Salty prey drive would propel it toward Shannon anyway.

Luke lifted the cat off Shannon and set Narci on the desk, stroking her to keep her still.

Leaning back into the couch cushions, Shannon cast the lavender. Salesti's images formed.

Salesti shows the Becky-thing peek through a door that leads to the stairwell on the near side of elevator lobby. Becky eases the stairwell door closed. Sneaks across to the conference room at the opposite end of the lobby from the Legal Office door. Wraps her hand with a towel, pushes out the glass. Reaches in, unlocks the door. Slips into the conference room and disappears.

The conference room connected with the Legal Office by way of a second door.

Narci and Salesti watch Becky fiddle with the second door's lock and enter the Legal Office right-hand hallway. Then the cat runs hell bent for leather back to Shannon.

Without a word to Luke, Shannon jabbed her finger several times down the dark hallway Narci had fled.

She cast the lavender into the dark, looking for the Becky-thing. *There.*

Shannon concentrated. Her scalp prickled.

Becky's body crouched waiting in an office two doors down from Shannon's own. Becky's images: running shoes motionless in the thick carpet, back stiff, in her hand, a knife, long, sharp, curved, as cruel as a guillotine.

Drom can see Shannon, now, right? Shannon imaged to Essi. Image erased.

New image: *Drom doesn't see Shannon, doesn't cast a black haze.*

Why? The same thing had happened with David—Drom hadn't seen Shannon's images and emotions at the Dickson reception.

Essi: Shannon casts the lavender over the crowd at the Dickson reception. Drom tries to cast his black, but it falls to the floor and dissipates. Essi's friend Toss tries to cast his turquoise and he fails too.

Only Essi and Shannon could cast?

Essi shows her mother casting a deep lavender haze out over a crowd. Then someone older, Essi's grandmother, perhaps, casts an even deeper midnight purple.

Hereditary then. *Ah.* Drom would also covet Essi so she could cast for him. Tharm had lied. Not that Shannon could cast the first stone.

Shannon said out loud for the Becky-thing's benefit, "Let's go wait in my office." Shannon took off at a measured, unhurried pace down the hall, thumping her hand against the wall as she proceeded, drumming an offhanded beat. Luke, Indy, and Narci followed.

When the group had trooped into her office, she flipped on her desk lamp, closed the door ,and leaned against it, as if she could keep that thing out if she didn't move a muscle.

Her heart, along with her head, pounded. Even though Shannon was well-fed, the hospital escape, the wait for Luke, the trip here had taken their toll. *Not much energy left.* But this job required mental strength. She'd made a living out of mental strength. When the time came, she'd pull it from every pore in her body. She'd burst with it.

Becky opened the door of the office where she'd waited.

Shannon listened for Essi's hum. The child did her best to send out a calm, brave signal. Shannon imaged wrapping her arms around the child and kissing her forehead.

Becky stepped into the hall, her knife raised in front of her.

Shannon caught another image: Juneau lifts her head, and a rush of wind, like a night sea storm, surrounds Shannon. Juneau, her wild one, ready to fight. Shannon imaged rubbing the whale's smooth, white back.

Becky crept toward Shannon's door.

They expected the Becky-thing to attack at full speed. Shannon would charge at the same instant. Like two rams butting heads, like two armies meeting on an ancient battlefield, axe to axe, sword to sword.

Shannon popped yet more sugar cubes, more candy into her mouth.

The Becky-thing stopped just outside Shannon's door.

Shannon stopped chewing and touched her braid for luck.

*   *   *

"It's time," Shannon said, her voice low, and gave Indy the signal to lay down. She placed her hand on Indy's head. Then she touched Narci. Salesti flowed from the cat, through Shannon, and over to Indy where it secured Indy's spirit and brought her to Shannon. Once again Narci slumped, exhausted.

She could feel the dog's presence, sweet, loving, loyal, yet with a wild ferocity hovering in the background, much like Juneau's. But where Juneau was born and bred wild and would ever be so, Indy had been born tame and tethered to Shannon by her millennia-bred nature and six years of love and care. Shannon could sense the dog's bewilderment, and Essi's gentle thrumming, calming Indy, as she so often calmed Shannon and Juneau.

Shannon imaged in a quick flash, conveying her plan to Juneau, Salesti, Indy, and Essi: Essi stays out of harm's way, avoiding Drom and the croc. The child locates Becky, takes her to Shannon's mind for shelter. Indy stays safe by following Shannon's commands. The dog barks and growls, pushes at the two invaders when Shannon and company push, but Indy *will not* attack either of those beasts alone under any circumstance. Indy backs off at Shannon's command.

All the while, Shannon's eyes focused on the door knob.

It twisted.

Nothing else existed but that twisting knob.

Luke grabbed her wrist. "Essi, change of plans. Bring me over."

Shannon, her mind on the door knob, reacted a fraction too late. Essi pulled Luke in; his body collapsed.

"Hey, I can smell the perfume even in here," Luke said inside her mind.

"Oh no, Mister," she said, "You will head straight—"

The door burst open and slammed against the far wall. The Becky-thing paused a moment, a black silhouette holding a long curved blade against the light behind her, then took a step into the glow of Shannon's desk lamp, its eyes full of hate, arrogance and anticipation.

Not Becky's eyes.

As Shannon prepared to ram the Becky-thing, a voice shouted down the hall.

"Hey, you, what're you doing there?"

The Becky-thing turned.

Someone in the office at this time of night? No way.

"You get your pretty little ass down here right now, young lady."

Portman. *Why in Odin's name had he come here at this ungodly hour?* He'd ruin everything.

The Becky-thing started back toward Shannon's boss.

Shannon stumbled to her office door. "Matt, run, she's a psycho, she's armed, she'll kill you."

Portman had been striding down the hall toward them. He halted at Shannon's words—and at the sight of that huge, curved knife.

Shannon leaned on the door jamb, her eyes on the Becky-thing, her body weakening. *So soon?*

The Becky-thing leaned toward Portman, her expression intense, feral, predatory.

Portman leaned back, his mouth a wide O.

But his face scrunched itself into indignant haughtiness and he started forward again.

"You, I want you out of my office now," he said in his best booming courtroom voice, stretching a pudgy arm forward and pointing a pudgy finger at the Becky-thing.

"Listen to me," Shannon said. "Don't come down here."

The Becky-thing charged Portman. Old Salty. Pure prey drive. Seek and destroy.

Shannon screamed at him "Matt!"

Move! Go after the creature.

Her feet refused. So tired.

From within her mind Luke said, "Go, Shannon."

As if he'd shoved her, Shannon took off, wobbling her way along the wall. But the Becky-thing had gained on Portman.

Portman's bravado melted in the face of the blade; he turned, charged into the reception area, threw open the office door and escaped out into the elevator hallway.

Then he pushed the elevator down button and waited for the door to open.

Idiot.

"The stairs, Matt," Shannon said, closing on the Becky-thing inside the office door.

"Come on, come on," he said, muttering to himself.

The Becky-thing slammed into him. He fended her off as well as he could, but her long curved knife slashed at his loose suit jacket again and again.

"No," Shannon said to no one in particular, as she reached the two grappling figures, grabbed the Becky-thing by the arm and yanked it up and off with all the strength she could muster. Good thing Becky, already petite, had kept herself trim and slim. The thing stumbled away and fell.

Portman lay still, red blood spreading out on the carpet. Shannon crouched beside him. *Stop the bleeding. Think. Use his jacket.* She slid it over his arms and head and bunched it up.

Before she could locate the worst of the wounds, the Becky-thing began scrabbling back toward them along the floor, a growling sound coming from deep in its throat. Blood lust.

Shannon kicked at her. The Becky-thing sprang to her feet, the knife in her hand; she backed up two steps, then charged. Shannon pushed herself up and away from Portman. She turned sideways to avoid the knife, but the move sent the Becky-thing's body on a collision course with hers. It rammed into her, the knife slicing open her left hand, and the two sprawled together on the floor.

The Becky-thing landed on its stomach, Shannon on top of her.

Move inside Becky's consciousness and take Drom and Salty unaware. Now!
Gathering herself, Shannon shouted the command. "Essi, now!"

Sprawled on top of her friend, Shannon grabbed the Becky-thing by the arm. All of them—Essi, Shannon, Juneau, Luke, Indy, and Salesti—raced over into Becky's mind, and landed in her cavern, her unused brain space.

Essi veered off in search of Becky's spirit.

Drom held back, behind Salty. A coward as usual, he counted on the croc to take care of these paltry but troublesome visitors.

Salty laid in wait, awake and active in Becky's mind. Shannon called to Juneau and Indy with images. *Block Salty, hold him at bay while we deal with Drom. Take extreme care.* Juneau's wild ferocity and Indy's instinct to protect at all costs would make the croc hesitate.

Salty didn't cooperate. Or hesitate. He ignored the challenge in Juneau's clacking jaws, in Indy's deep growl and headed straight for Shannon.

Indy charged between Shannon and Salty with a vicious snarl, then sprang at the crocodile.

"Indy, no, come. Come to me," Shannon said, commanding the dog to obey. Shannon's voice and hand signal meant "right now or else, Independence." Indy had never disobeyed her after the "and I mean NOW" command.

Until now.

Huge mastiff jaws clamped onto the crocodile's throat. Salty's long jaws locked on Indy's chest. Juneau whacked, battered him with her powerful fluke. But the pair, locked in a death grip, rolled over and over, nearer and nearer to the edge of Becky's mind.

Shannon searched for a way, any way, to help Indy.

Salesti, who'd been fighting Drom with Luke, flashed toward them, but the crocodile shook Indy off and slithered after Shannon once more. With a growl like a jet engine, sounding of fury and courage, Indy, bleeding from her chest, glanced for one moment at Shannon, her golden, intelligent, loving eyes full of knowing, and flung herself back in front of the croc, grasped its head in her huge iron jaws and threw herself out of Becky's head, hauling Salty with her.

"Indy, no!" Shannon's voice broke. She would have followed her mastiff out into eternity if Juneau had not blocked her way. Luke wrapped his arms around her chest and held her tight.

"Let go," Shannon said, struggling against Luke's hold.

Before Luke could reply, Drom's roar filled Becky's cavern. He rose before them, much larger than before, five times the size of an ordinary man, radiating much more power than before. Without Salty's grip on him, his power bloomed like a nuclear mushroom cloud. The stench of the sewer overwhelmed them, choking their throats and stinging their eyes. Although it seemed impossible, their feet sank in swampy quicksand.

Juneau, Shannon's wild ferocious sea creature, swam up beside her.

Meanwhile Essi's search for Becky had succeeded. She sparked past them, ferrying Becky's spirit. Becky trembled and tossed back and forth with pain and madness. Essi carried her back, through Shannon's body into the quiet, safe recesses of Shannon's mind.

Essi. So brave and competent. How far that little punkin had come since she'd landed in Shannon's mind a week ago.

But the swamp. Drom loomed over them. Shannon couldn't breathe. Juneau, swimming in water that wasn't there, maneuvered between the two human figures and Drom. Her powerful fluke slashed across Drom's face and he grabbed his eye, bellowing in pain. The whale flashed back down and floated in front of Shannon.

Shannon grabbed Juneau's fluke and the whale heaved. Nothing. Juneau heaved again. Shannon's feet came clear of the swamp.

Wait a second. What had Andy said about Tharm? The alien influenced emotions; don't listen to her, he'd said.

Of course. If Juneau could float through this huge black chamber, why couldn't Shannon? Nothing stopped her but her own notion of reality. Shannon closed her eyes. She imagined she swam with Juneau in the sea. She let go of Juneau's fluke. She…she swam, swam in water that didn't exist.

Juneau pulled Luke free.

"Luke—we see swamp because Drom imagines it. Fight him. Reimagine."

Luke swung from Juneau's fluke, then steadied himself. And he flew.

Drom's great arm, with his fist doubled up, came slashing across like a tennis racket, and backhanded Luke, who soared up and away like a brand new tennis ball.

Drom's eye, still bleeding from Juneau's blows, turned his glare Shannon's way again. The pain propelled him forward, more furious than ever.

Shannon and Juneau charged toward the demented, perverted alien, crashed into his giant chest and they pushed him. Pushed hard. Luke reappeared.

Together Shannon, Luke, Juneau, and even little Salesti battled Drom. Shannon focused every iota of concentration on Drom until a glimpse of Salesti distracted her. Had Salesti grown somehow? Had Drom set the tiny fuzzball on fire? Shannon chanced one quick look straight at the tiny creature. No, Drom had set no fire. Salesti's body remained small enough to cup in Essi's hand as always. But around her floated an aura, a flaming crimson ring that transformed it into a small sun, a force to be reckoned with. *Odin's eye.*

Together they pushed Drom back, and farther back, to the edge of Becky's mind.

They could do it, they could throw Drom out.

But Drom pushed back with everything he could muster, frantic now, aware, for the first time in eons, of his mortality. He gained a step and then another.

Luke backed up and flew forward again, ramming the dark alien, who bellowed and staggered backward.

Almost.

Drom could move no further without falling away. Shannon could see the disbelief building in his eyes.

"Salty." Drom's desperation rang out. But the powerful beast couldn't help him anymore.

Because of Indy. Gone. With that thought, Shannon lost her will to fight.

Drom seized upon Shannon's sorrow. With an unexpected lunge to one side, he regained precious space between himself and oblivion. He maneuvered toward Shannon.

Kill the leader, kill the resistance.

Juneau rushed in and her powerful fluke once more battered the same eye she'd drubbed before.

Drom emitted a great shriek. Juneau and Luke rejoined the front line.

A flash of black lightning, another shriek from Drom and he forced them back.

Shannon sensed all of her friends' strength draining away. They'd never beat the alien if the battle wore on. Even Salesti depended on Shannon's energy to create her own. Shannon made one attempt to stop the killing.

"Drom. A moment's truce. What would it take for you to agree to leave the Earth and never come back?" she said.

For a moment all the combatants paused and turned their heads to stare at Shannon.

Yes, a crazy thing to ask.

"A moment's truce, then," Drom replied and stepped away, but to the side, not toward the edge of Becky's mind. He kept his eyes on his attackers.

A surprise, that. His strength had drained as much as theirs.

Of course it had — Becky's body — They'd all drained her, and they all weakened as she weakened. Shannon's group all backed off a step and rested. But they watched his every move, his every breath, ready to spring if he attacked.

"What would it take?" Drom laughed. A gust of putrid air blasted them. "Nothing you are and nothing you own can keep us from this planet. We have chosen it as our new home. We shall rule."

"You'll be discovered and destroyed."

Drom rumbled from some deep dark place.

"We will remain hidden, careful. No one knows we are here until we enslave them. I will take you and—" He turned an eye to Luke. "—him, and no one will know we exist." His face twisted for a moment. "Although now I must also retake Becky and David. Congratulations, woman. No one has ever rescued one of my slaves before and you have freed two. In any event, Tharm is even now—"

So Drom didn't know that Tharm had been, uh, expunged.

Shannon still hadn't mastered the suppression of images in her mind that accompanied her thoughts. For the briefest moment, she remembered the struggle to push the foul, damaged alien out into eternity; revisited the moment when Tharm vanished.

Drom stopped mid-sentence and bellowed. "You killed Tharm?" His voice, twisted with anguish and his hatred, pure hatred, filled the cavern of Becky's mind. He lunged at Shannon.

Luke and Juneau hadn't let their guard down for a moment. They lunged as Drom lunged.

Shannon glared at Drom. Power stolen from the Selador and its people. Essi's planet dead. The planned destruction of Earth.

No. By all the gods and all that is good, not in my house. Shannon shoved aside her sorrow over Indy and rushed to help her friends. They heaved against him. Drom roared and resisted, his power frightening. He fought like a crazed beast now, fueled by revenge.

At that moment Salesti rejoined the fray. Though it seemed impossible, the little alien's flame grew even brighter and more intense than before. How in hades did it *do* that?

They fought Drom to the edge, struggled to push him out, but he managed to turn them sideways to the edges of Becky's mind, forcing both sides into equal danger of slipping beyond existence.

Shannon would slip out into nothingness without a second thought if Drom accompanied her. But Essi and Juneau, Luke, Salesti, never. She struggled to maneuver Drom between the walls of Becky's mind and her team.

The battle raged, a few steps back, a few steps forward, neither side able to gain the advantage.

Becky's body would give out on them soon. If the body died, they'd be trapped. Salesti had tried to explain why it couldn't continue to burn energy from the fat cells of Becky if she died. It had something to do with the fact that Essi and Salesti existed in Becky's spirit. Her own spirit called upon her body's energy, not Essi or Salesti. Shannon's team must go, and soon. Shannon's jaw tightened. But she'd stay and die if it meant Drom stayed and died with her.

As if on cue, out of the darkness, the small fierce figure of Becky rushed toward them, back from her refuge in Shannon's mind, Essi at her side.

Drom didn't see them coming as they hurtled into him. Shannon did, though, and backed off to join them for one last attack.

Pull it together. All the mental energy, every bit she possessed. *Gather it, explode it.*

The three rammed him.

Drom staggered backward.

He howled with rage, clawed at the air.

And fell out into the void.

Becky's mind settled into dead quiet. No one moved.

They'd done it. Salty, the primitive predator and Drom, with his dream of a sick, twisted kingdom, gone.

Indy. Gone too.

Some part of Shannon, also gone. Her face felt as heavy as stone. The rest of them, except Becky, exhausted, smiled at each other, patted—or rubbed, in Juneau's case—each others' backs and arms with weak arms and hands, and savored the stillness.

Shannon hesitated. Something had gone wrong.

Deathly silence. More than Drom's departure accounted for this eerie stillness.

Odin's eye. Becky's body neared death.

Essi, quick, take us all home, Shannon imaged. She wanted to examine Becky's body. Everyone flowed over except Becky.

When Shannon had regained her body, lying flat against the floor, she lifted her head and glanced around her. Indy's still body lay next to Shannon's. She couldn't bear to look at her brave, loving mastiff. Narci sat on Shannon's chest, kneading her T-shirt like bread dough. Shannon's hand stung, throbbed, pain from her palm shot down into her wrist and arm.

She sat up. Her eyes watered, her head swam, her head wobbled on her weak neck. *So tired. She wanted to lie down. To let go.* So many souls on board and the fierce battle, coming so soon after their encounter at Otter Bay, had had stolen too much from her. She would die in moments if she didn't act now.

"Narci, I'm sending Salesti back, and Luke too, just long enough to get him back to his body.

"What?" Luke said.

"I'm dying. I have to offload," she told him.

"Do it," he said.

"Bring food."

"On it."

Hugging the cat, Shannon imaged for Salesti to take Luke over. They departed. Narci jerked her head back and forth, as if a flea had invaded her ear. She rubbed against Shannon and shivered. Her sleek black cat looked up at Shannon with reproachful eyes that said, "Another one?"

Shannon wrapped the gaping wound on her hand with a sock she slipped off her foot. She caught the image of Luke, slipping away to curl up in a corner where he could ignore most of what transpired in the alien world of Narci's feline mind. Salesti stayed to sustain him there. The cat jumped up and skittered for the back of Luke's unconscious body.

Gauze smothered her mind. Something urgent she needed to do. *What was it?*

Becky. Her form sprawled face down on the floor wedged next to Shannon. She slid several inches away and eased Becky's body onto its side.

No. After everything they'd come through. Not this.

Six inches of knife lay buried deep in Becky's torso. To the hilt. The knife Becky had used to stalk Shannon.

Juneau and Essi drew in a deep, quivering breath along with Shannon.

So much blood.

*   *   *

"This will turn out okay," Shannon said. "It will."

She slid Becky's body over onto its back, taking care not to dislodge the knife or bang her friend's head. Shannon placed two fingers on Becky's neck. *Don't die, Beck, hang on.* Her heart still pulsed, a slow, erratic beat. Blood gushed from Becky's wound. Shannon ripped off her shirt and pressed it around the knife.

"My phone, where's my cell phone?" Shannon asked, looking around her.

"Essi, go bring Becky over, we'll—"

Shannon's hands on Becky's chest brought her spirit close. For the first time, Shannon could hear her thoughts, so much more than reading her images and emotions. "No," Becky's spirit said. The voice sounded weak, but hard, like obsidian, like diamond, like a blizzard.

"We can deal with it, Beck. I have friends who—"

"—My body's dying," Becky said. "I'm staying, and you will leave me alone. If it's over for me, fine."

"But you can come over here with me if your body…. It'll work out all right. I mean, not all right, but okay. Maybe not okay, but better than…." Shannon's anxious voice cracked, right along with her heart.

"This is *my body*. It's dying so *I'm* dying. I will never, repeat never, live somebody else's life instead of my own. No offense, but I don't want to be you."

No surprise there.

Shannon's mind traveled far away, as if she were standing at the other end of the universe watching this moment. Cotton batting folded itself down over her spirit. She couldn't hear, couldn't see, couldn't think. Maybe it was over for her as well.

Or maybe it should be. She looked at the knife in Becky's chest.

She longed to use it, end this struggle to stay alive. She—

—a great swirling arose all around her, clicking and jaw snapping, high squeaks and long calls, rubbing all along the edges of her mind, and a small black eye, one with a spark in it, a twinkle of ever-present amusement, a flash of deep and unknowable intelligence. Juneau, pulling her back, away from that knife.

Essi hugged her, the child's soothing hum surrounding her too, huge green eyes staring at her, unblinking, holding her, staying her hand, a humming that filled Shannon's senses with cherry blossoms on a warm banana-bright day.

Luke ran back into the elevator lobby, restored by Salesti. He lugged the cooler over and began loading edibles into Shannon's lap.

All right. For Juneau, for Essi.

Shannon gazed down at her friend. She must decide. Bring Becky over against her will? Or leave Becky in her body to die? Of course Becky should stay with her body, just as David wanted to stay with his. But eye of Odin, this was *Becky*, her truest friend, her cherished friend, no one else had been close to her since Georgey. And Georgey had died. Not Becky, too, please not Becky too.

Shannon's mouth pressed into a grim line. She would choose the kindest way, the best alternative, even if all the alternatives appeared grim. Even if the kindest option would be the hardest for Shannon.

"You have to be sure," she told Becky. "If you stay, you might die, or you might live to become a monster ruled by Salty and Drom living powder."

"I'm sure. I'll take my chances."

"But you're my best buddy. I can't let you die." If she could take charge of Becky and her body, she could fix this terrible mess. She always succeeded if people just let her do things her way.

The kindest choice. Shannon's shoulders fell.

"I love you, my friend," Shannon said. The tears fell like meteors from the night sky. "Stay with me. Don't give up. You don't know how to quit."

And then, "Call for help, Luke."

"Already on the phone."

As Shannon listened to him converse in low urgent tones with 9-1-1 dispatch, her gaze followed the pattern on the wall down the hall a few feet. Another body there…. Portman! She let out a tiny groan.

"…Three people in critical condition. We need ambulances. Hurry…."

Help Portman. Go.

But she couldn't hold the notion. She stared at the blood circling under her friend and shock dissolved her thoughts. She shivered. She couldn't get the shivers under control. She should go….

…Where did she need to go?

Shannon's mind threw out a white screen. Not a thought crossed it. The shivers continued…

…Luke came into view, kneeling by Becky, keeping Shannon's sweat jacket over her wound, talking to her in that wonderful, low, calm, quiet voice. *How she would miss it.*

Indy's inert form several feet away. *Her Indy.* How would Shannon bear life without her?

Her eyes wandered.

Oh, hades. Portman! Shannon gathered herself up onto all fours. She crawled the few paces to her boss's side.

Lots of blood here, too. She checked his pulse. Heart still pumping.

Portman groaned. His jacket remained bunched on the wounds where Shannon had placed it. *Good, she'd staunched some of the blood.* She used a corner of one jacket sleeve to wipe blood splatters off his face.

His eyes opened. He focused on her and shifted his body.

"Stay still," she said, her voice gentle, her hands pressing on the makeshift bandage. "You'll make the bleeding worse. I can hear the ambulance coming."

He continued to stare at her, his eyes glazed.

"The woman?" Portman whispered.

"Badly hurt. You're safe."

"Who is she? Why was she here?" he asked.

She replied with a question of her own.

"What're you doing here in the middle of the night?"

"I was afraid this attacker of yours would come after me too. So I talked to the Police Chief and got my own police protection."

Yes, Portman always took advantage of his connections.

"My wife and kids are at my house. If anything happened to them because of my work, I…I'd never be able to live with myself. So I came here to sleep on my couch. I figured an attacker would follow me and leave them alone."

His words floated toward her from far away. *So tired, so goddamn tired.*

"So where are your bodyguards now?" she asked.

"They don't even know I'm gone. I wanted them with my family."

He'd worried more about his family than himself. Who'd have thought? Portman had a redeeming quality.

She patted his hand. "It's over, Matt."

He passed out.

Sirens.

She craved food. Didn't she have a lapful here a minute ago? *Too weak to get to her cooler now.*

Luke's face appeared in her blurry vision. He pulled the cooler over to her side and handed her a box of doughnuts. She lay down, curled, shivering, on the floor between Becky and Portman and ate until the medic crews arrived.

The white screen that had absorbed her every thought enclosed her again, then turned black.

*   *   *

When she regained consciousness, she inspected the scene. Two paramedics hunched, deep in concentration, over Becky and Portman. Another medic handed Luke a blanket for Shannon. He arranged it over her with great care, as if she might crack like blown glass if he moved the wrong way. He handed her another doughnut. She ate it without sitting up.

As the medics loaded Becky and Portman into one elevator, Chen erupted at full bore from the second one, then stopped short. The fury on his face disappeared and turned to disbelief as he took in the gurneys carrying her friend and her boss, the bloody floor, Shannon curled like a fetus under a blanket, Luke hovering over her, Indy lying dead and Narci curled tight against Shannon's stomach. He eyed the doughnut in her hand.

So what, Chen? By now he should be accustomed to finding her lying in blood, the dead and dying strewn about her, eating her inappropriate little meals.

As she watched him, Chen's form blurred, wavered like a desert mirage. She blinked. Her vision didn't clear. She must watch what she said. But for the life of her, she couldn't remember why. She couldn't think. Her mind....

"Luke," she said. "Salesti?"

Luke took her hand. Salesti flowed across to her.

Chen pointed at Luke and said, "I'll deal with you later. Move." Then he frowned at Shannon and said, "Right now I have some questions for you."

A paramedic pushed Chen aside and examined Shannon.

Perhaps Chen chewed her out then. She didn't listen. She watched Luke cross over to talk with another police woman. Officer Taney, wasn't it? Chen's fuzzy form knelt beside her, blocking them off.

"Can you ID the woman the medics just took downstairs?"

Shannon forced the words from dry, sticky lips. Chen knelt closer to hear her. "Becky Anderson, from the SQ," Shannon said, her words like bricks. "My best friend. Andy Fernando's girlfriend."

Chen's eyebrows lifted. "Andy Fernando, the suicide from Otter Bay?"

Shannon winced. "Yes.".

An officer handed a clear plastic sack with Becky's knife in it to Chen. He held it up. "Is this the knife used on Becky Anderson and Portman?"

Shannon's head moved in slow motion up and down. She refused to look at the knife.

"Whose prints am I going to find on it?"

"Becky's." Every word became an effort. Shannon responded more and more slowly.

"She stab Portman?"

"Yes."

"Why?"

Cleverness eluded her now. She lifted her hands as if helpless to explain.

"Not her fault. She knew about the attacker. When Portman turned up, she…Confusion…." *There. Do with that what you will, Chen.*

Tears again. *Would she ever stop?*

"She tried to kill herself?"

"No. Accident. Fell on the knife. As far as I know." *And if that made Chen wonder, so much the better.*

Chen waited, but Shannon offered nothing more. He shifted gear. "What's Quintana doing here?"

"I called him. Needed help. As you can see."

"He help you run from the hospital?"

Shannon's head moved left to right in slow motion. "I called later." She waved a hand around the elevator lobby, didn't speak. If Chen thought her gestures meant she'd called from here, well, his mistake.

Shannon's voice sounded to her as if she'd covered her head with a lead-lined bucket.

The paramedic interrupted. "Officer, I want to transport this woman now. Her vitals are plummeting."

"Go," Chen said, and added, "Tell them at the hospital that she's been dangerously sick for a week or so."

Words crackled over his radio. He turned away and listened, then said, "Our esteemed prosecutor, on the way to the hospital, insists that I know *right now* that you saved his life. Congratulations. Tell it to the judge at the mitigation hearing."

To the paramedic she said, "Can you fish out a peanut butter sandwich from my cooler there? I'll eat it on the way."

"No can do. You're going to get a glucose drip, which I will attach as soon as this gentlemen moves." He frowned at Chen.

Chen moved. "You have anything else to tell me about this whole sorry mess?"

Shannon couldn't have told Chen the story even if she'd wanted to. She couldn't summon any push to make words move. Her head moved in a slow "no." Or she meant to. No movement, as far as she could tell.

"We'll talk later," he said and moved over to talk to the officer who'd examined Becky.

She glanced over at the body of the dog at her side. *Her Indy.* Luke caught her stricken face and said, "Shannon, I—"

Chen held up a hand. "You two will not talk to each other until I've taken a full statement from you, Luke. And until I've finished with you." He pointed at Shannon. "Do I make myself clear?"

"Perfectly clear," Quintana said.

"Perfectly," Shannon echoed.

What had Luke wanted to say? Ill, in shock, Shannon cast the lavender and searched Luke's emotions without a conscious thought.

Shannon nodded. Luke felt sorry, deeply sorry about Indy. But confused. Distant. He'd withdrawn from her again. Well, who wouldn't, after this day in hell? *He'd ended the evening in the mind of a rat-catching, half wild, half looney cat, for Odinssake.* If he'd backed off when he thought her a drug-addicted gambler, he would want nothing to do with her now that he'd experienced her actual mind, her new skills, the hair-raising company she kept.

As the paramedics loaded her onto a gurney, the tears dripped.

By all the Dragons of the Sea, how she'd tired of crying.

Someone had fetched Narci's kennel from the parking garage and Officer Taney lured her in with an open can of cat food. Shannon begged Taney to let the cat eat as much as she wanted.

Taney agreed, her face solemn. "Because the cat has a disorder just like you."

Did Shannon catch a tiny glimpse of laughter in Taney's eyes? Taney was a good egg. Shannon must remember to tell her….

Shannon rode in the ambulance to the hospital, half aware. She could feel the glucose drip coursing through her vein and spreading energy. She could *feel* it. She yearned to close her eyes and savor that feeling for hours, for days. But she couldn't spare the time.

When the ambulance stopped and the back door popped open, she struggled into a sitting position and said in a voice so weak the paramedics leaned in to hear her, "This is where I get out. Hand me the release form."

The paramedics stared, stunned that she'd contemplate leaving.

"*Now,*" Shannon said, trying for strong and authoritative and achieving perhaps glazed and insane. "I know my rights. I'm an attorney and if you don't let me out of here, I'm suing." *Shameless and bad. Worse, even, since they didn't know that Chen hadn't finished with her.* He'd blow a gasket when he found out she'd gone. *So?* He must be used to her ways by now.

Shannon wove her way out to the curb and found a taxi line. She begged the driver to break every speed limit in the City to reach the Dickson, promising to make it worth his while. She couldn't pay him, of course, as she didn't have her purse, and she heard him calling in a complaint even as she limped into the Dickson.

To her surprise, a number of people, late hangers-on from the reception, still wandered around the Dickson's main floor. "Moon?" she asked the first person she encountered inside the atrium. A student who looked as if he'd managed to get his hands on a handsome volume of champagne, backed up, repelled by her blood-soaked clothes, and pointed down the stairs. "At the pool," he said. Shannon shambled down the stairs.

The door to the pool room stood open. *Not good.* Shannon used the wall to make her way through it and paused. Todd stood by his desk, hands fidgeting with a clipboard for no apparent reason, his face pink and puffy. He turned when Shannon clattered against the door.

"Food," she said. He threw down his clipboard and rushed out like a man on a mission.

Moon knelt by the water, shouting to someone in the pool. All traces of his normal confidence and calm had vanished. The group he'd introduced to her before she'd run off earlier stood around him, even at this improbable hour, intent on the activity around the whale, stiff with concern.

"How is she?" Shannon asked as she knelt by Moon.

He didn't pause to voice the anger Shannon knew he held inside. "Her condition's plummeted," he said. "Her system has rejected the respiratory equipment. We're just about to remove her from it, but she cannot function on her own. Her sole hope of survival, a slim chance, is to breathe on her own again. We have run out of options. If you cannot bring her back, she is about to die." Moon pulled his grim study of the whale to glare at Shannon. His glare melted into astonishment and then into concern as he registered her bloody clothes, her ice white and near-skeletal face.

*   *   *

Juneau is about to die. The blood in her head sank into her stomach like a cannon ball. Her belly pitched. She would've burped every bite of her last snack into Moon's lap if Essi hadn't already converted it all into desperately-needed energy. She gagged on dry heaves. Juneau battered along the walls of her mind, as if trying to escape. Shannon's headache swelled.

A short muscular woman pulled herself out of the water. Shannon squinted. Her hair glinted blue, as blue as the aqua pool itself. "You Shannon Kendricks? About bloody time. You've got your wet suit on?"

Shannon hiccoughed up a sad laugh. "No wet suit. Screw it. I'll go in like this."

Todd joined them. "I have wet suits." He held up several.

"No time," the woman said.

"Let's do it," Shannon said.

Without waiting for further permission, she slipped into the water. The SQ kept Juneau's pool cooled to 50 degrees. This water felt twenty degrees colder. Maybe subzero. Her blood thickened, as if she'd plunged into a freezer.

For one startling moment her lungs didn't expand, her heart didn't beat; she didn't breathe. Then the tremors started; her teeth chattered, her hands shook. She forced her legs, one at a time, toward Juneau. Three men in the water blocked her way. Moon shouted to them; Shannon could no longer distinguish words; her ears rang with the shocking cold of the water. The men eased back.

Juneau looked thin, grayish yellow. Much too thin, too gray.

Essi? Ready? Shannon imaged Essi and Juneau at her fingertips.

Essi hummed. Juneau's flood of anticipation tingled Shannon's nerve endings.

Shannon didn't dare wait. She stretched her hands to Juneau's lovely round head, placed her fingers flat against the whale's forehead, and imaged Essi to take Juneau home.

As she focused on Essi and Juneau, she sensed, as if from far away, the tense conversations in the water and on the pool deck cease. Everyone watched her, watched the whale.

A familiar sensation brushed against the side of her mind as Juneau moved past. Juneau's high, gentle call sounded, resounding at first, then fading as Essi pulled Juneau's spirit into the whale's own body. Juneau's warm tingling on Shannon's skin ceased—one moment there, the next gone, as if a door had closed.

Wait!

Juneau had gone.

The whale left behind an emptiness as huge as a football stadium. Shannon stood alone in the middle of that emptiness. She uttered an involuntary cry, and sank below the water.

Juneau had gone home. Shannon could sleep. *Too tired, too cold to stay awake.*

Shannon's system started the shut down process. She drifted. Drifted. *She didn't mind. She'd done enough…*

Wait. Some sort of humming buzzed along her arm, and up to her mind. She recognized it…but she couldn't remember. She *needed* to remember…something important…*Essi!* If Shannon slept now, Essi would die.

But she wanted to stay here on the floor of the pool. So tired. Nothing left to give. Let her sleep.

Essi's big green eyes floated in front of Shannon. Her pale silvery blond hair. Her silvery lavender skin. She imaged going home. Home to Toss.

All right, Essi. For you, I'll try.

Her legs moved a few inches. She pushed with feeble legs toward the surface. Her face emerged. *So warm. The air felt so warm.* Shannon's legs gave way.

From Juneau's other side, the blue-haired woman had seen Shannon sink, had ducked under the whale, had caught Shannon as she dropped a second time. "Steady on, " she said. "Look." One strong arm slid around Shannon's waist and she lifted Shannon's chin with the other. "Check out Juneau" she said.

Shannon focused.

Juneau's eyes opened, those lovely black eyes so full of impish intelligence, and looked straight at Shannon. The whale wriggled in the harness, her body powerful even in her weak state. She fought to break free of the straps and tubes. The staff in the pool backed off, talking to her with strong, calm voices, commanding her to rest, but staying well clear of her thrashing fluke and body.

Moon shouted to her. "Shannon, can you calm her?"

The woman helped Shannon float to Juneau's side. Waves born of Juneau's rebellion washed salty ice water into Shannon's eyes, her mouth. Her new supporter held her upright.

"Be still, sweetheart," Shannon said, her voice tender, and she laid the side of her face and her arms on the beluga's back. Perhaps the whale still sensed her mind through her touch, or perhaps Essi managed it alone: the whale calmed.

The woman murmured behind her. "Impressive."

Shannon raised her head in time to see the surprised faces of SQ staffers and Dickson researchers gathered along the poolside. Moon, Todd, Ambika, Saunders and Tremaine had approached, other Research Center Directors behind them.

Ambika beamed down at her.

Soon the staff had loosened Juneau's harness, though not removed it, released the breathing tubes.

"Out of the pool," the tall woman said. "Your lips've gone blue."

"You'll call me if something goes wrong?" Shannon asked.

"Of course," the woman said, her face crinkling into a smile. " My name is Dakota."

Shannon took one long last look at Juneau's intelligent black eyes and slid her hand along Juneau's jaw as she moved around the whale.

Nice job, Essi.

zhoo.

Essi would miss her too.

At the edge of the pool, a big guy leaned down and hoisted her out of the water and onto the cement. Cold and shivering, she struggled to sit up. *So many people. Crowding her.* Full of congratulations, shaking her icy hand, patting her frigid back.

Hypothermic, severely compromised, about to crash again. Maybe for the last time. The crowd crushed in on her…she couldn't breath…. "Please," she said, her voice so weak few could hear her. "Please, I—"

Moon forced his way through the group, a polite steam engine, with a mug of hot coffee and a wool blanket. Shannon took both with shaky hands, cupped her hands around the mug and pulled it close. She gave the director a grateful nod as Moon wrapped the blanket around her shoulders. The hot steam swirled into her face. Moon and the same fellow who'd pulled her from the pool raised her to her feet and led her to the work desk, where she sank into the padded chair. Todd returned with a brimming hot plate of food and stood guard, waving well wishers away.

"Frankly," Moon said without preamble, "I didn't think you could bring her back, and not with a touch of your hand." His eyes remained locked on her face, his look direct and puzzled. Intrigued. A new respect contained there.

And a hard new intellectual scrutiny.

Uh oh.

How strange, how unlikely Juneau's rescue scene must have looked to Moon. A comatose whale, unconscious for six days, dying—and in hobbles this frantic stick of a woman, not even a bona fide marine biologist, but an attorney, of all things. She jumps into the pool, lays hands upon the whale and voila! The whale returns to life.

Odds on, Moon, an inquisitive man, had vowed to learn how she'd accomplished it.

No way.

"I've got to scare up some warm clothes," she said, interrupting Moon's train of thought. She stood. Blackness closed in. Her legs noodled. *Woo, not going anywhere yet.* She sank back into her seat.

Todd brought over two large lab coats and more towels.

"Start with these. A research specialist's bringing sweats." He pointed. "Hot shower's in there."

A great guy, Todd.

Then a thought hit her like an incoming stone. *Loki's luck.* In her rush to help, she hadn't secured the promises to go forward with the Project, to free Juneau.

Had she saved Juneau's life, only to ruin the whale's chance to go free?

"About the Project—"

The woman from the pool, Dakota, popped up next to Shannon and held out a slick black swim bag. Todd handed it to Shannon.

He pointed to the young woman.

The girl smiled. "Take anything you need."

Shannon smiled back. *Who knew people could be so helpful?*

Her first step away from her chair sent her stumbling. Todd clamped onto her elbow and escorted her to the shower room door.

"Fantastic—you and Juneau. We'd lost her. Someday tell me how you did it." He gave her a salute, his hand snapping from his bushy red eyebrows, and turned back to the pool.

Shannon made her uncertain way into the women's room. Beyond the sinks and private stalls, she spotted a row of curtained showers. *Glory be.* If the water ran steaming hot, Shannon might never come out.

The water did run hot and Shannon did take a long time to emerge, but when her skin began to wrinkle, she toweled off and reappeared in a warm pair of red fleece sweats, rather too short on Shannon's long legs and arms. As if she cared.

Moon paced nearby. "There you are. Juneau is well. She is eating on her own. A mash to begin with. The equipment irritated her throat. Come now, let me take you to meet your new partners."

A moment passed before Shannon's slow thoughts caught up with the word. Partners.

"Partners? They've agreed? Project Juneau is a go?"

Moon permitted himself a pleased grin as he nodded.

"Oh, yes, the demonstration in the pool has quite convinced them."

He offered a handshake. Shannon grasped his whole arm, leaning into him for support. His other arm wrapped around her to keep her on her feet.

Since she found herself close, she gave the director a big hug. And bawled.

Still bawling in Moon's embrace, she caught sight of his uncomfortable look of surprise and then she entered a universe of blackness.

CHAPTER TEN

TIME NO LONGER MATTERS

SHANNON AWOKE in a dark hospital room, alone, the insulin drip stinging her wrist, the ping of a machine out of view penetrating the thick fog tumbling in her mind.

"Is Becky alive?" she asked. But no one answered and the fog closed around her.

*   *   *

Shannon's mind drifted. *Essi? Salesti, Jun—no, just Essi and Salesti. Juneau had gone home…. Narci. But Indy gone.* Such a terrible, terrible word, *gone*.

*   *   *

…Shannon is lying on the asphalt in the parking lot in front of the White Wolf. *So tired, can't wake up.* She opens groggy eyes and notices two black polished shoes beside her head. Someone bends over her.

"Help me." Shannon's voice croaked. "Please."

The man remains silent. He fingers her necklace, as if examining the stone. He tugs hard. Shannon's neck stings as the chain breaks.

"No, don't. Becky's. Can't lose it. Mustn't lose it." She grabs the man's leg but her grip falls away. He ignores her. As he stands up, he snatches her purse, climbs into the black jaguar and starts the engine. Shannon rolls over to escape its tires, then props herself up on one elbow. The car backs out. As it turns and pulls away, Shannon memorizes the license plate. "TOMSTOY," it says.

The man in the high stakes room. Tom Willingham. *Remember. Remember black jag tomstoy willingham.* Shannon fell back into a deep black well.

* * *

Shannon opened her eyes. *Remember,* she'd told herself that morning at the casino. But she hadn't remembered. Until now.

She called out, her voice small and dry."Officer Taney." The door remained closed. She called again and a third time. No use; no one could hear her. She buzzed the nurse's station.

A nurse strode in on soft-soled shoes, smiling. For some reason Shannon could not look away from one long nose hair hanging from the nurse's nostril. "You're awake. Can I get you anything?"

"Please. Ask Officer Taney to come in. Is she still here? It's important."

The nurse retreated to the door and called in the officer. "I'll let the doctor know you're awake."

"What can I do for you, sugar?" Officer Taney said.

"Please. Call Chen. The man who took Becky's emerald. Tom Willingham. Black jaguar. Tag says TOMSTOY." *Great Odin, she sounded like Todd, with his abrupt short form talk.*

Taney cocked her head and puckered up her face. "You came up with that *now*?"

"Please. Just call."

Taney's dubious look remained, but she pulled out her cell phone.

Shannon sank back into the pillow and drifted off.

* * *

The door swung open.

"Everyone ok in there?" The night nurse.

"Is Becky alive?" Shannon whispered, but her voice, like rain in the wind, blew back into her face, and no one answered.

*   *   *

"Luke?"

No one answered.

*   *   *

She listened, as the doctors argued about why Shannon continued to lose weight. No one knew the answer. Except Dr. Bennett, who watched Shannon with worried eyes.

"As soon as you're strong enough to take Essi home," Dr. B. said to her when they were alone. "I'll arrange it." The words scattered, like leaves on a breezy street.

No, she meant to say, *let me go now.* But the words wandered from her mind.

*   *   *

Shannon stared at the ceiling. She'd stared at it for several minutes now. Then lavender haze appeared at the door. Jane and Picker entered. Picker placed roses on the bed stand, sat and squirmed, as silent as Shannon. Jane laid a box of dark chocolates next to the roses and sat by Picker, full of office gossip. But Jane's stories disappeared even as she spoke, as if Shannon's mind were a river, as if Jane's words floated downstream and out of sight.

Scott Cross, Jane informed her, had become engaged and disengaged within a matter of eight days. Scott, too, floated past Shannon's view and out of sight. Jane held Shannon's hand and only this mattered.

*   *   *

Light filtered in along the edges of a pale green-striped curtain.

Essi?

Shannon caught the child's faint pulsing by attending with every fiber of her being. *Too faint.* Shannon imaged: *what's the matter? Show me, sweetheart.*

No response.

Odin's death. *Her little alien child hovered close to death.*

Of course. She'd forgotten. Essi could not recover if Shannon didn't.

All right then.

Shannon would not die.

*   *   *

Chen visited one morning.

"Dr. Bennett tells me you are getting stronger. I'm glad to hear it."

Well, Chen wasn't such a hard—

"She said I can ask you a few more questions today."

Or, yes, yes he was.

Chen proceeded to interview her again. Her intruder. David. The SQ warehouse. Andy. Becky. The Law Office. Luke. Detail by excruciating detail. She answered like a programmed computer. Her story hadn't changed. Every question, though, every answer kindled a memory that burned her heart one more time.

When he finished, he regarded her for a long, silent minute. Shannon watched the second hand tick its way around the clock. At last he stirred and told her he'd dropped the charges for murder, accessory, assault, and aiding and abetting. She would, however, face the music on two counts of eluding the police. Bail had been arranged on her behalf. When she left the hospital she could go home until the date of her hearing, which hadn't been set yet. Shannon lifted an indifferent shoulder. Even if the charges stuck, the penalty would be a small price to pay for the chance to send Juneau home and to take Drom and Salty down. To save the damn world. His words floated away down the river.

"What about Luke?"

Chen's face tightened. "You know and he knows and I know that he got too personally involved in this case. You realize, I hope, that the Chief should've fired him. But Luke's popular, has a boatload of commendations—a lot of them from me—citizen letters praising his work, medals, awards, yadda yadda. So maybe no one ever asked him some pertinent questions they should've and maybe they never will. If he manages to keep his nose clean from now on. You get my drift?"

Shannon nodded.

After Chen finished chewing on her about Luke, he broke the news about Becky.

"She made it through surgery, but it was a close thing. She's recovering right down the hall."

Becky lived.

Lived!

Becky had confessed that she'd stabbed Portman, Chen said. David Fielding confessed he'd been present at several killings, resulting in the ghastly contents of his freezer. Chen still worked the open case, of course, of some "other" killer that had forced David to participate in those deaths. But Shannon and her friends knew the police would never chase down "the other."

Both Becky and David, aided by their attorneys, had already struck plea deals: once they recovered from their injuries enough to visit the judge, they'd enter into voluntary commitment at a high-security mental facility to the south, where they'd stay until they no longer exploded into episodes of rage and aggression. *Poor David.* Another ruined life. *And Becky.* Alive, but without Andy. Innocent, but incarcerated. Full of Drom and Salty's living powder.

Chen stood. "That's about it. Oh, almost forgot." He held a package in his hand.

Shannon eyed it. Another box of chocolates? Nope, not unless the pack contained four pieces of candy, max. "What is it?" she asked, her voice hoarse.

Chen grinned. *Must be something big, for Chen to break a full smile.*

"A certain large green emerald."

Shannon tried to sit up. "Becky's emerald? You found it? I take back every bad thing I ever said about you, Detective. Thank you so much."

His grin vanished. "Every bad thing? What?"

"This is such a good thing, the first good thing for me in a long time. Are you going to give it to her now?"

"This very moment," Chen said, and took his leave.

* * *

Shannon pitched and twisted in her hospital bed. She'd believed since childhood that she couldn't *hurt* her friends if she *had* no friends. She'd let her guard down with Becky and Luke and look what had happened.

Memories floated through Shannon's mind. Becky and Shannon laughing, a hundred times, laughing; Becky bleeding, a curved blade in her chest. Andy fondly scratching the whiskers of Wally, the big old walrus; Andy sprawled on his back, his face blown to ruin. Georgey giggling on the swings; Georgey, red, choking, gasping for air, long minutes of dying as his throat swelled. Luke, leaning in and gently kissing her, just the once; now, she expected, suffering nightmares in which Shannon assumed a prominent role.

Should she have pushed them all away before she hurt them?

Essi's humming interrupted. *Wrong,* Essi protested, *wrong.* She imaged Shannon holding tight to Becky, to David, to Luke.

Shannon nodded. Right, Essi. Pull them close and do everything possible to keep them safe. That's all a person could do.

Shannon pitched and twisted.

* * *

Officer Taney bounced into her room to report that Narci had eaten enough in two weeks to feed a pride of lions. She produced flowers in a white vase. She fidgeted.

Shannon couldn't resist a wan smile. She motioned for Taney to sit down. She said, "I don't know your first name, Officer Taney. I'd like to."

"Londelle," Taney said.

"Londelle. Lovely. Do you mind if I call you that?"

"My friends call me Londy. You call me that."

"Well, Londy, my friend, I owe you. Thank you."

"Sugar, being around you and this cat, what with your escapes, your disorders and killers and what not, it's cured a lifetime of boredom. Thank *you*. Don't you worry about Narci. I'll take care of the little thing until you go home." She paused. "I'll miss that little thing. You know, sometimes I catch her staring at me with those big baby blues like she knows exactly what I'm thinking. And she runs to the door every time Luke comes over to say hello to her. But she gets there before he even drives up to the curb." Lordy shook her head. "Some disorder she's got."

Odin's eye. Essi's living powder. Narci had acquired new skills.

Narci. The diminutive cat had carried her weight in this disaster, bless her heart. Shannon looked forward to the moment the cat would curl her warm body into Shannon's lap. She could feel Narci's velvet fur against her hand, her sandpaper tongue across Shannon's face. *Looked forward.*

*   *   *

Shannon propped herself up to read the Ocean City Chronicle late one afternoon. Something must be happening beyond these hospital walls. *Time to find out what.*

She rustled the pages. New movies coming out this weekend up at the Ocean City Mall TwentyPlex. She'd been too busy to go to the movies for a long time. She loved movies. She would go. *As soon as she could escape from this damn hospital.*

And to remind her why she hated hospitals, here came another lab tech to draw some more of her blood now.

*   *   *

The lavender haze drew her eyes from the Heather Anderson romance Jane had given her, announcing, as always that someone's arrival. *Phooey, not now!* The bodice was about to be ripped. She sighed and put the book down.

And someone did arrive. In handcuffs.

*   *   *

"Becky," Shannon said, a smile cracking her dry, chapped lips. A small, gangly police officer followed her friend into the room and stood by the door with his arms crossed on his skinny chest. Shannon's mind paused and focused on him for a moment. Didn't a person have to be tall to be gangly? She stared until he shifted, uncomfortable under her gaze, and walked like a gummy to the other wall. Guess not. *Focus, now. Becky's here.*

Becky sank into the chair facing Shannon. The hardware on her wrists clanked into her lap.

"The hospital released me. So now I get to trot off to a nut house instead of prison," Becky said, her words like cold steel, watching Shannon with unblinking, unfriendly obsidian eyes.

Shannon's smile faded. "We could still get that changed. I'll talk to Portman and Chen—"

"Don't bother. Drom and Old Salty left their marks on me. I *should* stay under lock and key."

"I'll try to—"

Becky interrupted. "You won't try anything that involves me. If it weren't for you, Andy would be alive. I wouldn't have a huge scar on my chest. I wouldn't be accused of attempted murder. I wouldn't have the memory of the slimiest alien in recorded history taking my mind and squeezing it until I agreed to do everything thing he said. I wouldn't wake up screaming because a killer crocodile has ripped out my throat."

Becky stopped to take a breath. She shook so much her handcuffs never stopped rattling.

She continued, "All your fault. I don't want to see you, talk to you, think about you, acknowledge that you ever lived. I wanted to tell you that."

Shannon had known this conversation would come. She'd braced for Becky's fury. Still, the force of it hit her broadside, a tidal wall of hurt, drowning her.

But then, a strange thing happened. Shannon had berated herself over and over with the same message Becky had just unloaded on her, had screamed this message at herself so often it had become old news, Shannon's mantra: *all her fault.*

Yet, hearing it from Becky, the untruth of it crashed in on Shannon, the wrongness of it overwhelmed her. *Not* all *her fault. Not.*

A weight so heavy it had bent Shannon to the ground lifted away.

Becky sat, stiff, still, staring at Shannon, awaiting a reaction.

At length, Shannon said, "You know what? I hope you throw everything you've got into erasing every trace of that bastard Drom in your system. Then I hope you get back to your sea creatures somewhere, somehow. Fight for that, *that's* where you belong." Shannon reached for her glass on the bed table and sipped some water.

Hold it together. She cleared her throat.

"Drom would laugh to think you've broken down. Well, go stuff that laugh down his rotten stinking throat. You're stronger than him."

Not good enough. Becky deserved better.

"I'm on your side. I always will be." Shannon's lips quivered. Essi squeezed her hand.

Becky looked at her a minute longer, a look full of bitterness.

Then she said, "I'm no victim. You got that part right." She paused, began to speak, then stopped, as if she found the next words distasteful but necessary. "Also thanks for getting my mother's emerald back. Chen told me you remembered who'd taken it, and they tracked it down from there. But that changes nothing." She stood up and whipped around to leave. The guard who brought her in secured her arm, and led her toward the door.

"You didn't have to come in person to tell me you never want to see me again," Shannon said to Becky's retreating back. She shouldn't have struck back at her, but she couldn't help it. *She hurt. She hurt so much.*

Becky didn't turn around.

But as they reached the door, she stopped and she said, "I'll never forgive you for what's happened, and I can't start over unless you're out of my life. But when I asked you to, you let go of me, let me stay in my body, even if it meant I would die. That was the best and hardest thing a friend could do."

And she disappeared through the door.

Shannon lay back on her pillows and exhaled a big breath she hadn't realized she was holding. For a long time, she didn't stir.

The best and hardest thing a friend could do.

Weight as heavy as iron stone lifted away as if moon gravity now governed the Earth. She might float right off the bed.

She'd give Becky the space she needed. But she wouldn't give up on her. A friend wouldn't.

Shannon rested.

*   *   *

Shannon, even with her aliens still aboard, grew stronger under strict bed rest and the constant glucose drip—not strong, but stronger. The time had come to talk to Dr. B about getting out of this place so she could send Essi and Salesti home.

*   *   *

The next day, when Dr. Bennett came to check on her, Shannon said, "I'm well enough to go out to the SQ to send Essi and Salesti back to their Riverworld. No sense in keeping me here. I won't get any better until they leave."

The doctor frowned. "It goes against the grain, but I know you're right. You'll still need nursing care for a while. I wanted you back here after you released them, but Dr. Moon stopped by to see me. He's offered to pay for your home care. Okay by you?"

Moon? A shrewd protector of a valuable asset. But also a good man.

"Sure. Great. How soon can I leave?"

"I'll have everything arranged by tomorrow."

Shannon watched Dr. Bennett's departing back. Her eyes still rested on the door when lavender haze announced another visitor.

A small round woman in overlarge glasses wheeled in Matt Portman. He looked pale, gaunt.

"Hey Matt. You look like you've been through a wood chipper. How're you feeling?"

"Feeling alive, thanks to you. I, uh, came to thank you again for saving my bacon. When do you get out?"

"Looks like tomorrow. You going to stay at home for a while?"

"Yeah, the wife insists. Oh, sorry, this is my wife, Alice." His hand waved toward the woman who'd wheeled him in. The last conversation between Portman and Shannon rippled across her mind. "Another two or three weeks anyway," he continued. "You? You do understand you can come back? You're unfired." He coughed into his hand.

Shannon laughed. "Thanks, but I'm not coming back, Matt. I'm going on to something new."

When she'd reaffirmed the decision to walk away from the legal profession altogether a few days ago, lying here on this blasted bed, pounds and pounds *more* weight lifted from her back, weight she hadn't even known she carried. And this weight she could afford to lose.

Portman relaxed back in his chair, relieved for some reason. "You've needed this for a long time. I could never figure out why you stuck with it when you hated it so much."

What? Portman—*Portman?*—had understood Shannon better than she'd understood herself? *Portman?* Had Shannon slipped into a parallel universe?

"If you change your mind, of course, you can always come back. But, I've announced for Mayor, so I might not be County Attorney for long." Portman showed the good grace to look sheepish as he said, "The story of me sneaking out to lure the killer away from my family has boosted my ratings. Anyway, I'll write whatever recommendation you need anytime."

* * *

Luke had never come to visit.

* * *

And now one important task remained.

* * *

On this late autumn day, a light gray veil dimmed the sun's sparkle, although a light blanket of soft solar warmth pressed against Shannon's skin. A breeze from the west lifted her hair and smelled of brine and bulwarks, shells and sea gulls.

Shannon had resigned in writing from her volunteer position, turned in her keys and now paid the SeaQuarium entrance fee to pass through the turnstile the same as any ordinary visitor. She'd become an outsider here. A forlorn gloom settled over her.

Think about Juneau. Soon she'd join the team from the Dickson—Todd and Dr. Moon and other biologists and scientists to start the work that would set Juneau free for good. Juneau. On her way to freedom. *Freedom.* The word shot through Shannon's bloodstream like electric thread. Together the team could make it happen; a victory she could never have accomplished on her own. Warm pleasure washed over her. She—

Salesti interrupted. *Hurry.*

Yes. Back to the moment. Shannon gripped the railing that circled the 200-foot shark pool to prop herself up. She glanced at the sleek shapes that glided in the pool's depths. She'd substituted as a docent here from time to time, and she recognized the resident Broadnose Sevengill, the Shortfin Mako and, of course, the Great White. Beautiful creatures in their way.

Salesti had guided Shannon to the pool, above which the moving portal back to Essi's world now hovered. Not that Shannon could spot it, though she'd stared unblinking, until her eyes stung.

Salesti buzzed about inside Shannon's mind, dipping and diving even more than usual.

Shannon imaged that she'd miss the little dynamo. *Take care of Essi, will you?*

Salesti's reply came not as an image, but as the luxurious blanketing of a warm, scented cloud that held Essi and Shannon safe.

Shannon imaged: *you're sure your world can replenish now that you're rid of Drom and Tharm?*

Salesti, as happy as always, buzzed and imaged. *Yes. With Drom and Tharm gone, the Selador River will, over long times, recover and give birth to a plenitude of new Seladorans.*

Well, if anyone would know, Salesti would. Wait, though. Had Salesti imaged those thoughts, or had it spoken? *Spoken?* Shannon cast back. *Not sure.*

Essi imaged: the child grabs Shannon's neck, and holds tight.

Shannon imaged back: her arms encircle the child. She kisses the top of Essi's head and her soft, pale curls.

"No more portal rooms for you, sweetie. Go home to your friend Toss."

tosss.

Remember, Essi imaged, moving away, *living powder stays with Shannon.*

The little girl's hum vibrated faster and faster until it sounded like Salesti's buzz. The child opened her hand and Salesti settled there.

Yes. Shannon counted a great deal on the presence of their living powder. Not the creatures themselves, but more than memories. For comfort. For company.

It's time. Send them.

She stepped up on a small stool she'd carried with her, her legs secure against the railing—well, secure enough. Well, not secure, but better than if no railing existed. She glanced down at the water below. *Good thing the SQ fed these sharks well.*

Shannon couldn't steady her tremor as she stretched to her full height, hand extended, her weak muscles objecting.

A whisper: *shenen. esssii lofss shenen.*

Shannon smiled.

Rose red and lavender lightning sparked, the images of the child and tiny creature faded, and for one moment, Shannon could make out the portal, the white-gold flash that filled it, and the two wisps of color, her friends, as they slipped through it and disappeared.

Gone.

She blinked, stepped down and leaned hard on the railing. She looked up at the place she'd last seen them, her vision blurry.

Gone.

And yet not altogether. Their living powder remained, a small, real part of them.

A glorious, swirled haze formed beside her.

Oh. Right. Even without Essi, the living powder gave her the power to cast the haze. *The living powder.* She leaned against the rail and closed her eyes to see if she could enter that empty cavern in her mind. She concentrated.

Yes, there. Heaps of the stuff, swirling together. Shannon's own cobalt blue powder, Essi's lavender and Juneau's white. David's palest yellow. The raven's iridescent night hue. Salesti's rose red, the glow of color that surrounded all the salesties. Becky, in Shannon's mind for so few moments, had left a smattering of her living powder, a glorious sky blue. Even Luke's, by Odin, even a small amount of Luke's, a forest green, a deep deep forest green.

But another powder: a deepest midnight purple. Where had it come from? And on the cavern floor—an unusual shape, perhaps a package.

Shannon imagined herself in the cavern, hands on hips, staring down at the object. A book? A disk? *Something in between.* She picked it up.

A rose red glow infused the object. Salesti had left it behind, then, an image, like a letter for her to read. *No way.* Salesti could *do* that?

Shannon opened it: her great mastiff grapples with Old Salty inside Becky's mind, her deep purple powder shedding all around her; Salesti flies through it again and again, collecting it, even as Shannon's beloved dog throws the croc and herself into the void; Salesti carries the deep purple powder back to Shannon's mind.

A small measure of her Indy, glowing and alive. Tears welled in Shannon's eyes.

Thank you, Salesti.

Shannon's focus returned to the shark pool. The color-swirled haze had announced someone's arrival. She waited. After a few moments she sensed someone behind her.

A deep, quiet, calm and familiar voice spoke over her left shoulder.

"Amazing. That incredible perfume hasn't worn off *yet?*"

Shannon grinned, reached for her braid, fingered its thick, firm weave, squeezed it for luck, and turned.

THE END

It would be my honor if you would review this book on Amazon.com and I would be delighted to hear from you at **cathy.parker@icloud.com** or receive your comments at my author profile on bublish.com.

You can also visit my website at
AuthorCathyParker.com

www.ingramcontent.com/pod-product-compliance
Lightning Source LLC
Chambersburg PA
CBHW071119180726

48291CB00007B/2091